MW00425289

DISTURBING THE BONES

DISTURBING THE BONES

ANDREW DAVIS
AND JEFF BIGGERS

MELVILLE HOUSE
BROOKLYN · LONDON

Disturbing the Bones

First published in 2024 by Melville House
Copyright © 2023 by Andrew Davis and Jeff Biggers
All rights reserved

First Melville House Printing: July 2024

Melville House Publishing
46 John Street
Brooklyn, NY 11201

and

Melville House UK
Suite 2000
16/18 Woodford Road
London E7 0HA

mhpbooks.com
@melvillehouse

ISBN: 978-1-68589-145-9
ISBN: 978-1-68589-146-6 (eBook)

Library of Congress Control Number: 2024937687

Designed by Kyle Kabel

Printed in the United States of America

1 3 5 7 9 10 8 6 4 2

A catalog record for this book is available from the Library of Congress

To Andy's grandchildren Edie, Devon, George and Leo

and to Jeff's billie boys, Diego and Massimo

May they someday live in a world without weapons of mass destruction and witness global peace and understanding.

You know what Einstein said:

If there's a World War Three, I don't know what weapons we'll use, but I know the weapons of World War Four: Sticks and stones.

Now, think about that.

—Studs Terkel

SEPTEMBER

—

Prologue

Freddy Evans gazed at the freshly excavated set of human remains with a peculiar feeling in his stomach. It made him pull on the strap of his denim overalls as he towered over Anchee Chang, the young archaeologist who held her brush beside the bones encased in dirt with the touch of an artist.

"Something wrong?" he asked.

"We shouldn't move anything until Dr. Moore gets here," Anchee said, a microphone dangling from her earbud. "Dr. Moore, we need you at quadrant 14."

The urgency in Anchee's voice unnerved Freddy. This was his first dig. He ran a hand through his dreadlocks.

Anchee waved a small yellow pickax in the air, motioning for the archaeological site director to come over a small hill. Freddy remained transfixed by the bones. He looked at the intact skeleton sitting atop a lattice of other remains. The skull dominated the shattered ruins, as if it had been rearranged on different terms.

An arena of mud had been excavated from the valley, divided into cross sections, revealing burial mounds, rafts of skeletons, and stacks of crates and equipment. Staircases descended into pits. Ladders scaled down. The flattened quadrants of land stretched like a football field marked by dark pockets, earthen holes, and moving figures.

Everyone had shed their long sleeves with the heat. Anchee, a graduate student researcher at Southern Illinois University, had kept the floppy hat. She focused on the edge of a skull at one end, which looked like it had been cushioned by the other bones. It reminded Anchee of her first dig

3

near her university in western China, when a flood had swept centuries of history into a gorge.

As Dr. Molly Moore trudged within sight of the quadrant, Freddy held out his hand to create a protective border to hold back a small group of curious volunteers. The constant movement at the archaeological site came to a halt.

"We haven't touched it, Dr. Moore," Freddy said, his voice shaking. He looked at his site director with a mix of awe and horror.

"Molly, dude, call me Molly," she said, moving with a clear authority, and then she knelt by Freddy and Anchee. It seemed to Freddy like Molly was leading them in some sort of ritual. Both looked proud but also overwhelmed by their discovery. Crouching down, the site director pulled her reddish-blond hair into a ponytail, a red bandana dangling around her neck. Molly looked younger than her twenty-eight years. She was fit, with a freight-train metabolism that kept her on the move.

As Anchee clicked off a series of photos, Molly pulled out a thin brush from her pocket, and then started to shave away dirt from the skull and a set of teeth.

"Sandeep, we need you down here," she said into a microphone from her cell phone, which hung from the top button of her blouse. She knew their ground-penetrating radar could examine the level of disturbances to the soil.

Freddy rose, leading the group of volunteers as he stepped away. One of the few locally hired crew—and one of the only Blacks from the nearby historic town of Cairo—he seemed more at ease with the volunteers, despite being in his early twenties.

"I'll get another sifting screen," he said to Molly, who nodded without saying a word, and then he walked away, taking lanky strides in his overalls.

Molly put her mouth just above the trace of the skull's jawbone, and then blew off a veil of dust. Using a penknife, she cut a line from the teeth across the dirt, scraping off a clump from a plant. Her knife gently nudged the dirt until she heard a click.

"We need to get the laser scanner to map the interface," she said, looking back at Anchee.

The graduate student pointed at Molly's knife. Something glimmered with a metallic edge. Molly pushed the knife forward, popping out a heart-shaped locket.

Her brush grazed the locket like a goldsmith, until it caught a flicker of light.

"This sure isn't prehistoric," Molly whispered.

There was an eerie silence about her as she climbed up to her knees, crouching by the display of bones. She pushed away more soil.

As the locket dangled from the tip of her knife, a latch suddenly opened, revealing the remains of a faded heart-shaped photo, which had been eroded by the elements.

"Definitely not prehistoric," she mumbled, breaking a pained smile, though it didn't last long.

Molly didn't want to alarm her students—or the crowd of volunteers at the site. Rumors could get passed quickly. She insisted on keeping ahold of the information in the same way she gripped the locket inside her fist.

"Back to work, folks," Molly announced, trying her best to act casual. "We'll let everyone know what we found once we do some tests."

The workers in the crowd slowly dispersed, though not without a last lingering look over their shoulders at the pit. Warned by Molly to keep to the rules, everyone had resisted taking a photo, other than Anchee. All discoveries at this site remained a secret until Molly made the first public disclosure.

Within an hour, the crew's lead technology expert, Sandeep Agarwal, had scanned Anchee's photos of the burial site, and then projected a 3D recording of the soil, moving magically through time.

With Molly and Anchee by his side, Sandeep stood at his outdoor lab station, refusing to take a seat. His turban was plastered in dust. His lab looked more like a game center than an archaeological site. A set of scratched music speakers rested to the side, awaiting a DJ. The constant, though quiet, thump of Punjabi hip-hop, in fact, kept the beat. A canopy of tents and plastic walls protected it from wind and dust. A large grid map of the archaeological site was posted on one of the plastic walls. To the side, two more tables were covered in trays of bones and artifacts gathered from the dig.

"What do you got for me?" Molly asked.

She recruited Sandeep after she had read his academic paper on using remote sensing at a dig in his family's native Punjab region on the border of India and Pakistan. She promised him a potential archaeological discovery that would justify shifting his postdoctoral studies from Canada to southern Illinois.

Sandeep pointed at one of the screens, now commanded by Anchee, which displayed a map in various colors from the remote sensing scans.

"Look there," he said.

Sandeep enlarged the image on the screen.

"Those are alterations of the soil," Molly said, placing a finger on the screen.

"Someone was digging here long before us," Sandeep laughed.

His sarcastic tone had a seriousness about it.

More images of the bones popped up on the other screens.

"The question is when," Molly said quietly. "No way to know how long ago just by looking at this. Could have been a farmer ten, twenty, a hundred years ago. Maybe two hundred years ago. There's no way of knowing at this point."

"This whole area is strange," Sandeep went on. "I haven't had time to really understand it, but the radar is picking up disturbances way below this grid."

"We're dealing with twelve thousand years of history," she said, "but I think it's important to focus on the top layers of soil right now."

"Still, these laser maps are odd," Sandeep continued, pointing at the screen. "I need to look deeper into this area."

"Listen, right now it's more important that we get a sample of the bones and a mold of teeth to the FBI lab in Chicago," Molly said, stepping away from the computer table.

"FBI? Are you joking?" Anchee said, alarmed. "What about the forensic unit right on the SIU campus? They can handle this."

"Uncle Sam's paying the bills on this dig," Molly said, moving to the edge of the tent wall. "And federal protocol says he has first dibs on anything that might be considered fresh bones."

She lifted up one of the side flaps as Freddy entered the lab area carrying a tray of bones.

"I've sealed off the area as you requested," Freddy said.

"Thanks," Molly said, walking back to the table. She picked up two plastic bags, which held the newly found locket and a shoe. "We had enough delays with the pandemic," she added. "I don't want to give the feds any reason to shut us down again."

1

Patrolling an old riverside warehouse, Detective Randall Jenkins was working on his own "dig." He had stationed himself on the stern of a twenty-seven-foot Defender-class police boat, which hovered in the middle of the Chicago River Canal. His presence cast the confidence of three decades on the Chicago PD as a veteran investigator.

A stealth police drone pivoted to the opposite side of the river. A police officer operated a radio from the stern as two more cops stood at the railing of the boat.

Chicago's canals may have drained this city's swamp, reversing the current of the Chicago River and the history of the city in the process, but Randall knew it hid secrets. It provided the cover for crimes and unknown bodies.

The Chicago River canal system wound through the city with the dark green sheen of something unnatural, cutting through the steel and concrete of high-rises with the precision of the water's blade.

Randall focused on the old warehouse. The remnants of a retired boat slip were still visible on the ground. Garbage and broken bottles surrounded a riverside deck that once loaded ice.

Randall's first assignments as a detective, having risen through the patrol ranks in his bureau, took place under the faded signs of the meatpacking houses that covered the walls from another time, another set of rules. The veterans of the Afro-American Patrolmen's League had updated those rules for Randall. Not that he had changed his professional wardrobe in years. In a corduroy jacket and dark jeans, he carried himself with the build of an ironworker, and the inquisitive gaze of a scientist. His Glock 19 handgun was concealed.

A lot was concealed about Randall, at least in the mind of Nikki Zanna, his longtime detective partner. He was a South Side kid; his Bronzeville apartment was his private getaway. "Nicoletta," the granddaughter of Sardinian immigrants from the West Side and twenty years Randall's junior, could not have been more different, and yet, the partners moved with the unspoken agreement of veterans who had solved enough cases to foretell their next steps.

Nikki always wondered if Randall's unflappable expression masked some other emotions. He carried a pleasant grin that seemed eternally amused. He had a knack for asking the same question in a hundred different ways, in order to get to the answer, without losing his cool. There was something about Randall's manner that made the far-fetched appear possible. She had never seen him break down—in anger or sadness, or side-splitting laughter, for that matter—and she was not quite sure if that amazed or concerned her. It made her slightly uneasy, though; his self-possession somehow challenged her own.

That knowing look was etched on his face now. Nikki glanced at Randall, and then followed his gaze toward the targeted building in the Fulton River District, surrounded by grids of streets crossed by train tracks and looping highways.

All that bird shit. The windows of the warehouse had not been opened for years. It did not look abandoned, though. The warehouse seemed shrouded like a stalled renovation project that might have lost its investors and now languished like a forgotten building on an inspector's list.

Randall texted his command.

In place.

As the lead detective on this case, he was ready to move forward.

Within seconds, with the force of a cannon, a loading door came unhinged, flying from the building almost intact until it made impact on the water of the canal. The warehouse suddenly came alive, clouds of smoke pushing out of the door frames.

A SWAT team emerged from the side of the building, toting assault rifles that bumped up against their protective helmets.

Waved in by a lieutenant, the SWAT team two-stepped their way into the smoking hole of the door, weapons in hand.

Arriving from the boat dock, Randall and Nikki headed to the warehouse as the SWAT team fanned out on the flanks.

A backup team stepped from the shadows. A team of sniffer dogs added their bark. Police congregated outside the blown door hole as Randall and Nikki moved into the warehouse. Nikki held her handgun aloft; Randall had put his away.

The detectives walked to the middle of the vaulted room as if planning to make an announcement. Floating particles of dust wafted around them like flies caught in streaks of light. The SWAT team crouched with their scopes along the perimeter of the room with the precision of surveyors.

It was as empty as it appeared from outside. Still with their guns drawn, the SWAT team huddled around Randall in the middle of the room. Daylight now revealed all four walls. The glare was almost too harsh for the police who had entered in the darkness of the smoke.

"It's goddamn empty," Nikki said, sticking her gun into its holster. "Someone was tipped off."

The SWAT leader touched the camera on his helmet, confirming its presence and his own confusion. He motioned for the SWAT team to fan out again.

Randall had moved to the corner of the room, standing under a set of windows that faced the canal. All of the windows had been covered with some sort of tarp. Pieces now fluttered in the wind, ripped by the blast of the exploding door. Randall tugged at a shipping rope that hung from the ceiling.

"Sorry, Randall," Nikki said. "Someone blew this call."

She kicked at a pile of rubble in the middle of the warehouse, which became more cavernous with the increasing light. It had been emptied of any goods years ago.

That knowing grin stretched across Randall's face in a way that amused Nikki.

"*Intzà?*" she mumbled to herself, in her grandparents' language. "Talk to me, man," she added with a hand gesture that reflected her irritation.

Following the rope to its end, Randall glanced over his shoulder at Nikki, looked back at the rope, and then at the floor. He slowly knelt, withdrew his handgun, and then used the end of the barrel as a stick, scratching at the dust on the floor. Randall reached down and pushed away a pile of trash as a stream of light cut across the side of the room from the top windows.

"Check this out," Randall said.

One of the cops moved to the side of Randall as a couple more SWAT team members shifted into position. It took Nikki a second before she realized Randall had motioned for her to come by his side.

Outlining a slab in the floor, Randall clipped his forefinger and middle finger under a latch, and then pulled. The frame of a door came into view. Randall leaned back and pulled up the trapdoor, revealing another chamber below. A waft of mildew and mold stung his nose.

"Get me Milan and a bomb squad," he said, over his shoulder.

As the SWAT leader radioed his command, Randall withdrew a light from his jacket and shined it below.

"But how?" Nikki gasped.

Randall nodded to the trash pushed aside.

"Layers," he said.

He didn't say anything more, as a heavy-duty robot was lowered into the cellar, its flashing lights capturing all of the attention like a carnival ride. After the bomb squad made a sweep of the warehouse and lower chamber, Randall descended a narrow metal ladder that dropped from the trapdoor. Nikki stayed on the floor level to deal with the communications. A team of bomb-sniffing German shepherds yanked at the chains of two policemen, who strained to hold them back from the action. One dog lunged for the darkness of the trapdoor, nearly pulling its master with it.

"Packed," came Randall's voice from below, sounding on the radio.

In full body armor, Lt. Milan Delich grunted his way into the underground room with Randall, followed by three other squad members. With a clipped gray mustache and rounded double chin, Delich moved slowly, betraying his proximity to retirement, but with a precision that had gone through the fire too many times. Their presence filled the tightly packed space, where crates had been stacked from the floor to the low ceiling.

Pointing at one of the crates, Delich grinned at Randall like he had figured out a riddle.

"Rocket launchers?" he said.

"Assault rifles, explosives, ammunition," Randall responded.

"Randall, I just received a message I need to share with you," Nikki's voice on the radio sounded.

Amid the clatter in the room, Randall didn't hear Nikki.

As Delich bent over a crate to pick up a metal rod, Randall grabbed his arm. A stunned Delich halted his movement, and then looked down again. His black boot came within an inch of a set of drone propellers, which jutted out like a bear trap.

"Jesus. My son's units used those in Afghanistan," Delich said. "Who the hell would have access to this kind of military hardware here?"

Randall stepped around another crate, opened a latch, and then pulled out an M4 carbine assault rifle.

"Sure as hell not the Disciples or the Vice Lords."

The buzz on Randall's phone broke him from the exchange. Nikki was texting, which surprised him, since she was nearby.

FBI needs you down at lab now. Herby says it's important.

Randall looked around at the cache of weapons, caught between a feeling of satisfaction and uncertainty, and then stared at the message.

"You going to call the deputy chief?" Delich asked.

Nodding, Randall didn't say anything. He read Nikki's message again. A few seconds passed before Nikki followed up with another text.

Getting car. Will be outside.

2

—

BALLROOM, MCCORMICK PLACE
CHICAGO, ILLINOIS

The overflowing crowd jammed the Chicago ballroom. Extra chairs lined the walls. The top archaeologists in the country ringed the tables, along with graduate students and young professors who had sat in a classroom with a young Molly Moore only a short time ago. What a difference an archaeological dig could make in shifting time and expectations.

Dr. Moore, wearing a chic gray blazer over a black turtleneck with dark slacks, now walked up to the podium at the front of the ballroom with the ease of someone entering her own home. The rural image on the giant screen behind her, in fact, was taken near her childhood home—a photo of green rows of corn that fanned into a series of large mounds, guarded by a sentry of woods.

"I appreciate this honor to speak at the national conference," Dr. Moore began, clicking on her remote to display drone images of one of the mounds, which appeared more like a distinct earthen platform. The aerial shot captured the precision of the mound's boundaries, which seemed like they had been laid out by a surveyor.

While she exuded an aura of confidence, the young archaeologist couldn't believe she was keynoting at the annual conference for the American Association of Archaeologists. But she knew she had earned it. She was about to reveal one of the greatest discoveries of her times among her colleagues. Whether she was Molly or Dr. Moore, she was also terrified.

She cleared her throat. "Our Moore Creek study is under the federal aegis of the new Ft. Defiance Highway corridor linking the geospatial and cyberspace command centers at Scott Air Force Base outside of St.

Louis to the loading docks on the Mississippi River at Cairo, Illinois," she went on. "I was honored to receive the contract to head up the mandated survey for the Illinois Department of Transportation and Federal Highway Administration."

A handful of insiders in the room exchanged glances. Some had questioned the contract going to Dr. Moore's upstart Moore Archaeological Group, instead of the more established Center for American Archaeology in Chicago. Such gossip had dissipated, including charges of nepotism, when Dr. Moore began to release the findings from her work. The backstory added its own dimension.

Her prize-winning Yale dissertation on high-tech breakthroughs in excavations in prehistoric Vietnamese sites was not Dr. Moore's only bona fide. Molly, as she preferred to be called, had grown up within miles of this highway project. As a child she had walked barefoot with her daddy through these fields, collecting arrowheads and pottery shards.

"Those hills are not natural," he had told her, referring to the mounds. "Best leave them be."

"Thanks to the initiative of retired general Will Alexander, the first engineering survey conducted by the Ft. Defiance Construction and Engineering Company found evidence of hunting sites," Molly continued, suddenly pausing. "Gen. Alexander, to his credit, informed me and the regional archaeological organizations of the initial discovery."

A new image appeared on the screen. Standing on a mound to the side of Molly, with a field of corn in the background, the gray-haired Gen. Alexander posed in his usual attire of tan fatigues, a black T-shirt, and sunglasses, holding a ceramic pot. He looked more like a modern Indiana Jones than a military figure.

"This is Gen. Alexander." Molly's voice sounded embarrassed to use his military title. She repeated, "Gen. Alexander brings years of experience of working at archaeological sites around the world as a military officer. We're quite lucky to have him in our region."

In his early seventies, Will Alexander considered himself a godfather to Molly and a handful of kids from Cairo and the hard-scrabbled region that had managed to make it to the university or military academies. Alexander, a direct relative of the county namesake, prided himself as a dream maker who had provided the introductions, written the letters of recommendations, and made the crucial phone calls.

Alexander had viewed Molly as a special case. He had followed her archaeological pursuits at Yale and around the world. Over the years, he had sent her shards of pots and ancient artifacts from his operations in the Middle East, North Africa, and Europe. He loved archaeology with the passion of a history buff, especially in war zones, where the ruins littered the ground with their own stories.

"We've been building forts forever," he told her when she returned to Cairo. "It's time to show the world how forts have been crucial parts of our culture for thousands of years."

Molly moved on to the next photo, which juxtaposed an aerial shot of the fields and mounds and a seemingly impenetrable corridor of forests on one side. On the other side was a LIDAR (light imaging, detection, and ranging) X-ray image of the same area. The green sheen of the nearby river couched the site on the bottom of the screen.

"This delta region of southern Illinois is referred to as 'Egypt' due to the confluence of the Mississippi and Ohio rivers," she noted.

The reference to the ancient world came alive in her photo.

The audience gasped at the illuminated indicators of prehistoric occupation. The outlines of living areas, the straight lanes of walkways, the spread of an open gathering area in front of a mound. The farm field transformed into an underground urban compound. The mounds radiated, somehow still alive. Another image produced a three-dimensional point cloud of the same field, casting the area into an otherworldly aura of colors.

"Using light technology, mounted on a drone," Molly continued, "we were able to pinpoint some stone structures in detail, discovering earthworks such as mounds, canals, and roads."

Working with her hand-picked international team, along with volunteers from the nearby Southern Illinois University, she followed up with remote sensing tests, as well as ground-penetrating radar waves, which cut more than 150 feet through the low-conductivity soil. The ground-penetrating radar might have looked like an overgrown lawn mower, but it could even cut through concrete to detect images.

As more photos and video flicked onto the screen, drawing reactions from the crowd, the young archaeologist paused and drew a long breath, overwhelmed herself by the significance of the find.

"Due to the delays from the pandemic, we haven't even touched the surface of the whole site, let alone what is below the twenty-six layers of soil, which we know goes back twelve thousand years," Molly said. Her voice was getting more serious, finding its confidence, as she added, "but our initial survey demonstrated we had not simply stumbled on a hunting camp."

She hesitated before going on.

"We believe we have discovered the largest permanent series of villages in the Early Archaic Period in the Mississippi Valley, and what is one of the most important archaeological finds in North America."

A huge applause waved across the room.

3

The huge lab on Chicago's West Side always reminded Randall of the chaotic kitchens he found in the back of large commercial restaurants. Metal stands of shelves leaned with boxes, instruments, and towels. To the side sat refrigerated autopsy cases flanked by long counters. Nothing ever appeared to be in order.

At this late hour, the veteran FBI lab tech Herby Harper walked with a limp from a hallway at the far corner of the laboratory. With his face mask pulled below his chin, Harper looked like he had a beard. Randall thought Harper was too thin, almost too sickly to be around so many cadavers.

The detective's attention shifted for a moment toward the hallway, where he had noticed someone walking back and forth. Randall assumed it was a security guard. He couldn't quite make out the person's shape, standing to the side of the door. Randall glanced at Nikki as she leaned against the wall on the side. She looked concerned, but expectant, and that somehow comforted him. He knew he wasn't alone—Nikki understood this visit to the lab was no routine investigation.

Randall struggled inside to keep his composure as Harper ambled over to a spread of bones and skull fragments, including a mold from a set of teeth on the counter.

Harper's gloved hand reached down toward one piece of bone. He moved the molded set of teeth and bones to the side, next to a file he had held for years.

"This is unreal," Randall said. His voice suddenly got hoarse. He tried to clear his throat. "I've waited over forty years for this."

"It's your DNA, Randall," Harper said.

"You positive this matches up?" Randall asked. His voice was quiet.

"It's definitely your DNA," Harper said, staring at the bones. "These were sent by an archaeologist working on a federal highway project near Cairo."

"Archaeologist in Cairo, goddamn," Randall said.

Harper looked over his shoulder, and then back at Randall.

"She's out in the foyer, actually."

"In the foyer?" Nikki spoke up. She could tell Randall, absorbed by the evidence on the table, had not heard Harper's last line. Her eyes scanned over his shoulder, past the files and shelves, at the door leading to the hallway. Nikki had not seen an archaeologist in the foyer or hallway or wherever, only a young woman dressed for a night on the city.

Harper nodded. He understood Nikki's confusion.

"She's in town for some convention," he added, "so I had her drop by in case we have any questions."

Randall still didn't respond. Stepping away from the counter, Harper unpeeled one glove, picked up a folder, and then handed it to Randall. "Here are the dental records."

Randall hesitated before taking the folder, and then opened the first file. Harper had also printed out additional photos from the archaeological site, but Randall's eyes shifted toward a photograph clipped at the top. A Black woman in her late thirties smiled from her journalist ID card.

Randall, near tears, repeated himself. "I've waited over forty years for this."

Nikki joined Randall at the counter as Harper moved to the side. In a natural gesture, she placed her arm around Randall's shoulder for a moment, looking down at the files.

"God, your mom was so beautiful," Nikki said.

Randall nodded. That was his father's line, when he was a kid: "Your mom is so beautiful."

Randall would never forget the classy way his mother always smiled in these moments, dismissing his father with a simple hand gesture, and then clutching his child body into her arms. The memory of their voices together comforted him for a moment, as a buffer from his emotions, and then his eyes fell onto the newspaper headlines in the files.

MISSING PERSON REPORT: FLORENCE JENKINS, 1978, CAIRO, ILLINOIS.
Chicago Defender Press Reporter Missing. Civil Rights Writer Disappears in Cairo.

Seeing the name of Cairo in print always struck Randall with a jolt, and then a flood of memories from his childhood. He rarely spoke about his family's past in the southern town. His ex-wife, Gloria, assumed he was born in Chicago until she stumbled onto his birth certificate. Randall's daughter, Teresa, learned more about his childhood and his mother from her grandfather, whose stories about river town life sounded like something from another country. And yet, Randall had lived in Cairo until he was eight years old, returning every summer until his mother's disappearance.

That was another life he had left behind. Cairo had added a final blow in 1978 when his mother never returned from a family trip down south.

It wasn't another country for Randall, though; it was another part of his life he had chosen to close, as if he could condemn its memory from existence. The name of Cairo, Illinois, had always sounded like a threat to him—a threat from a past he didn't fully understand.

Randall backed away from the counter. The abruptness of his movements startled Nikki, who shot a look at Harper.

"Herby," Randall said, his voice low. "Can you sit on this for a while?"

The lab tech looked at Nikki, and then back at his old friend.

"Just for a short time?" Randall went on. "Let me check this out first. These things can get complicated."

Harper studied Randall's face like it was another artifact. He nodded. "Okay, just for a short time," he said. "I'll give you some time."

Randall nodded his thanks, though his eyes were elsewhere.

"You okay, man?" Harper said.

"Got a bathroom round here?" Randall said, wiping at his nose.

"Yeah," Harper said, pointing at the door at the far end of the room.

Nikki watched Randall walk to the opposite side of the room in a hurry. When the door closed behind him, she could only imagine his state of mind.

Randall burst into the bathroom with his fists. He let the emotions come out in waves—the confusion, the anger, the hurt, and then the gut-wrenching emptiness of loss. Holding the wall for support, he stared into the mirror, forced to face his own fate, and his own misery, without anyone around. Just as he had done as a child, as a teen, and as a young man who had been forced to live with the unresolved mystery of his mother's disappearance.

But he wasn't alone. He had never felt alone. Wiping at the tears streaking his cheeks, Randall saw his mother's fingers in the mirror. He saw her cheekbones, and then the curve of her eyes, the slope of her nose. He could barely breathe. He knew the only way to control his emotions was to unleash the anger again, so he turned and kicked the garbage can into the wall with a crushing blow. He attempted a breath, and then another, and then breathed as if his life depended on it.

"Let it out, slowly," Randall heard her voice tell him. "Breathe in, coolly." It was his mother's voice. The mother to her child, as he struggled with asthma in those early years. Randall saw his mother's hands in the backyard as he tried to breathe as a child, his thin legs crumpling into her arms. "Let it out, slowly," she would say, her words as soothing as any balm on his chest, and as calming as any rescue inhaler. He felt a semblance of life returning to his lungs, the rest of the world a blur. Her face became clearer with each breath.

Randall saw his mother in the mirror now, just as he had done for years. For decades. Her presence had always been around him; her disappearance had always held out a shred of hope of return.

Closing his eyes, Randall now breathed deeply through his nose, exhaled through his mouth, and then opened his eyes to see himself again.

He knew what he had to do next.

Turning toward the door, Randall could imagine the others were waiting for him. They were waiting for Detective Jenkins, not Randall the child who descended into asthma attacks, or Randall the teenager who refused to fall asleep at night, forever hoping to hear his mother's return to their home, until he fell asleep in exhaustion. Until she never did.

Harper nodded at Nikki when Randall came back through the door. The detective tugged at his belt and then approached the counter ready to finish their official business. Nikki stepped toward Randall, and then embraced him, placing her arms around his neck. He buried his face into her shoulder. Harper looked away, unsure what to do.

"Perhaps we should go take some fresh air and talk," Nikki whispered. "You don't have federal clearance on this, man."

The embrace didn't last long. Randall unlocked Nikki's hand, and then stepped back. He looked at Harper with the aplomb of an investigator. Running a hand through her hair, Nikki wasn't sure if Randall had returned to his old self, or if he had transformed into someone else. Either way, she realized he had returned to the table with a new mission.

"The DNA," Randall began to say, sounding like he was in the middle of a sentence. "That's where we start."

On the side of the counter, Randall noticed the plastic package that had contained the bone samples. Across the label, like a warning, was the handwritten explanation of the contents, as well as the signature of the archaeologist.

DR. MOLLY MOORE, Moore Archaeological Group, Cairo, Illinois.

"Moore? In Cairo?" Randall said, his voice returning to his role as a detective. The Moore surname stung him as much as the Cairo location. "Moore?"

"You know it?" Nikki asked. Her finger underlined the last name: Moore.

"I knew a Moore family." Randall's voice faltered. "They terrorized the town when I was a kid. They were Klan. I'll never forget that name."

"Common name," Nikki said almost dismissively. "Is this Moore Archaeological Group a federal outfit?"

"There are scores of private little firms out there picking up highway clearing contracts," Harper said. "I should probably bring her in, since I got her here."

Harper walked toward the door, opened it, and then waved for another person to come inside.

When Molly walked into the laboratory—her first time in an FBI facility—she seemed both intrigued and intimidated. She looked like a young lab assistant to Randall; Nikki pegged her as a scientist, her hair pulled back, a pair of black-rimmed glasses perched on her nose. In their eyes, this Dr. Molly Moore couldn't have been more than twenty-five.

Shifting to the side, Randall gathered his mother's papers in the folder. His actions seemed strangely nervous to Nikki, like he was treading in new territory.

"This is Dr. Molly Moore," Harper said, a step behind as she approached the counter.

She held out a hand with the eagerness of meeting another professional in the field.

"Please call me Molly," she said.

Randall hesitated before he offered his open hand in a hasty handshake.

"Randall Jenkins. I'm a detective with the Chicago Police Department," he said.

Nikki nodded, showing her badge, stepping back from the counter.

As Molly's eyes fell onto the bone samples, she realized there was more to the discovery than she had imagined.

"You're not FBI?"

Randall looked at Harper, and then back at her.

"This is related to a civil rights cold case," he said.

"I hope our samples were helpful to you, then," she said, turning back toward Randall. "We followed federal protocol."

Randall nodded.

"Samples?" he asked. "There's more?"

"Definitely," Molly said. "We've sealed everything in a locked case at our dig site. We made photos of the bone positions and findings, of course. That's how I've handled this kind of finding at other sites."

"In Cairo?" He pronounced it Kay-row, like the syrup, with a southern inflection.

"Just outside of "Care-o," she responded. "That's how locals pronounce it. I grew up there."

"Care-o," Molly repeated.

"Kay-row," Randall repeated. Looking over at Nikki, who stood on the opposite side of Molly, Randall handed Molly the first sheet on his mother's file.

"Me too, Dr. Moore, I also grew up there, at least for a few years," he said.

Randall paused for a moment.

"The DNA on those samples you sent matched my mother."

Taken aback, Molly set down the paper, and then looked away. Her chest tightened. Her eyes darted, unable to hold Randall's gaze. Nikki picked up on the body language and its air of denial.

"Your mother? I don't understand," Molly said.

Turning back, she looked directly at Randall.

"I don't either," he said.

"Who was your mother?"

"Florence Jenkins."

Molly hesitated. She wondered if Randall was playing some kind of joke on her. The seriousness in his face, though, which had shifted into a glare, disturbed her with its intensity. This was no joke. Despite her archaeological training, accustomed to surprises, Molly was nervous about learning any more facts.

"Flo Jenkins, the writer? Who wrote the book on the United Front?"

Randall opened his mother's file to the newspaper headline.

Civil Rights Writer Disappears in Cairo.

Molly stepped away from the table.

"Oh my God," she said. "Why? Why would her bones be found at my dig site?"

"That's what I'm going to find out."

"Oh my God, on the Henson farm."

Molly sounded like her voice was going to crack. Something snapped inside of Randall, too. He did everything in his power to not cry or shout— or do something he would regret. He stared at Molly for an awkward moment. She wringed her hands.

Randall pushed off the table, shielding himself from its contamination. His movements stirred the papers on the file again. A news clipping on Florence floated to the edge of the table, and then everyone watched as its brittle yellowed page cascaded to the floor.

In his haste to catch the clipping, Randall tore the paper in half.

"Careful," Molly said, and then she corrected herself. "I'm sorry, I meant, any contact can chip the edges."

Holding the two pieces of brittle newsprint in his hands, Randall's stern look sobered Molly. She moved back from the counter as Randall placed the torn clipping on the stack of papers and closed his mother's file.

"You need to secure the site and all of her remains right now."

Molly wasn't sure if she had been dismissed from the room or not, but she felt a palpable sense of suspicion.

"Until I get down to Cairo," Randall said, "the identity of my mother is to be kept a secret. Is that understood?"

"Absolutely," Molly said. "We keep everything confidential."

"You understand the seriousness of this?" he added.

Molly nodded, knowing he wasn't asking for her word. It hit her that she was indeed standing inside an FBI facility, with a Chicago detective. Whose mother she had found. And a set of bones from a missing person. From her site.

Walking out of the laboratory, Molly could feel Randall's eyes on her back. She knew she was being watched as she scrambled into the dark parking lot. She couldn't wait to put her car in drive and get out of town.

4

───

A streetlight outside a courtyard window shined over Randall's shoulder and onto the small kitchen table in his elderly father's apartment. Randall sat to his side, fork in hand, trying to get the eighty-nine-year-old to eat his dinner and take his tray of pills.

Her arms crossed in exasperation, Randall's daughter, Teresa, perched on the opposite side of the table with a look of complete disdain. She shook her head, again, unconvinced by Randall's motives.

"Why the hell do you have to go down to that godforsaken place?" she said. Anger coated each word like a hard fist. "Can't you just send someone else down there?"

To the side of Teresa, like a reminder of his failures, a photo of Randall and his toddler-age daughter at the beach had been framed on the wall. It might have been the first and last vacation together.

Feeding his father, Isaac, a round-faced man who wore a bib, Randall felt the blows of her words. He knew his last-minute call to his daughter was an inconvenience. It was her one night off, but this was an emergency.

Their relationship had never been close. Coming together rarely seemed to make it any closer, especially when he asked her to take care of her grandfather. There was something false about Randall's close rapport with his father—or, at least, that's what Teresa thought. His thirty-six-year-old daughter had never truly forgiven him for leaving her mother and splitting up their family. Randall had been an absent father for Teresa, more attentive to his detective work than her schoolwork or games or recitals. His decision to put his father into a county center for dementia patients also bothered her.

24

It seemed like he considered his family a burden. This whole scene made Teresa feel conflicted, angry, but also sympathetic at the same time. Teresa wanted to despise Randall for his disappearing acts, and yet, she couldn't deny the compassion he showed his father, gently offering him food. A fragile bond holding the torn family together still offered a chance to her.

"It won't be for long," Randall spoke up. "I need to follow up on what was found in Cairo."

"Your mother's bones," she said.

Teresa had never used the word "grandmother," because she had never known her. But she understood the rupture in his own life after Randall's parents got divorced when he was a kid, a transplant from Cairo to Chicago suddenly without his extended family, forced to find his way in a big city. Only a few years later, Teresa knew well, that kid in Chicago had been devastated by the disappearance of his mother; of waking up every day for the rest of his life without knowing where Florence was or what had happened. As his daughter, Teresa knew he carried the wound of feeling abandoned by his own mother.

"I've got to go back to Cairo," Randall said. "Open up, Paps."

"I want to go home to Cairo," Isaac said, eating a spoonful of rice and beans.

"You are home, Pappy," Teresa said. "We're in Chicago."

She noticed a southern Illinois calendar taped onto a small fridge as she took the spoon away from Randall.

"I'm worried about you going down there alone," Teresa went on. "It may be Illinois, but it's still south of the Mason-Dixon line. Who knows what could happen to you?" She stopped feeding Isaac, and then looked straight at Randall. "I don't want you to disappear like your mother, too."

The word "disappear" had always hovered around Florence Jenkins, as if her last trip to Cairo in the late 1970s had been a portal to somewhere else. There were plenty of rumors. Some suggested she had run off with another man, having divorced Randall's father before the incident.

There was a minimal investigation. It became a missing persons case. The idea of a crime or murder was out of the question. Others thought it should have been a civil rights case, but with no direct evidence of wrong-doing there was nothing to pursue.

When his father remarried, some encouraged the teenage Randall to let go of the pain and move on with his life. Others knew better; that

Florence, as a dedicated writer who had filed so many articles on the civil rights struggles in the Mississippi Valley, had most likely taken a wrong turn on a dangerous story.

"She didn't disappear," Randall said, trying to look calm, though he fell short. He turned to Isaac. "Paps, I've got to go away for a few days."

Isaac ate the food quietly.

"Paps. It's me. Randall."

"Do I know your mother?" the old man asked Teresa, earnestly.

"It's okay, Pappy," Teresa said, offering him another scoop of food. She looked back at Randall. "You promise to come back soon?"

"Not too long. I need to find out something."

Randall rose to leave, hugging his daughter with a long embrace.

"I love you for being you," he said, "and for being here for us."

Teresa shook her head, and shifted back to feeding Isaac.

"Listen, you fool, just get back safely."

5

——

LAKE SHORE DRIVE
CHICAGO, ILLINOIS

The world was still dark, unknowing, and even calm with the lanes of semitrailers steadily on the move. There wasn't commuter traffic on the Dan Ryan Expressway in Chicago before dawn. The buildings downtown appeared to wall off the highway, and the sun had not crept over the lake until after Randall made the exit onto Interstate 57.

The journey to Cairo would take six hours—or, rather, six albums of music. McCoy Tyner's thunderous piano to get through the suburbs. Nina Simone's ballads would navigate the loneliness across the prairies. Donny Hathaway's soulful tunes would get him through the small towns and yearning cornfields. Once you got south of Interstate 64, the old Mason-Dixon line for the heartland, it was nothing but Chaka Khan's funk, John Lee Hooker, and Muddy Waters's blues for Randall.

The signs for the upcoming presidential election changed with the geography, too. The blue banners for the Democratic presidential candidate, US senator Elaine Adams from Illinois, vanished downstate with each mile away from her Chicago base.

With each new sign for President Richard Waller, Randall felt a new blue-red line had been drawn across the country, no longer beholden to geography, but a cultural segregation of beliefs.

REELECT THE PRESIDENT:
DEFEND YOUR GUNS, DEFEND FREEDOM,
DEFEND THE WALL.

27

Randall drove with the window down. He played the music loud. He knew the trip was more than six hours; it was a lifetime of regret.

"Vanished"—that was a default term, just like "disappeared." "Murdered" was another, but no one had ever dared to mention it since there had been no discovery of a body or any details of violence.

Not that murder had eluded Cairo during the Jim Crow days of his childhood. Florence had brought the stories and images to a national audience herself, covering the assaults of the racist White Hats that fired into the housing projects from the levee in the late 1960s. Fire-bombings ravaged neighborhoods. One downtown street was known as "Sniper's Alley."

His family had left Cairo in the early 1970s for a reason. Randall had lived through Cairo's troubling times as a kid long enough to retain the pain and appreciate the departure. He didn't just read about the picket lines in front of segregationist stores, as Cairo made the national news—he had joined them with his mother. He had heard the story so many times about US Army private Robert L. Hunt Jr., a young Black man found hanging in the Alexander County jail in 1967.

The farther away from Chicago he got, the more Randall felt ready for the trip to Cairo. He knew he was returning to his childhood trauma. The ghosts of the United Front rode in the front seat, leading boycotts of whites-only shops and restaurants. The National Guard tailgated behind him in a convoy of soldiers, occupying Cairo and maintaining the peace. He was passed on the highway by Nazis and Klansmen, who ground Cairo to death with their white hats.

As a detective, Randall had followed every guide—and still, years later, he had come up empty-handed. He had not given up, but decades later, the case had gone unmercifully cold.

Until now.

The images passed through Randall's mind on the highway with the clarity that he was witnessing history for the first time.

"Black people can't meet in the local parks or even on the streets without being harassed by Buster Moore and his White Hats or the police," a young Florence had once said on TV. "They're taking sniper fire every night. How much longer will the state of Illinois let this go on until someone else dies?"

That question—and rare footage of news film—had reeled through Randall's mind for over forty years. As a teenager, his mother's voice had resounded in his mind with the fervor of a superhero. As a detective, it had always made him wonder about the backstory of his mother's prophetic statement. She had returned as a writer for *Ebony* magazine, among other journals and Chicago newspapers, to cover news stories that no other venues would cover. She wrote two notable books, including one on the Cairo civil rights movement.

Now it was bringing him back to Cairo. "No one really leaves Cairo," his mother had told him.

On his drive down the state he couldn't get the headline of Cairo's newspaper out of his mind:

FLORENCE JENKINS MISSING.

That was the right term—missing. She had been missed by so many people, starting with Randall.

6

___

The sign on the train overpass leading into Cairo, Illinois had lost its exuberance: WELCOME TO CAIRO! It seemed like a warning amid the overgrown weeds, rusted side bars, and chipped concrete walls that arched over the two-lane road.

Randall saw the signs of abandonment before any signs of life. He slowed his car to a crawl, passing empty lots that collected clumps of garbage, shopping carts without wheels, and a glittering of broken glass. Rolling down his window, he was hit by the acrid smell of a swamp that lingered from the nearby riverbanks. Boarded-up storefronts and taped windows covered with a collage of materials. Weeds the size of small apple trees emerged from the broken sidewalks. Second-floor windows were sealed with cinder blocks and planks of wood, the green paint now a faint riddle of squiggles. Walled in between two old buildings, a collapsed apartment house had not been cleared—even the yellow police tape had broken from a telephone pole on the corner, surrendering any attempt at safety.

Randall pulled up to a stop sign, and then lingered when he realized no one else was in sight. The lights of a hair salon should have reminded him that he was not alone. A food cooperative cast its neon sign with a light of hope. One car finally trundled down the side street like a reflection.

This was not the Cairo he had heard stories about from his grandfather when he raced around the downtown streets on his bike as a child. Cairo during the Civil War was where Ulysses S. Grant had built his command headquarters; it was where they had published five newspapers, saw ten steamboats arrive daily at the wharf, cranked out thirty tons of ice from the factory, featured a US customs house, and heard the screech of seven rail lines that connected Cairo to the rest of the world. Randall drove through the intersection, then turned left with his own sense of abandon.

When he pulled into the parking lot, the late-afternoon glare struck across his windshield. Wearing sunglasses, black jeans, boots, and a collared shirt, Randall reached in the door panel, emerged from the car defensively, and untucked his shirt, which now covered his pistol. It felt like the Caribbean down here, not Illinois.

The cascading steps of the Alexander County sheriff's office, however, looked like the backside of a strip mall. Narrow windows and anonymous doors lined the building. The courthouse was adjacent.

Randall wiped at his brow with the back of his hand, slammed the door of his car, and took a breath. Randall never liked entering police stations. He preferred the streets.

Before he could get his bearings in the hallway, the first thing Randall noticed after the chill of air-conditioning was the blare of a ball game from inside the sheriff's office. It was a St. Louis Cardinals baseball game—either on the TV or radio—but the shouts following every crack and update drowned out the announcer's voice.

"You Card fans crack me up," came a voice into the hallway, forced out of the room in jabs. "Even down by six in the ninth inning."

Randall saw the door was open to the office.

"After all these years in town, Sheriff, and you still haven't come around to the Cards," came another voice.

Only the chatter on the TV, which was perched to the side, like a framed window into Busch Stadium, continued when Randall walked into the room and leaned against the front reception counter. There didn't seem to be a lot of action in the lockup section. A handful of deputies in light brown shirts and dark pants chatted in the background, while one deputy sat at the counter on a stool. An older man with short gray hair, Sheriff Charles Benton, slumped against the wall, watching the game.

"That loser should've been sold years ago and had his ass extradited back to Santo Domingo," Benton roared, scanning the room.

Benton didn't budge from his roost, aware of Randall, but not bothered enough to make eye contact. The deputy at the reception counter, however, just stared at Randall.

Removing his sunglasses and placing them on the counter, Randall nonchalantly pulled out his badge from his pocket. He looked up with a

grin, and then put the badge by his glasses. Thrown off guard, the deputy
shot a furtive glance at the sheriff, and then picked up the badge without
a word.

"Good afternoon," Randall said. "How you doing? I'm a detective with
the homicide unit of the Chicago Police Department, in town to follow
up on a missing persons report, related to the disappearance of a Chicago
resident in Cairo."

Sheriff Benton peeled off of the wall, hardly breaking his concentration
from the TV, and moved toward the counter with a curious look. Sizing
up Randall's presence, the sheriff scratched at his chin. He was a thin
man, with the build of a short second baseman. The gray in Benton's hair
was slicked back. His wrinkled forehead, without his cap, gave him an
older look of someone who might be ready for retirement. The star badge
above his left lapel carried a sign of power.

"Sure you got the right town?"

Benton's voice had a hard accent from Chicago, not Cairo, which
threw Randall. The sheriff still swaggered like a local. He faced off with
Randall as the deputy stepped to the side, holding Randall's badge in his
hand in disbelief.

"Can't say I recall any missing persons report from a Chicago resident
in Cairo," he went on. "I'm Sheriff Charles Benton."

No one offered a hand of greeting.

"Yeah," Randall said. "This goes back to the 1970s."

"Holy cow, 1970s?"

Benton's laugh allowed the deputy to loosen up and break his own
smile. The sheriff handed back Randall's badge. The seriousness of the
moment had been dispelled. Randall scooped it up.

"You're out of luck on that one," Benton continued. "Most of the old
files were destroyed in the flood in 2008."

To make his point, Benton swirled around and pointed toward the
office window. "Big river out on those banks, if you hadn't noticed, you
coming from Chicago and all."

"I'm here about new evidence," Randall responded.

Benton motioned for the deputy to turn off the TV with the remote
control.

"What are you talking about?" Benton said to Randall, both of his
hands on the counter. "New evidence on what? As sheriff of Alexander

County, I think I'd know if there was new evidence in a missing persons case in my area."

Benton sounded confident. His posture looked the same to Randall, who picked up on the territorial nuance of the office. But his Chicago accent. Randall had expected to find some potbellied Southern sheriff chomping on a cigar.

"We need to discuss this in private," Randall said.

Benton motioned for Randall to follow him to his office in the corner, and then he sat down, pointing at a chair where a stack of newspapers sat.

"You can drop them on the floor," Benton said.

The papers slammed to the floor as Randall took a seat.

"The FBI contacted my office with lab reports from a federal highway archaeological site with new forensic evidence on the Florence Jenkins case," Randall said.

Randall tried to act as detached as possible. He had bluffed his way through jurisdiction issues many times in the past, but with this one, his insides tore at the mention of his mother's name.

"Florence Jenkins?" Benton scoffed. He tried to laugh. "Hell, Florence Jenkins disappeared years ago. That case was closed decades before I ever became sheriff."

"Forty-six years ago," Randall said. "It was never closed."

"Missing persons case was never closed?"

"It was a civil rights case," Randall insisted.

"Civil rights case . . . in 1978?" Benton asked.

There was a moment of stillness between the two men; neither wanted to show their cards.

"You think hate crimes ended in the 1960s?" Randall said quietly.

Benton held up a finger. The point was taken.

"Just saying," Benton went on, "those kind of things had quieted down in Cairo by then."

"I'm aware of that," Randall said. "Florence Jenkins was my mother."

Benton sat up in his seat. His eyebrows arched across his wrinkled forehead. He lowered his guard.

"My God," he said. "I didn't know. I'm sorry."

Randall nodded. "That's why I came by your office. There's been some new evidence found."

The two exchanged looks. An awkward silence passed.

"New evidence, huh. It's kinda odd the FBI would fail to contact me on this, though," Benton finally said, sitting back. "But I sure understand how you would have a personal interest in this."

For the first time, Randall felt cold in the air-conditioned room. Expecting the confusion, he was prepared with a backup story.

"I've been sent down by a Chicago PD and FBI partnership on this as lead investigator," Randall said. "I'll report back to both. "

Clapping his hands in a sudden gesture, Benton stood up from his desk.

"Well, this is something. In my jurisdiction. I'll need to be updated on all of this. I've only been sheriff for the past couple of years, but I'll check to see what we have on file. I'll do whatever I can to help." Benton hesitated for a moment, and then added, "And where did this new evidence emerge? At the riverfront? Lots of things floating down the river as far away as Ohio end up here."

"An archaeological site," Randall said, cutting off Benton's words.

"Archaeological site? Oh, that's right, you mentioned that. You mean that highway project?"

"The Moore Creek Archaeological Site, I believe it's called."

Benton smiled at Randall.

"Right, the Ft. Defiance Highway project for us. If you're looking for directions to the site, we'll be happy to lead you there."

Randall shrugged.

"I can find it," he said.

"Well, let us know if we can be of help."

In a final gesture, Benton held out his hand for the first time. Randall looked at it hanging over the counter like a challenge, and then reached out and shook Benton's hand.

"To preserve the integrity of this investigation, I need your cooperation in keeping this confidential, and not made public," Randall said.

Benton nodded.

"Of course, you can count on me. It won't leave this room."

Benton stared into Randall's eyes while they exchanged the pro forma parting words of law enforcement colleagues. Randall didn't trust this fellow cop and didn't know why.

As he walked down the hallway, he heard the cackle of a Cards fan mocking the Cubs.

7

CAIRO, ILLINOIS
ALEXANDER COUNTY

Randall's drive picked up on the details of Cairo's street life, the wave of a hand from an elderly person on a front porch, the suspicious looks of youths checking out his unmarked sedan with Cook County, Illinois, license plates. He sped through town in a minute, leaving behind the remnants of a waterfront life that disappeared years ago.

Experience had taught him to zigzag his way out of town. There were too many deputies in that office, with too much time on their hands. He had no desire to be bothered by a racist local sheriff's interference.

The first billboard out of town, as Randall turned onto a rural route, set the tone of the outer borough politics: GET THE U.S. OUT OF THE UN—OATH KEEPERS.

The billboard was a modern-day warning of a right-wing militia group of ex-military and defiant police armed with semiautomatic rifles, whose vigilantism had ranged from Ferguson, Missouri, to Charlottesville to the US Capitol. Randall knew what the Oath Keepers meant.

"How about getting your ass out of the US," he said to himself, rolling down his window despite the sweltering humidity. Rural routes called for an elbow on the windowsill, the wind in your hair, and the radio doing its best to transmit the static-filled R & B tunes from a remote Cape Girardeau station.

The next billboard brought Randall back to the present time: REELECT PRESIDENT WALLER, DEFEND THE WALL, DEFEND THE AMERICAN WAY. The backcountry was Richard Waller country, the solid Republican strands of rural America that wove a red quilt across the maps with invincibility. The upcoming election plowed through the state of Illinois—and the country—like a highway. You were either on the side of the swaggering Republican president or his liberal Democratic challenger, Sen. Elaine Adams from Chicago.

There was no meeting ground in the middle—not in this election.

Randall followed the directions of a map from Dr. Molly Moore that had been enclosed with the FBI report. Street signs on the dirt road didn't exist, only route numbers that curved along a heavily forested area of bald cypress and tupelo gum trees that seemed to suck the light out of the sky, and then those numbers disappeared with a series of turns.

A hand-scrawled sign—MOORE CREEK ARCHAEOLOGICAL SITE—sat on the edge of one side road. Soon after, another sign—STAY AWAY: TRESPASSERS WILL BE PROSECUTED—seemed to invite trouble.

He turned and sped onto the dirt lane.

Whether anyone had been waiting for Randall or not, there were enough signs at the haphazard parking lot of the dig site to ward off onlookers. Honeycombing ancient pottery sites had been a time-honored sport for most of the locals for years, so the advent of a new archaeological discovery drew the most lawful residents in the region. The warnings of danger, even death, made Randall laugh. The hurried handwriting on the signs abounded. It reminded him of homemade signs warning of guard dogs in Chicago, dogs that wagged their tails and licked the hands of officers right under the signs.

As he drove up to the site's entrance, he counted six cars, a pickup truck, a Southern Illinois University van, and a CBS-TV remote unit. The presence of the media confused Randall. He felt a pain along his neck, his hands stiffening into a clutch, and a feeling of uncertainty stretch across his chest. Had the young archaeologist tipped off the media on the discovery of Florence's bones? Had the sheriff? Was the TV news already spotlighting the new evidence in the cold case?

From his windshield's vantage point, he could make out a few structures on the opposite side of the lot, including an old barn. Along with tables and stakes, the rest of the area appeared to be cordoned off with yellow tape, like a crime scene.

Walking across the dirt lot, churning up dust with his boots, Randall waded through a crowd of people at a central tarp area to the side of the site. The closer he got to the edge, the more the excavation seemed to expand. Anticipating a site the size of a street lot, Randall began to feel the immensity of the rural expanse, as the archaeological boundaries stretched far longer than he ever imagined.

It was huge.

Randall realized that he had never been at an archaeological site, let alone investigated one. Standing at the rim overwhelmed him. For the Chicago detective, the array of deep pits unfolded like an underground library. All the subterfuge of urban life—the high-rise apartments, the back alleys, the storefronts, the underground tunnels—seemed so accessible compared to the gaping mounds and stretches of thick forest that surrounded the area.

"This is a restricted area, sir," came a voice.

It was Freddy, with his tall, thin presence, wearing denim overalls over a muddy T-shirt, like a young farmer ready to plant at the site. The attire of the rest of the crew and volunteers suggested to the Chicago detective that a casual reality was the norm here in the outback. At least on this sweltering day.

Randall stepped back. He didn't anticipate seeing any Black people, especially with dreadlocks, at the archaeological site.

"We have some fragile prehistoric sites here, and there's a no-entry rule," Freddy went on, unimpressed with Randall's silence. He assumed Randall was one of the many curiosity seekers from outside the region. "Sorry, but you're going to have to leave."

Randall stepped to the right of Freddy, wanting to keep his view of the site from being blocked.

"My God, this place is massive."

Randall took in the expanse of the pits and piles of dirt in quadrants. With all of the survey tape and mounds, volunteers marking off areas and carrying trays of artifacts, it almost appeared to Randall like the prehistoric village was in the process of being rebuilt, not uncovered.

Reaching into his pocket, Randall withdrew his badge and ID card. "I'm looking for Dr. Moore."

The Chicago Police Department badge didn't scare the local Cairo kid. At least it wasn't one of the Cairo cops he had dealt with in the region. Randall didn't look too threatening; he was alone, for starters, and looked out of place.

"Well, ah," Freddy said, looking over his shoulder at the far end of the site, "she's a little busy right now."

"Tell me, why's the media here?" Randall asked.

His voice was irritated. So much for secrecy; the damn archaeologist had told the world about the discovery of Florence's bones.

Freddy cleared his voice.

"You're standing at one of the most important archaeological finds in history," he finally said.

"That's it?" Randall questioned.

Freddy looked at Randall with a quizzical smile.

"That's not enough for you?"

8

—

Cheryl Harris, the veteran correspondent of CBS's *60 Minutes*, hustled down a sunken muddy set of steps of the dig site in rubber boots. She had been warned about the 95 percent humidity. She wore a long-sleeve blouse and long cotton pants to ward off the mosquitos, but her clothes now hung in matted clumps of sweat and mud.

"This is the best shot," said Harris's cameraman, who had already set up in front of the tarp-covered walls. The view behind Harris captured the deep layers of the dig.

Harris nodded as one hand touched up her sweaty hair, pulled back in a bun. She held a microphone with the other.

"Coming through," a voice rang out.

Harris spun around as Danny, a young worker carrying a long tray of skeletal remains, dodged her microphone, kicking a clump of mud onto her shoes and pants. Danny attempted to right the tray as a few bones fell into the mud.

"Sorry ma'am," Danny said as he held the tray with one hand, and bent over to scoop up the remains of a femur with the other parts of a skeleton. Wearing a fading St. Louis Cards baseball hat, Danny was muscular in his Megadeth concert T-shirt, and stocky as a baseball catcher in his shorts and black boots. A pair of headphones rattled with the thunder of heavy metal. A skull tattoo snaked down his arm and onto his hand, which took a fervent yank to pull one bone out of the mud.

"Danny, careful with that, for this soul's sake, you got someone's life in your hands." Molly suddenly appeared as Danny continued to wobble along the dirt path with the tray of remains. Molly could barely hide her amusement. She hustled over to his side and picked up a heavy crate blocking the passageway between burial sites. The reporter marveled at the young archaeologist's strength.

Standing opposite Harris, Molly put her hands on her hips in a pose of authority. She acted like the site director. She referred to her crew as Arkies, a silly term she had picked up in Vietnam. She grinned at Harris, enjoying the chaos. She liked keeping the media off guard. "I'm a redneck," she would tell reporters with a twinkle in her eye, especially when the research language at the laboratory degenerated into academic phrases too far removed from the dusty soil. But the redneck reference to Molly was about history, her militant coal mining family roots, when her striking great-grandfathers donned red scarves and rifles in solidarity with other union miners in the labor wars of a century earlier.

With a Yale T-shirt and khaki pants, Molly tried to exude the same aura of defiance, though Harris viewed her as an upstart. When they first met, the veteran reporter asked Molly the same question she had heard from so many others: "How old are you?" No matter; Molly was determined to put Cairo back on the map, instead of allowing it to wither into oblivion.

That had not always been her plan. When she first hopped on a Greyhound bus as a teenager heading northeast to an Ivy League scholarship, she vowed to never return to her hometown, ever. And she didn't—for years. First undergraduate, then graduate school. Then the doctorate at Yale, and summer digs in Mongolia and Tunisia, and then the big discoveries in Vietnam.

As far as Molly was concerned, her past in Cairo and southern Illinois was the past. She was more interested in someone else's prehistory.

Then came the phone call from Gen. Will Alexander.

"I don't trust anyone else to do this important dig," Alexander had told Molly. "It's mandated by the laws, you know, as we carve out this new highway, and I need someone I trust to get it done right."

After retiring from nearly forty years of global services in the Military Missions of the US Army Corps of Engineers, Alexander had returned home and founded the Ft. Defiance Construction and Engineering Company in Cairo as the headquarters for his private operations around the world.

Retirement wasn't quite the proper term. Alexander had quit in protest of the Obama administration's decision to abandon a missile shield defense system in eastern Europe. He had hailed it an act of treason to appease the Russians. Returning to southern Illinois, Alexander positioned his global company near Ft. Defiance in Cairo for more than familial ties. It was a remote part of the state—and country—that he considered outside the bounds of Washington's scrutiny.

Alexander, however, was always one click away from his deep Pentagon ties, and the backroom deal-making in Washington. He had his own network of high-level planners, strategists, and military brass, which he commanded with the chutzpah of a paratrooper jumping into battle, just as he had always done around the world. This time, however, he was determined to go beyond his reputation as "the bunker builder." The Ft. Defiance highway contract would be the beginning of a larger enterprise and a legacy that wouldn't be complete in his mind until he had set the foundations for his son and his burgeoning arms manufacturing empire, Gunnor, Inc.

Gunnor needed this highway to expand. The road to success in weapons development, however, was paved with required archaeological surveys in this part of southern Illinois. You couldn't walk across a field without kicking up an arrowhead. This meant quick and dirty digs to satisfy the state and feds for the highway project, Alexander had reminded Molly, just like the archaeological firms had always accommodated the green light for the coal companies. Not that Alexander didn't encourage her to expand her archaeological survey. He knew the region's archaeological treasury had yet to be fully unveiled. But for the sake of timing on his highway project and weapons depot, he had simply asked her to divert her work around his operations.

It did not take long for Molly to realize that this dig would evolve into such an important archaeological site and attract national news interest. After she filed her first findings, Molly had been flooded with local and regional media requests for interviews. With reporters looking for local hooks and headlines, these interviews had been easy, almost like rehearsals for the real show. Each interview was followed by an even larger media venue, forcing Molly to refine her presentation of the site and its meaning to the public. She felt like she was treading a line between academia, archaeology, and entertainment, with the fate of her home region's central role in ancient history suddenly in the balance. And this weighed on her. It was not a matter of getting the story wrong; it was more of an issue of not letting down the place of her roots.

The arrival of a crew from America's top national TV news magazine show had thrust Molly into a spotlight that forced her to be extremely deliberate with her words.

This was true when it came to Florence Jenkins's remains. In a closed meeting with her staff, Molly had given strict orders, on pain of immediate dismissal, to not mention that any contemporary bones had been discovered. None of the other archaeologists or staff knew of the many connections Molly now realized she had with Florence Jenkins. Molly had kept her promise.

Standing to the side, the cameraman gave Harris a thumbs-up. Molly looked at the camera.

"We're just outside the town of Cairo, Illinois, standing on the edge of one of the most important archaeological finds in North America. With the help of new high-tech equipment, researchers may have discovered the largest permanent village in the Mississippi Valley, thanks to Dr. Molly Moore, who is overseeing this extraordinary dig."

"Oh Lord, get ready," Molly thought, on hearing her name.

"As part of federally required excavations for the incoming Ft. Defiance Highway, this site is just the tip of the iceberg," Harris went on, "of the astonishing remains that have been hidden for more than twelve thousand years." She turned to Molly. "Dr. Moore, please show us where you first discovered this site."

"We've always known this was a historic site round here," Molly said. "As kids we found lots of arrowheads and pottery remains after the floods. I actually dreamt of finding a site like this."

"So, with history hidden for more than twelve thousand years, now your dreams have come true?" Harris asked.

"We found some of the earliest burial remains of domesticated dogs here," Molly continued, "which might place them around nine thousand years." She paused for the punch line. "In human years, of course."

Even if no one laughed at her jokes, Molly couldn't resist retelling them.

"So, this is a federally funded project," Harris stated.

"Yes," Molly answered. "The National Interstate and Defense Highways Act created by the Eisenhower administration requires new road development to assess historic archaeological sites before construction. We're very lucky because this section of the Ft. Defiance Highway cut through a remote area no one would have ever found."

9

——

Approaching from the opposite end of the site, Freddy guided Randall along the passageways through the pit houses, trash mounds, and burial grounds. Randall sensed Freddy's growing ease; the young archaeologist acted like he was giving him a tour of his own home. Freddy leaned against the stacks of pots and pottery shards like they were furniture pieces. He pointed at the tables of screens, where volunteers worked to separate mud and dirt from the skulls, dismantled rib cages, and other bones, with the detachment of gossiping in one's kitchen.

"Sounds like you like your job," Randall said.

"I learn something new every day out here," Freddy laughed. "The past is our prologue, as they say. And it pays quite well."

Descending into some pits as deep as thirty feet, Freddy showed Randall how Danny and a cadre of some students from the Cairo area had been trained to insert soil moisture measurement devices into an embankment.

"This looks like an explosive container," Randall said.

"Same concept," Freddy said, bending down to the dirt. "It measures the flow of electricity in the soil, which allows us to figure out differences in the soil moisture, and everything below."

Impressed by Freddy's technical language, Randall stepped back as he saw Molly with the television crew in the distance. She brandished a handheld magnetometer in front of her. Hoisting the long bar onto her shoulder like a rocket launcher, Molly showed how the instrument could measure the magnetic field around them, revealing underground landscapes.

The world of archaeology—something he had never considered—suddenly fascinated Randall. The archaeological site expanded like an ancient crime scene.

"We gotta keep it down near the interview," Freddy said, lowering his voice.

Randall moved toward the huddle of people around Molly and the CBS-TV crew.

"We first thought it was a hunting site, but with the help of the radar scans and remote sensing, we were able to go through layers of soil strata," Molly was explaining.

Molly pointed at the top of the archaeological pit, where Sandeep and two other Arkies worked at computers set up on tables under a tent.

"You see, the floodwaters over thousands of years have preserved this prehistoric site by depositing layer after layer of rich earth that supported the overgrowth in this semitropical region. We're setting up a GPS-linked virtual reality of the entire area," she added, motioning for Harris and the cameraman to follow her up a dirt staircase, "which allows us to understand what is going on below the ground, before we start to dig."

"Sounds like a video game," the cameraman laughed.

"Or a 3D map of history," Harris added.

Molly moved in her brisk way toward the tent, where Sandeep bounced back and forth, flipping through the three-dimensional images of the archaeological site between two large computer screens and keyboards. He moved like a disc jockey scrubbing vinyl records on a turntable. When the cameraman focused on Sandeep, Molly signaled for Sandeep to turn down the level of a hip-hop hit that cast an urban feel to the workspace. To his right, Anchee operated two other computers as Harris and her *60 Minutes* crew quizzically observed.

"I finished the new algorithm this morning," Anchee said, smiling at Molly. "Well, it was almost morning. More like four a.m."

"Check out these sick images," Sandeep added.

Molly stepped up between her researchers, looking at Sandeep's computer. A three-dimensional map of the valley appeared on the screen as red lines sliced across the soil strata into quadrants that formed settlement patterns.

"Holy cow, did you manage to mount the radars on the drones?" Molly said, impressed by Sandeep's quick work.

"We now have our own private laser up there in the sky," Sandeep gushed.

"Laser drone?" Harris said, looking over Molly's shoulder.

"No, it's not a laser drone like the military use, like a weapon," Anchee explained, "but we mounted our drones with this technology called LIDAR, which allows us to record what's in the earth below."

"They get a little carried away with their drones," Molly said to Harris, trying to hold back her own laughter. "But these two helped us prove that six thousand years ago these people were trading rare minerals as far away as Montana."

"Drones, radars, remote sensing," Harris said, holding up her microphone. "Indiana Jones's whip has come a long way in modern archaeology."

"Well, I wouldn't mind having a whip, now and then," Molly said, smiling. "But we haven't found any signs of conflict or weapons or a holy grail, or at least none yet that we're aware of."

Molly saw Freddy waving from the far end of the site. She knew the man with sunglasses and dressed in black was not a pot hunter. Molly recognized Randall from Chicago.

"I'll be right back," Molly told Harris as the cameraman shifted to the side.

Molly walked quickly toward Freddy, traversing the passageway through the main site. Motioning for Freddy to leave, Molly threw a concerned look over her shoulder. She wanted to maintain enough distance from Harris and her camera crew. Randall appeared from the side.

"So, you made it down," she said. "Wish you would have given me a heads-up."

"Listen, I'm here to see whatever else you found. Evidence you said you had for me," Randall said, taking off his sunglasses. His words stung with the challenge of mistrust. Molly knew Randall viewed her with suspicion, as if she might have held back the evidence on purpose.

"I just meant I could be more available to . . ." Molly said, her words drifting off.

"I've been officially designated the point agent on this investigation," he said. "We have a partnership with the FBI, especially on cold cases."

"Cold cases?"

It was the worst-case scenario for her work; to have her site shut down over some criminal investigation.

"I'm here to open my own investigation into your site."

"An investigation into this site?" she said.

Nodding, Molly bit her tongue at her openness. She wondered if she should not have gone to the FBI in Chicago.

"You got a problem with that, Dr. Moore?" Randall asked, his tone point-blank.

She looked over her shoulder at the cameraman. She lowered her voice.

"Look, can we deal with this after the interview? They arrived from New York last night."

Randall didn't seem threatening but imposing. As he looked out again at the vast site a crease under his tired eyes caught her attention. His face appeared concerned, and that suddenly worried Molly. As an investigator herself, she knew finding Florence Jenkins's body now revealed she had stumbled onto something of great consequence, not just auxiliary to the site.

"Shit, the dust," the cameraman was suddenly shouting, as he and Harris approached Molly and Randall. A gust of wind had swept across the area like a dust devil.

"Freddy will take you up to the barn," Molly said to Randall, "where the rest of the findings are stored. I'll join you as soon as I'm done."

Randall looked bothered by the situation; his own clock was set to another timeline. The reality of the national media had already scuttled his plans. He nodded at Molly as Freddy motioned for Randall to follow him up the hill. They didn't get far. As the two men were departing, the honking horns of incoming vehicles could be heard. A Hummer barreled down the dirt road. The county sheriff's sedan and two trucks followed in the clouds of dust.

Fearful of a sheet of dust on their equipment, Sandeep and Anchee hurriedly moved to cover their computers and instruments, though their frantic gestures gave the appearance of wanting to hide something.

Harris threw a vigilant look to her cameraman, who panned his camera toward the incoming cars.

Molly shook her head, striding out to meet the vehicles, which had blasted by the warning signs that had been posted on the outer boundaries of the archaeological site. All cars were supposed to park at the far entry of the excavation perimeter. Instead, the Hummer bumped over a mound of artifacts, and then swerved around a set of tables and screens, where the dig workers were meticulously combing through layers of soil.

"Stop those fools before they wipe out a thousand years of history," Sandeep cried out.

The Hummer jerked to a stop, raising a shroud of dust that drifted toward the tent. The sheriff's car and trucks grounded into their own pit stops of haze. Standing only a few feet away, Molly held up her hand to her face, pulling her bandana above her mouth to filter out the grime. She looked like some masked outlaw defending her outpost.

Watching from outside the barn, Freddy and Randall stood at its doors. Randall wondered why the sheriff had taken so long to arrive. He knew they would have tailed him. The entourage seemed like overkill.

"Stuff's inside," Freddy said, opening the heavy barn door.

"I'll come in a minute," Randall said, nodding at Freddy.

Far from being intimidated, Molly motioned at the Hummer with her magnetometer, threatening the reckless occupants who dared to override her security arrangements.

Indeed, she knew them. There was only one Hummer in the county. Emerging from the passenger's side of the vehicle with an incredulous smile was her mentor, Gen. Will Alexander, dressed in his usual attire of aviators, tan fatigues, a black T-shirt, and a tan vest.

His grin was anything but threatening. He looked more like a gung ho drill instructor who had arrived for boot camp.

Nonetheless, Alexander's visits were stressful for Molly, like an annoying weekly reminder to wrap up the operation as soon as possible. Molly had always shrugged at his demands.

"Will you look at this, Dr. Molly Moore," Gen. Alexander bellowed like a proud uncle.

Alexander was a generous man. He could certainly afford to be one. With the military ramp-up under President Waller's administration, Alexander's bunker-building expertise and military connections had won him more lucrative contracts than he could hardly manage.

"Molly, since the last time I came out here, your little sandbox has suddenly grown into a whole playground. My word."

Kicking through the mud and dust, the general came over and gave Molly a hug, and then he stepped toward the edge of the open archaeological arena. Sheriff Benton and a deputy had also stepped from the vehicles.

Randall remained in the background by the barn, his hands on his hips, like a surveyor still charting out the boundaries of the site.

The sheriff joined Alexander, gazing at the sprawling excavations.

"Reminds me of the diamond and gold operations in the Congo," Benton said.

"Good old days," Alexander laughed.

With the meter tool still in her hands, Molly joined Alexander at the edge of the site, where he stood with his hands on his hips. He looked down at her and smiled, and then turned and widened his smile to include Harris, who had arrived with her microphone in hand.

"What a beautiful day, ladies, hot and muggy like I like it," Alexander said, his voice more of a pronouncement than a greeting. "I tell you, Molly, first the local media, then the *Chicago Tribune* and *The New York Times*, and now CBS network television. You write a book, and they'll make a movie! You'll pay off your student loans in no time."

"General, please, you have to be more careful coming onto the site," she quickly responded, trying not to beg.

"Good morning, Cheryl Harris," Alexander said. "I sure love your program. Watch it every week. I'm Gen. Will Alexander. I'm in charge of this highway operation, which our officials at Scott Air Force Base are anxiously waiting to complete, and we sure are proud of Dr. Moore here. She's the star of Alexander County."

"Thank you," Harris said, stepping away. "We were just wrapping up here."

"With all due respect, General," Molly said, putting the magnetometer on the ground, marking a line between the two of them. "You're interrupting an interview on our work."

"Someone told me you found an effigy pot with a human head on it?" Alexander said. "I'm just so curious about what you're finding. I haven't seen any of those in years. We'll be more careful with our vehicles, I'm sorry."

Alexander's intrusion derailed the filming. With a deadline looming to catch her flight in St. Louis, Harris sent off her cameraman to take some B-roll footage of volunteers loading up crates and screens.

Motioning for Danny to bring over a little box, Molly moved away from Alexander's reach. Harris drifted away to another area.

"I think it's Early Archaic," she said.

"Really?" Alexander said. "My word, Molly, they didn't even find that at the Kincaid site."

Danny stepped up and then handed the box to Molly. Lifting up the cover, she reached in and pulled out a small, five-inch human head effigy pot. The general lit up like a little kid. Molly had to restrain him from touching the pot, which she kept firmly in her hand.

"Wow, that's a death mask, Molly," Alexander said. "Check out the headdress."

She looked at the top of the small effigy.

"I hadn't really examined it closely yet," Molly said. "You're right, General."

"But that's probably more Mississippian Period than Early Archaic," Alexander went on. "The shape of the eyes. It's just like the find at that Koster Farm site near Peoria on the Illinois River."

"Of course, General, I know the site," Molly said.

"But that's a beauty," he said. Alexander gave one final poke at the effigy, and then gazed out at the site. "You know, Molly, I hate to say this, but the feds are bustin' my butt to get this phase done." He shrugged, in a gesture of sympathy. "I'm sorry, but you need to hurry up your work. The funds for your project on this highway have to be expended by a certain date."

Molly closed the lid on the box.

"General, you know we've only begun the initial stages of the survey. The pandemic pushed us way behind."

"Well, I know, it's not me, honey. I'd be here every day helping you dig if I had the time. But I'm serious, we've got Washington breathing down our necks. And I got workers on idle. Every inch you dig deeper is costing the government a lot a time and money."

"I'm going through twelve thousand years of history here, General."

"Come on now, Molly. You've got more than enough layers of history and bones here for the rest of your life. What if you started with this section of your research, and allowed us to continue on the highway, and then you could come back at a later date to finish the rest?"

"It doesn't work that way, General." Molly laughed at the thought. "We have twenty-six layers of this site to examine."

"Well, to be honest, I'm in charge of those twenty-six layers," Alexander insisted. "And you were hired because of my recommendation," he added. "Not that I would have them revoke that, but let's be clear."

Molly turned her back to the general for a moment, thinking of a proper response. She lowered her voice, not wanting to draw attention on national TV.

"No, sir. My company was given the federal jurisdiction. This site is under our jurisdiction," Molly shot back.

An awkward moment of silence jutted between the general and Molly. Neither of them heard the soft approach of shoes on the dusty path behind them.

"Federal jurisdiction or not, this is my . . ." Alexander began to say quietly.

"Well, actually, this is a federal crime scene now," Randall suddenly injected.

His words stunned the other two with an air of indisputable jurisdiction. Having walked down from the barn, he had made his way toward the gathering without much notice. The comment cemented the jarring moment of silence between Molly and Alexander, as if Randall had flashed his badge with the finality of authority. Throwing a frantic glance in the direction of the news team, Molly worried the encounter would end up on tape. Fortunately, Harris and her cameras were still far enough away, chasing after volunteers. Benton and his deputies had moved to another area, focusing on Sandeep and his equipment under the big tent.

"This is Detective Randall Jenkins," Molly said.

The general turned to offer a handshake. His directness seemed a contrived act of concern to Randall.

Alexander took off his sunglasses.

"Gen. Will Alexander," he said, his voice low, seemingly moved by the meeting. "I understand you're the son of Florence Jenkins. I'm so sorry to meet under such circumstances."

Randall shook Alexander's outstretched hand. It felt like they were making some deal in the field.

"Our good sheriff will be at your service, detective, so you can properly carry out your investigation."

"That's good to hear, General."

Alexander's condolences delivered, Randall shifted to his side, angered at the thought of Benton violating their confidentiality agreement.

"I had asked the sheriff to keep this quiet," Randall went on. "This is a civil rights case now. The FBI, working with my CPD homicide division, has asked me to oversee this investigation."

Molly seemed stunned by the sudden intrusion of so many agencies on her site. Nor had she ever heard anyone so confident of their position and power speaking to the general on his own domain.

"Certainly," Alexander said, expecting Randall's announcement.

When Alexander placed his sunglasses back on, Randall thought the general seemed ageless in a way, both a relic of another era and still a physically fit soldier ready to attack at any minute. The general motioned for Molly back in the direction of the reporter and her TV crew, who had returned to the front part of the site.

"Go and finish your interview," Alexander said. "Again, apologies for the intrusion, and congratulations. You're prime-time now."

Relieved to be done with the two men, Molly shook her head in dismay and made her way over to Harris and her camera crew.

"Listen, Detective," Alexander said, walking Randall over to another pit. "As the contractor on this site, I understand your request to the sheriff that we need to keep this confidential, in order to keep our highway operations moving along, and your investigation untainted. You have my word on this. Don't be upset about the sheriff. He's required to report something like this to me, as head of the highway project." Alexander paused, and then continued. "It's in all our interests to keep this quiet."

The last line had a familiar air to Randall. It sounded like bullshit.

10

___

Flipping on the lights of the old barn, Molly motioned for Randall to follow her inside. "Over here," she said over her shoulder. "I'll show you what we found."

She didn't just turn on the lights; Molly pulled back the curtains on a complex station of investigation, revealing piles of artifacts, weighed-down tables, and lines of shelves stacked with labeled bones and pottery shards. The walls were plastered in maps and grids. The barn hayloft contained boxes and more cases.

Molly felt the tension between the two of them, leaving her ill at ease. Sighing, she thought carefully about her next words. She needed to play by the book and not allow herself, as a trustee of this found history, to be complicit in any wrongdoing, especially if it compromised her work. She wondered: What was going to be allowed in the process of investigating the death of the detective's mother? The destruction of her site? Or worse, a cover-up?

Randall was at home here, as he would be at any crime scene. But deep down, he felt strangely at sea. The emotions triggered by his mother had disarmed him for the first time in his life. At the same time, he recognized a difficult connection to Molly and her way of speaking. She was local, and that concerned him, and their entangled history with the Moore family would prevent her from being honest about stirring up the past, especially when it came to Cairo's civil rights woes.

The side wall of the barn, with stalls from years ago, caught Randall's attention. Molly had set up computer stations, with large screens and video-conferencing technologies. A stockpile of instruments foreign to Randall, such as LIDAR technologies and drones, sat on the tables like watchdogs.

Molly walked Randall over to her desk, which was covered in a sea of printed-out sheets and charts, as well as her notebooks. When Randall reached down to pick up some paperwork, Molly took it from his hands, feeling somewhere between outraged and intimidated.

"Please don't touch any of the research."

"This place looks like our crime lab," Randall said.

He couldn't help picking up a map with a series of grids. He looked at Molly in an impressed yet mocking way.

"Ph.D. at Yale? Dissertation of the Year from the American Archaeological Society based on your research in Vietnam. You worked in Tunisia, Mongolia." He hesitated for a moment. "What the hell are you doing back in Cairo, Illinois?"

Taken aback by his comment, Molly set down the map.

"A professor at Yale once reminded us that some of our greatest discoveries might be in our own backyard," she said.

"You found my mother in your own backyard."

His tone was anything but sympathetic to Molly's moment of honesty. Randall sounded pissed off. When she realized this, Molly took a breath and then pointed for Randall to follow her. On the opposite side of the barn was a long table covered with bones, skulls, stones, and hoes. Molly always referred to it as the puzzle table—the pieces still in search of a body or instrument or larger piece of pottery.

Randall found the table to be a macabre display of ruin. But Molly's unflinching arranging and sorting of the bones fascinated him. It took a certain kind of person to handle ancient skeletons and skulls while determining the details of the lives of those recovered.

She picked up a separate rectangular box marked with the exact geo-synchronous location where it was found, opened it, and delicately pulled out a skull, which had a tag dangling from its eye socket. Molly read the tag, to be sure of her finding.

"We have everything labeled and stored," she said, handing the tagged skull to Randall. "This is what we found."

Randall leaned back against the barn wall. He wasn't expecting to be handed his mother's skull in such a direct fashion. The light weight of the skull pressed into his hands, which Randall cupped, as if protecting a baby.

Molly understood the meaning of the moment, and suddenly she felt guilty. When Randall looked up at her, his mother's skull in his hands, Molly felt like he was holding her responsible for her death.

Molly knew that this was not a moment he wanted to share with anyone, especially someone like her.

"Let me, ah . . ." she started to say, but the words didn't come out.

Randall turned his back to her, and then leaned against the worktable. Molly wanted to comfort him, but when she moved in his direction, she felt a troubling sense of danger. She stepped back as Randall wiped at his nose with one hand, his other hand holding the skull.

"I closed off the part of the site where we found your mother," Molly went on. "No one has messed with the area or the rest of the evidence."

She wanted Randall to believe her, but when he spun around, glaring at her with an intensity she had not anticipated, she realized her words had resulted in the opposite effect. Randall looked like a changed person. Walking back to the table, he tenderly placed his mother's skull on the table, and then stared at it.

"I'm sorry," Molly said, trying to be close but not too close to Randall. "So sorry."

Her concern didn't appear to mean much to him. He continued to glare at her.

Molly walked away from the table. Randall, unable to look further, turned his mother's skull to the side. His face had shifted from a look of sheer bewilderment to a look of angry disbelief. His silence tugged at Molly. She wanted to leave the barn, as soon as possible, and she knew Randall could see that in her stammering manner.

"Look, we just discovered all of this," Molly said, now standing in the middle of the barn, "and I immediately turned in the evidence to the FBI. I'm not here to hide anything. My team will do whatever necessary to help."

Randall finally let go of his mother's skull, unloading a burden, gently placing it back in the marked box.

"You understand you are responsible for protecting this evidence," Randall said. Molly nervously nodded. "The investigation will be left up to the law," he added.

Both of them quieted when a commotion erupted outside of the barn. Molly recognized Freddy's and Danny's voices, and then the exchange of shouts with others.

"I need to talk to someone in town," Randall said. "I'll be back."

II

CEDAR STREET

CAIRO, ILLINOIS

She called it an "evening drink," especially the rosemary bushes, which emanated an intense, almost dizzying fragrance in the humid evening. Standing on the front porch on her 1920s bungalow, two side streets off the main drag of Cairo, Liz Hoskins was watering her herb garden.

Everyone in town referred to her as "Librarian Liz," from the kids to the old-timers, since everyone Liz encountered had walked away with a book in their hands, thanks to her school library. And everyone admired the abundance of this eighty-four-year-old's front yard garden, which straddled the broken sidewalks and nearby abandoned properties with the precision of a crop farmer. Boxed-in lanes of leafy zucchini sat next to rows of carrots, celery, broccoli, and brussels sprouts. Tomato vines climbed along a front gate, with little cherry balls of fruit hanging along the mailbox. Her front porch, which sloped to the right, was stacked high with crates of soil, which she had fashioned into an overflowing herb garden of rosemary, oregano, parsley, and sage.

When the black sedan pulled up to the curb, Liz tipped her watering jug, and then set it down. She looked closer, unable to recognize the driver. It was too dark, and outside of a little light on the side of her house, the street remained as obscure as a rural route. This driver didn't appear interested in the blooming eggplant or squash crop.

"I can't believe it," Liz finally said.

Liz wore a summer dress. She touched up her gray hair, which had been pulled back into a ball. She looked ten years younger than her driver's license would admit. She had never changed to Randall.

He emerged out of the car, slammed his door, and then stood, capturing the moment with a contented smile. Liz was his mother's sister. His dear aunt. That same gaze. That same pose.

"Is that you, Randall?" she called, carefully stepping down the porch. By the time she made it to the bottom of the stairs, he had already arrived and embraced her.

"Oh, son, it's been years," she whispered. "What brings you down?"

Randall held on to Liz, and then whispered back.

"Auntie, they found Mama's body in a field here."

He continued to hold her tightly as she burst into tears. Randall felt the years of turmoil pour out of her. His aunt shook, and that shook Randall's own resolve. Clasping Liz closer, Randall finally let himself feel the grief of a broken family, and a child who had lost his mother.

A voice from the porch suddenly broke their embrace.

"How long are you staying?"

Standing to the side of the cracked door, Pauline stared at Randall with a suspicious gaze. Strands of hair fell into her face like a mask. With one hand on her hip, Pauline looked ten years older than her age, even though she was Randall's younger cousin.

"Hello, Paulie," he said as he helped Liz up the stairs.

"I said, how long you staying this time?" she said with a relentless voice.

"Pauline, not now," Liz said, making it to the door, not revealing the news.

"Just saying," she went on. "We don't need any cops down here."

As Pauline disappeared into the house, Randall helped his shaken aunt slowly enter, and then looked back at his car on the street. His license plate may have shared the same state as Cairo, but he knew he was in another territory here—outside of his jurisdiction. He was from Chicago, in everyone's view now. He was an outsider, at least in the minds of people like his cousin Pauline, who had forever seen his side of the family as a broken branch. Those who had gone away. Those who had betrayed their hometown.

Randall had planted himself in the corner chair of her sitting room. Pauline stood by the door on the opposite side of the room, refusing to commit to sitting down.

"I can't believe what you're telling us after all these years," Pauline bemoaned.

Liz moved slowly but intently. Shaken by the news, she brought a tray of snacks and drinks into the room and hovered over the coffee table, reading glasses dangling around her neck.

She had never failed to be a gracious host with her defining Southern hospitality. There was only one main room in Liz's home—the sitting room, with ornate bay windows and bookshelves from the floor to the ceiling. Liz had not only been the school librarian; she was a living archive herself. As a child, Randall had always envisioned her as a sort of wizard whose library was where everything of importance took place. His childhood memory was surrounded by books, a tender image of two sisters, his mom and aunt always laughing together like a call-and-response team of jokesters.

"I need more time, I almost never have time to freshen up," she chided him. "Since that virus, I haven't had too many visitors."

"Especially from outsiders," Pauline added.

Randall did his best to smile, took a drink off the tray, and then looked over at an old *Ebony* magazine calendar, a gift from Randall's mother from Chicago in 1978, that had remained on the wall. Time had been frozen in that year.

On the coffee table in front of him was a stuffed scrapbook that Liz had retrieved at Randall's insistence from her bookshelf.

"Oh, I know this one well," Randall said.

Walking behind Randall to get a better view, Liz pointed at one of the faded color photos.

"I told you when you were here years ago that's the last picture we ever took of her," she said, wiping at her eyes.

Randall had framed this same one in his South Side apartment. He had looked at it every morning of his adult life. It was a photo of Florence Jenkins, standing next to the trunk of a 1974 Chevy Impala. Florence looked beautiful, vibrant, glancing over the top of her sunglasses like a movie star. A heart-shaped locket dangled at the edge of her blouse. She wore a scarf in her hair. In a red-and-white summer dress, her red shoes leaping from the otherwise faded photo.

"She'd come down from Chicago for Uncle Alfred's funeral," Liz said, taking a breath. "I remember it well."

"Summer of 1978," Randall said. "She didn't bring me, because she said she had to finish that piece for *Ebony* on the breakup of Stax Records in Memphis."

"That's right." She laughed quietly. "Sam and Dave days."

Lizzy turned more wistful.

"She pulled out of here in the morning. Last time anyone saw her was at that gas station on Mounds Road, heading back home."

Liz had relived that morning a thousand times in her mind. Flo's dress. Her promise to return to Cairo later that month for a special harvest dinner. Her jokes about life in the big city. Nothing seemed too out of the ordinary in her life then, after so many years of conflict in Cairo. For Liz, Flo appeared to have found her place in Chicago as a writer and journalist. After an unhappy marriage, she had just made the big decision to divorce, and had spent hours talking to Liz about her concerns for the young Randall in the process.

Her disappearance that summer day never made sense; her new life was just starting. Some jealous folks whispered about an old flame down in Memphis, but Liz knew that was not true. The remnants of the United Front claimed she had been murdered. Yet, the late 1970s had been calm compared to the late 1960s and early 1970s. By transplanting herself to Chicago, Flo had not played a role in local civil rights protests in years, outside of her writing. That didn't make sense to Liz either.

"That Mounds Road gas station still in business?" Randall asked, turning back to Liz.

"As far as I know," she said. "Old Leon's son runs it now."

"We don't need you digging up trouble down here," Pauline blurted out. "Things are bad enough as is. Know what I mean? Folks barely getting by down here. Last thing we need is some outsider creating problems."

"Pauline," Liz said, her voice troubled. "This is your aunt we're talking about."

"May she rest in peace," Pauline said, hesitating for a moment. "In peace, know what I mean?"

Randall took a deep breath. He knew Pauline was baiting him. She always did when they were kids. He felt a sense of sympathy for her, and that surprised him. Randall knew his presence was not easy. He had never come down "to visit," as Pauline would remind him. He had only come down to investigate his mother's disappearance.

"I've gotta do this," Randall finally said. His voice was small, but insistent.

"Do what? Pick some scabs? Reopen some wounds? Rustle up some bad apples down here, and then leave, and let us clean up the mess?" Pushing off the wall, Pauline wasn't finished. "I'm sorry to hear about Flo, but we buried her a long time ago. We had to. We had to move on. You understand me? Last thing we need right now is some cop digging up her memory in search of a crime."

Liz could see Randall's unflappable presence was cracking with each word from Pauline. His mother, Flo, had that same sense of self-possession about her. That grin.

"Let's celebrate Flo's beautiful memory then," Liz interrupted.

Randall turned to a rare photo of himself with his mother and father on a fishing boat, down at the Mississippi River. He looked like he might have been six or so. They were happy then, or so he thought. Holding a fish in his hands with a wary expression, the young Randall stood in front of his parents. The divorce had left him in a state of sadness, estranged from both parents, as if his mother had abandoned him in the boat by himself.

That feeling of abandonment and distrust had stayed with him all of his life, even after Randall had moved into a strange new house with his father after Flo's disappearance. The absence of his mother's voice was felt, unable to fill the gaps in his father's distant relationship.

"How's your daddy doing?" Liz asked.

Randall shook his head.

"He's hanging in there," Randall finally said. "He's getting the kind of attention he needs."

"You see him often?" she asked, looking at Randall.

"Whenever I can," Randall said. "But this dementia. Sometimes I feel like he's gone, and he's just refusing to leave his body."

"He's still living, Randall," Liz said. "But now your mother is gone. You need to accept that."

Randall's hand landed on another album page, right on top of a photo of young Nazis wearing swastikas as they picketed in support of the local White Hats white supremacist group in the late 1960s in Cairo. Randall pointed at the photo. His mother was in the line of defiant locals. It always shocked him. It had made national news, too. The Nazis defiantly broadcast their racist views on their placards: Back to Africa, Support White Police, Shoot Black Snipers, all adorned with swastikas.

"Back to Africa," Randall said under his breath.

He stopped speaking as his finger outlined the placards, and then he leaned in, looking closely at one of the photos. It was clearly a young Charles Benton, the county sheriff as a youth in a white shirt.

"What the f . . . This guy looks like that sheriff," Randall said, looking up at Liz.

"How do you know Benton?" Pauline said, still fixed at the door.

"That is Sheriff Benton," Liz went on. "He was elected just a short time ago, but he's been with the general for many years. Worked abroad with him, and then came back when the general retired," Liz said.

"He's from Chicago, too," Pauline said. "Just like you."

"Pauline, hush," Liz said.

"The general," Randall said.

"Gen. Alexander, of course," she responded, turning the page in the album to another protest scene.

"He came back, too," Pauline interjected. "But at least he's bringing jobs and some investment with him. No one gives a shit about Benton."

Randall felt like his finger was burning on the photo of the young Nazi Benton, who sucked on a cigarette, holding a sign that said Shoot Black Snipers. The burning sensation moved to Randall's stomach; it made him want to wretch. How could someone who openly marched in Cairo with a swastika armband now brandish the sheriff's uniform as an elected police official?

Randall remembered being a young police trainee looking into the dark history of Cairo. He had sat for hours in the state archives learning about how outside Nazis supported local white racists who refused to integrate their lunch counters and shops into the 1970s. In the end, their racist defiance had brought Cairo to its knees and ultimately left the town in ruin. The white businesses pulled out of town, gutting the foundations of the economy. Store windows soon became boarded; the sidewalks disappeared. The stately mansions retreated behind weeds. Those who remained, largely Black folk, were the last anchors in a river town swept away by an unforgiving tempest.

Reaching over to close the album, Liz cut off Randall's hold on history. The album served its purpose. She kept it as a living witness to history, at least as long as she was still living. The photos and newspaper articles on Flo's disappearance held a deep personal meaning for her.

"You need to remember this, Randall," she said. "The disappearance of your mama broke something in all of us. All of us." She paused. Randall looked toward the front window, then at Pauline, and finally turned back at the Chicago calendar.

"She didn't disappear," he said. "She's been here the whole time."

12

—

Molly worried about her mom's drinking. Especially in the evenings. Especially when they were alone on the back porch of her cabin in the Shawnee forests, where the isolation amid the trees and thickening bush and limitless stars lent itself to another drink.

Harriet Moore wasn't alone, however. Her companion Earl Karnes sat next to her on a bench, buried in a stack of old cushions. A retired plumber, he also hired out as a river guide on the Cache River, taking birders from the Chicago and St. Louis Audubon Societies, and then hunters from Kentucky and around the region. Locals knew him as one of the last Shawnee in the area. He kept Harriet company. He wasn't local, except that everyone accepted the fact that all Native people were local at one point.

"Think I'll get something to eat," he said, rising from his seat. "You already eat, Molly?"

She nodded.

"Thanks, but I'm good," she said.

The back screen door slammed as Earl went into the house.

Molly worried about something else—and someone else's mother. Sitting in a wicker chair on the porch, under the night sky, Molly looked over at her mother, who nursed a ceramic cup that she held in her hands. Harriet lounged on a wooden swing on the opposite end of the porch. She preferred the ceramic cup, which she had shaped herself, to hide whatever was inside. Tonight was bourbon, with her box of Marlboro Lights.

Molly smiled at her mother, who lightly pushed the swing back and forth with her foot.

"Do you remember a woman named Florence Jenkins?" Molly asked.

Taking a quick drink, Harriet looked askance at the comment; she was either offended or irritated. She halted the swing with her foot.

"You gotta ask your father about that shit," she said. "He's the local boy. So many stories, I don't know what's true anymore and what's a tall tale."

Molly smiled, as she had learned to smile in a strained way whenever she was reminded of her parents' bitter divorce. Her father was a distant presence in her life, now living down in Kentucky; his extended family even more. She had never known her grandfather. She had only heard stories about him, no different from the way she had collected stories about the prehistoric peoples in the region. He seemed as mysterious, contradictory, and strange as other figures in the black-and-white photos of the past. In many respects, he was just another person in a historic photo or newspaper clipping to her. His fame or infamy disgusted her. Some considered him a legend. Others were more muted, refusing to offer any details other than his daily bona fides.

In truth, Buster Moore's shadow and his involvement in the White Hats, as a Klan leader in the 1960s, had not escaped Molly. It had dogged her. Cairo was a small town. Teachers tended to teach multiple generations of students. Molly remained "Buster Moore's granddaughter" for years, at least until she graduated high school, and left town on that Greyhound bus. With each year it had become a fainter moniker, and with each retiring teacher it became even less important to note. The only exception was on Martin Luther King Jr. Day, when Cairo, now majority Black, was reminded of its brutal racist past and the civil rights heroes who had brought the town's troubling story to the nation.

When she returned as "Dr. Moore," the Yale scholar who had run off to Southeast Asia to chase her dream as an archaeologist, some locals accepted her new identity with pleasure and put her grandfather's reputation to rest. But not all. A few of the old-timers from Buster Moore's era were still alive or had clear enough memories to matter. The Moore name was not forgiven.

Harriet, though divorced from Molly's father after six years of a rocky marriage, never forgot a single word or story or accusation. As a young woman from outside Cairo, Harriet had paid dearly for her broken marriage, especially among those who considered Buster Moore the face of Cairo's racist past. Forced to remain in the area due to custody laws, Harriet had lived with Buster Moore's ghosts, because she had posed with him in more photos than she cared to admit. Those photos, like prehistoric artifacts, never vanished. They kept reemerging at the wrong moments in people's lives.

"One thing I do know," Harriet suddenly said. "Your grandpa Buster Moore died of a rotten heart."

Kicking a small bench in front of her, Harriet rose from the swing and stormed into the house. The back screen door slammed. It wasn't the first time for Molly. Staring at the same Leo constellation that kept her company in Vietnam, Molly wondered if her true home was elsewhere. Living in a trailer at the archaeological site was no real home, for sure.

She closed her eyes, and listened to the cicadas and buzz of insects.

Within seconds, Harriet was back on the porch. She held a large box of materials with both hands. Dropping it in front of Molly, Harriet was amused by the fact that a pointy white Klan hat fell onto the floor in front of her feet.

"Here," she said. "I've saved this goddamn box for a long time. Wanted to burn it so many times, but I never did. I'm haunted by it every night. Haunted by how long I stayed with your father and that family of White Hats. I was so young when I got married. I didn't understand nothing then. And I don't understand anything better now. Perhaps you will."

Harriet walked over to her swing and slumped down, without a glass or cup or anything but her bare hands, which she wringed in an intense way.

"But, poor Flo Jenkins," Harriet suddenly whispered. "She was a fine woman."

Easing out of the sink of the chair, Molly bent over the box and started to go through the Klan souvenirs, the pamphlets and books, and even a few photos.

"What does my grandpa have to do with Florence Jenkins?" Molly said, looking over at Harriet, who stared into the darkness of the woods.

"Hell if I know, Molly. And I don't want to know. There's so much blood on Buster Moore's hands, I don't want to know anything."

13

———

Liz had over a dozen albums, intent on chronicling the history of Cairo, not only her own family. Sitting alone on the small bed in the guest room, a lamp by his side, Randall continued to flip through his aunt's scrapbook. Each album had been dated and the themes and issues noted on the side of the binding. Randall understood the shared investigative talent in his family. Not that this bedroom had changed in the three decades he had visited the house.

"Still up?" Pauline said, standing at the doorway of the bedroom. She carried a clean towel in her hands, and then set it on the bed. "You get hungry, there's more peach cobbler in the fridge."

Randall smiled, looking up.

"Thanks, cuz."

Pauline was finally softening, or at least adjusting to his presence.

"I'm going home now," she went on, "but you gotta promise me something."

Randall nodded.

"My mom's elderly," Pauline continued. "I know it's hard for you to be down here. I know the discovery of Flo's bones is difficult for you. But it's also difficult for all of us, especially Liz." Pauline hesitated for a moment. "Those bones have been buried in our hearts for years like a stake."

"Mine too," Randall said.

"I'm a nurse, Randall," Pauline went on. "I bandage people up. I help them get better. I don't know what your intentions are, but I'm hoping you don't plan on ripping off the bandages just to take another look at the wound. I'm not sure everyone, including my mom, can handle that."

Randall looked down, flipping a page in the album.

"What do you want me to do?" Randall finally asked, peering up at Pauline. "Just walk away from this? From my mother's murder?"

"Murder?"

The word jolted Pauline. She looked down in silence, unable to respond.

"I can't walk away this time, I can't. I'll never heal. None of us will until we find out what happened to her."

Randall inadvertently flipped the page of the album, landing on an article about the 2008 flood, which had swamped the town from the deluge of the Mississippi and Ohio Rivers. A news clip featured a photo of a teenage Molly Moore, with the same hairstyle as her later years, assisting with the flood recovery operations.

"You know this girl?" Randall said, motioning for Pauline to join him on the edge of the bed.

"That's Molly Moore. She's Buster Moore's granddaughter. She's kinda like the town star."

Randall shook his head, closed his eyes, exhaled in shock, and then looked closer at the photo. Molly looked like a kid.

"Buster Moore's granddaughter?"

"Uh-huh, his granddaughter," Pauline said, "but she's a good kid."

The tone of her voice unnerved Randall. He couldn't hide his disgust, again shaking his head.

"See, this is your problem, Randall. You don't know how things are down here now. They're not all bad, the Moores," Pauline went on. "Some of the better apples fell far enough away from the tree."

"And let them keep their secrets buried?" he scoffed.

He flipped the page out of anger, turning to an article on a Black history exhibit.

"After the big flood in 2008, Molly Moore set up an exhibit at the customs house on Black history. She was just a child then. That's when she was at school. Made the town proud. Just like she's doing with that big archaeological site now."

Randall quickly shut the album.

"Easy for white folks to talk about Black history, like it's over," he said. "Diverts them from talking about the present."

Pauline wagged her finger at Randall.

"You don't know anything about what's happening in Cairo, or that girl," she said. "Molly Moore is digging up the past to understand it."

"That's why I'm here, Pauline," Randall said, his voice almost pleading. "That's why I'm here."

14

—

Molly climbed into Randall's sedan.

"Thanks for asking me to come along," she said, closing the door.

He didn't respond, nodding in a way that somehow confirmed her presence without actually condoning it. Randall knew Molly could be useful in his investigation. When she had phoned him that night, inviting him back to the archaeological site, after he had demanded to view the exact plot where Flo's body was found, Randall said that he needed to visit the Mounds Road gas station first thing in the morning.

"Old Leon's place, I know it well," Molly said. "If I come along, my site is on the way."

Randall didn't say no, even though he honestly wanted to keep his distance from Molly. From the Buster Moore family. After going through the box of Klan memorabilia, Molly felt the same. She just didn't know how to tell Randall.

For the first minutes in the car, he didn't say a word, following her indications to turn left and then right onto a rural route.

Small talk had no place in the car. Not between the two of them.

Molly decided to break the ice—with a sledgehammer.

"I assume you know who my grandfather was."

Randall nodded his head.

"Of course I do."

"You know, I'm not . . ." she said, her words trailing off. "I mean, that's not me."

68

Randall looked at Molly briefly, and then back at the road. He wasn't in the mood for denial.

"That's real good. I'm so glad you told me."

Molly flinched at the shade of sarcasm in his tone, and still she wanted to say more, but it didn't come.

"I wanted to say . . ." she tried again.

"Turn here?" Randall asked, cutting her off.

She nodded.

As the car bumped onto a dirt road, she tried to talk again, but the words didn't come out. She wanted to apologize for what she despised about her family—and herself. She wanted to plead with Randall to recognize her own life decisions. But Molly knew such apologies and pleas were empty words to Randall.

Old Leon, as he was known, was standing in front of a gas pump and his 1950s-era station when the sedan pulled into the lot. He was an old man, indeed. Probably in his nineties, he still came to the station every day, though he had passed the operations down to his son Leon Jr., and then his grandson, Little Leon. Leaning on a cane, Old Leon wore a straw hat, and a set of suspenders that held up his pants to his rib cage.

Without mentioning the discovery of the bones, Molly had called him in advance, alerting him of Randall's intentions. Old Leon was waiting. He had been waiting for this moment for years. His son, who resembled him closely, watched from inside the station almost like an old window display.

"I remember it well," Old Leon said after Randall and Molly had stepped out of the car together, an imposing sight of Black and white for the elderly man. He didn't offer them a place to sit inside. He didn't say he was sorry for Randall's loss. He wanted to make his peace outside, by the pump, exactly in the place he had witnessed the event years ago.

"Not like you'd forget the sight of your granddaddy Buster . . . and Florence Jenkins standing together," he went on.

"Buster Moore?" Randall said, his voice tense.

"And Florence Jenkins together?" Molly said, startled by the admission.

Randall adjusted his sunglasses. Molly stood on the other side of Leon, by the pump, trying to shade her eyes from the glare of the sun. Her jeans were smudged with dirt; her T-shirt was edged with sweat.

"When was this, spring or fall?" Randall said. He didn't find the old man charming. Nor did he trust the select memory of someone in his nineties.

"Spring? Well, wait now, no," Old Leon said. "It wasn't no spring. It was a hot summer day. Summer, it was. 1978."

Randall nodded. The old man had passed the first test.

Old Leon spoke like he was back in the 1970s—or even the 1960s. The default language of the present tense intercut into his language, reliving the moments of history again. For he had been part of history, part of the group of white supremacists in the late 1960s that launched countermarches and attacks against civil rights advocates who had simply demanded the right to shop at the local stores, have decent housing, and have access to jobs.

"Buster was an old friend of mine, you know," Old Leon said. "Went way back. I hadn't seen him in a long time, though. So, on that day in 1978, I didn't think much of his visit. But soon enough, I knew something strange was up."

"Strange?" Molly asked.

"See here now," Leon went on. "Buster pulls up in his pickup truck." He pointed on the opposite side of the pump. "I come out to meet him, 'cause in those days we do the pumping for the customers. Buster is as mad as all get out. As I pump the gas, he's railing about Alexander."

"Alexander?" Randall said.

"The general," Molly answered. "There is only one Alexander down here."

Old Leon continued, oblivious of Randall's question.

"Buster says Alexander has made a lot of orders for pipes and construction equipment, and hadn't pay him yet, so Buster was going up with a load to get paid."

"Were you a White Hat with Buster?" Randall asked.

Old Leon cleared his throat.

"I know what you're thinking, but Buster Moore was a changed man then. The days of United Front and White Hats battling was over. Lord Almighty, Buster Moore had found the Lord."

"My grandfather never set a foot into a church in his entire life," Molly blurted out. "For Christ's sake."

She shook her head. Leon's story had already fallen apart.

"Go on then," Randall said. He had dealt with racist deniers before.

"We seen Flo Jenkins walk up to the station. She's hot, sweating, carrying a bag and her cameras. Everyone knows her. That she's gone off to Chicago and all. So when Flo Jenkins walks up to the pump, she says her car has broke down, just over the road, and she needs a ride into town. Now, here she is, all sweaty from walking, carrying all those cameras. I remember she had on real nice red shoes. Real nice dirty red shoes, I remember them now."

"Red shoes," Molly echoed.

Randall turned back to Old Leon, trying to not lose the thread of his story.

"You're sure it was Florence?" Randall interrupted. "She'd been gone from Cairo for years. How did you know it was her?"

Old Leon stared at Randall, wiped the edges of his mouth, and then continued.

"Sure as can be. It may have been years, but I have never forgotten her face."

"Why's that?" Molly said.

"This is gonna sound funny, young lady, but you gotta understand. I knew Flo Jenkins very well, and I'm not proud of it, and I feel ashamed now, but I'll never forget her face for I had once hit her on a picket line."

"You hit her?" Randall said. Enraged, Randall stepped forward and glared at the old man. "The fuck?"

Old Leon flinched, bracing for Randall's response.

"Go on," Randall said. "And don't you lie to me . . . tell me the truth."

"I knew who she was when she come walking up to the station, and I felt bad. And so did Buster. Your granddaddy wasn't proud of his White Hat days neither," Old Leon went on.

"Damn, Leon," Molly spoke out again. "We all know he went to his grave with a white hat."

"I said tell the truth, old man," Randall said.

"You gotta believe me," Old Leon said. His voice became small, whispery. "Buster didn't have no intentions to harm your mother. So, he up and offered her a ride into town. I saw 'em. He filled up the truck and off they went."

"I can't believe my mother would get in the truck with Buster Moore," Randall said.

"I saw it with my own eyes," Old Leon insisted.

Leon paused for a moment. Randall looked at Molly with utter disgust.

"I know about my granddaddy," Molly finally said. "He died an unrepentant racist. Don't tell me he had turned around."

The comment made Randall kick at the dirt and step away.

"Wait a minute. They found Buster's body the next day," Old Leon said, his words halting Randall's stride.

"So what? How does that clear Buster Moore?" Randall said.

He turned back toward Old Leon. Molly crossed her arms, staring at the older man with the knowing gaze of someone who had spent her life listening to storytellers.

"They said Buster had a heart attack, but I don't believe that one bit," Old Leon said, shuffling toward Randall, beseeching him with a plea. "And no one ever found Florence neither. They never found her body. But nobody ever questioned what happened to Buster neither."

"What's the connection?" Randall said. He glanced at Molly, then back at Old Leon.

"I can't tell you that, but they done 'em in."

"They?" Randall said. "They who?"

Old Leon trembled, clutching his cane; it was the only thing keeping him afoot.

"Well?" Molly said, her voice adamant.

"Lot of people didn't like Buster," Old Leon said, his voice barely audible. "Lots of people didn't like Flo Jenkins neither."

The old man's explanation didn't add up to Randall. It almost made Buster Moore, the infamous leader of the White Hats, seem like a victim. That was one image that didn't belong in the same picture with his mother.

"Okay, I'm done here," Randall said.

Molly looked at Randall, unsure what to think, though she knew enough to not trust Old Leon. It was an old story to her; the old ones looking for redemption as they faced their reckoning with a lynch mob past.

"My grandfather died from a heart attack," she said, her voice quiet.

Randall appeared to be unfazed; he had heard enough conspiracy theories on the streets of Chicago to keep him from trusting any source. He nodded at Molly to head back toward the car. The signal was clear. This interview was over.

There was no final word with Old Leon, no handshake or farewell. If anything, he had only added to the tension between Randall and Molly;

he had placed them back into the same car with a match ready to inflame the engine.

As Randall opened the car door, however, his phone buzzed. He leaned against the outside of the sedan as Molly climbed into the passenger's seat. She looked out her side of the car, barely managing to stay so close to Randall.

The voice on the other end of the line didn't surprise Randall. His daughter Teresa, in fact, spoke in an unusually soft manner.

"It's Pappy," Teresa said, her voice faltering. "I just got word from the hospital."

There was a long pause. Randall hunched over the phone. Looking outside the window, Molly could see his body lean against the car.

Something important hung on Teresa's words.

"Are you still down there?" she said.

"Yes, in Cairo," Randall responded. "I'm coming home now."

Leaving the flicker of Old Leon's gas station in his rearview mirror, Randall knew the trip back to Chicago would be a grueling one.

"I'll drop you off," Randall said to Molly. "I've got to get back to Chicago. This old man is just telling lies, anyway."

Molly could see a strain tighten Randall's face. She picked up on his distraction in the last minutes of the interview, his attention trailing away. Randall had not even muttered a goodbye to Old Leon. Getting into the car, he had been too preoccupied to follow up with any notes, or any of the new details. The just-ended call had shattered his investigation, and any new evidence would be left behind.

"Another case?" Molly asked.

Randall shook his head, and then stared ahead at a road sign for Cairo. He felt condemned to leave Cairo and its entangled history for the rest of his life.

"No," he finally said after a long pause. "My father just died."

Molly gasped.

"I'm so . . ." she began to say, but the words petered out into a gush of emotions.

"Don't have to . . ." Randall mumbled, disgusted by the thought.

He put the pedal to the floor and peeled down the dirt road.

15

Molly's daddy always said they were *hainted* by the unseen things in their lives.

For the first time since she had come back for the big highway contract and discovered this monumental site, Molly felt overwhelmed by her situation. She felt haunted—or *hainted*, in the old dialect—by a family she couldn't escape.

Maybe Gen. Alexander was right, Molly thought. She had enough material from the dig to justify several academic papers, if not a book. Perhaps she should just wrap up her work on one section, and let the dead bury the dead.

The chorus of a riverboat song came to her, "Goin' Down to Cairo." She had learned it from her father, who had learned it from Buster, when she was a kid shucking beans on their back porch. "Black them boots and make them shine."

The river levees had broken too many times to remember some stories, at least for the handful of people who had stayed in town after the floods. The alleyways were haunted with the remains of so many battles that people had lost track of the dates when the lights once shined in the local movie theater, when streetcars clamored up busy streets, and when a lynching brought thousands to an intersection to witness the spectacle of a Black man hanging from the steel arches welcoming folks to the historic downtown.

Molly had wanted to run away from this history so many times.

But Cairo called her home.

History was below the surface of these ruins now. It had faded to unsolved crime stories. The firing line of racial strife left behind bullet marks in the 1970s, which had disappeared into the rubble and weeds. Bridges led out of town to somewhere, but they could not span the one river of peace the town had never managed to cross.

Molly thought about all of this as she drove out to the archaeological site. She thought about Randall Jenkins and his mother, Florence. She had thought about them ever since her trip to Chicago—and Randall's visit to the site. They had never left her side. They haunted her.

Randall had driven off leaving the dust of an impasse that would linger between their families and their own rapport for the rest of their lives. Or, at least, that was how Molly felt, and it tasted like a bitter brew in her mouth.

Molly pulled her car into the excavation site with a sense of defeat. On the other side of the old barn, three mobile trailers sat on a hillside at the far end of the parking lot. Molly had insisted on round-the-clock oversight, given the high interest in the dig by local prowlers and souvenir seekers.

Stepping into the old barn, Molly went for the box of remains from the Florence Jenkins excavation. Overwhelmed by his father's death, Randall had left town without them. What would he do with them, she wondered?

Molly bent over a large burlap bag, and then halted for a moment. Someone had kicked over a pot. Molly wasn't alone in the barn.

Standing at the front door of the barn, Sheriff Benton appeared with a cadre of deputies. Benton, his hat tipped to one side, breathed out of his mouth. He looked incensed, like he had been left out of a party.

"Molly," he said.

"Sheriff?"

"You know the general's getting more impatient and uneasy about his highway project," Benton said.

"We're working as fast as we can," Molly said.

Benton's intrusion into her enclosed research space bothered her. Yet, Molly knew how to play the game of local politics.

Looking around at all of the bones, skulls, and pottery shards, Benton seemed uneasy about the confines.

"As the county sheriff," he went on, "I do hope you keep me posted if you've found any more information on those bones. The newer ones. If you have any other evidence, you need to keep it in our office for safekeeping."

An awkward silence passed.

"Just want to make sure things are kept safe," he added, acting concerned that Molly might have misunderstood his intentions.

"All the artifacts have been sent to the federal authorities, following their protocol," she said. "If you want to check out some skulls and bones and pottery from 900 A.D.," she said, "be my guest."

Benton flinched, almost shocked by the offer.

"No, absolutely not," he said.

Molly felt she was in deep now, lying on behalf of Randall. She did not trust Benton or anyone in the sheriff's office.

"Dr. Moore, Dr. Moore," came a voice from outside the barn. It was Sandeep, who appeared with Freddy and Anchee. "Excuse me for interrupting, but we need your help on the radar, Molly."

This was a good moment to break the conversation, Molly thought.

"We must be on our ways, Sheriff," she said, reaching out a hand to bid Benton goodbye. "My team and I need to get back to our site work."

As Benton walked to his car, Molly picked up the box with Florence Jenkins's remains, heading in the opposite direction to the far end of the site. Wind had already begin to whip up the dust along the edges of the pits as the team struggled to tie down tarps. It may have been sunny, and clear in the sky, but Molly knew what the winds from the southern delta could bring. So did the unemployed highway workers, in Molly's mind, who hovered nearby with their waylaid bulldozers and equipment. These road crews had been denied a roadbed that, according to the law, first had to be cleared by Molly. The area was a treasure trove of indigenous history.

Flo's remains would be protected. Molly promised herself that.

16

—

NATIONAL GEOSPATIAL CYBER INTELLIGENCE CENTER
SCOTT AIR FORCE BASE, SOUTHERN ILLINOIS

Less than twenty-five miles east of St. Louis, Scott Air Force Base sat off the highway in the dense woods of southern Illinois. Dark asphalt ramps followed the hardwood forests that trundled south, passing abandoned farms and boarded-up houses, until they disappeared into the darkness. Barbed wire mixed with the wild ivy. The base buildings were nondescript, like large warehouses with offices.

An end-fire helical antenna perched among other vast satellite installations. The flat roof did not divulge any other information. It stretched down a quad like the rest of the buildings, as drab and unmarked as a block of storage units. A small window above a door interrupted the side walls.

Special operations agent Alison Foreman was back in a new arena at the cyber intelligence center. She had only been stationed here since the launch of a special operation to monitor a new Russian weapons project. Her mission involved navigating a small sliver of the cyber world, but an important sliver. As a liaison among agencies, Alison pivoted between her military past and posts at the Defense Threat Reduction Agency and the National Geospatial-Intelligence Agency (NGA) cybersecurity center at this secret outpost in southern Illinois.

She stared out the window of her office with a longing expression, knowing that her face remained in the shadows. For the native New Englander, the warming temperatures had changed her favorite season of autumn into hell in this godforsaken part of the heartland. It may have been Illinois, but it seemed more like the South.

The nomadic life in military intelligence had given Alison insight on everyone's life on the front lines from the Middle East to Eastern Europe to secret operations on military bases in the United States—and left her lonely. Alison looked at her reflection in the window. She ran a hand through her short dark hair, and wondered if she would celebrate her fortieth birthday the next month in the same room, alone, her identity a secret to all but a handful.

At times, stranded in this strange world of southern Illinois, Alison had often wondered if she had failed in her life's ambition to eventually become the head of military intelligence. She had to remind herself that, in fact, this new cyber program may have been based in the backwoods, but she was in the center of all things global, monitoring nuclear and modern warfare. The cyber world had put everywhere on the frontlines.

"It departed from Sredny Ostrov Airfield," came a voice in her earbuds.

It disrupted the moment of distraction she had allowed herself at the window.

Wearing the civilian clothes of a stylish corporate executive, Alison walked down a hallway. Emerging from an elevator four stories below, she entered a cavernous room filled with two rows of large-screen computers. A massive cybersecurity map illuminated a screen that dominated one entire wall; flashing lights thrust the signposts of Siberia and a dozen other locations onto the forefront of the screen. With monitors and a large global map in the background, the silhouette heads of several operators in uniforms fronted computer screens. More than a dozen others with earphones typed at their keyboards like telemarketers. The swirl of languages filled the room. English and Russian were the most frequent.

Alison looked across the shoulder of a computer operator, who acknowledged her presence, and then pointed with a single finger at the right side of the screen.

"Don't fuck this up, whatever you do," she said. "We're being monitored for detailing what's happening."

The operator looked terrified by her tone. Alison may have been relatively new, but everyone feared her.

"Intercepted," he said. "Encrypted code." He pointed again as a new code popped on his screen.

```
FS2ewR22ServerCallback onThrottleReceived =
new ServerCallback (@009ZwOverride public void run(String
json Log.e(TAG, "Throttle command received "} + json);
```

"Activate," came another voice on a radio.

"Signal confirmed from Deveselu," responded another.

"Record it," Alison said, "and prepare a Level 3 intel report by the end of this test." Alison knew the Russians were not just trotting out their new nuclear hardware; they were treading on the edges of a mutual treaty violation.

Without another word, she turned and walked away.

17

___

EAGLE 2 STRIP MINE
JOHNSON COUNTY, ILLINOIS

The strip mine looked like an abandoned bombing range. The black pools of coal waste were encircled by clumps of wild grasses, while stretches of pockmarked land were nothing but gray wounds, demarking the toxic afterburn of explosives. It could have been anywhere on anyone's radar in coal country, from the plains of Wyoming to the hollers of West Virginia. This strip mine, though, was the creation of Gen. Will Alexander; its latitude and longitude coordinates were a county away, within shooting distance of his headquarters in southern Illinois.

From the view of a drone, the strip mine seemed like a gap in the forest. Gen. Alexander had been reduced to a small pixel of a stump in the field below.

At the base of the mine, with earbuds hanging from both ears, and a microphone to the side of his mouth, the general strode in his boots and tan fatigues like an entertainer on a stage. On a direct remote, he was watched by a brass section that included Gen. Walter McCarthy, the Air Force general and vice chair of the Joint Chiefs of Staff, and Gen. Tayler Priest, the head of the US Missile Defense Agency, ensconced in a secret office.

"Hope this trip has not been for nothing," Alison said, grinding her boots into the dirt.

The intelligence agent had been assigned to attend Alexander's demonstration in person, given her nearby location at Scott Air Force Base. As a representative for her boss at Intelligence, Surveillance, Reconnaissance, and Cyber Effects Operations, her presence was familiar to Alexander, though he had never really understood her role. She stood in her Lord and Taylor boots, blazer, and skirt, uncomfortable at the outdoor event. Young enough to be the daughter of these gray-headed generals, Alison clutched an electronic pad, prepared to take field notes.

Alexander's dramatic staging had been chosen for a reason. With the presidential election only weeks away, everyone on the strip mine knew that their military dynamics could change in a heartbeat, if a less-than-receptive Democratic administration came to power.

Alexander moved away from the remote huddle, in order to get a better look at the strange clumps of land that had been reshuffled from the mining.

"Is it even safe to be here?" Alison asked one of Alexander's technicians. "Smells toxic. I should have brought that damn mask."

She didn't receive a response.

Alexander knew ground-level observations of the battlefield were the most convincing, especially when it came to new contracts for hardware. He operated from experience. And this included the roles of his fellow generals, McCarthy and Priest.

In the same room, the three men would look similar for a reason. Graduates in the same class at the Air Force Academy, they had all gone through the ranks as young officers together, and even received their first medals at the same ceremony at the tail end of the Persian Gulf War. But after the war they had climbed the ladders of military leadership in their own separate ways—in different branches. Enamored with war zone operations, Alexander had chosen to shift from the Air Force to the Army and its Military Missions, a "blue to green" shift in military parlance, but he had never lost touch with McCarthy and the Air Force. McCarthy might have been the most ambitious out of the three, opting for a career at the Pentagon, but Priest eventually rose to command the top agency that wrote the checks for the contracts to develop the enabling technologies for high-tech weapons.

In secret, they referred to themselves as the "quad." The fourth counterpart in their lifelong group, Gen. Bill Egerton, head of Intelligence, Surveillance, Reconnaissance, and Cyber Effects Operations for the Air Force, had been waylaid on an urgent matter at Scott Air Force Base.

Gen. Alexander did their bidding. He always had, in war zones around the world. While the scale of his contracts grew, so did the concern that his inside track in the Pentagon could be traced back to his fellow "quads." Alexander's garrulous personality may have been uproarious at a bar or a backroom gathering, but his unrestrained boasts had embarrassed the others more than once, especially Priest, a patrician officer who considered the southern Illinoisan crude.

Alison—she preferred using her first name, never her last, to preserve the enigma about her—had observed Alexander abroad for many years. As an intelligence officer, gifted linguistically with a computer programmer's grasp of cyber languages and coding, she had parachuted into some of his combat-area military missions to take control for any cyber intrusions. Alexander seemed impressed by her appearances; others under his command had marveled at her ability to remain anonymous and nondescript, someone who could move in and out of war zones without a trace. Still, the two remained distant, rarely exchanging a word or two, almost if to protect their positions.

Alison knew these men needed her as much as she needed their entry into the theater of war. The flicker of military hardware at this testing station triggered the fond memories of other battlefields. She felt that surge of thrilling energy that came from the end of a barrel. So did Alexander.

On the opposite end of the strip mine, a battery of fatigue-clad operatives hovered around a small launch station. Another cadre swiveled a laser device set up on the edge of the mine that looked like a robotic version of a machine gun nest. These operatives stood out in appearance, wearing blue Gunnor, Inc., coveralls; they were technicians, not soldiers. None of them had the covert look of the secret weapons test that was in play. Straightening his sunglasses, Alexander craned his head to the side, as if to hear the sound in the earbuds better.

"Go ahead, son."

With the giddiness of a newcomer to technology, the veteran Alexander loved the videoconferencing leap of the unfolding scene. Here he was in a hidden area of southern Illinois, and with a click and a verbal command, the window into his secret world would open to a secret boardroom in Chicago.

"Watch this miracle in the making," Alexander continued.

Framed by the high-rise windowed backdrop of the Chicago financial district, Tom Alexander stood at the front of the room of the Gunnor, Inc., corporate board meeting with an uncontained smile as he watched his father's image come onto the big screen.

Tom, with his short hair slicked back and dressed in a tight-fitting suit, may have traded his father's military swagger for a Wall Street sophistication, but he still possessed that irreverent look of assumed authority. His tie was loosened at the neck; he had already started to wage the battle. Thanks to his father's military contacts, Tom had the stance of a contestant who was about to announce his own victory.

But his confidence belied reality. Tom's position as president of the company was as tenuous as the whims of the light switch, which he clicked off into darkness as a screen descended from the ceiling and illuminated his presentation. Tom knew he was one click away from losing his job—and his fortune. The Gunnor company's last deals under his command had either flopped or failed in gaining an expected bid.

Every one of the older men sitting around the long oak table shared two traits: silver hair and a distrust of the young Alexander's showmanship, which had led the aerospace and defense company from its *Fortune* 500 standing to its shaky financial circumstances. An exposé in *Forbes* magazine had referred to Gunnor as a "modern-day Remington company, visionary, but with defective rifles and all."

"With the expansion of the Ground-Based Midcourse Defense program on track," Tom said, his voice shrill, as the hardware images on the 5K screen came alive, "the Air Force will be updating its future strike and deterrent capabilities as part of the program."

"Last I checked, we've got an election nightmare staring us in the face," came an older voice from the darkness. "Are we living in the same universe?"

"Elaine Adams's platform is insane. She's gonna cut the balls off the military," another voice added at the end of the table.

Tom's staged momentum deflated in a flash. He stuttered, cleared his throat, and then attempted to regain his marketing assurance.

"When it comes to weapon programs, as my father likes to say, great guns always trump political parties," Tom said. "With all due respect, elections come and go, but America will always need the best weapons."

He grinned at the stoic and unconvinced room, impressed with his own punch line.

"Didn't your father call for invading Mexico last week on TV?" came the same doubting voice.

Tom hesitated for a moment, accustomed to the chuckles about his father. He clicked his remote control. Across the brilliant screen, the huge Eagle Mine test site appeared, with Gen. Will Alexander in the background.

"Gentlemen, we are about to change the history of air combat," Tom said. His voice dropped an octave dramatically. "I don't need to remind anyone in this room of the old adage," Tom continued. "He who hesitates at the trigger, loses the bid. We lost a huge hunk of an eighty-billion-dollar bid on the long-range strike bomber contract last year because we failed to put the resources in play to execute an agreement to compete with Northrop."

The board members' somber faces revealed the losses.

"For a company that has built critical components for the bombers that have defended this nation, we should never let this happen again. And it won't. With the phase one contracts of the Air Force and US Missile Defense Agency completed, we will soon break ground on the new Ft. Defiance Airborne Laser Complex in Cairo, Illinois, and establish our laser system as the best, most sophisticated value for the nation."

The board members didn't look entirely convinced as Tom allowed his father to take over the presentation.

The focus jumped back down to the abandoned strip mine bombing site, where Gen. Alexander was in command. Being monitored in Washington by two of his oldest friends, the older Alexander relished the return to action he had shared for decades.

"This is not simply a new frontier of weapons," the general went on, speaking into his microphone. "Our Mobile High Energy G System can protect against drone attacks within thirty miles. In the current age of global warfare threats and domestic terrorism, development of this laser system will be the most profitable path for Gunnor company and its stockholders."

The silence in the room was awkward. Alexander had an aura of light behind him.

"Forty years ago, the liberals mocked President Reagan's Strategic Defense System," the General declared. "They called it 'Star Wars.' But today, gentlemen, 'Star Wars' is no longer science fiction. Our G System is the future for Gunnor and our bottom line."

Suddenly, an image from an aerial drone that looked like an attack grid on a digital readout took over the room. A high-definition, razor-sharp picture of the scarred mine's vast scope revealed technicians on the ground, with real-time sweat unfolding the new arms package.

"Reminds me of Afghanistan down here in this shithole," Alison said to one of the technicians in a quiet voice. "What a godforsaken place."

The audio link crackled into play. Alexander muted his mike. Like a referee on the fifty-yard line, he juggled conversations from two different war rooms, toggling to the different groups from a wireless fanny pack.

"Ready," the General declared.

"Launching Eagle 1 and Eagle 2," came a voice on the audio track. Shifting his focus back toward the two generals, who shared his veteran gaze of authority, Alexander broke a smile of confidence.

Alexander continued to balance the multiple conversations deftly between his secret Pentagon brothers, his boardroom, and the field. They were one and the same in his grip.

"Prepare yourself," Alexander said. "We're three years ahead of schedule."

"Three years?" McCarthy cut in as Alexander's hand cupped the earbud and microphone. "Christ, might even catch up to the Russians."

"Russians?" Alexander laughed or feigned a laugh. "I'm talking about countering nuclear weapons. Their hypersonic nuke program is still a mess. No platform, no bomber."

"Not what our intel says," Gen. Priest said.

Two drones circling over the vast wasteland like turkey vultures shifted their attention from the horizon of the strip mine to the possibilities of the black operation unfurling in front of them.

"The four-thousand-watt laser has already been proven capable against drone attacks within seventy-five miles," Alexander began his introduction. "But it's limited to stationary positions."

From the launch station, the working cadre signaled they had made contact with the drone in the air. Motioning for Alison, Alexander referred to a nearby monitor, which displayed a graphic design on the screen. "The second drone is deployed in this situation for precision targeting." On the screen one drone in the air aligned with the crosshairs of a target, a six-story strip-mining dragline relic called the Captain, whose bucket jutted out with the teeth of an alien monster. At the launch station multiple images from the aerial drones themselves appeared. The general and techs down below looked like ants. Alexander then pointed back at the sky.

"Three, two, one," came the radio voice.

Within seconds, the huge strip-mining Captain dragline groaned as it burst into a glitter of shattering pieces, completely incinerated.

"Damn," McCarthy said.

"Yes, gentlemen, this is the weapon of the future," Alexander said, unable to contain his glee. "Laser drone warfare." Then, in dead seriousness, he added, "Generals, this is not a video game."

The first drone made another loop, celebrating its role of victor in the battle in the sky.

On playback, with the precision of a missile, the camera's angle from the avenging drone captured the lock and load of the laser weapon on its target, and then the flash of light of its beam. The destruction of the monstrous machine took place in seconds. Debris sprayed the gorge below.

There was a gasp in the board room. Tom swelled with pride.

"You did it, Will," McCarthy said, imbued with Alexander's enthusiasm.

"Damn right." Alexander nodded in victory. "This is the first and only weapon in the world equipped with such a highly lethal and truly functional laser." He couldn't resist crowing. "Three years ahead of schedule."

"Still doesn't mean much if it's not in the pursuit of another aircraft," Priest said, staring at the screen of the computer. "Especially a hypersonic."

"Gentlemen." Alexander laughed, accepting the challenge. "That was just the opening salvo of our operations."

Alexander adjusted his microphone and rattled out a series of orders. The frames from another drone churned out a series of images that loomed nearby as the drone circled over the abandoned strip mine with the swoop of a predator.

"What you are about to witness is the final phase," Alexander said. Staring at the sky with the intensity of a true believer, he added, "Fire at will."

"Ten-four," came the voice on the radio.

With the computer pad in her hand, Alison realized before the others could understand what they were witnessing. Multiple camera perspectives showed up as two drones appeared and then wildly raced past the vast valley ridge, when the main drone suddenly fired a laser blast that downed its drone target, incinerating it with a flash. Flickers from the hail of tiny parts drifted down to the strip mine floor. The ash sprayed like confetti from a tremendous celebration.

The spectacle moved like a stock market surge across the Gunnor boardroom in Chicago's Waller Tower. A roar of applause boomed. They had not taken their eyes off the screen.

Alexander clicked off his mute, took a deep breath. "There's big money here." The board of directors understood it. He clicked on the mute again.

"Goddamn," McCarthy said, clapping his hands. "That was beautiful."

"Fired at one hundred and sixty miles an hour," Alexander said.

"Three years ahead of schedule?" Priest chimed in, suddenly convinced. Alexander grinned like a proud father.

"The Russians can launch all the hypersonic bombers from outer space that they want," he said. "But here on Earth, this program will turn them into popguns. We can now do more than equip drones with laser weapons and destroy all command and control. Imagine the lethal capability of our greatest airmen with laser-equipped fighter jets. Just imagine."

Tom Alexander seized on the euphoria of the moment to intervene.

"With the contract for the new Ft. Defiance Highway corridor linking Cairo to the geospatial and cyberspace command centers at Scott Air Force Base and the loading docks on the Mississippi River," he added, "the proposed Airborne Laser Complex at Ft. Defiance will not only protect our land but help revive a dying heartland area by bringing in an estimated twenty-five billion dollars with the next expanded defense program."

The applause in the background drowned out Tom's next words.

"I like your enthusiasm, Will, and this is impressive," McCarthy said, looking at Alexander in the camera of the remote, "but we're not the only ones on a secret test site right now. The Russians are on a race to beat us."

"We're still behind the Russians," Priest added.

This was not the sort of reaction he had anticipated. Priest had been a wet blanket since their academy days, and it had always bothered Alexander, with his sense of surrender.

"We have to prioritize our focus and today that is the hypersonic warhead challenge," McCarthy explained.

"As I told you before," Alexander said, "I'm never behind the Russians."

Alison made note of his last line. Her training had given her an uncanny ability in remembering people's attitudes and positions, and the words they hung on them like trophies. With the demonstration over, she moved from the staging area of the strip mine as guards opened the doors of her unmarked black SUV.

"Damn, it's hot down here," Alison said.

OCTOBER

—

18

___

The instructions from Alison were simple. The control center operator only had to monitor and signal the coordinates of the hypersonic bomber employed during the Russian test. Floating peacefully in orbit, the Pentagon's NRO intelligence satellite eavesdropped with its transponders snapping and humming, as it had on other occasions.

Monitoring inside the top security room, the Air Force team watched the icon of a Russian missile as it zipped across the earth's outer atmosphere like a meteor. The hypersonic glide vehicle could pinpoint its acceleration, racing twenty times the speed of sound. It could approach new continents in minutes as the missile and warhead raced with precision and unimaginable speed. The unmanned hypersonic missile could glide at seventeen thousand miles per hour over the planet.

"There's been some sort of . . . mistake," came a voice.

Alison looked at the jumble of data on the monitors. It didn't make sense. The signposts of Siberia and across all of Russia on the screen scrambled. When the coordinates of the hypersonic bomber came back into the command center's view, the screen exploded with a ripple of never-before-seen data.

"What the hell just happened?" Alison whispered.

Her question was met with five seconds of terrifying silence.

Finally, a soft voice came. "It appears the Bardiche missile has been launched."

Alison sat back in her chair for a moment. She stared at the loop of sequenced codes and signals on her screen that made no sense, other than one possibility; a nuclear-tipped hypersonic missile was hot, armed, and out of control.

On the screen, it all came clear.

Standing in front of the illuminated wall of screens, Alison could imagine her counterparts at the remote Siberian command center fidgeting in their uniforms. They understood the risk of their bomber test. The Russian president had deemed this effort, unlike the last times, to be fail-safe. He wanted to show that his hypersonic bomber Bardiche (pronounced "bardeesh"), named after Ivan the Terrible's famous battle poleax, was capable of delivering his new nuclear weapons, as if they were infallible.

The nuclear weapons were indeed delivered; the hypersonic bomber was not infallible. Gulping the atmosphere, the nuclear warhead launched from its hypersonic vehicle so unthinkably fast it disappeared from the most sophisticated missile shield defense systems.

Alison had no idea what her counterparts saw on the large screens of computers at the Russian Command Center on the Sredny Ostrov military base in Siberia on that day. The Russian soldiers would have been dressed in camouflage and wool. They would have been bored by the lines and links on a screen in a dark room that didn't vary much from the eternal gray sky outside.

One operative would have noticed the slice on the screen, and rubbed his right eye, checking to see if he had a speck in it, and then shook his head.

"What was that?" he said, loud enough to be heard, though soft enough to be a question for himself.

Before he could answer, a siren blared with such urgency that they all leapt out of their seats. The room illuminated in an instant. The operatives exchanged looks of terror, and then went back to their computers as the commanders spoke into the microphone that hung down from the headphones.

Under an expansive sky and gray clouds, three Siberian farmers in heavy jackets and hats, loading crates in the potato fields, would never have any idea that a secret hypersonic Russian bomber had pierced the sky like a mythical creature losing its grip on its fabled saber. They just looked up at the darkening clouds, as a gust of wind blew their hair. Then, they saw a wave of light rip across the horizon of the field like a fireball, and then in a flash that fireball grew into a wall of light that incinerated the fields and farmers and everything in its way.

Two flashes, actually. The distant sweeps of brown and green on the blue ball suddenly bulged with a herniated thrust as two mushroom clouds expanded on the border of Siberia and Mongolia.

A ripple of sensors alerted the world; the earth felt the tremors before it happened.

The Russian control room went dark. No one said a word as they sat amid the spotted blackness of screens that still resonated with the last horrifying realities on their grids.

"Oh my God," Alison said. She may have been in her secret cyber office in southern Illinois, but she had a direct window to the disaster on the other side of the planet. She felt very alone, even if she knew she was hardly alone. Everyone's actions this day would have a ripple effect and impact the lives of those on the opposite side of the world. And that horrified her.

19

_____

The illusory age of fail-safe systems had come to an end.

Miscalculations had always been part of the nuclear past, and yet fate had remained on the side of humanity. The explosion of a B-52 bomber carrying two nuclear bombs came one switch away from detonating in North Carolina in 1961. Three decades later, Russian president Boris Yeltsin activated the nuclear briefcase, only to pull back when the perceived threat was discovered to be a Norwegian rocket studying the northern lights.

This weapon, Bardiche, the unstoppable hypersonic missile, was supposed to be the weapon to end all accidents. Speed somehow could make up for malfunctions.

The chasm between speed and human error was slight, but forever waiting for an opportunity.

The fireball of a detonated nuclear warhead froze time in the rest of the world. Footage from Siberia and Mongolia swirled in the background of phones, computer monitors, and TV screens in every village and city, from the remote tip of Cape Town, South Africa, to the bridge communities in Alaska, which frantically checked the radiation fallout with nonstop clicks. Unimaginable images of the vaporized communities and their radiating ash remained online as a magnetic force field, mesmerizing viewers with their hold—and their tragedy. The ash and soot turned the hemisphere to a dirty gray. Attempts to explain the indescribable, taken largely from drone images, rattled in every language. The area had simply been leveled and eradicated of any life.

Instead of some clarity, the searing images of suffering from the shock-wave of destruction in Siberia soon turned into an impenetrable wall of incomprehension. The reality of the nuclear disaster was unthinkable even in a world of endless wars.

"We still do not know if it was an accident or an attack," said a reporter in Paris. "All we know is that a nuclear warhead detonated in the remote stretches in Siberia from a Russian hypersonic missile."

"Authorities raised the death toll from the multiheaded nuclear device to one hundred fifty thousand in the central Siberian region near Novosibirsk," another reporter said, standing against a dead gray background, "as a five-mile-wide fireball shattered windows more than five hundred miles away." The Mongolian death toll was yet to be determined. The capital of Ulaanbaatar reeled from the shockwave.

And then, setting up for an after-game analysis of a game no one had attended, the media from rival centers of power unfolded their equipment and attempted to say something—anything—that might serve as a word of sanity.

"There's no doubt this Bardiche was a colossal disaster of Russian malfeasance and negligence," a Canadian voice chimed in from one side of the world.

"There's no doubt this was an act of aggression or terrorism against Russia," responded a Hungarian pundit from another side.

Down in southern Illinois, the flickering of the images on the TV screen cast off a strange afterglow in Gen. Alexander's enclosed media room.

"They're going to blame us?" he bellowed to the Fox News pundits. "You stupid fucks, you blew your foot off with your hypersonic pistol! Morons! They don't know their asses from a Siberian hole in the ground."

In state media channels and on the Telegram platform, Russian president Kasimir Serov attempted to deflect any blame for the "Bardiche incident" or accident, disaster or sabotage, as it was being called, and suggested the tragedy had been the result of a cyberattack on the controversial Russian hypersonic spacecraft and secret stealth bomber. A string of accusations followed immediately, as Russian, Chinese, and other global media outlets posted interviews with tantalizing images of possible culprits, first pointing at Ukrainian forces or a dissident Chechen terrorist group, and then landing directly on the US military, NATO, and attendant intelligence agencies.

The briefing room at the White House was no less defiant—and confused. Instead of shock and sorrow, though, an air of denial created a tense atmosphere as reporters stood shoulder to shoulder, leaning over others jammed in the seats with their phones in one hand and a pen in the other.

President Richard Waller, who had gambled much of his administration on a massive rearmament program, tripling the size of the military budget and nuclear weapons, fiercely rejected the notion of any American involvement in the Bardiche disaster. In fact, he nearly mocked Russia's misery.

"American military intelligence had no role, I repeat, no role in this *Barday* tragedy," Waller said, mangling the weapon name. "Believe me, no role. Russia, don't blame us for your faulty program." He repeated his words again.

Waller's off-the-cuff remarks on military attacks had already given rise to Sen. Elaine Adams's campaign for the Democratic nomination a year before; now his flailing over the Siberian disaster had pushed her campaign over the brink of success.

"It is not whether we can trust President Waller's assessment," Adams said in a cable news interview, "but whether we can even trust the president at all."

As a ranking member of the Senate Intelligence Committee, Adams gathered the top Pentagon officials to examine the causes of the nuclear disaster; emerging from the meeting in front of the cameras, flanked by the brass, Adams was a sudden source of stability for the nation.

While denying any American involvement, Adams now framed the "Bardiche disaster" as an opportunity for global cooperation, and a long overdue time for weapons reduction and world peace, especially as the global economy teetered on the edge of a depression. She appealed to a nation in need of rationality, not the unpredictability of saber-rattling.

"No other issue matters in this campaign," she declared, "for any party, for anyone who believes in a future for our children."

In fact, the arms race had many players. And envious ones.

From the corporate boardrooms to the politburos, from the laboratories to the testing fields in remote areas that had become staging grounds for the next wars, the race for the hypersonic had been one of the holy grails on the global market for weapons. The truth remained that the American hypersonic missile at the Navy's Conventional Prompt Strike program was far from ready. The Chinese lagged even further behind. Everyone in every meeting, in every country, understood the missile gap behind the Russians in the hypersonic race. Speeding at three times the rate of the supersonic Concorde aircraft, the Bardiche could absorb the radio waves and elude the radar systems of the Americans and NATO—anyone on the planet. If the missiles functioned properly and accurately, the Bardiche could strike at will, "invincible," in the words of the Russian president. The experimental nature of the missile, however, and a recent failure that had been leaked to the press, had made "invincible" more aspirational than incontestable to military observers.

Until the disaster—and the scorched earth rings of fire, ash, panic, and death.

Waller then made his administration, and himself, the victim of the human tragedy. In front of world media he countered.

"This blaming the US, and me, is a hoax," he declared. "Just a desperate last-minute effort by the Insane Elaine Clown Show to rob me of the election."

The president's line didn't just bring ridicule.

"You stole that 'Insane Elaine Clown Show' line from me," Gen. Alexander railed. He aimed a finger at a huge monitor. "Waller is a TV show warrior, not a soldier. This is a dangerous and incompetent imbecile."

The media unfurled satellite shots of Russian naval warships at sea, edging toward American waters. The carriers stretched into the tides, hellbent and charging, as white waves framed the edges of the runway of departing fighter jets. This combatant image of warships and their fighter jets preparing for war became even more terrifying as the news networks cut between the Russian generals and their correspondents at the White House and Pentagon, who seemed as out of place as a Russian aircraft carrier off the Pacific Coast. When Waller was asked if he was in communication with his Russian counterpart, he refused to discuss the ongoing strategies, invoking his role as commander in chief.

"A Russian show of force" went viral globally with images of two Russian Sukhoi Su-27 bombers equipped with nuclear warheads breaching the airspace over Alaska.

With a NORAD map of the Bering Strait behind her, Billie Tipton, a veteran TV correspondent whose crusty voice always seemed to underscore the seriousness of her reports, told her viewers how unprecedented Russia's violation of American airspace was in her broadcast in front of the White House. With corresponding images of Russian jets and warships, she noted that it was not uncommon to intercept Russian bombers, but this was the first time Russians had defied the American F-16s and E-3 Sentry airborne warning system and refused to turn around. The NORAD command, still stunned by the nuclear detonation, had actually allowed the Russian fighter aircraft to do as they pleased.

"Russian naval warships and fighter jets appear to be rewriting their own international rules," she announced, the camera returning to her profile framed by the White House.

Those rules, however, went beyond airspace. In fact, Russian counter-measures shut down US and European airspace. Exploiting a critical command injection flaw, Russian hackers gained access to the air traffic control infrastructure in the United States and transmitted a signal that brought all operations to a halt for an hour. While the Cybersecurity and Infrastructure Security Agency revamped efforts to assure government leaders, Adams moved again to refashion her campaign into a mission of peace.

"We cannot and we must not fall into the spiral of a reckless arms race," she declared at a campaign event in New York City, "in an age when cyber warfare knows no borders."

In a Fox News video roundtable of retired generals, Alexander elbowed his way to dominance in the discussion, silencing the others with his declaration: "Now is the time to upgrade, modernize, and expand our military capabilities, not run away from the realities of the world."

The White House denounced "Insane Elaine" as a pawn. NATO commanders met in an emergency session as missile defense systems were bolstered. Regional military alliances renewed their plans. Dealing with the radiation fallout, the Chinese premier put that country's military forces on alert to deal with the flow of refugees to its borders, and any subsequent military conflict. China stepped in as the surrogate for Mongolia, adding a further ripple to the global impact. The Security Council of the UN debated resolutions on nuclear weapons.

The world was now awash in leaders and experts denouncing such weapons and further arms development. Counter-voices held their own, reminding viewers and readers that the hypersonic race was literally the fastest way to mutually assured destruction, and therefore a deterrent to any war.

But war—or, at least, the fallout of nuclear weapons—had already been breached with this so-called accident. There was no deterrent to a past event, which radiated its fallout to the future. Within hours of the disaster, the streets flooded with protesters for disarmament and peace in every capital in the world, as if an alarm had been triggered on everyone's phone with the same recognition of the historic moment. Slogans topped banners and popped onto social media: "Disarmament and peace now means no more war."

Within forty-eight hours, millions of marchers worldwide jammed the streets in a coordinated sit-in, refusing to leave until their governments acted on the crisis. Traffic came to a halt; businesses closed; school classes were canceled. The chill from Siberia had darkened the skies with a moment of truth. Nothing else mattered.

Looking frazzled and angry, Waller appeared again in front of the cameras, though this time he issued a chilling warning: "The United States is prepared to respond to any threat of its borders with a full-throttle military response."

Gen. Alexander's frustration wasn't only with the dangerously escalating world situation. He had failed to inject his perspective at the highest levels. Gen. McCarthy, among others, had kept Alexander out of the room of decision-makers. When the cameras on the president turned off, Alexander picked up his phone and made his one last stand to Washington. "Listen, morons, if you are prepared to respond, why don't you return my calls and I will give you a military response that will put an end to this bullcrap!"

Adams introduced an urgent resolution in Congress to strip the president of any power to launch military action.

As a former attorney general for the state, Adams had fought her way through the backroom Chicago politics with a potent mix of courtroom drama, community organizing, and chutzpah. And she had won. Her rise to the US Senate had been predicted for years. Invoking both her father's African American heritage and her mother's Serbian roots, Adams had cast herself as the quintessential American story of success for a new era.

"We must not allow ourselves to get any closer to the brink of war," Adams said only days before the election as millions of Americans had taken over the streets in peace marches. "We must halt this new era of weaponry and warfare, so such a tragedy will never happen again. We must rid our nation of this dangerous man in the White House."

The war of words between the candidates—and the extremely polarized views in the nation—became as important as the negotiations with the Russians, who had slowly pulled back from the abyss of an escalating nuclear war.

Within hours of Waller's defensive comments, the largest peace march in American history ringed the White House and the outer edges of downtown Washington, DC. A counter-march toted America First flags on the perimeters as police and federal forces attempted to separate the opposing sides. The White House communication's staff claimed the AP estimates of one million protestors were wrong; the National Park Service confirmed the numbers in an aerial shot on X-Twitter.

"Today I announce my pledge," Adams said to those gathered in DC, her voice hoarse after speaking at rallies across the country, "to change American policy and enact a 'no first strike' weapons policy on my first day in office and bring all nations together to immediately eliminate nuclear weapons worldwide." This message immediately went viral.

The outpouring for disarmament grew in unbelievable numbers as the counterprotesters in support of the president faltered with each replay of the horrific images from Siberia. The thunder of the crowd could have been heard as far as the Washington Monument, where tens of thousands of others had stationed themselves in a blockade.

Waller referred to candidate Adams as delusional and treasonous in a blizzard of posts. He threatened to arrest her for inciting insurrection. Defying the president's warnings on social media, Adams staged a new press conference in front of the US Capitol, now joined by former presidents and their spouses. The ripple of cheers from the crowd was sent across the internet like a get-out-the-vote message. The headline in *The New York Times* served as the best indicator of the presidential polls:

ONE DAY AWAY, ELECTION IN TURMOIL

The Washington Post saved the latest endorsement for their headline:

GENERALS TAKE STAND FOR PEACE AND DISARMAMENT

In a remarkable show of unity, most of the Joint Chiefs of Staff, led by Gen. McCarthy, decked in their uniforms, caps in their hands, insisting they were being strictly nonpartisan, called for a peaceful resolution to the crisis. The Joint Chiefs of Staff, in fear, secretly and illegally removed the nuclear codes in the "football" and emergency satchel from the control of the president.

En route to her final campaign event in Chicago, on the eve of the election, Adams declared one of her first historic acts as president would be to instruct her new transition team and Pentagon officials to lay the groundwork for an international disarmament summit in her hometown of Chicago. She declared that Gen. McCarthy, with the Joint Chiefs of Staff, would be the leader of the summit negotiation team, along with her possible secretary of state, Alistair Freeman, the liberal senator from California.

"Just as the Atomic Age began in secrecy under the stadium stands at the University of Chicago's Stagg Field in 1942, with the first sustained nuclear reaction," Adams told the nation on the eve of the election, "we will assemble an extraordinary gathering of military and political leaders to Chicago as the place to openly bring the age of atomic weapons to an end."

Something else was coming to an end—at least for one voice in the darkness of a room with no windows.

"McCarthy to lead a disarmament summit? Are you fucking kidding me?"

Gen. Alexander's lone voice rattled the walls of his hidden headquarters in southern Illinois. He knew he stood out as one leading retired general who did not join the other brass in celebrating Adams's possible ascent to commander in chief. Alexander relished the darkness, preferring it to any illuminated stage bearing Adams and her weapons proposals that he perceived as treason. Stunned by his longtime military friends and their betrayal in his mind, Alexander had worked his phones in vain. He had been cut out. All communication from McCarthy and the other generals had been silenced. Now he was forced to watch the events unfold in front of him, powerless and voiceless, and seemingly at the mercy of the current commanders.

For the first time in his life, Alexander felt like he had been abandoned in a bunker of his own making.

20

Beside his daughter at the Oak Woods Cemetery in Chicago, flanked by his father's quartet of gray-headed friends, Randall stepped away from the placing of his father's headstone and the last words of the benediction. The ceremony to place Isaac Jenkins's ashes in the ground had been delayed until his closest friends could be in Chicago together.

Randall still felt the pain of the unresolved questions in Cairo. He wondered if his dear mother would ever have a proper burial. Even her remains were in an archaeologist's cardboard box, hardly a resting ground of peace. Randall knew he needed to return, but it was a different world now. What mattered before didn't matter in the same way. He didn't even know if Molly Moore and her team were still at their operations.

Randall's cell phone suddenly imploded with messages. At first, Randall didn't believe the messages, which had come in bits and pieces of truth. Then, the final line made it clear: Multiple death threats had been issued for presidential candidate Elaine Adams on the eve of the election, as she returned to Chicago for the final night of her campaign.

"Where are you going?" Teresa demanded as Randall walked away from the crowd of onlookers milling about as a pastor greeted everyone under a tent by the gravesite.

Randall looked at Teresa, and then stepped forward and hugged her. The embrace was so immediate and intense that it took her by surprise. For the first time in her life, she felt like her father had needed to comfort her. Or, even needed her to comfort him.

But he was leaving, again.

"I've got to go," Randall told Teresa. "Elaine Adams is back in town for her final event."

"So? Aren't there other detectives to watch over her? And what about the Secret Service?" Teresa went on. "That's their job, not yours."

"It's not that simple," Randall started to say, but his words drifted away as Teresa looked over his shoulder. His partner, Nikki, stood at the far end of the cemetery, leaning against her sedan, her arms crossed.

A gust of wind caught Randall's attention. Storm clouds had been threatening all day long, and he felt lucky to have made it through the funeral without a drop. A darkness now rolled into the sky with a final warning.

Randall could read her mind as Teresa turned back to the gathering: "Your family is always second, even as you bury them."

Sen. Eleanor Adams was not just the Democratic presidential candidate, in the final throes of her historic campaign. Nikki, who had silently greeted Randall and then climbed behind the driver's wheel of her car, understood what Teresa did not know; Randall had been tracking the death threats on Adams before she even announced her run for office.

"The red cap character is back," Nikki said, pulling away from the curb.

With the panoramic stretches of the lake in the dramatic background of Grant Park, Adams had launched her presidential campaign in Chicago more than a year before the election, invoking her father's role as a first-generation steel mill worker who had drifted into Chicago during the great migration from the South.

Striding across the stage at that kickoff rally like a veteran rock star, she pulled the crowd to its feet with the verve of her inspiring stories, her biting wit, and the power of her vision. Adams had been spellbinding, especially for Randall, who had been in the crowd in plainclothes duty at the kickoff rally. He couldn't resist the energy of the crowd. Stepping out of his detective role for a few minutes, he had even allowed himself to melt into the euphoria of the chants for Adams.

It wasn't just Randall's South Side pride, or Adams's pioneering role as a female candidate, or her progressive campaign for a "Great Shift," which called for massive cuts in military weapons as part of a new peace policy and transition to a green economy. There was a far older bond between the two that no one in the vast crowd would have known, not even Nikki. Adams and Randall had attended the same elementary school, not long after his arrival from Cairo as a child. He had called her Ellie. She had been the only kid to welcome him into the neighborhood. In that first year of big-city bewilderment, she had been his anchor—and defended him more than once from bullies.

Nearly a half century later, Randall's flipped role as Adams's protector took on a personal mission, far beyond that of a detective. He may have lost touch with Adams—she had moved on to a different middle school, on a fast track for academic success—but he had never forgotten her generosity as a child. He still referred to her as Ellie. He still remembered the curls of her dark hair, which now had been straightened into a short bob cut.

On the day of her presidential launch, though, his distraction had been brief in the huge crowd. Tracking a credible death threat, Randall had roamed the rows of supporters in search of a particular identity—a man wearing a red cap, carrying a black bag. The crowd, however, had grown beyond the expectations of the organizers. Thousands of Adams supporters and peace protesters poured into the park; some put the crowd at twenty thousand. A noisy handful of Waller devotees, swirling America First flags in the backs of pickup trucks, trolled Lake Shore Drive in support of the president. Working with his crew, Randall felt overwhelmed by the task.

Randall had never anticipated interacting with Adams at such a historic moment. Checking in with the Chicago police security force backstage, he appeared behind the Secret Service line to verify an update of information on his target. In that moment, Adams and her entourage had arrived in their SUVs, unfolding onto the stairwell of the backstage in a swarm of activity. Standing on the top step, flanked in all directions by the Secret Service, Randall watched as Adams came up the steps, a funk version of "Power to the People" sounding in the background.

Two aides hustled in front of Adams, searching for their advance team. Then Adams reached the top step, only a few feet away from Randall, who peered out from beside a Secret Service agent.

"Ellie," he said.

Elaine Adams, radiating with the adrenalin of a candidate aware of her sudden rise to power, halted her stride, and turned toward Randall.

The head of Adams's security team stepped in front of her, blocking her direct access to Randall, who wondered why he had blurted out her name. He had broken the protocol of his job, like a starstruck kid at a rock concert.

"Randall, is that you?" she asked.

"Ellie," he said, smiling.

Adams pushed by her security chief, giving Randall a big hug as a huddle of Secret Service agents formed around them. Randall pulled back and looked into Adams's eyes and saw the same kid who had protected him in another time.

"You win this, okay," he said, hearing the words himself like a spectator.

Adams winked.

"So good to see you," she said.

As an aide tugged at her arm, Adams smiled and allowed herself to be escorted away, the pounding of the music and the crowd growing closer.

"What's your name?" the security chief said, stepping in front of Randall.

"Randall Jenkins, CPD," he said.

"Don't ever do that again, Randall Jenkins, CPD," the security chief sniped. "I'll remember you."

The Chicago detective wasn't impressed. The security chief stared at him, making an imprint of Randall in his mind.

"Get out of my way," Randall said as he darted down the steps, and then walked around the side of the stage. Feeding himself into the jaws of the crowd, Randall took some solace in the Secret Service agents flanking the sides of the stage. He knew the roofs of the nearby buildings had snipers with telescopes.

In the very moment that Randall had allowed himself to feel the energy of the crowd, the roars of "Adams, Adams, Adams" ringing in his ears, he saw a man in a red cap, carrying a black bag, who matched the description. Randall moved on him. The man shifted quickly toward the left side of the crowd, pushing his way into the front rows, not far from a short metal fence set up in front of the stage.

Randall had remained a couple rows behind the man, maneuvering the squeeze of the final push of the crowd at the front. And then he was blocked. The pushing crowd sealed up any passing lane. Randall tried to nudge his way past two women, who turned and intentionally shifted their hips, thwarting his attempt to make it beyond their well-won spot.

"Let me by," Randall said.

The women didn't budge.

"It's urgent," he said.

When the man in the red cap reached into his black bag, Randall didn't wait for a response. He pushed one of the women to the ground, darting toward the man by the fence. Randall's action, though, had the opposite effect. Several in the crowd screamed at him, pointing at Randall as a violent interloper in the otherwise joyful crowd.

"Stop that dude," one man called. "He just pushed down a woman."

The commotion set off a ripple of attention, including that of the man with the red cap, who realized Randall was heading his way. A section of the crowd descended on Randall, however, surrounding him in a scrum, intent on bringing him down.

"I'm with the Chicago police," Randall called out.

He wasn't sure if he was desperate or outraged. The circle broke up around him, backing off with the terror that Randall might pull a weapon on them. It was too late. The man in the red cap had run off to the opposite side, and disappeared into the crowd.

Randall didn't hear a single word of Adams's speech.

Twelve months later, as Nikki and Randall again pulled into the same park along the lakeshore, she reported the latest: "Daniels says the red cap suspect is gone."

"And Adams?" Randall asked.

"She's safe onstage," Nikki said.

21

MOORE CREEK ARCHAEOLOGICAL SITE
ALEXANDER COUNTY, ILLINOIS

Molly and her team had sat in the trailer on the archaeological site, glued to their computer screens. The turmoil of the prehistoric world underneath them couldn't compete with the contemporary drama.

They watched the images of the aftermath in Siberia for the thousandth time, and repeated shots of a bewildered Russian president Serov at a press conference in Moscow, and then the election banter on competing networks. They were heartened by the rise of Sen. Elaine Adams's campaign, and the outpouring of support for peace in the urban streets and in the small towns. Other than a few peaceniks in the college town of Carbondale, life in the Shawnee forests and swamps had remained an outpost of wilderness. While work at the archaeological site was put on pause, Molly and her core group of Arkies continued to catalogue their findings.

The sunset had clipped the first tips of the Shawnee pines before Molly turned down a side trail in the woods. "I need to take a walk," she had told the others, staggering out of the trailer in exhaustion. Where she now stepped wasn't really a trail—more of an eroded creek bed—but the last sun rays cut through enough to illuminate a passage.

The faint trail had intrigued Molly. It was not far from the archaeological site, and somehow seemed like a connecting fork to another prehistoric settlement. She knew the stands of trees could be deceiving; that the slope of a hill held signs of habitation even if it now appeared like an impenetrable forest. The prehistoric Mound Builders did build mounds, as she had lectured many times.

Alone, tired, and feeling the chill of the setting sun, Molly marked off her pacing. She identified a few landmarks, aware of the coming darkness. She scanned the area, making an inventory: a huge sandstone boulder that had a broken craggy nose, a blooming slope of purple wildflowers, and the pockmarks of cottonmouth snake holes.

A rustling in the woods nearly took away her breath. Molly flinched, and then turned.

"Oh shit, Earl, it's only you," she said.

Standing in his overalls, Earl was beside three knee-high stumps, where the fresh remains of eastern red cedars covered the ground, recently chopped down and left behind. He carried a little day pack, which bulged with leafy plants and flowers.

"Didn't mean to startle you," he said.

"Well ya did, Earl," Molly said, easing out a laugh. She nodded at his backpack. "You 'senging?"

"No, haven't found any ginseng in ages," he said. "Goldenseal and echinacea."

"Check this out," she said.

She removed the small five-inch human head effigy pot from her backpack that she had revealed when the CBS News reporter had filmed the archaeological site. It was a marvel.

Molly explained that in the turmoil of the last months, she had forgotten it in her pack, intending to send it off to the lab at Carbondale.

"That's a death mask, Molly," Earl hissed. He stepped away, wary of the effigy. "You're messing with some serious spirits."

"It's archaeology, Earl, not a weapon. We've still got to do the carbon dating," Molly went on, "but I'm guessing the shell-tempered ceramic puts it around nine hundred years old. That's what Alexander thought. He always has a good eye for this stuff."

"It's wrong to be digging up burial sites," Earl went on. "How would you like me to go into the town cemetery and dig up your ancestors' bones?"

"Earl, let's not go over this again. If I didn't save these sites, contractors would blow them up in a second and then cover the pulverized remains with asphalt for a new highway. Thank God there are laws that allow us to do our work first."

"You really think laws and folks like Alexander give a shit?"

Molly laughed.

"I think he does," she said. "He could have contracted a quick-and-dirty assessment of the area from another firm and built his highway by now. But he didn't, did he? He insisted we should be here for a reason. To do the job right. Now he's pushing us to finish up."

Molly placed the figure back into her backpack.

"You keep this up and you're going to find things that are better left unfound," Earl went on. "You know what I mean? Let the past stay buried with the past. You're messing with an underworld you don't understand."

Molly dismissed Earl's omen as part of the regional lore. She respected his indigenous perspective. In fact, Earl had shown her several prehistoric sites in the woods, and along the river, and Molly had promised to never excavate any of the sites. She believed in archaeology as a road map for knowledge; that we could learn from the ways, and even the mistakes, of those in the prehistoric past.

"I'm not a tomb robber," she told Earl once. "I'm an interpreter who seeks to learn from the guides of the ancients."

"Well, what if the ancients don't want to guide you?" Earl countered.

Holding a finger to his lips, Earl now turned to his right. His body language always unnerved Molly. He was a step ahead of her. Earl looked back at her with a forehead tense with concern.

"Follow me," he said in a low voice.

They walked through the woods without a trail, sliding through the thick overgrowth, pushing grapevines aside, and heading into a darker canopy of trees. Slowing his pace, Earl came to a halt near an outcropping of limestone, which provided a lookout into a lower gorge. Earl motioned for Molly to crouch down. Squatting on his haunches, Earl pointed through a stand of pine trees about three hundred feet away, where a circle of a dozen men in fatigues with assault rifles had gathered. One man appeared to be in charge, pointing out instructions to the rest.

Molly felt herself leaning into the limestone wall, trying to hide, and then moved closer to Earl.

"I've run into them a few times now," Earl whispered.

"Who are they?"

"Don't know, really. None of them is local."

At first, the idea of armed outsiders in the sparse backcountry of southern Illinois didn't appear so strange to Molly. Hunting parties from St. Louis and Chicago were common, though typically in the fall for deer or pheasant seasons. When one of the men in fatigues turned their way, aiming his automatic rifle toward the limestone bluff, Molly froze in horror.

"They look military," she whispered.

With their guns drawn, the men in fatigues broke up into twos, and then darted down the gorge, executing a military training operation. The main leader remained stationary.

"Alexander is bringing 'em down," Earl said quietly. "Militia. I've been watching."

"Training to invade Missouri?" Molly joked.

"I hope so," said Earl.

A little ripple of Earl's smile calmed Molly's nerves. She watched as the main leader walked away, as the gathering disappeared into the cloak of the woods.

"Getting ready for the election, I guess," Earl whispered. "Everyone's talking about civil war around here."

"Dude, don't joke," Molly said.

She choked on her last word when a series of automatic rifle fire exploded in the woods. The sound of gunfire in hunting season had always sickened her. She had once put on an orange jacket, toted a boom box of disco music, and strutted through the Shawnee forest to alert the animals of incoming hunters.

This time, despite Earl's presence, she felt like hiding deeper in the limestone bluff.

22
—

PATRIOT RANGE TAVERN
CAIRO, ILLINOIS

The Patriot Range Tavern hid in a forest off a dirt road. Locals referred to it as "the firing range." It was just outside the city limits north of Cairo, heading on the blacktop tucked along the winding curves of the Cache River. However, once you turned onto the dirt road, you couldn't miss it: a neon sign illuminated the showcase—Guns, Straight No Chaser.

"The firing range" was its true name. Inside the tavern, you either felt at home among the camouflage attire and unconcealed weapons or menaced by the air of military occupation. Displays of antique guns hung on the walls like crosses at the stations. Veteran flags covered the walls. There were a couple of deer heads, a black bear, a mountain lion, and a wolf—but this was no hunting tavern. With a huge mirror behind the bar, several giant TV screens aired in the background as fatigue-clad men sat at the bar counter and either watched the television monitors streaming from the shooting range or hollered along with Fox News at the latest scandal.

Several of the TVs broadcast Fox News's coverage of the final rally at Grant Park in Chicago for Democratic presidential candidate Adams.

"As part of her 'Great Shift for Peace' campaign, Adams announced a major effort to remove assault weapons, including a gun buyback to reduce the estimated three hundred fifty million firearms owned by Americans," the reporter announced, the image of Adams's huge rally in the background.

"Buyback, my ass," said a younger man at the bar, aiming his invisible rifle at the TV. "I'm voting with my two hands."

His drinking buddy, dressed in camouflage and black military boots, spit out his beer in laughter.

"I hate these commie fuckers," the younger man went on. "They think they can run our lives with their bullcrap laws. This Great Shift is a Great Shit."

His drinking buddy laughed and then held up his forefinger, pretending to aim a gun.

"Boom," he said, pretending to blow away the smoke.

With the tavern packed on that night, and the firing range booked in advance, a handful of men wandered to the back of the building, passing through an ornate door. An armed guard stood to the side. The back room was not off limits, but restricted to only those who had been invited by Gen. Will Alexander, who owned the tavern, firing range, and ammunition warehouse that supplied the patrons.

Alexander kept the back room like the den of a mountain lodge, with a massive stone fireplace on one wall. Paneled in dark wood, the room was adorned with leather sofas and large wooden chairs. The setting granted the general's select minions, those who had previously made the military-grade pay, an impressive sense of class.

In front of the fireplace, Alexander and Sheriff Benton held court with a few men in fatigues. From a distance, it looked like a gathering of soldiers. From the side window, the men could watch the exchange of weapons at the outdoor firing range, where a gaggle of men in camouflage outfits fired assault rifles at human-shaped targets. Other men with guns juggled drinks in their hands, standing in a line that resembled a golf driving facility, an air of celebration about them.

Alexander pointed at one of the TVs in the room, where an NRA spokesman discussed the implications of candidate Adams's proposals for new gun laws and weapon reductions. Lighting a cigar, Alexander somehow felt amused.

"*Cogito ergo sum armatus*," he said, blowing out a streak of smoke. "I think therefore I'm armed."

Benton smiled, as did the other men. One fatigue-clad soldier turned toward Alexander with a sense of urgency.

"You know, General," he said, "I haven't bought a new gun every year since 9/11 just to put it away in a closet. I'm seriously worried about this bullshit, General. They say she's leading in the polls. I'm worried that woman might win this election."

"Don't you worry, son, she's not going to win," Benton said. "Remember, you're in Alexander County. You can lock and load, and relax. All orders from the feds for maintaining control of our weapons we disavow."

The General pointed at an encased Colt revolver above the fireplace.

"During the Civil War, Sam Colt defended our right to weapons. He sold to the South as much as the North. He understood gun rights come from above and our Constitution, not from any political party."

"It's time again to defend those rights," Benton said.

"Yes, sir," a soldier chimed in. "We've served you proudly in war zones around the world, and we're proud to do it here."

"Well, thank you, boys," Alexander said. "Makes my old heart swell to hear that."

23

Alison stood along the wall of windows, the curtains pulled back, taking in the illuminated spectacle of the monuments in the night. The night sky seemed incredibly peaceful to her. The embroiled streets below, which had dissolved into unruly encampments of supporters of the two political candidates, were nowhere in sight from this penthouse suite.

Turning back to the room, Alison sized up the gathering of brass. This ensemble of generals was anything but calm. The three men had all removed their military jackets and ties. It almost felt like she needed to serve them a drink, on the rocks.

"Lord help us if this goes wrong," said Gen. Priest as he dropped onto the sofa.

In the background, a television carried the story of the upcoming presidential election. His campaign riddled with scandals, President Richard Waller, a former professional wrestler, reality TV star, and hotel chain owner who had danced his way through *Dancing with the Stars* to a surprise victory four years earlier, now clutched at the podium of his press conference for support. Waller thrust his flushed face forward, accentuating the pink pockets of his eyes, a stack of hair attached with the delicacy of a spray can gone awry. He held up a small hand that somehow disappeared in the backdrop as cameras flashed.

"Adams is going to win in a landslide," Gen. McCarthy said, sitting across from Gen. Priest. Another general sat beside them now: Gen. Bill Egerton, with the Air Force, a stocky figure, most apt to dip a chew of Copenhagen tobacco than sip a glass of wine in public settings.

Egerton put his cowboy boots onto the coffee table with a natural ease.

"She's calling for a fifty percent cut in the military budget and an elimination of new weapons programs to fund her 'Great Shift,'" Priest responded. "That's before she even starts this disarmament summit."

"I know that, goddamn it," McCarthy barked back.

"Got anything to drink in this room?" Egerton asked.

McCarthy shook his head, looking at Alison by the windows. He nodded for her to sit down with the others.

"Russians aren't happy either," McCarthy said. "I had a little visit with Ambassador Ushakov."

"Ushakov?" gasped Egerton. "He's already agreed to join Adams at the table for her arms reduction treaty in Chicago."

"I know that," McCarthy said. "That's why we met."

"Fuck Ushakov. We can handle him and any summit," Priest said, interrupting. "You raise the stakes so high that every party throws in their cards. Every arms agreement has been derailed the same way since Reagan and Gorbachev at Reykjavík. Ushakov is an idiot. He's perfect for the summit."

Egerton responded with a laugh. "Adams's proposed secretary of state, that Freeman guy from California? How could they put him in charge of leading the negotiations with you, McCarthy? I bet he's never used a gun in his life. How can you be nominated for secretary of state and never have used a gun? That I'd like to know."

"Don't worry about Freeman. We have ways to tip his cards," Priest spat back.

He leaned back with a grin.

"Elaine Adams is no Reagan," McCarthy stated. "She won't let go. She's hell-bent on removing everything in the arsenal, even if she winds up surrendering this country."

"Funny you would say that," Egerton said, his tone pointed. "That was Will Alexander's line on Fox News last night."

"Damn Alexander." McCarthy laughed. "He left me more text messages than my mother."

"He's talking about civil war if Adams keeps pushing the gun control plan," Egerton said with little humor in his voice.

"Did you set him straight?" Priest asked. "He's like a mad dog to me."

"Alexander can play a better role for us," McCarthy said, clearing his throat. "Let him play his part for the networks, stir up the hornet's nest," McCarthy added, his voice dismissive. "He's a mad dog, but he's our mad dog."

Alison pointed to the TV, a rerun of the Fox interview with Alexander suddenly appearing with his intense gaze. The background of the Pentagon framed Alexander in a studio location. He wore a navy blue suit with a tie. The TV reporter had introduced him as a former general and military weapons expert.

"He's turning into a celebrity on Fox News and other networks over this," Priest added. "He keeps saying Adams is committing treason if she follows through with her plans."

"He's a good mad dog, as long as he doesn't turn on us," Egerton said. "We don't need anyone goin' down a QAnon rabbit hole again. At least Alexander digs his own."

"I don't know," Priest countered. "This can get out of hand. All of this treason talk. She's not even elected yet. Someone needs to bring Alexander down a notch."

Egerton took his feet off the coffee table. Sitting next to him, Alison moved to her right.

"Alexander doesn't know shit about what's happening," McCarthy said, looking at Alison, and then back at the others. "Better that way. We all know he's all bark, no bite. He's got a raft of development and construction contracts around the world he's worried about. Besides, he's a good distraction on the TV. His outrage makes us look good. As he raises the heat on Adams, we can do what needs to be done to keep us on track and straighten out this mess."

"Keep an eye on him," Priest added, nodding at Alison. "We can't have anyone turning this into a circus, especially during a transition of administrations. We can't allow him to get in our way."

McCarthy looked at Alison, giving her a cue, and an assignment. She rose from the couch and nodded, facing the three generals.

"I plan to be back on base in southern Illinois after the election," she said. "I'll pay him a visit and keep you updated."

Alison understood her role in the room.

In her mind, Alexander was no match for her military intelligence prowess. No one was, including the rest of the generals, who couldn't set up their own end-to-end encryption in a high-tech world that already surpassed their brawn on the battlefield. This secret meeting was no more secret than a hotel key. They were relics, like Alexander. But they were in power, and she had sworn an oath to serve them. Still, she couldn't wait to get out of this hotel and back into the field, where she belonged.

24

Gen. Will Alexander watched the unfolding drama of the election night from his office. He was preparing for his own war. Instead of a tragedy for the nation, in Alexander's view, this election could have been an opportunity for the United States to recommit to its role as the world's unabashed supreme leader. Wars passed, like caravans, and the barking dogs of insignificant nations would always fall to the wayside of history. What mattered, to the general, was victory. And victory for the United States. A time of global threats was not a time of capitulation.

There were no surprises in the election. The peace vote had overwhelmed the flailing accusations and threats of the Waller administration, whose support had dwindled to a fervent base of true believers in his call for a new arms race. Networks called the election for Elaine Adams within minutes of the first results.

But elections were only battles; Alexander had his eyes on the war.

"We stand our ground," Alexander announced to two guards, who stood by his office door. "To those who surrender, you will be remembered."

The two guards at Alexander's door, unlike the rest of the nation, understood that the general was referring to the brass that had joined the incoming new president on the stage. The other generals, in Alexander's mind, had already chosen sides—the side of the losers, even if they would be victors in the election.

"We will prevail," Alexander said.

Another issue crowded his mind with the fallout of the election. The Gunnor laser weapon system was three years ahead of schedule. To scrap it now, as part of some pathetic peace offering, would be the last straw, and a devastating one for himself and his son, Tom. But this was not the only matter disturbing Alexander. In fact, the general didn't even consider the weapons contract a priority. The nation's very security was at stake. We could never give up command and control of the nuclear arsenal.

Alexander knew he had only one option. The outlet of the conservative media would carry his voice of dissent. In defiance of his fellow generals, Gen. Alexander had taken to the airwaves to sound the alarm on the other generals' stand for peace. Words, for the soldier, were meaningless without follow-up action.

"We are on the precipice of surrender," Alexander declared on Fox News, appearing from his own private studio, as the stunning results flickered at the bottom of the screen. "The incoming administration better take note. Any attempt to disarm our military, disable our weapons systems, and disarm the American people is nothing less than a threat to turn our country into the next battlefield. You cannot win the war without weapons. Any pursuit of a peace summit must be based on superior firepower, not surrender. We must never disarm or give up our superiority."

For the outside observer, Alexander's admonition was too late. People were voting with their feet, as millions flooded the streets in cities from New York to Des Moines, Iowa to Los Angeles—and Chicago, as Randall watched thousands of people line the lakefront like a seawall.

Down in the outskirts of Cairo, inside the barn of artifacts, the Arkies had set up a large-screen TV to watch the election results. Their own dirt-floor research seemed entangled with the nation's fate.

"There it is," Freddy called out, pointing at the screen.

The screen sat on top of a couple crates, with a collection of chairs ringing it in horseshoe fashion. Anchee, Danny, and Sandeep leapt to their feet, as Molly stared from her chair, astounded by the results.

"My God, they did it," Molly said.

"We did it," Freddy added.

The banner across the screen announced the final verdict:

ADAMS WINS PRESIDENCY IN LANDSLIDE
RUSSIA AND CHINA AGREE TO JOIN
DISARMAMENT SUMMIT IN CHICAGO

"You think this might mean a new normal?" Anchee asked as Freddy and Danny high-fived and then hugged Sandeep.

"Not sure 'normal' is the right word," Molly said, crawling out of her chair, "especially down here."

Down in southern Illinois, at his Ft. Defiance headquarters, the outraged Alexander held the attention of the two armed guards, who watched the general pace along the windowless walls. The guards traded looks with each other. Alexander came to a halt in front of his desk. Everyone heard the ping on the general's phone—and it echoed on his computer screen. Alexander had altered the sound on the phone to ring like a pistol shot. It was a text from his son Tom, from the headquarters of Gunnor, Inc.:

> Preparing for the worst. According to our meeting at the US Missile Defense Agency today, all funding for the laser weapon program will be terminated immediately with the new administration. The day after inauguration, the Ft. Defiance project will be over.

"This is betrayal," Alexander declared. "She's placing our country in the crosshairs of the world in the name of her treasonous peace plan without one viable goddamn defense system to protect ourselves."

President-elect Elaine Adams appeared on the TV screen in his office, waving to the crowd at her victory party.

Alexander kicked his chair across the room.

"And we were three years ahead of schedule."

FIVE MONTHS LATER

—

25

Randall and Nikki stood along the wall of the huge conference room in the basement of the nation's largest convention center. Funny enough, other than his work as a cop he had only been at the famous destination one other time in his life—as a kid wandering the pedestrian promenades and sky bridge to get to a Stevie Wonder concert.

Called the Chicago International Global Arms Reduction Summit, or CIGARS, the disarmament summit's central staging area for the security team now had all the tension of a war room. An air of bravado hovered among the thirty or so officers, some of them equipped with sidearms and uniforms. Others sat in their suits, including representatives from the FBI, Homeland Security, and military intelligence. Another flank of assistants and guards lined the walls like bookshelves. Edwin Ford, the silver-haired Secret Service director heading up the security arrangements, commanded everyone's attention with a veteran's aplomb in the face of war.

A giant screen illuminated behind him, showing the outside image of police in riot gear, flanked by enough military hardware to launch an invasion in another country.

"This is part of the mixed-team troop deployment from city, state, and various federal offices involved in security for the NATO summit in Chicago in 2012," Ford said.

"Every day is a NATO summit to us in Chicago," said Chicago Police chief Nathan Daniels.

The laughter in the room should have cut some of the tension, but it didn't. Daniels wasn't known for his sense of humor.

"Not sure if that's something to brag about," Ford quipped. Ford wasn't known for his sense of humor either.

"We've picked up chatter from extremists of every persuasion, including some white supremacist operation calling itself the New Underground," Ford continued.

He looked over at his Russian counterpart, Igor Sergun, who oversaw the Federal Security Service of the Russian Federation and had been selected by Russian president Serov to run the summit security operations.

"Might I remind you all that this is an international collaboration here," Ford added.

The turnout of all the Chicago Police Department honchos, six US federal agencies, the Pentagon, and foreign security operatives from most of the world's nuclear-armed nations duly impressed Randall. The role of the Russian and Chinese security heads and their two high-ranking generals also concerned him, opening a back door to something out of American control.

Checking his watch, Randall had this nagging feeling that the whole security apparatus was not up to the task of defending a meeting of world leaders with such complicated logistics and short lead time. A commotion at the door somehow dispelled his thoughts. Three armed guards with machine guns stepped to the side.

"Hope those machine guns understand who's in charge," Randall quipped to Nikki.

"Not you and me, that's for sure," she answered.

Flanked by a military police escort, Gen. Walter McCarthy strode into the room, followed by the Russian ambassador, Yuri Ushakov. Silent and intense, everyone around the tables stood for the leaders as they took seats at the head of the table beside the Secret Service chief, Ford. Trailing behind, Alison Foreman shadowed the general's entrance, handing him a folder, and then she retreated to the back wall next to Randall. Alison looked at Randall, nodded, and then focused back at the table.

The detective couldn't quite make out Alison's identity. She didn't wear a uniform or even an ID tag around her neck like the others. Alison looked over again, checking out Randall. He knew she took notes with her eyes.

"Know her?" Nikki said, nudging Randall.

Randall shook his head.

His presence towering over the large group, McCarthy cleared his throat, even before several of the agents had returned to their seats.

"Gentlemen, sorry to interrupt, but Ambassador Ushakov and I only have a few minutes."

Randall and Nikki sized up McCarthy, who possessed a tremendous aura of power. Even the Chicago Police chief seemed demure in his presence.

"We must underline the significance of assuring the security of all participants at this summit," McCarthy went on, "and the need for sharing intelligence with Ambassador Ushakov's team. To be clear: this summit must succeed. Understand, the fate of the world may be at stake."

That line silenced even the slightest of coughs or shuffles in the room. The Russian ambassador nodded, right on cue.

"We must have the utmost cooperation between nations on all security details," McCarthy continued. "Again, I can't underscore the heightened state of trust necessary between the participating nations involved that we must demonstrate."

The two Russian generals at the side tables glanced at the Russian ambassador with stone-faced expressions as their translators whispered in their ears. The Chicago Police chief checked his watch with the clear signal that McCarthy had overstayed his welcome.

"As a National Special Security Event, Gen. McCarthy," Ford spoke up, "our Department of State has designated the FBI and Secret Service as the lead agencies here and have shared their work with our respective Russian and Chinese counterparts."

McCarthy continued. "Agreement on the arrival time of the world leaders is being hammered out as we speak. Our expectation is that the presidents of Russia, China, and the United States will arrive together."

"We've got NORAD on the skies," Ford went on, not responding to McCarthy's interruption, "the Coast Guard on the lakefront, and the FBI on counterterrorism." He threw a dismissive look at the Chicago Police chief. "We're assuming Chicago police can keep the streets clean."

The Chicago chief, Daniels, picked up a glass of water, swallowed, and then nodded his head. Randall knew his boss wanted to add a few more words.

26

___

Standing at the edge of the dig site, Sandeep worked the remote control of his drone with both hands, like a handheld version of a video game. He preferred the drones with the powerful Altitude Hold, allowing him to maintain its position in the air for the safest amount of time. It was essential for aerial shots. Using the ultrasonic sensor, Sandeep worked the Wi-Fi camera for real-time video transmissions, which he could download directly on his computer.

Sandeep called this drone his "ghost bird," because it never seemed to be noticed.

Molly would not have seen his drone as she walked away from the active site. Then looking left and then right, checking for any intruder, she stopped and knelt on the ground in her khaki pants. She reached into her backpack and withdrew a short metallic cylinder, and then set it into a shallow pit and hurriedly buried the instrument.

Standing up, Molly moved her right boot over the darker shade of earth with the nonchalance of a dance step. She looked over her shoulder, adding another layer of dust with her boot. Grabbing her backpack, Molly set off for the main archaeological site, dusting her hands on her pants.

Molly didn't notice Sandeep until she stumbled into him on the trail leading away from the end of the site. She hesitated for a moment, startled by his quiet presence, and then looked up to the sky to follow his quadcopter toy.

Molly had always trusted Sandeep as her main aide-de-camp, but his sudden appearance somehow spooked her. Sandeep wore the same T-shirt he had sported all week, the "Go Salukis" emblem of the Southern Illinois

University Egyptian mascot. It amused him. His Sikh turban was the same red color.

"You're far from the launching pad, no?" Molly said as they returned to the archaeological site. She adjusted the heavy backpack on her shoulder.

"Just taking it out for a spin," he said, grinning. "I wanted to test control with distance on the open field. It's been kept in storage since the last lockdown, so I thought I should take advantage of the new freedom."

"Very good," Molly said. She stepped away.

"Everyone's getting together later tonight," Sandeep said, still looking at the images on the remote control. "Care to join us? I'm blending my beats with Punjabi hip-hop. You won't be able to resist."

"We'll see," Molly said. "I've got a lot of new data to enter, so I'm not sure when I'll finish."

Even though Sandeep picked up on Molly's distraction, he remained adamant about discussing his work.

"Okay, but we should talk soon," he said. His voice took on a more urgent tone. "I'm not sure what it is, but my radar scans indicate to me that there's an extensive network underneath this area."

Molly shrugged her shoulders, and then flipped the backpack to the opposite side.

"This area is full of underground shafts. Enough tunnels in this region to hide an army."

"Well, when you have time back at the lab, I need you to check out some of those scans."

Relenting, Molly nodded.

"Maybe I'll see you later this evening then," she said. "Punjabi hip-hop?"

"DJ Waley Babu, baby," he laughed.

Lugging her backpack with a groan, she smiled and then made her way to the barn. With stacks of crates lining the walls like bales of hay, Molly had moved some of her more fragile and important artifacts to a secret off-site location. In fact, Molly hadn't been in the barn in months; she had turned over the inventory job to Danny, who fashioned his own unique system for the collections of bones, tools, baskets, pottery, hides, beads, and other findings.

Molly walked over to the corner of the barn. Several metal canisters held soil samples from the various quadrants. She placed the backpack next to a couple of bucket augers as she searched for an empty cannister.

Wedged between a couple of sort-and-file piles in the corner, something shiny caught her eye. It was a transparent plastic bag. Molly reached down, picked up, and unzipped the bag. It was a shoe. A red shoe. Florence Jenkins's dirty red shoe.

"Jesus Christ," she said.

Spinning around to see if anyone else was in the barn, Molly shook her head in denial. It wasn't that she was mystified by the shoe's appearance, but the reality that in her haste to follow up Randall's sudden departure, and then the chaos of the nuclear accident, she had allowed the shoe to literally fall through the cracks of her storage containers. Somehow it avoided being placed in the box with Flo's remains.

Still holding the shoe inside the plastic bag, Molly turned it over and looked at the sole, and then studied the heel. Dried mud remained inside a few of the crevices. A darker clod was crusted on the edges. It had plant and seed material still in it.

"I still have to test this," Molly said. She meant it for Randall.

Molly could only imagine what the detective would have thought of her apparent sloppiness—the opposite of her diligent work. She knew he had harbored suspicions about her own role. She had replayed the last interactions with him at the archaeological site a thousand times in her mind. The encounter at Old Leon's place made her cringe at her failure to assist him in his investigation. She felt like she had failed him, and failed Florence Jenkins.

The idea of doing something for Randall, and not just offering empty words, imbued Molly with new energy. The tables of artifacts came back into focus. The purpose of her work galvanized her resolve.

She hastily zipped up the plastic bag and placed it into her backpack.

Walking outside the barn, Molly could see a drone hovering above the site like a crow.

The attached camera fired a burst of its synchronized images.

As his drone landed thirty feet away, Sandeep lowered his remote control for the first time, and grinned at Molly. To her the childlike nature of Sandeep fled in these moments. He looked like a scientist, and a DJ.

27

―――

Illuminated by the flashing police lights and neon signs, the dark side of the alley was a blur of power lines that tangled into iron staircases, cascading down into walls of air conditioners and garbage cans.

Arriving in the Chinatown alley, Randall and Nikki encountered Russian ambassador Yuri Ushakov sprawled out in a pool of blood. Russian and US security agents stumbled over themselves and garbage cans jammed next to their vehicles. Everyone was still bewildered by the direction of the silent shot. The ambassador had left through the back door of House of Wah Sun, a three-star Michelin restaurant, when it happened.

The alley looked more like an obstacle course than a passageway. There was hardly enough room for the police cars, including one car that blocked the side street. The two cameras outside the restaurant were being accessed, adding to the mess.

There was a bigger problem for Randall and Nikki, who made it to the crime scene less than two hours after the security meeting and within minutes of the shooting. The media was there before them, three TV crews and their satellite vans scaling the walls with their spotlights. Reporters had set up a front line of microphones.

Randall and Nikki elbowed their way through the back, stepping over the remains of fish and garbage that had spilled out the back doors. It was too dark for Randall to get a good sense of the terrain.

A circle of other officers stood near an ambulance, whose light swirled with a red strobe. Onlookers filled the entrance to the narrow alley, making it feel claustrophobic. Yellow crime scene tape and uniformed cops held back those armed with iPhones. Everyone seemed to know it was someone important on the ground.

"He'd just left a private dinner with the Chinese ambassador," Lt. Recker told Randall, who leaned down to the blanket-covered body on the filthy pavement. "This is really a mess." His voice trailed off with a tone of dread.

"Just give me what you've got," Randall said.

As police photographers and an FBI forensic team continued their work, Recker could barely talk, overwhelmed by all of the attention. This was not your run-of-the-mill murder. The veteran lieutenant had always prided himself on his gym fitness, buffed and ramrod straight in posture, but losing an international political figure on his call was like taking a blow between the shoulders.

"We had two officers stationed in front, but he exited with his security out the back door. One of his guards was still inside. We identified two gunshot wounds. Looks like .45 ACP, maybe 9-millimeter. Must have had a suppressor on. No one heard anything."

Two police officers shouted for onlookers to move back as they cordoned off the area behind the ambulance. Randall nodded, watching the Chicago Fire Department ambulance crew load the ambassador into the back of the vehicle. Blood lined the edges of the blanket.

Nikki elbowed Randall, nodding at a Russian general, who had attended the earlier security meeting. Sitting in the backseat of a limousine, the general appeared to shrivel up with the commotion. He had remained unscathed from the attack. A small crowd of Russian and Chinese officials stood on the sides, some of them peering from the back doorway of the restaurant.

"And the Russian general?" Randall asked the lieutenant.

"The Russian general was in the limo. I can't get much out of him. He doesn't speak good English. But he didn't get touched. Ambassador took a shot to the left side of his head and neck. Severed his fuckin' jugular vein, man."

Turning to the ambulance, Randall motioned toward the roof.

"Had to have come from over there. Sharpshooter."

"I'll have them check the storefront," Nikki said, "and offices on the other side. I'll call Rotini in organized crime. He'll know who runs this street."

"This street is beyond borders," Randall said.

The flash of cameras, even from the side street, flickered onto Randall's shoulder.

"Get the media out of here," he said. Randall knew it was too late.

From the opposite end of the alley, two younger policemen walked toward the gathering. Three TV cameramen followed them as they escorted a towering man with a red beard. By the time they reached the ambulance, Randall could see the man had noticeable tattoos on his neck.

"This is him, Lieutenant," one policeman said.

Recker pointed at the burly man. He was wearing a ball cap and a jacket, unusual in the hot summer evening. Randall looked at his black military boots. He seemed like a veteran, perhaps in his forties.

"Everyone has a different story for where the shots came from," Recker went on. "We stopped this guy in the corner, who said he saw someone running away."

Recker waved for the man to come over. Randall greeted the man, who towered over him.

"Detective Jenkins, and you?"

"Fritz Mueller."

"Tell me what you know, Mr. Mueller."

"I've told *them* all I know," the man griped. He looked at the other police with contempt.

Randall stared at him, sizing up this character.

"I was over there having a smoke, heard the gunshots," the man went on. "I was afraid, so I took off. Then I saw some kid in a hoodie run down that way."

"Kid? See his face?" Randall asked.

"Well, no. Didn't see his face. He was wearing a hoodie, like the rest of the punks around here. Like a gangbanger. Brown, Black, who knows . . . but he was short."

Randall traded looks with Recker, and then turned back to the man.

"Where were you coming from?"

"The restaurant. Down there, on the corner."

Randall nodded at Recker.

"Take him down and get his statement, and make sure the FBI finds out . . ."

Before Randall could finish his sentence, the Russian general appeared outside the limousine, shouting in Russian at the driver, who tried to deny something.

Returning to Randall's side, Nikki held a list on a notepad.

"The feds, FBI, and Secret Service will be all over this, calling all the shots," Randall said. "Make sure we get the gunshot residue test and bullet fragments first."

"All ballistic summaries have been requested," Nikki countered. "What about talking to the Russian general?"

"We'll leave world diplomacy in the hands of the feds, for now."

When Randall's phone rattled with a text, he took a deep breath and prepared himself to hear a barrage of fury from his chief. This was a colossal disaster for the police department.

Randall stared at the phone. It was a text from Molly Moore—*that fucking little Molly Moore*. That Moore name had stung Randall with its reminder of his mother's death.

Molly Moore, Randall said to himself; the two names belonged together.

It had been ages since they last communicated. The blast in Siberia had created its own sequence of time. The election frenzy, and now the new administration and peace summit, had taken place in a timebend, squeezed between the nuclear disaster and its fallout.

Everything else, including his Cairo investigation, may have fallen to the side in his workday, but Randall had never stopped thinking about the Ft. Defiance archaeological site and its meaning. Randall had never liked unfinished assignments. In the case of his mother, it felt like an open wound that burned, not a cold case. But his trip to Cairo, even at her burial ground at the archaeological site, had left him feeling more bereft than ever.

Can you call tonight? Molly had texted.

Molly's writing surprised Randall. But he didn't trust Molly; her need to assuage her own guilt seemed more important than finding the mystery behind his mother's bones. She was in denial, as much as anyone else down in southern Illinois. Another text arrived.

A lost piece of evidence was found.

The archaeologist's use of that word—evidence—unnerved the detective.

He reread the text: a lost piece of evidence?

Irritated by Molly's sense of urgency, Randall wanted to call immediately, but the blare of the backstreet and its crime story swirled around him. As the lights flickered along the streets of Chinatown, Randall stuffed his phone back into his pocket and waded through the crowd.

Damn the ambassador. Damn all of the media flocking around this crime scene. Damn even this disarmament summit that now tethered him to a new position of security. It all fell to the wayside of Randall's thoughts as his beloved mother emerged back in his mind. Her bones. That skull that sat in his hands, beseeching an explanation.

As the lights whirled around him, the noise clashing on all ends, Randall retreated into his heart and mind, conjuring another reality. Molly's text had put a spell on him.

28

An hour after filing their reports, Nikki looked up at Randall, one hand on her beer at a Riverwalk bar, where she and her partner had sought to process the ambassador's death away from the camera lights. Nikki saw that Randall had hardly touched the beer she had brought him—the special Ichnusa from Sardinia he liked.

It was like he could never get away from Chicago's crime scene. The ambassador's shooting was being blamed on local gang activity. On the TV at the bar, a news report put up a graphic on the screen that robbed Nikki's attention.

RUSSIAN AMBASSADOR SLAIN IN A WEEKEND OF GUN VIOLENCE
8 DEAD, 45 INJURED IN CHICAGO

The news report shifted back to an image of President Adams and a group of generals, including Gen. McCarthy.

"Thank God Almighty for her," Nikki said. "If that buffoon was still in the White House, who knows where we'd be tonight."

Adams and her secretary of state announced that the Russian premier had agreed to remain in the summit, despite the ambassador's murder. No one knew what concessions Adams had already made on security arrangements. It was understood that she had no other choice but to move forward, and Russian intelligence and security would now be lining the summit halls in large numbers.

"Hey, you," Nikki said, trying to get Randall's attention.

They had been more than detective partners at one point. But their relationship had crossed that line of professionalism—a line waiting to be crossed like a bridge whenever they felt the need. They were more than friends. At least, Nikki felt that way.

In the last few years, however, Randall had drawn a new line of no return before they could cross it again. He told her they needed to be nothing more than colleagues on the force.

It wasn't Nikki's choice. She wasn't even sure if it was his. Randall shielded his emotions with a wall of silence. And that grin. Nikki had always wondered if the damage from his mother's abandonment had affected Randall's fear of losing a loving female relationship again.

Nikki understood how important Cairo was to Randall. The discovery of his mother's remains had changed something about him. Randall had never veered from a certain neutrality on every assignment in the past. No one could push him over the edge; no one could goad him into a fight or even a first punch.

For the first time in their partnership, Randall seemed to be rattled. Nikki picked up on how many times he would check his iPhone, scroll through the photos, reread old messages. At first it made her wonder if Randall was implicated in something beyond his control. When Molly called, Nikki recognized that Randall had been swept up in the Florence-Cairo investigation with a pull that he could barely withstand. And this Molly—whoever that was—played a beguiling role.

"Who is this Molly?" Nikki asked as Randall spoke on the phone.

Randall held up a finger, and then turned away with the phone.

"I'm sorry to bother you, given all that's happening in Chicago with the summit, but I went ahead and did a quick analysis on your mother's shoe," Molly told Randall on the phone as she sat in her car on the side of the road.

"My mother's shoe?" Randall said.

"I believe so," Molly said. "Remember at the gas station, Old Leon referred to your mom's shoes? It fits the description. A red shoe."

"I thought you had shown me everything . . ."

"I thought I did, but the bag with the shoe was accidentally left out."

Her words eked out in a weak tone, and Molly knew it. She paused for a second. She wanted her words to sound deliberate, even professional.

Molly looked out at the darkness in the woods, where she had parked alone.

"The heel of the shoe contains some residue from a plant," Molly went on. "I tested it, but . . ."

As Randall listened to Molly, his mother's photo had appeared on his phone. Randall had linked his mom's face to Molly's contact. He traced her cheekbones. His finger went down then to another link from his mother's FBI chart on her disappearance.

"The residue or pollen is from a plant, a ficus, but I'm not one hundred percent sure what kind," Molly was explaining.

"Ficus?" So what, everybody's got a ficus plant.

"But this is not a common ficus. In fact, you wouldn't find it anywhere around here. It's the kind of exotic species you'd find in a tropical forest— or a nursery."

"Did you go around and check the nurseries in the area?" Randall said.

Molly paused for a moment.

"I'm not sure it's my job," Molly said. "Besides, there's no such nursery down here. Except, uh . . ." She paused for a moment. "The general has a greenhouse. It's been profiled in a few gardening magazines."

"The general has a greenhouse?"

"Yes, he's an avid collector of plants."

Randall exhaled and swallowed.

"A goddamn renaissance man," Randall added.

This sounded as far-fetched as Old Leon. Stories abounded like this in southern Illinois, where truth often came second to an absorbing tall tale in the woods. The connections and implications were evident.

"Listen, you need to get a sample from his greenhouse."

The line went silent.

"I'm not sure it's my job," Molly repeated. She cleared her throat. "But I know your aunt worked for the general in the past, setting up his arboretum. Maybe you could ask if she would help."

She paused.

"I can't do that myself," Molly went on. "It's not like I can barge into that greenhouse without permission. He's my sponsor. I can't get too close to this, especially if this is just a goose chase and it just brings embarrassment to everyone involved." Molly added to herself, "Or worse, if the general was involved."

Randall felt Molly's voice quiver with doubt. He didn't find it helpful, despite her attempt to make up for her sloppiness on the shoe. In fact, it pissed him off. The idea of genuflecting in front of "the general" appalled him. It seemed like Molly needed to operate under the sway of the local hero.

"I'll ask her," Randall said, "but, not over the phone. It's complicated with my family." He added, under his breath, "I mean in Cairo."

"I understand," Molly went on. "We can compare the DNA right in my own lab if I can get a sample. You won't need to send it away." Molly cleared her throat again, though this time it sounded false. "We need you to come down to do this. I mean, when can you come down?"

Randall was the one who paused this time. It almost seemed like she was setting some sort of trap for him.

"Listen, kid, my heart is down there, but I'm in the middle of this summit security." Randall added, "My professional responsibility is to this situation."

His voice sounded adamant.

Confused by his conversation, Nikki looked at Randall, his strained face, and his troubled brow. Nikki knew Randall was making a decision in that very moment. The sound of a news report blasting from a television above them erupted in military gunfire.

Staring out into the nearby forest, Molly understood Randall's promise.

"When are you coming down?" Molly pressed. "This stuff is outside of my . . ."

"I'll be there," Randall interrupted. "As soon as I can. You keep this to yourself. And whatever you do, don't lose track of anything, especially my mother's shoe. You hide it somewhere."

"I understand, yes, okay," Molly said. "But, you're coming down?"

Her pleading voice sounded more than worried to Randall. She sounded almost terrified.

"What's wrong?" he said.

"I'm just, ah . . ."

Molly's voice seemed to crack. It sounded like his daughter's, for a moment. For the first time, Randall allowed a fatherly emotion to intrude into his hunch. He blew out a steam of frustration, drawing Nikki's attention. He knew he was in the process of deciding against his best judgment—but didn't all fathers?

"What's wrong?" Randall repeated.

"Just, ah, all of the rage and turmoil, I guess," Molly finally said. "The weapons thing, you know, here and in the world. I'm frazzled by all of the war talk."

She trailed off, losing reception.

"I can't hear you," Randall said.

"It's just, it's not easy down here," Molly said, surprised by her own words. "I mean, I'm not sure I can handle this crime stuff on my own. I'm an archaeologist, not a detective. But I want to get this right."

There was another pause on the phone. Neither one knew what to say.

"I'm coming down, Molly," Randall replied. "Thank you, and don't be scared."

Randall placed the phone back in his pocket, and then picked up his beer. He didn't take a drink. He just stared at the crowd in the room.

Nikki knew it was time to press for details.

"Molly?" she said. "Oh, the young archaeologist. You into that stuff now? Archaeology."

Randall turned toward her with a look of frustration.

"She found something connected to where my mother was killed," he said.

The comment set Nikki back a notch.

"Killed?"

"There may be a direct link now with some location," he said.

Turning toward the twinkling city river again, Randall tried to visualize where Molly had been calling from—the crossroads in the woods that she had described.

Farther down the blacktop road, beyond the turnoff for the Patriot Range Tavern, Molly had actually turned onto another dirt road that jutted to the left, winding back into the thick cypress tree swamps of the Shawnee National Forest. No one ever took this turn, unless you lived on that dirt road. And only one family resided there.

"You hurry up, Randall Jenkins," she mumbled to herself as she drove along the broken dirt road.

Across the table in the Chicago bar, Randall finally took his beer, drained it to the last drops, and then stared at Nikki.

"You've got to cover me for a bit," he said.

"Now?" she blurted out. "The bosses and chief will shit a brick . . . in the middle of this Russian hit investigation?"

"You can handle it," Randall said.

"You don't have federal clearance on this, man. You don't have permission from the chief, " Nikki admonished him. "You really want to do this on your own?"

"Yes. This can't wait for all of the interagency approval. That would take forever. I need to know what happened now."

Randall looked more serious than Nikki had seen in a long time. He looked deadly serious. She understood there was no turning back.

"You know I won't be able to cover for you for long," Nikki snapped back. "Promise me you'll be back soon. Just a day or so."

Randall touched Nikki on the cheek with kindness, only to quickly withdraw his hand.

"As soon as I shake this out," Randall said, "I'll be back. I promise, partner."

29

—

A crowd packed the auditorium with the vigor of a coal-mining hearing. On one side sat an array of gray-haired locals and note-taking students, fascinated by the national media coverage over the archaeological site. On the other side of the room, though, the hulky frames of laid-off highway construction workers wedged into the chairs with a feigned discomfort and rage. A few held up signs: COMPLETE THE HIGHWAY. BUILD THE ROAD.

Sloping down to the central stage, every seat had been taken; other onlookers stood along the walls. A few SIU students had been allowed to sit on the staircase, in violation of the fire codes. The administration was thrilled to host what they had hoped to be a positive community event, especially in a time of local tensions and a global crisis. TV cameras lined the front.

With images beaming from three huge screens behind him, Sandeep operated the laptop computer at a podium on the right side of the stage. Molly and Anchee stood against the wall as a support team while Danny and Freddy flanked the opposite side, filming Sandeep's presentation.

The huge community outpouring inspired Molly. She recalled attending numerous lectures on campus as a kid, soaking up the readings and performances from visiting writers and scholars. She could imagine a few local teens with the same excitement about her own project. After making the introduction of their work, she turned the show over to Sandeep, in order to grant him a little more experience lecturing in front of a crowd. Besides, he was the technology wizard who had put together the slideshow of photos, as well as videos from his drone cameras.

Molly didn't need to claim all the credit. It was enough to see her work appreciated by the wide array of locals.

With a mic on his lapel, Sandeep strode across the stage with the mastery of an expert presenting a TED Talk. He made sure to make eye contact. He smiled at the kids and older folks. He answered questions from the college students.

Alison Foreman, the military special operations agent, blended into the audience of locals without much trouble. She applauded like the rest of the crowd. Her appearance had no defining detail that would place her away from the others.

Alison had created an intelligence chart on Gen. Alexander, which included his operations at the dig site. The Arkies at the site, including Molly and her tech specialists, had their own file. They were outliers for sure, but Alison viewed them like the rest of Alexander's crew: operatives for hire. Sandeep was one member of the crew that intrigued her. He and his family had been under surveillance for months, ever since one of his former professors in Canada had been implicated in a spy ring in Syria and Iraq. His hiring on to Molly's crew, in fact, seemed odd to Alison. Most of the SIU faculty, she discovered, had no idea how he had been recruited by Molly. Sandeep didn't work for SIU or have a postdoc research grant, as Molly had once incorrectly written in a proposal, but had been hired for her newly formed archaeological study firm based on his expertise in LIDAR technology that he had used in Syria, as well as the Punjab region.

"Thanks to breakthroughs in ground-penetrating radar technology," Sandeep explained toward the end of his lecture, "we have established the Moore site as arguably the most significant Archaic Period discovery."

A round of applause erupted from most of the audience.

"I'd now like to reintroduce the lead researcher from the Moore Archaeological Group, and our team's hero, Dr. Molly Moore," Sandeep continued, walking back to the podium.

Molly walked onto center stage and waved as the crowd got to its feet. It was the first time she had received a standing ovation—at least in her own southern Illinois. Most of the highway workers remained seated.

Taking off his lapel mic, Sandeep darted to the side, and then scurried up the aisle to the exit door at the top of the auditorium. He looked back at the large crowd, which had taken its seat again, as Molly answered a question from someone on the lower right.

"Thank you," Molly said. "We've called this special forum to let every-one know why it is important to keep working on our archaeological site, regretfully resulting in delays of US 251, which you all know as the new Ft. Defiance Highway."

Sandeep didn't hear the rest of her presentation. He had to go to the restroom. It had been a long night. Outside in the reception area, unsure where the restrooms were located, Sandeep hustled over to a university employee who stood behind a table laden with punch bowls. She directed him to the restrooms. A special reception was planned by the university president after the final presentation.

As he turned to go, however, Sandeep nearly bumped into Alison, who had followed his exit from the room. Dressed in blue jeans, a light blouse, and boots, Alison appeared like a local in the room, or even a casually dressed professor.

"I'm sorry," Sandeep said, shifting his step.

Alison smiled. She ran a hand through her hair, and then looked at him from the side. Her presence beguiled Sandeep with a certain allure and sophistication he had never seen in southern Illinois. She looked at him intensely, wanting to engage, and that flattered him. He wondered if she was a faculty member.

"That was a great presentation," Alison said.

Sandeep didn't move.

"Thanks."

"Sounds like your dig has turned up some real surprises."

"Yes, indeed."

Turning back to the table and SIU employee, Sandeep awkwardly reached over and offered Alison a glass of punch.

"Thank you."

"Certainly." He held out his hand. "Sandeep."

"I know that," she said, widening her smile. "Alison." She shook Sandeep's hand with a strong grasp. "Impressive work. I was curious about your GPR system."

With a drink in hand, Sandeep faced Alison, pleased at the atten-tion, especially from someone who seemed like another scholar. He had heard that a group from Washington University in St. Louis had come to the presentation.

"Ground-penetrating radar," Sandeep started. "We've got new equipment but depending on the subsurface material and the frequency of the antenna, we can go pretty deep."

"Couple of feet?" Alison asked.

Sandeep laughed.

"Couple of feet, sure. But this is limestone territory. Low frequency on the antenna, and I can go really deep." His voice rose. "Hundreds of feet."

"Really, hundreds of feet?"

"You can't imagine what's down there," Sandeep went on. "We're still sorting out images of underground shafts and disturbances in the soil."

"No kidding? Sounds fascinating."

Freddy appeared near the table. He stared at Alison, then back at Sandeep.

"Dude, you're back on."

Sandeep nodded. He still hadn't gone to the restroom.

"Please excuse me. It was nice meeting you," he said, walking back to the auditorium.

Alison nodded, pulled out her phone, and made a few more notes.

30

Randall chose the winding river route, driving back to Cairo through the stormy night, taking a two-lane road that could barely handle the traffic of a single wide load. The back road scuttled under the river levees. The road stretched from the shipyards in Mounds until it followed the first stretches of the tugboats and cargo ships that moored along the banks of Cairo, which is where he emerged at dawn.

Randall fiddled with the radio. There was little to listen to outside of the evangelical fervor of preachers, old country tunes, or a static rebroadcast of a St. Louis Cardinals baseball game. He turned it off.

The long night of darkness made Randall think again about what had happened on his mother's last night in southern Illinois. Did she know she was going to die? Did she struggle to the last breath? It was painful to think such things, and yet it obsessed Randall. He needed to resolve what took place, to clear the blur of her memory in his mind, as if ensuring her soul could finally rest.

Strangely enough, he had only kept beautiful memories of his mother, even with the divorce of his father. The way she always read to him, made sure his schoolwork was understood and complete. The way she made him feel he could do whatever he wanted in life. There was an élan about her, that extra bounce in her step, the sashaying across the room like a dancer that would always light up anyone around. Randall remembered the joy he always felt when she came home at night. He would wait up as a kid—against the rules—and yet, she would hug him at the door, swing him around the room in a dance step, and then take him to bed. She always came home. As a kid, he relied on that. She always came home, and then she didn't.

With his window down, Randall gazed out at the storm sky—the darkness before the dawn. The levees looked reassuring, even if he knew the force of the powerful river behind them; that flooding came and went and left behind its wrath. That the river remained a mystery behind those levees, even down at the boatyards or embankments, where towboats dragged their loads onto shores.

Randall had no idea he had been followed for two miles by operators from Alexander's company, and when he passed the pullout to the lower river dock, speeding on to downtown Cairo, his presence had been registered. He was no longer a danger to the activities taking place on the river.

Two men in jumpsuits were on watch by the side of the dock. In the dark, with the steel truss cantilever bridge in the background, several workers unloaded a long shipping container from an unmarked barge. There were no lights on the cargo ship. Not even the white sheen of the stern light. The operators worked in the darkness, in near silence. Using a crane, they locked up the container with a steel chain and rotated it toward an open forty-foot semitruck, lowering it into the bed and securing it. The huge decal of a dragster race car adorned the shipping container. Working quickly, they unloaded several other large crates, which also appeared to be part of a race car operation.

The rain provided a bit of cover. The docks were quiet.

Within minutes, the truck pulled out of the dockyard, ascending the dirt road over the embankment, and onto the river route.

Two pickup trucks escorted the semi along the narrow road as they splashed in the puddles of mud. The small convoy weaved down the river road until it turned at a railroad crossing and entered a rural route into the wooded swamp areas. The trucks bumped down the dirt lane. With every turn, they descended deeper into the forests, where massive oak and cypress trees leered from the side of the road like ancient spirits. Tree frogs serenaded the entry.

Coming to the end of a narrow and muddy road, squeezed on both sides by dense bushes, the trucks arrived at a closed gate in the middle of the forest. Spotlights powered on, triggered by a sensor. When the gates opened, two armed guards emerged out of the dark forest. They wore rain jackets. They waved the trucks forward, as the rain began to pound even harder.

When the last pickup truck in the convoy passed through the gate, disappearing into the darkness, the guards retreated back into the forest. The gates closed, and then locked. The lights turned off, leaving only the croaking frogs and sprinkling of stars in the sky to rule over the premises.

Randall had pulled his car off the road to wait out the storm. As the rain pounded on the roof, flooding down his windshield, he cracked the window, smelled the rain, and the musty aroma of herbs and corn.

Randall had driven all night, but for a moment he wasn't tired. He was invigorated. He had somehow gained strength from his destination. Randall wanted to be at the archaeological site at dawn, despite the warnings from Nikki about his need to be part of the investigation over the Russian ambassador's murder.

He felt it in his bones. He needed to be in southern Illinois now.

He didn't want to bother his aunt, yet—or even provoke the wrath of his cousin Pauline. He was better off alone, as he had been ever since his mother never returned home that night. He soon fell asleep, exhausted, as he would when his mother took him to bed as a child, knowing the morning would come.

31

———

MOORE CREEK ARCHAEOLOGICAL SITE
ALEXANDER COUNTY, ILLINOIS

It took less than two seconds for the crack of thunder to follow the lightning. It rippled in the night sky outside the trailer's window like a string of broken Christmas lights, and when the rain splattered with the wind across the window it seemed like the lightning was knocking on the door.

"Dude, I, for one, am happy to be inside this trailer," Freddy said, shuffling a deck of cards.

"Just don't make us listen to Kendrick Lamar all night," Danny scoffed.

"Shit, better than that head-banging AC/DC junk you play."

Into the wee hours, the cadre of Arkies had lost track of time, sitting around a card table in the trailer, which looked more like a dorm room than a research station. Huge piles of beer cans lined the walls in boxes. Dirty dishes sat in the basin of the adjacent kitchenette. The trailer served as one of the unofficial housing units for a few of the Arkies that resided on site, while others made the hour-long trip back to the Carbondale campus in the evening. Some, like Anchee and Danny, lounged on the narrow couch behind the card table, where they scrolled on their phones. They shared photos of their families from China and nearby Dixon Creek. They both had overbearing fathers and resilient mothers.

For the first time in her American experience, Anchee felt like she had found a real community among the Arkies. There weren't just fellow scholars—she had plenty of those, who admired her acuity with spreadsheets and analysis. Danny and Freddy felt more like her best friends, perhaps her first real friends in the United States, who shared the mud of the dig and the tiredness at the end of the day in the trailer and listened to her without any judgment.

"As long as the trailer doesn't blow away," Sandeep said across the table, looking at the hand of cards Freddy had dealt him.

The wind rustled so loud that Freddy felt compelled to reach over and turn up the radio on the kitchenette counter. A tune from Alicia Keys cranked out from a nearby Cairo station. Freddy looked content, but the clash of sounds outside made Anchee glance outside the small window above the couch.

"These American trailers don't seem so safe," she said.

"What are you talking about?" Danny laughed. "Got the best vinyl and cardboard around."

"Cardboard?" Anchee mumbled.

"They call it 'tornado alley' for a reason," Molly said, holding up her hand of cards.

"That's comforting," said Anchee.

"Don't worry." Molly laughed. "We're fine."

Molly rarely joined them for an evening of entertainment. It wasn't that "Dr. Moore" wanted to separate herself from her underlings—hardly. She felt like one of their peers. She liked to play games. She could drink most of the river runners under the table. Facing a growing timeline, Molly worked every evening at the site, documenting the day's research, analyzing pieces of pottery, tools, or bones. She was operating on four or five hours of sleep.

"Does Molly, like, date?" Freddy had asked Anchee one night, when Molly had begged off an evening game of poker at the trailer.

Anchee told him to mind his own business.

"There was someone in Vietnam, or at least that's what I heard," Danny said. "So I was told by a friend in town. A friend of the Moores."

"As in another archaeologist?" Freddy pressed. "Doesn't she want to date normal people?"

"Mind your business," Anchee repeated.

"She's private in that way," Danny said. As a local Cairo boy, he had grown up with people who had attended school with Molly. "She's always been intense. Not unfriendly, but intense. It's like she has one objective right now, and everything else is a distant second, including, you know . . ."

"Leave her alone," Anchee said. "Can you imagine the pressure she has with this dig? Not like she has time to worry about some guy's insecurities."

With Molly present now, the card game was dealt out as a diversion from the stormy weather. Molly knew most of the poker games, and Texas Hold'em was her favorite; her mother had taught her those. But she preferred to play a local card game called Somerset, which had been created by an evangelical group with its own set of rules and suits and deck. Molly found it wonderfully archaic—and contradictory, in a religious way.

The Arkies opened another round of beer, determined to wait out the storm. "You guys are sharks," Molly said. "I see how you'll pay off your student loans. I'm gonna need to get to bed, before the sun rises."

32

MOORE CREEK ARCHAEOLOGICAL SITE
ALEXANDER COUNTY, ILLINOIS

Molly and the Arkies weren't alone. The predawn darkness hid several figures moving with the wind and water, who began cutting the cords on the tarps over the more recently exposed areas of the archaeological site. The cruel team added to the storm's ruinous power.

The destruction of the site was underway. This was just the beginning.

Rain pounded across plastic sheets that had been slashed, pouring into the sensitive quadrants with the rush of filling up a swimming pool. Research stations and tables, which had been tied together, were ripped apart and pushed into the pits below.

The destroying of the rain tarps around the dig site seemed as frantic as the weather. The howling wind turned the loose ropes into whips.

The Arkies would not see the makers of destruction—and with the weather and rocking music it took too long before they would hear them.

In the darkness, a tow truck roared onto the parking lot. It backed up, lowering its vehicle lift fork, which fought against the mud to rip apart one of the supporting walls of a trench, allowing for a stream of water to cascade into the pits below.

The tow truck's wheels spun in the growing muck like an angry gyroscope. Without the lights on, the driver appeared to be getting sucked into the collapse of the archaeological walls. The truck finally bucked the mud, pushing off with the blade of the shovel. The wheels spat out a storm of sludge. As the rain continued to beat down, the driver attempted a more panicked maneuver, plowing through the side entrance to the site. He flashed on his lights, desperate to pull out of the ruts.

A final blast from the tow truck in the mud sounded like a herd of elephants. The truck crashed into a storage unit, shattering it into pieces, and then knocked over a fence by the entrance to the site.

At the distant sound of the crash, Molly looked at the door, threw her cards to the table.

Sandeep followed Molly's gaze toward the door. The rumbling grew louder.

"We need to check the tarps," she said.

Looking over her shoulder at the small window, Anchee stretched for a better view.

"Wait," she shouted. "I see truck lights out there."

Several unknown figures emerged out of the darkness. They splashed through the mud, hopping into their own pickup trucks left by the side of the road.

Freddy, Sandeep, and Molly bolted from their seats for the door. Danny had already grabbed his jacket and a flashlight, holding open the trailer door.

His T-shirt soaked in seconds, Freddy reached the barrier of the archaeological site first, and then Molly, Sandeep, and Anchee saw the back of his head disappear into the rain as he sprinted for the road. Stomping past the others, Danny knew exactly where Freddy was headed.

"Their trucks, man, their trucks," Danny shouted, splashing through the puddles. His ball cap fell off as he raced toward a pickup truck near the road, which swiveled in the mud, and then disappeared into the darkness behind Freddy.

Molly shifted in the opposite direction. She knew it was too late to chase the intruders. The gunning of the truck's engine howled its departure as the rest of the pickup trucks followed.

"Oh my God," Anchee screamed.

Sandeep reached the main archaeological site. Always prepared, he fixed on his headlamp, shining the light into the rain, and stood at the sloping staircase entrance to the main pit. "We've got to divert this runoff," Sandeep yelled.

"Sandeep," Molly shouted. "Come back. It's too dangerous."

A sheet of rain whipped across Molly's face, forcing her to hold a hand to her eyes. With more cracks of thunder, the rain deluged the area with torrents of sludge, nearly knocking Molly to the ground. She felt the hand of Anchee on her arm.

"Sandeep," Molly screamed.

She and Anchee watched as the rushing runoff destroyed the edge of the deepest pit as Sandeep's figure wobbled on the edge. He slipped, struggling in the mud, and collapsed with the swollen earth falling over the edge of the largest pit. Sheets of muddy water covered his crumpled body in seconds as bits of wood and bones floated around him. Sandeep didn't move. His headlamp had disappeared into a pool of darkness.

"Sandeep!" Molly cried.

As she made her way down the other side of the larger pit, using a walking stick to steady her balance in the wind and rain, Molly continued to call out for help. She slipped herself, barely able to keep from falling into the pit, which dropped more than eight feet below.

Sandeep's body sank in the eddies of mud.

"Don't move," came Freddy's voice; he took Molly by the shoulders and placed her to the side of the pit.

Danny had already tied up a rope to one of the posts on the side of the pit, and then he tossed the rope to Freddy. Wiping the rain and mud from her eyes, Molly crawled to her knees and watched as Freddy lowered himself to the bottom of the pit. Danny held the end of the rope at the post.

Molly saw blood oozing from Freddy's muscular arm as he landed on the swampy ground of the pit, reaching down and pulling Sandeep out of the mud. His headlamp fell to the ground with a splash.

"Pull me up, man," Freddy called to Danny.

Straddling the mud, holding Sandeep's limp body in one arm, Freddy stumbled up the staircase against the cascading water. The rope tightened. Danny leaned onto the end of the rope, locked his arm against the taut hold, and then pulled on the rest of the rope toward Freddy and Sandeep.

Struggling to the top of the staircase, Freddy handed Sandeep over to Anchee and Molly, each one wrapping one of Sandeep's arms across their shoulders. Sandeep babbled like a drunk, asking about his headlamp. His turban had been lost in the mud. Neither Anchee nor Molly noticed Freddy drop to the ground as he applied mud to his wound.

"Come on," Danny called out, picking up Freddy from the mud. "Let's get out of here."

"Been shot, dude," Freddy said, getting to his feet.

Danny saw a streak of blood break through the mud Freddy had packed onto his arm.

He had seen a light flare in the darkness as the two of them had pursued the trucks, but Danny had no idea anyone had fired a gun. The trucks had disappeared quickly into the dark night.

"Damn," Danny gasped. "Solid hit?"

"It hurts like hell, but no, just a graze," Freddy said, trying to get to his feet. "But I got them."

"With a piece?" Danny asked, surprised at Freddy's assertion.

"With this," Freddy said, raising his cell phone, and then he wobbled a bit, overwhelmed by the blitz of energy.

Barely able to lift Sandeep, Molly and Anchee hoisted their shaken colleague into their arms, and then dragged him toward the trailer.

"Get inside," Molly shouted behind her. "It's too dangerous. We're going to have to wait for this to pass."

The rain continued to drench the site.

"Molly," Danny shouted, toward the dim light of the trailer. "Freddy's been shot."

33

MOORE CREEK ARCHAEOLOGICAL SITE
ALEXANDER COUNTY, ILLINOIS

Randall arrived at dawn, the rain having retreated to the south, pulling his sedan through the muck of ruts that had been a parking lot. Crawling out of his car, where he had slept and waited out the storm, he stepped into the remains of the ruins with an eerie sense of having arrived too late.

The huge archaeological site looked like the aftermath of an all-night rock concert, strewn with bits of plastic, ropes, branches, and broken boards. The puddles of water were dark and swampy.

Randall moved slowly as he gazed in awe, stunned by the damage. Following a set of entrenched truck tracks in the mud that led from the edge of the archaeological site to the parking lot, he observed the markings of double-wheeled pickup trucks, and perhaps a wheel lift with at least six tires.

He sized up the ruins in an instant; no storm had created all the destruction without a little help. Randall took it all in. It was a professional job.

The trail of destruction was obvious, even with the havoc from the rain and wind. Tables and research stations had been knocked down. Tent cords and stakes had been ripped to pieces. The plastic tarps covering the quadrants, which had been painstakingly preserved and protected, now glittered in the morning light like tiny bits of plankton in a sea of muck.

From the far end of the site, Randall saw Sandeep crack open the trailer door at first light. His long hair was disheveled. A bruise spread across the left side of his face.

Molly, Anchee, Danny, and then Freddy, his arm wrapped in a bloody gauze, emerged from the trailer in single file. They were still covered in smudges of dirt and caked mud.

No one said a word.

A mud-clad Sandeep pointed his hand toward the site, walking toward Molly. He motioned at a few bones floating in a pool of muddy water. The whole site looked like a small brown lake. It reminded Molly of a coal slurry impoundment. Freddy and Danny kneeled in the distance, pulling bits of pottery and other artifacts out of the mud.

"Careful," Molly called out. "No one should enter the pits yet. It's too dangerous."

It was hard enough to lose months of work. Molly couldn't bear the thought of someone getting injured in a sinkhole, or cutting their hands on a piece of metal or wire. She grimaced at Freddy's arm in a bandage, and Sandeep full of bruises.

As the sun rose over the valley, and the sky unpeeled its darkness into a blue morning, Danny was the first one to spot Randall on the far end of the site.

"That Chicago cop is back," Danny whispered to Freddy, who had stayed up the entire night with him, on guard, sitting by the card table, prepared to take out the first person who entered the trailer. He didn't plan to get shot again.

He glanced over his shoulder at the far end of the site, near the parking lot. Molly was on her knees, picking up the shards of a large pot that had been unearthed in the evening. Mud covered her from the bandanna tied in her hair to the cakes of dried earth on her pant legs. "Heads up, that Chicago dude is walking over," Freddy said to Molly.

Randall approached the others with a careful pace.

Molly got to her feet. She looked toward the far end of the site, where she had found Florence Jenkins's bones. So overwhelmed with the rest of the site, she hadn't even checked that spot yet.

When she finally saw Randall, Molly couldn't stop herself from shouting, so elated by his presence that it made Freddy look at Danny with an inquisitive expression.

"Randall! Over here, Randall!"

Dropping a stack of shards, she hustled in his direction. The rest of the Arkies followed behind her.

In his clean, mudless jeans, Randall seemed conspicuously removed.

"Who did this?" he said, stepping up to Molly.

She didn't hesitate. The emotion of the night overwhelmed. She reached up and gave Randall a tight hug, throwing her arms around him. Freddy and Danny watched as Randall awkwardly held Molly for a moment, and then stepped back.

The two site workers picked up on Randall's standoffish posture. They noticed he wiped at the mud on his sleeve.

"Thank God you're here," Molly said, suddenly embarrassed at her actions. She wiped at her eyes. "You were right. Someone shot Freddy. It's a crime scene now."

Noticing Freddy's bloody gauze, Randall didn't need to say anything. The destruction of the archaeological site also spoke for itself.

With the morning sun rising to their backs, they all stood on the edge of the site.

"Goddamn it," Molly said. "Goddamn them all."

Randall turned to Freddy and Danny, who held up a broken sifting screen.

"Did you get any glimpse of the trucks or anyone?" Randall asked.

Danny nodded his head.

Pulling his phone from his pocket, Freddy jumped in. "They're blurry, but I've already enlarged them to get some numbers on the plates."

"Good work," Randall said.

Molly patted Freddy on the shoulder, and then retracted her hand, afraid she might hurt his injured arm.

"You're amazing," she said. "Paid in blood for those shots."

Taking notice of Randall's presence, Sandeep quietly walked away, carrying a backpack of equipment. He still didn't trust Randall.

Molly reached down, picked up two pieces of pottery, and then put them together.

"They certainly want us out of here," she said.

"They?" Randall asked.

"Could be anybody," Molly said. "A lot of folks are pissed off that we're here and blame us for preventing crews from finishing the highway. Local jobs, I guess." She paused for a moment. "The road is still being worked on west of here."

Molly saw Randall's attention turn toward Freddy.

"Did you take him to the hospital?" Randall said.

"It was just a graze," Molly said.

The comment jarred Randall with her casual dismissal of a wound— and an attack.

"Someone here would shoot a kid over a job?"

Molly tried not to laugh, but the fallout of the morning had already unleashed her fury in a scoff.

"Folks have been shot for less around here," Danny offered.

"Did anyone call the sheriff?" Randall asked.

Danny looked at Molly, and then at Randall, as Freddy shook his head and started to walk away.

"The sheriff is the last person Freddy would call," Danny said.

"He's the law," Randall said. His voice sounded irritated. "Got to report it. And if he doesn't act, we can."

Molly looked at Randall, surprised by his seeming obliviousness to racist attacks in the area. Involving the sheriff was the last thing Freddy would do, as well as Molly, who didn't want to risk some further excuse to close the site.

"The law works in different ways down here," she said.

"Not sure you understand the way people are down here," Danny added. "Jobs are hard to find. Over in the coal fields, people waged wars over jobs."

Randall didn't hesitate to snap back. "You may not know it, but I am from down here. You don't need to lecture me on the racist bullshit of bad cops. But this sure isn't just about road crews losing their jobs."

"Then who?" Molly responded.

No one mentioned Florence Jenkins's name. No one needed to; it was too obvious.

Standing toward the front of the site, near the parking area, Freddy's waving hands attracted everyone's attention. He held up a ball cap in his hands.

Freddy had wiped most of the mud off the cap by the time everyone arrived at this station. He handed it to Randall. The cap was made from camouflage material, with an air mesh tactical design.

"Found this in the mud by the truck tracks," he said. "It's fresh."

"It's military issue," Randall said, turning it over. "You should be able to get a DNA sample off this." He glanced down at the tracks. "And make molds of the truck tire tracks."

"We can do all that," Sandeep said, stepping up to the group. Molly stood behind him. Bending down to the ground, which was still covered in mud, Sandeep scooped up some dirt near the tracks.

"It's wet," he said, "but a 3D scanner still can work here."

"Hell yes," Freddy said.

Randall raised his eyebrows, impressed by the technological jargon.

"We've also got images of the vehicle lights, but blurry," Freddy spoke up.

"Said you have some numbers of the plates?" Randall asked.

"Some numbers," Freddy said. "It was fast and dark."

"I'm guessing the truck was a dark blue or black Ford 250," Danny added.

"How do you know?" Randall said.

"I chased them as far as I could," Danny said, edging closer to Freddy.

Randall nodded his approval. This investigation team didn't lack for guts and talent. The first bits of evidence gave him a start. What it led to, however, was another question. And one which Randall and this new crew still needed to sort out. Molly shook her head and smiled. The resilience of her team inspired her.

"Think I recall you saying something about this being under your jurisdiction now," Molly said, looking at Randall.

Crossing his arms, Randall still didn't respond to Molly. He looked down at his shoes, and then his pant legs, which were now crusted in mud.

Randall looked up.

"I'm here to make sure the law can find out what happened. Then and now."

34

———

It didn't take long for Benton and his deputies to arrive. Randall expected them, and in fact wondered what took them so long. Their police lights flickered in a convoy like a parade.

It may have been a multiple crime scene now, but Randall knew a more complex role rested in his hands with its own responsibility. His duty as the son of Florence Jenkins, the woman who brought him into this world and raised him with love, had been brutally taken away; his badge as a detective remained. He felt no need to explain this entangled role to everyone converging on the crime scene, including potential suspects in the cover-up of his mother's murder. To the contrary, instead of cordoning off the site, Randall understood that the pits could serve as a useful spider's web.

But Alexander's Hummer, with the Ft. Defiance construction logo, surprised Randall with its sudden presence.

A team of TV vans followed the three vehicles from the sheriff's crew, led by a whirling satellite dish. Even in this remote area of the country, the television networks were never far away. The site was beginning to look like a roadside attraction again.

Taking a deep breath, Molly looked intimidated. She doubted her control over the site. Something about the police lights terrified her, especially when they broke through the ramparts of her site's parking with a line of vehicles, encircling the Arkies, measuring their strength.

Randall's presence felt reassuring to Molly.

"What the hell are the TV stations doing out here?" Danny shouted at Molly, who had begun to assemble a new fence.

"I don't know," Molly said, "but look, the general's here."

The brown Hummer slogged through the deepest pits of mud. Cutting in front of the other cars, the Hummer pulled by Molly and the Arkies, who had returned to their work on the edge of the site.

Gen. Alexander emerged out of the Hummer with his usual urgent stride.

"Molly," he said, hustling over to the side of the pit, his hands in front of him, anxious to console her. "I am so sorry."

"General, look at what they've done," Molly said, meeting Alexander at the edge of one pit. They embraced, at his insistence.

Standing nearby, arms still crossed, one foot on top of a broken piece of fencing, Randall wondered how and when Alexander was informed about the site destruction.

The rest of the Arkies and volunteers distanced themselves from the police. Positioned on a slope, where he had reassembled a simple research station and refashioned a new tent covering, Sandeep covered some of his equipment with a plastic bag.

The flanking Arkie counterparts, Freddy and Danny, looked over their shoulders at the small crowd of deputies and media correspondents, including a local TV broadcaster who wobbled through the mud in boots and a dress, carrying a microphone in her hand.

Framed by the cameraman, Alexander walked over to the edge of the site and held out his arms.

"Just look at this destruction," Alexander shouted. "It's dangerous out here, girl."

"The site's been sabotaged," Molly said. "I need your help."

Randall finally walked over to Molly and Alexander as the general waved at the sheriff with one hand. Benton joined the others in haste.

"We've got safety issues, indeed," Alexander said, seizing on the word for help. He turned to Randall, looking for a little backup. "I see you're back, Detective," he said. "Just in time. Don't you agree we've got safety issues out here?"

"I would," Randall said, "there are definitely safety issues here."

Placing his arm around Molly's shoulder, Alexander shifted to his role as mentor in chief.

"You gotta listen to me for a minute, honey," Alexander went on. "I'm a veteran builder. I know this area like the back of my hand. And this place is honeycombed by old mines and oil lines and waterways.

It's dangerous out here, Molly. So many sinkholes. We got an accident waiting to happen here."

"More than an accident has already happened here," Molly said.

"Exactly. We're talking about liability concerns," Alexander went on. "I mean, you're on your own out here. I don't even know about your insurance coverage."

Sheriff Benton stepped into the ring; that was his cue. He nodded at Randall, acknowledging a fellow law enforcement officer, even if he resented the Chicago cop's intrusion on his territory.

Alexander continued: "With all this rain and flooding, this whole area could give way, Molly."

"It's not safe out here," Benton added.

"We're cleaning up the site," Molly said, aware that this meeting had also become a public display for the TV reporters. She lowered her tone. "We'll have a federal engineer on the site soon as well, who will ascertain the safety issues. This is not my first dig, General."

"Well, all right," Alexander said, relenting.

Molly gave Randall a perturbed look. Why wasn't he getting involved and vouching for her?

"Don't delay on this one, Sheriff," Alexander went on. "Whoever did this terrible act of vandalism should be brought to justice immediately."

Benton nodded. He shifted for the cameras.

"I've already sent deputies to question people who have publicly threatened this site. We're on this."

Benton's tone jarred Molly. She may have received some dirty looks in town from laid-off highway workers, but she had never received any outright threats.

"What are you talking about?" Molly said. "None of the highway workers has threatened this site until now. Have you tracked down someone from last night?"

Benton shook his head.

"Highway workers don't have anything to do with this," Benton went on.

"Then tell me, who does, Sheriff?" Randall piped up.

"Yeah, tell us who does," Freddy added.

Benton stared down Freddy in silence, sizing up his overalls, his long dreadlocks, and the bandage on his arm. He avoided Randall as he looked back at Molly, and then toward the camera again.

"We've picked up threats by radical Native American groups, tree huggers, and ecoterrorists," Benton said. Nodding at one of his deputies, who entered the circle with a bag, Benton reached in and pulled out a couple of large feathers. Benton held them up like signposts. The cameras zoomed in on the patterns of the feathers.

"Eagle feathers were left at the Ft. Defiance construction trailer with a note to stop the dig," he declared. He displayed them to the cameras. "The statement was signed by a radical eco group and these symbols of a local Indian movement were left behind."

Molly looked at Danny, who leaned near Benton's hand for a closer look.

"Those are turkey feathers, man," he said. Danny shifted toward Benton. "Match the ones on your liquor bottle."

Shifting away from Danny, as if he didn't hear him, Benton went on.

"There's a certain element in the county—and across the nation, for that matter—that is lawless. It's my job as sheriff of this county to do whatever is necessary, including the cordoning off of this site, to protect our citizens from any further attacks."

Randall smiled at Benton's reasoning.

"This is bullshit, man," Danny barked at Benton.

Molly held up a hand for Danny to back off.

"Lawless, my ass. This guy harasses people all the time," Danny went on. "This is bullshit."

"Take it easy," Randall said to Danny.

"Glad you're back, Detective, so you can see our situation down here," Alexander said in a softer voice.

"General, this is bullshit, and you know it," Molly insisted.

Alexander threw up his hands. His brows turned in concern. He withdrew his sunglasses. He wore a look of apprehension, worried about Molly, and then nodded at Randall for support.

"This prehistoric site is too important to fall into the hands of vandals," Alexander said. Looking straight at Randall, he added, "And this is a tragedy when something like this happens to sacred objects. I mean, we can't let someone wreck such a repository of history. We've got to protect this site for many reasons. You would agree as well, for your investigation?"

Randall nodded.

"Instead of bothering us," Sandeep blurted out, having made his way toward the commotion, "why don't you track down the thugs who did this mess." Stepping toward Benton, he pointed at the road. "They're probably drinking down at the tavern."

Benton didn't take the bait. Not with the cameras nearby, and with Alexander's powerful presence within sight. He remained calm, in an apparent attempt to bring everyone together.

The sheriff didn't seem out of line to Randall. He was just asserting his authority.

"To secure the area, we're going to need to see everyone's proper ID," Benton announced in the most formal voice he could conjure. "Deputy Jackson, please check the identification of everyone on the site right now."

Molly kicked at the dirt. Randall watched Benton's orders unfold as deputies fanned out across the lot.

"What the hell, General," Molly said. "Are you really going to let the sheriff waste our time on this? This is my life's work. I'm not shutting down this site for a minute more."

"We're protecting it, Molly, not shutting it down," Alexander continued. "Don't fight me on this one. We'll work out some way for you to sort through this mess."

Alexander wheeled around toward Randall, pointing toward the barn on the hill.

"Detective, can I have a word with you?"

In his boots, Alexander walked in the mud, beside Randall, escorting him away from the media scrum. Trying to avoid the mud puddles, Randall chose a series of planks that had been laid out like bridges across the site. Watching his next steps, remaining silent, he moved up the hill strewn with rubble and piles of trash.

"I understand why everyone is upset, for sure," Alexander said. "We're doing our best to finish this important study, and still follow the regs, you know." The general suddenly stopped. "This is good enough."

Randall halted and shifted around, staring at the expanse of the site and the array of deputies among the Arkies.

"We kept our bargain, Detective," Alexander proclaimed.

Randall looked at the general with a blank expression.

"Which one is that?"

"As you requested, we've kept a lid on the discovery of your mother, awaiting the completion of your investigation." Alexander continued, "I know things for you in Chicago have been in disorder since the Russia disaster, the election, and that so-called summit in Chicago."

"No one knows?" Randall nodded at the media trucks. "No one?"

"Not on our end," Alexander said. "We know how to keep an oath down here."

Alexander turned back toward the site.

"And I assume Molly's kept it quiet. She's a good kid. Like a daughter to me. She knows what's at stake for her. This discovery here is her ticket to the stars, and she'll do whatever it takes to keep it going."

Randall heard shouting. He looked over at a huddle of deputies around Sandeep.

"Dr. Moore," Freddy called out. "They're arresting him."

"What's going on?" Randall said.

"Oh, dear me," Alexander grunted. "This sheriff is a bit of a stickler on ID cards, given a recent threat of terrorism around here."

Molly bounded ahead of the others, including the TV cameras, as Benton and his deputies surrounded the arrest scene. Sandeep looked more confused than afraid. His long hair still dangled around his shoulders without his turban. A deputy held tightly on to one arm, acting concerned that Sandeep might try to flee.

"Take your hands off him," Molly shouted.

The deputy turned toward Benton. He looked younger than any of the Arkies—and out of his element. The deputy pulled roughly on Sandeep's arm. Molly restrained herself from hitting him.

Seeing the commotion, and Molly's flailing arms, Randall hustled back down the hill.

"Do something," she shouted at Randall, moving away when he reached toward her arm.

Randall looked at Sandeep.

"Don't resist," he said. "Just cooperate. Show him your ID."

His words didn't comfort Sandeep, or Molly. Freddy stepped away from the scuffles, worried he might be the next one to be arrested. He had plenty of experience dealing with the sheriff. Benton pushed the others aside.

"This one doesn't have proper ID," the young deputy quickly said. "Don't have no ID at all."

"It's in my apartment in Carbondale," Sandeep responded.

"We're going to need to take him down to the station to verify his residency status," Benton said. "No big deal."

Benton motioned for the deputy to take away Sandeep.

Stepping in front of the deputy, Molly blocked him from moving, holding out a finger to his face.

"He's a Canadian researcher hired with my team, for Christ's sake, and has even given lectures at SIU as well."

Benton pointed to the deputy, who swiveled around Molly, dragging Sandeep with him.

"We have to follow the law," Benton said. "The Patriot Act expressly mandates we verify residency permits for these kinds of foreign . . ." Benton's words sputtered out.

Sandeep suddenly pulled away from the grip of the deputy, creating a commotion. He squirmed like he was having a panic attack. The cameraman zoomed in.

"Calm down," Randall said, pushing Molly to the side. "Tell him to calm down."

She looked at Randall with a scowl of betrayal.

"The fuck, man?" she hissed at Randall. "What the actual fuck, man. Are you part of this charade, too?"

"Calm down," Randall said, looking at the others.

"Don't tell me to calm down. I thought you were here to help. I can't believe this."

She stormed off toward the barn as the other Arkies followed behind her. Freddy threw a look over his shoulder at Randall with disgust. He had always distrusted the cop.

Benton turned to Randall. "Detective, see, you're not alone in this."

Alone—that word carried a strange threat to Randall.

"Sheriff," he said quietly. "I'm never alone."

35

The blaring noise in the background made Nikki close the door to the meeting room. Her own desk in the detective unit straddled three others, with enough privacy to scroll on the computer, but she hardly had room to make a personal comment aloud. She tended to take her private phone calls here.

Juggling the phone in her hand, she sat at the end of the table.

"Randall, you there? Okay, now I can hear you," she said.

No one in the station knew Nikki was talking to Randall. Not that his sudden disappearance had not been noticed. Most shrugged. Some of his colleagues assumed he was on family leave. That, in fact, was the official version so far. With all the federal law enforcement agencies in town for the global summit, a more-than-usual whirl of chaos had enveloped the station. Only Nikki knew about Randall's departure for Cairo.

"I'm not sure how much longer I'll be able to keep it from the captain," she said. "He's been leaving you messages. Even with the feds taking over, he's kept us on the ambassador's case."

Randall knew this, of course. He had deflected the messages with ambiguous answers.

"Listen to me, that's why I'm calling," Nikki pressed. "I finally got this out of the FBI. The bullet that killed the Russian ambassador came from an SR-25 sniper rifle. Twenty-inch barrel, not a .45 like that deputy thought."

They both knew the significance of the rifle model. Nikki looked over her shoulder. Randall faded out again. Nikki clicked on her keyboard, wishing to conjure his presence on the screen. She had no idea where he was in that moment, outside of some star of Cairo on the map. She pulled up the map on her screen, typed in Cairo, Illinois, and then zoomed in on the area. The snaking rivers on either side of the town seemed to strangle it; Cairo looked like the dead end of Illinois. She placed him in a car. Nikki imagined one of the rural routes heading up the Ohio River, dipping into some swampy valley without a cell tower.

Randall's voice became clearer.

"Those bullets were made for the Seals," he said.

Clicking at her laptop, Nikki juggled the phone again.

"Crededio's scanning the database now for how they could have been acquired," she said. "Trying to track down stolen military hardware." She paused. "When are you getting back?"

Randall seemed to say "soon," but his voice was still faint.

"Soon? What does that mean?"

Was that Molly with him? Nikki wanted to ask Randall, but she already knew the answer. The Chicago detective had done a little background research herself. Molly Moore beamed like the all-American success story in every news article, a small-town kid who swept through her Ivy League school with glowing marks, and then started to appear in archaeological journals with her breakthrough work in Vietnam. One writer called her a "MacArthur Genius in the making."

So, why would such a stellar academic return to her pit of a small town, the ravaged tip of Illinois that had all been abandoned by anyone left standing? Was it just a coincidence that a local Cairo kid, based thousands of miles away in Southeast Asia, would be the one to make the huge discovery at the Ft. Defiance site, instead of an older Illinois firm?

And why was Randall so taken with this Molly?

Nikki fought off that rasp of jealousy. Randall could be Molly's father, *per l'amor di dio*, as her mother would say. He wasn't that type, anyway. She knew that ever since his divorce, Randall had drifted in and out of short relationships like a mystery train. He worked too much. His work was too much, rather. They shared the reality that it was hard to come home at night and hug anyone else after witnessing the worst of humanity on the streets. It was something only they could share.

Randall's voice came back into reception.

"Do me a favor," he asked. "You know Mickey Berkes, right? Former military intelligence."

"Mad Dog Mickey? Of course."

Nikki typed the name into her directory index.

"Ask him to run the military data bases for a General William Xavier Alexander," Randall went on.

Nikki typed the name onto her screen: General William Xavier Alexander.

"That's Xavier with an 'X,' right?" she said.

The line had gone quiet. Randall was gone.

36

—

HARRIET MOORE'S CABIN
ALEXANDER COUNTY, ILLINOIS

The sun-dappled frame was perfect for the camera shot.

Sheriff Benton and his deputies hesitated at their cars, granting the two trailing TV vans just enough time to get out first and grab their cameras. Off a dirt road, beyond the labyrinth of draping vines and branches, a cabin sat back in the woods with an overlook of a dark green valley. A cord of stacked wood framed the slumping front porch. The rest of the shot for the cameras was an idyllic portrait of the Shawnee forests. Shutting the back door of the TV van, the reporter already had the news break image in his mind.

The arrest went as planned. Benton stepped out of the front door with Earl in the middle, two deputies on either side of him, as he looked down, strands of his ponytail in his face, his hands cuffed behind his back. Benton made Earl put on his favorite T-shirt, featuring a historic photo of Apache leader Geronimo and a group of Native American men with rifles, with the text: Department of Homeland Security since 1492.

At the bottom of the stairs, Benton halted the procession for a moment. He placed a hand on Earl's shoulder, making it seem like he needed to restrain him. The sheriff posed with the Shawnee activist—or, at least, that seemed like a good news tag to him. Earl looked up, dumbfounded, but incredibly calm.

It may have appeared tense to viewers, but to Earl it seemed like a joke. He knew all the police. Benton was hardly a stranger. Not that they were friends. But it had been twenty years since Earl's last activist work, when he blockaded loggers from clear-cutting areas of the Shawnee forest without federal permits. While the bib-overalled image of him being arrested had remained in the minds of locals, he was mainly known for his annual Shawnee Culture Day events, where he taught kids about indigenous ways in the forests. That was a friendly image, not a violent one.

One of the TV reporters stood in front of the camera, with Benton and Earl framed to the side.

"Just a few miles outside of Cairo," the reporter spoke, holding the microphone, "the Alexander County sheriff and deputies have taken Native American activist Earl Karnes into custody."

The camera zoomed in on Earl's T-shirt.

"According to Sheriff Benton, radical Native American groups affiliated with Karnes have made threats against the removal of Indian bones and artifacts on a nearby prehistoric archaeological site. Sacred eagle feathers affiliated with the group have been found at the site."

Benton motioned for Earl to take a step as the two deputies tightened their grips, puckered their mouths with a look of serious intent, and continued their march toward the police cars. It came off as serious as a mob bust in Brooklyn. Harriet Moore, cigarette burning, emerged from the cabin.

The lights of the police sedans flashed long after their departure.

37

___

As she stepped into the sunlit foyer of the sheriff's office, Molly could see Randall through the glass windows of the back office. It looked like he was having a standoff with two deputies. Not that Randall made any threatening gestures. To the contrary, he stood with a veteran's poise, his arms crossed on his chest, staring down two deputies, who floundered with their hands, offering up empty answers. Molly could hear Randall demanding to know the details about Sandeep and the other man under arrest.

In spite of her anger for his inaction at the site, Molly had called Randall in the car and told him that a native Shawnee activist named Earl Karnes had been also arrested on bogus charges. It had bothered Molly to plead with Randall for help, but she didn't know who else to call. Randall, for good or bad, was her law enforcement connection now.

One deputy took off his hat, wiped at his brow, and then held up a finger to Randall. It seemed to satisfy Randall, who pulled out his iPhone and checked the screen.

Sliding up to the front counter, Molly took little solace in Randall's presence. He suddenly looked like he belonged in the police station. He now looked like a cop to her. His lack of action at the archaeological site made it clear to her which side he was on when it came to her concerns. She suddenly regretted calling him.

When one of the deputies disappeared and then returned, flagging Randall to follow him, Molly wondered if Randall's allegiance to law enforcement superseded his commitment to justice. Could she really trust him?

She spent the next fifteen minutes pacing up and down the long hallway of the Alexander County sheriff's station.

The white walls seemed to go on forever. There were no pictures or posters. Her tracks were only obstructed by an occasional deputy heading to the front desk, and a weary grandfather, who loitered in the hallway, muttering about bailing out a family member for the last time. She could hear a ball game on a radio somewhere. Every time a door slammed or rattled, she stopped and looked up, hoping to glimpse Sandeep or Earl.

With little sleep, Molly straddled a line between being frazzled and enraged. Told to wait in the hallway, unaware of what was happening, she felt like crying one moment, and smashing down the doors in another. She poured herself a cup of coffee from a pot in the reception lounge, which swirled in an oily circle of brown water. Molly threw it out.

The corridor made her feel alone, and at the mercy of those who she neither trusted nor understood. This seemed like the story of her life—pacing the lonely corridors of academia, bureaucracy, and now law enforcement. Like pacing the cage, for Molly. Ever since she had been a kid, roaming the woods alone, exploring the river delta, Molly had felt more at ease as a lone wolf. She was quick, relied on her wits; her confidence girded her for any surprises, even attacks. It shielded her from the turmoil at home. It distanced her from the hushed comments about her grandfather. It made her make her own path by walking it. She buried herself in books, always alone, and yet always opening new doors with each page. By high school, Molly moved in her own lane among her peers, and among the rest of those in Cairo and the area. Her test scores unnerved the teachers. They told her to skip class and learn on her own. There was no looking back at this point. Molly felt like she could go wherever she wanted, because she had already blazed her own way. Arriving at Yale, Molly didn't feel any of the despair of homesickness or the crisis of insecurity like some of the rural kids. But she did feel alone.

Molly now felt alone in her hometown. She didn't know who to call or depend on; she didn't know who to trust, for that matter. Not that this was her first run-in with the law. As a teenager, she had even confronted a cop over the arrest of a young Black friend, Darnell, who had been illegally stopped, searched for drugs, and then detained at the station. Molly had paced the corridor then as well. But those times were different. Molly felt she had some element of moral authority behind her. To be honest, most people feared her family—or at least her Moore surname. No one feared an Ivy League archaeologist in these parts.

Everything now seemed so much more complicated.

At the archaeological site, Alexander had told her he could sort things out, as if he could put back the shattered, layered puzzle of the archaeological site. Sure, he had helped her in the past, but Molly was afraid of where he stood now. His actions confounded logic. He had set her up with this dig as an avid archaeology buff who wanted the research to end up in the right hands. The questions kept bothering her: Why would he want to shut down the operation now, just to finish a highway?

But another question, a still unasked and unanswered one, nagged at Molly's conscience: What was Florence Jenkins's shoe doing with such a rare ficus DNA, possibly from his greenhouse?

38

The room reminded Sandeep of a recording studio he had run as a student DJ. Soundproof walls, cinder blocks on one side, and a single window. Sitting at a table, he stared back at his reflection in the window, his loosened Dumalla turban now fixed, and then at the empty chair across from him.

He was cold. The air-conditioning was too high. However, a chill of fear forced him to rub his hands together. The ability to regulate that temperature, like the rest of his situation, was out of Sandeep's hands. He had never been in jail before; he had never even done a minute in detention in school, for that matter. His father's stories of being detained in Punjab as a young man, and tortured at the police station, always hovered in his mind.

Several people had warned Sandeep about joining the research team in the US, especially a remote southern area like southern Illinois. Wasn't that Klan country? How many Sikhs were down there, if any? (There was, in fact, a Sikh community in St. Louis.) He wasn't sure if he wanted to break down and cry, or shout out in desperation. Either way, he felt petrified by his confinement. Now the police had some criminal tag with his name on it.

When Alison Foreman entered the room, Sandeep could see two plainclothes officers to the side of the door. They didn't look local. But Alison's presence did. Sandeep placed her at his presentation at Southern Illinois University, and when she quietly shut the door, stepped around the table, and took the chair across from him, he wasn't sure if he should be comforted by that fact or terrified. If she was a researcher or university professor, then what was she doing at a jail?

Alison had changed her clothes for a different role. No blue jeans or tight blouse. She wore a dark navy suit jacket and a skirt. Her bob haircut was held back with a pin. She placed a folder on the table with the cold touch of an inquisitor at an exam. She reminded Sandeep of one of his dissertation committee members, especially when she looked straight into his eyes with the detached look of a veteran.

He now understood she was not a university professor. He felt she had manipulated him at the campus event, which meant she had wanted information of some kind. He felt like a fool.

"You asked me about the LIDAR equipment, didn't you?" he said.

"Sandeep, the sheriff brought me in to help. I need to ask you a few questions," she said. Her tone was direct, but not threatening.

Sandeep felt his heart jump. He pulled his hands back across the table and into his pockets.

"I've already told them everything," he said. Sandeep tried not to sound as panicked as he felt. "My visa work permit is at my apartment in Carbondale. It's an H-1B work visa. You can confirm that with Dr. Moore and SIU."

"Yes, yes, I know, don't worry about that," she said.

Sandeep stared at her. She didn't wear any makeup or jewelry. She looked like she had been taken by surprise as well. Glancing at the papers in the folder, Alison looked back at him with a straight expression.

"You a cop?" Sandeep blurted out. The tone of his voice surprised himself.

"You don't have to worry," she said. "I have some other questions for you, Sandeep. Just some basic questions."

Sandeep looked at his reflection in the window again. He knew a handful of others—most likely the two plainclothes officers—stood on the opposite side of the door. Alison seemed too slick to be a local cop. She must be a federal agent, he thought, perhaps an immigration official. This worried Sandeep. He wanted to ask Alison why she didn't reveal her true identity at the SIU event, but he refrained. He knew there was no reason to antagonize her inside a jail. Sandeep let his eyes fall into the back of his head as he searched his memory for what he had already told Alison.

"Your mother is from Pakistan, so you speak Urdu, right, and your father is from India, so you speak Hindi, and Punjabi, right?" she asked.

Sandeep nodded. "Punjabi is my native language, yes, but also English. I'm Canadian."

Alison was reading off a chart. His photo was at the top. He sighed again.

"But, ah, where did you pick up Arabic?"

The question threw him. He stared at Alison's brown eyes. They were distant.

"How did you know I speak Arabic?" Sandeep responded.

"Just answer the question, Sandeep."

He shrugged.

"I did two summer archaeological digs in Syria. In Palmyra. Temple of Baal, Diocletian's Camp, the Agora. Famous sites. I was there with the University of Toronto. I'm good with languages. I picked it up there." He paused. "I also speak French, if that matters."

"Palmyra, Syria," she said, nodding.

Alison reached into the folder and pulled out some aerial photos. She placed them on the table like pieces of a puzzle, and then turned them facing Sandeep. His lower lip dropped. It was like Alison had pickpocketed his wallet and spread it out on the table in front of him.

"Okay, so now let's talk about your work in Alexander County, Illinois. These photos are from your Walkera Voyager 3 quadcopter drone, right? Global satellite navigation?"

He stared at the photos, his right hand fingering one of the black-and-white images.

"How did you get these?"

"Just answer the question, Sandeep."

"These could be mine, yes."

39

The room next door had the same cinder blocks, but there was no window. That made it seem more suffocating, at least to Earl, who sat behind a table that touched the wall. His chair was wedged against the table and the wall, which made him feel protected but trapped.

Earl was rubbing his arm when Sheriff Benton entered. One of the inexperienced deputies had placed the right cuff on too tight, leaving behind a welt on Earl's wrist.

Benton took off his hat and tossed it to the table, and then lowered himself to the seat opposite Earl. Neither one looked the other in the face. With his chest heaving, Benton seemed to be either excited or agitated with the commotion.

This irritated Earl. Benton reminded him of an inexperienced hunter, with a loaded gun.

"I'm very disappointed in you," Benton said, moving his hat to one side.

"I haven't said anything," Earl said, his head fixed at the side wall. He rubbed his wrists.

"You telling me you can't control Harriet's daughter?"

"Wildcat plays by its own rules in the woods," Earl answered.

Benton leaned into the table, shoving it against Earl, who looked back at him. Trying to scoot back in his chair, Earl bumped against the back wall. Benton was fencing him in.

"We don't have wildcats in these woods anymore, Earl, you got that?" Benton said. "We eradicated 'em."

Earl stared at Benton.

"I haven't said anything," he repeated. He rubbed his wrist. "Teach your stupid deputy how to put on cuffs right."

Looking over his shoulder for a moment, Benton sighed and then shoved the table another inch. The two men stared at each other, defiantly, in a challenge.

"Don't want to have to bring you in again, you hear?" Benton said. "Next time won't be pretty."

Earl didn't respond, glancing down at his wrist. The pain throbbed now. The cuff had actually cut into his skin and left a dark bruise.

"Let me cuff myself next time you pull something like this."

Benton slammed his fist on the table, forcing Earl to lean back in a start.

"There won't be cuffs next time," he hissed. "There'll be a goddam body bag."

40

In the adjoining room Alison continued to set out a few images at a time, side by side. In Sandeep's mind, what seemed like a little folder contained multitudes. It also contained private images that only he had taken, downloaded, and stored. The more Alison reached into her folder and withdrew documents and photos, the more Sandeep felt like his entire life had been exposed. He had always prided himself on hacking; now he had been hacked by better hands.

Sandeep studied Alison's measured movements, her fingernails with no nail polish, her fingers with no rings. She didn't wear a bracelet. She had no tattoos—at least, not any noticeable ones teasing along her arms or hands. She didn't even wear glasses. There was something about her that was nondescript; she could disappear into the crowd without a second's notice. She reminded him of an assassin.

"This is Scott Air Force Base, and the National Geospatial-Intelligence spy center," she went on. "Why have you been photographing the base?"

"I'm so sorry, sometimes we just get carried away with the drones, and they get off target," he said, trying to act nonchalant. His voice was small, his breathing forced.

Sandeep shot a furtive glance at the door. His earlier sense of concern had given over to fear.

"We're still learning the technology," he went on. "We had no intentions of spying. We had no idea of the geospatial center."

He immediately regretted using the word "spying."

Alison nodded.

"No idea you just happened to be one hundred miles off course, hovering over the National Geospatial-Intelligence center? And what about this, the Whiteman base in Missouri, where nuclear missiles are stored?"

"Nuclear missiles?"

Sandeep reached over and touched the edge of the photo. The quadrants were well defined. The coordinates of the drone ran across the top like a frame.

"That's not my photo," he said. "I don't think it is."

Looking back at Alison, Sandeep let out a long sigh, and then shrugged his shoulders.

"Honestly, we've lost control of our drones so many times it's not funny. I've personally lost two. We send them out, looking for related mounds and nearby Hopewell campsites, and sometimes we just let them go too far. What can I say? We're amateurs still learning the technology."

"Amateur, you?" she said.

She collected the photos, shut the folder, and looked back at him, without any emotion.

"Nothing else you want to tell me, Sandeep?" She paused. "Better now than later."

41

Randall emerged out of the main office, stepping into the hallway, followed by Earl. Randall held open the door. The giant smile on Earl's face, his hair tied back in his ponytail, was the best thing Molly had seen all day.

"Earl, I can't believe this," Molly said as she skipped her way toward him, hugging him in front of Randall.

Molly released her embrace and stepped back.

"This is my mom's boyfriend, Earl Karnes."

"The terrorist with the turkey feathers," Randall added.

"Let's get the hell out of here," Earl said.

"Not without Sandeep," Molly said.

Letting go of the door, Randall nodded and told them to stay in the front waiting room. Molly took Earl's arm and ushered him down the hallway.

The click of a door caught Randall's attention. He looked down the hallway to the left, where Alison walked out of one of the rooms.

Picking up on Randall's presence, she waved to him in an awkward if curious way.

"Chicago, right?" she said, walking up to Randall. She held out a hand. "I'm Alison," she offered without a last name.

Randall nodded. He recalled her appearance at the security summit at McCormick Place. He had just assumed she was with the FBI or Secret Service. But Alison's presence now confused him. He had no idea of her affiliation. She was a fed, perhaps military intelligence.

"What are you doing down in Little Egypt?" Alison went on.

Randall had never liked that appellation of the southern Illinois region. It seemed belittling—always "little" Egypt, as if the meeting of the two great rivers in the delta was a trivial matter.

"Tracking down a cold case," he said. "What about you?"

"We're a little concerned over some breaches of security near Scott Air Force Base," she said. "Anyway, Chicago wants me back, and I'm truly ready to go." Her comment was intended to be an inside joke. "Can't wait to get out of this shithole."

"Understood," Randall said, though it wasn't clear if he was affirming her comment.

"Good to see you," Alison said as she turned and continued down the hallway.

Sandeep emerged from the same room as Alison, escorted by a deputy. His turban looked disheveled. Randall realized that Sandeep had been interrogated by Alison.

He didn't attempt to greet the researcher, who looked overwhelmed. Randall turned his head, pretending to look again at his phone, as the deputy escorted him out with the march of a military veteran. Randall just winked when Sandeep looked over his shoulder. Taken by surprise, it made Sandeep finally break a smile; he assumed Randall was part of his being allowed to leave.

42

___

Danny's deep voice boomed without any need of a microphone.

"Let's get the fuck out of here."

The crew was in the parking lot in front of the sheriff's office. They had gathered around Sandeep, each person taking a turn to give him a hug. Having gone first, Molly stood to the side, chatting with Anchee and Freddy.

Danny said it again: "We need to get out of here."

When Randall pushed through the front doors, Molly turned toward him and watched as he walked toward his car. There was something strange about the Chicago detective—how he managed to waltz into their archaeological site or the county jail unscathed, playing by different rules. He was the ultimate Marginal Man, able to play in many worlds.

Appearing out of the crowd, Earl walked toward Randall's car as well. It almost seemed like they knew each other, and yet, Molly couldn't remember introducing them before today.

"I'll be back," she told Anchee, and hustled to Randall's car. Earl stood at the passenger's side door, as if they had already made plans. By the time Molly got to the car, Randall had eased into his seat and rolled down his window.

"I don't know what your game is," Molly said.

She straddled the door's window between the two of them.

"There weren't any charges," Randall said. "There wasn't any reason to hold them."

"Then why did you allow the cops to arrest them?" Molly said, looking straight at Randall.

He didn't seem moved by the question. Randall didn't even bother to answer. He turned on the engine and shot a look at Earl, who had crawled into the passenger's seat.

"Why did that lady interrogate me?" Sandeep said, now standing next to Molly.

Randall looked at Sandeep, surprised by his sudden appearance.

"How did she identify herself?" Randall asked.

"She didn't," he said, "but I've met her before. She acted like a professor or something, but that was bogus. She must be some immigration agent." Sandeep paused. "She knew everything about me."

Randall peeked at the entrance to the sheriff's station. Cameras abounded on the building. He didn't feel comfortable speaking in the parking lot.

"Let's talk about it later."

Turning to his right, Randall motioned for Earl to put on his seat belt. Molly picked up on the exchange. The connection between the two men bewildered her. If only to placate her mother, she didn't want to get Earl involved in any more trouble.

"I'll take Earl home," Molly said. "Perhaps we can all meet up later."

"No, I'll take him," Randall said, shifting in his seat.

Taken aback by the comment, Molly hesitated as Randall revved the engine.

"Wait a sec," she said. "Who are you?"

The question jarred him, but Randall seemed to be in a hurry to get out of the parking lot.

"Someone I think you need," he said.

With the slam of his door, Randall quickly pulled away.

The departure of the car from the lot gutted Molly in some way, as a reminder of her lack of control over the situation. She stood there for a moment, alone and seemingly lost. Sure, she knew she needed Randall. Like an archaeologist with a fistful of broken pieces of pottery, she also needed to understand his role here in order to make sense of the shattering last days.

43

Earl told Randall to take a right at the fork, turn left after the huge oak, and then take the rural route across the valley until the turnoff at the ditch to the forest road by the swamp. That was the way to Harriet's cabin.

Randall glanced at Earl, and then back at the road. The Shawnee river guide was close to Molly; Randall had watched the two embrace at the sheriff's station like family. But that didn't concern Randall. Everyone was connected within two or three degrees by family down here. Instead, it was Earl's huddle in the corner of the hallway with Sheriff Benton that alerted Randall. Standing at the end of the corridor, Randall couldn't hear their conversation, but Earl's body language spoke for itself. The sheriff was repeating a warning, which Earl fended off weakly. There was an air of a stool pigeon about him.

Randall didn't wait for chitchat.

"So, you were brought in because you do know who's behind it, and they want to keep you quiet," Randall said.

Earl knew Randall wasn't asking a question. He rolled down his own window, sticking his hand out in the air.

"You're a cop, right?" Earl said, looking back over at Randall. "Listen, I don't know who wrecked the site, man. Honestly. But you're messing with some fucked-up, dangerous people out there, and I sure as hell don't want Molly to get hurt."

"Why would anyone want to hurt Molly Moore over an archaeological dig?"

Earl looked directly at Randall.

185

"Alexander Country has been run like a secret little plantation for decades," he said, turning back to the open window. The wind blew his hair into his face. "No one from the outside has ever given a shit about what happens down here, or who does what. Things been going down, you can't imagine. And now you're suddenly inside and the deeper you dig, the more shit you're going to discover. That's what worries me about Molly."

Randall stared ahead at the road without saying a word.

"Kids don't know what the hell they're getting into," Earl finally said, looking out the window.

"And you do?" Randall said.

"The huge oak up here," Earl said, pointing.

Randall slowed the vehicle, and then turned. There was no street sign. It seemed like all of these back roads had been left unmarked, to provide a getaway route for anyone in need of an escape.

"I know enough to stay out of this shit," Earl said.

"Why did they make it look like you had anything to do with the damage at the site?"

"That site is sacred to us Shawnee," Earl said, not flinching.

He cleared his throat; his chest heaved with a difficulty to breathe.

"Finding your mother is the tip of a lot of secrets buried down here," Earl said. "Lot of bodies out there that no one knows about."

Randall shifted abruptly toward Earl with a look of astonishment.

"How the hell do you know about my mother?"

Earl paused for an awkward moment. The car chugged toward a stop.

"Sheriff Charlie Benton."

44

Molly squeezed into the side booth in the tavern, pushing up against Anchee. Freddy made space for Sandeep on his side. A pitcher of beer dripped in the middle, glasses surrounding it like longing sentinels on guard. Freddy didn't hesitate, grabbing the pitcher, and then a glass, and started filling up the rest like a bartender.

The Arkies were not regulars at the Mounds Tavern, but they weren't strangers either. Danny didn't live too far away—though, tonight, he was missing, having been called by his uncle to help out on a back porch project. The others had stopped in for occasional beer runs and hamburgers.

It carried the aura of a river joint to Molly. Hunting, fishing, baseball, and the American flag. The TV screens barked from the corners of the room, from Fox News to ball games. The booths were packed with rural folks. These were Buster Moore's people. As a Cairo local, Freddy picked up on it first.

"Looks like we're providing a bit of diversity tonight," he said, taking his beer and batting his dreadlocks out of his face. "Cheers."

"Indeed," Sandeep said.

"So, what did you tell them?" Molly said, leaning across the table toward Sandeep. The urgency in her voice surprised the others.

"The truth about our surveys," Sandeep said. He was drinking a Coke. "This woman had all our images. Unbelievable. I was shitting my pants."

"All of our images?" Molly repeated.

"From the drone surveys of the site," Sandeep said. "Like the pits, and the valley site, and the mounds. She had a lot of questions about the site. I swear, there were some photos I'd never seen before."

Molly nodded. She drank her beer slowly.

"They confiscated a lot of our work at the trailers, too," Anchee said, "including some of Sandeep's equipment."

"What?" Sandeep blurted out. The sound of his voice made him look around the room. There was too much noise and commotion to disturb anyone else. With the TVs blaring, everyone was talking at the highest volume.

"Not much," Freddy said, smiling. "Danny held them off for a while, so I was able to hide the remote sensing equipment and a couple of drives in the safe box in the cellar below the barn. They didn't get the clone of the main drive."

His smile widened.

"And I hid the drones."

"Damn, you're good," Molly said, sharing a backhand slap.

"That Chicago dude, though," Freddy continued. "I wouldn't trust him any more than the sheriff. Not like he did anything to stop them from taking Sandeep away."

"I don't trust him either," Sandeep said. "He knew the woman that interrogated me."

"It was his mother," Molly said, her voice low. She looked around, the room blaring with the clashing noise of conversations and screens.

"His mother?" Anchee asked.

"That's why he's here," Molly added.

All of the Arkies looked confused by the comment. Molly leaned into the table.

"This has not been made public yet," she said. "You've got to keep this here. Randall's mother was a prominent journalist from Cairo who went missing decades ago, when he was a kid. The remains you found that we sent to Chicago to the FBI." She paused for a moment. "It was his mother, a woman named Florence Jenkins."

"What?" Anchee said.

"My God," Sandeep added.

"Florence Jenkins," Freddy said, almost in a whisper. "My uncle always talked about her."

The conversation at the table halted as two men at the bar started shouting at the TV screen with a bleacher bum's enthusiasm in the last inning of a game. Yet, this was no ball game. The men, both of whom were dressed in camouflage, heckled the newscast footage of President Adams at a press conference.

The Arkies' attention shifted toward a nearby TV in the corner, just on the opposite side of their booth.

"President Elaine Adams defended her intentions to propose the Weapons Reduction Act with Russia, China, and UN officials at the upcoming disarmament summit in Chicago, despite concerns . . ." the TV report continued.

The image of the Siberian disaster remained in the background as a series of shots of President Adams, and then the presidents of Russia and China, appeared on the screen.

"Lower the drawbridge and let the rest of the hordes come in," shouted one of the camouflaged men at the bar. He knew his outbursts were drawing attention. He was three inches of whiskey away from unloading his own weapons reduction act. Turning to address the rest of the tavern, he swiveled on his stool and stood up. "What a pathetic excuse for a president, this bitch is."

"Not my president," came a few hollers, and a couple of other supportive catcalls. No one really paid much attention to the camouflaged man, and his partner, and their wobbly perch at the bar. Drunk pontificators were a nightly occurrence at the bar.

"Bet you like this new president, don't you, raghead."

Everyone knew the recipient of this comment as the camouflaged man stumbled toward the table of the Arkies. The tavern patrons looked at Sandeep—and his turban. Some laughed. Others smiled. The old-timers in the tavern adjusted their seats accordingly, hoping the encounter wouldn't turn violent before they could finish their drinks. They had paid in advance.

"That's right, I'm talking to you," the man said, pointing a finger at Sandeep.

"Sit down, bud," Molly said, looking straight at the man. Her confidence impressed the others. "You should get back to your beer before it gets warm."

Bumping a table, which irritated an older man and his son eating dinner, both of them dressed in caps and farmwork clothes, the camouflaged man made his way to the Arkies' table.

"Oh, what da' we got here," he laughed, putting his hands on his hip belt.

Freddy regretted that he was sitting on the inside of the booth. The camouflaged man wasn't that tall; he was muscular, but the booze had put him a few strokes behind. Freddy thought he could take him out, if necessary. Not that Molly seemed concerned.

"Listen, I don't know about you," she went on, her voice so low that the man had to lean in to hear her, "but I'm related to just about everyone in this tavern. Do I need to call a couple of cousins?"

To make her point, Molly waved at the older man and his son having dinner. With a piece of fried chicken in his hands, the older man nodded back to her. Everyone knew Buster Moore's granddaughter.

That didn't impress the heckler. In fact, his friend at the bar egged him on, continuing his rants against the new president and her peace summit.

"Let's get out of here," Sandeep said.

"That's right, get out of here, raghead," the man said. "Out of our country."

"Whose country's that, bud?" Molly responded. Her words kept slapping him in the face. He stepped away from the table, unsure how to handle her defiance. "You're not from Alexander County," she said. "Not with that accent. What, working over at the fracking site or some pipeline? You from Wyoming or Texas? You take one of our local boys' jobs?"

Her barrage unleashed a ripple of laughter around her. Turning back toward the bar, nearly losing his balance, the camouflaged man attempted to sober himself into a fit of indignation. It didn't work. A wave of defeat pushed him away.

"The hell?" the man at the bar shouted, as the camouflaged man returned to his stool.

"Take it easy, Molly," Freddy said. "Jesus Christ, girl."

"This place has surely changed," Molly said. "Seems like every armed nut in the nation has converged down here. Hardly a single Illinois plate in the parking lot."

"I thought you said all of these people are your cousins," Anchee said, smiling.

Molly laughed, and then whispered, "Cousin is a loose term down here. I don't know anyone in here, except that nice old man and his son, and that's just because I bought a set of tires from them recently."

That bit of truth compelled the others to rise. Sandeep went first, then Freddy and Anchee. The empty pitcher of beer had served its role. Sandeep's glass of Coke had been drained to the ice. Walking toward the door, the Arkies could hear the camouflaged man and his partner taunt them from the bar. No one turned. Not even Freddy.

The humid evening tugged at the Arkies as they left the air-conditioned confines of the tavern. The relief from the rainstorm was gone; the sweltering follow-up was brutal, even in the night. When the door to the tavern clattered, Sandeep felt like they had left a tense scene for a frying pan of muggy weather.

"Oh my God," Anchee gasped as the four Arkies stood in the parking lot, "I was wetting myself inside." Everyone laughed at her comment as Freddy threw an arm around Anchee. "I thought Molly was going to kick that dude's ass."

Their laughter didn't last long. Wedged between two jacked-up trucks, the four Arkies looked back at the door as the camouflaged man and his partner stumbled out with a crash. They wore camouflaged hats. They also carried pistols on their belts. They didn't look like hunters. They walked with a gait straight out of an officer's canteen, albeit drunk and unstable.

"These guys are plastered," Molly said. "Let's go."

The Arkies made it to the middle of the parking lot—and then they heard the command. "I wouldn't take a step further," the camouflaged partner said.

They stopped in stride, all of them on cue, expecting the worst.

The man aimed a Sig Sauer–made 9-millimeter pistol at the crew. The first camouflaged man chuckled, wobbling his way toward the four. He had no idea that another couple had departed behind him, and quickly jumped into their cars. They revved their engine in an instant, and then spun out of the parking lot.

"Raghead," the man said. He took a swipe at Sandeep's turban, only to nearly fall to the ground. Sandeep stepped back, with Freddy at his side.

"Two on one," the first man said. "That's not a fair fight." He clicked back the trigger on his pistol. "This will even it up."

"Listen, bud," Molly said, stepping in front of Sandeep. "No hurt feelings. Let's call it a night and go home."

The camouflaged man wasn't having any of Molly's local diplomacy. He managed to rewind his arm and knocked ajar Sandeep's turban. Both men cackled. Frozen by the pistol, Freddy and Sandeep just watched the two men as Anchee looked around the parking lot for help. No one was in sight. The faint noise of music and chatter came from the tavern.

"Well, raghead," the first man said to Sandeep.

Then Anchee saw it—a black sedan bumped into the parking lot, speeding toward the gathering with no intention of slowing.

Bringing the car to a halt on the other side of one of the trucks, Randall barked at Earl like his parole officer.

"Stay in the car."

Earl nodded, but when Randall stepped out of the car, he reached over the seat and grabbed a duffel bag.

"Well, look at this," the first camouflaged man said as Randall stepped toward the Arkies.

"Three on one," said the man with the handgun, who stood several feet away. "I'd say that's still a fair fight."

He aimed his gun at Randall.

The veteran cop remained calm. His own pistol was inside his pocket.

"Put down your gun," Randall said. "I'm a police officer."

"We don't take orders from you," the first camouflaged man said.

He stepped up to Randall, daring him to take the first punch.

No one made a first move.

Then a booming shotgun blast, rattling the trees and dropping a hail of tiny bits of black walnuts, shattered the standoff, like an aftershock of an earthquake. The two men in camouflage looked stunned. The Arkies crouched in fear.

Only Randall appeared to know what happened. He shifted around and looked back at his car. Holding a sawn-off shotgun with both hands, Earl pumped the chamber and then aimed it at the man holding the handgun. Randall sighed. So much for anyone following his orders.

"I think the party's done here," Randall said, pulling out his pistol. "Everyone needs to go home."

Backstepping from the Arkies, the first camouflaged man chuckled as he kept an eye on Earl. Randall didn't hesitate. He grabbed the pistol out of the hand of the first man in camouflage with a quick move. Randall popped the weapons clip of bullets out in a flash, and then put it in his pocket. Shifting toward the other gunman, who wobbled to the side in fear, Randall held out his finger with the power that he could snatch anything in sight.

"Put that away," he said.

The man nodded, stuffing the pistol back into his holster. Randall handed back the gun to the first man with a gesture of dismissal. The two men stumbled to the side of the lot.

Randall picked up the turban. "Let's go," Randall said to Sandeep, a bit exhausted himself. "You've probably had enough fun for the day."

He and Earl escorted the Arkies to their cars; a few tavern bystanders had trickled out from the noise and watched in curiosity. Hugging the doorway, no one dared to wander into the parking lot. The militia drunks disappeared.

"You all get out of here now," Randall said, looking down at Molly, who sat in her car with a still-terrified look. "We'll follow you out."

Molly thanked Randall with a heartfelt nod, and for the first time, she felt like he had acknowledged it.

45

—

There was no going back to Chicago now for Randall. The discovery of Florence's bones was part of an active crime scene of history. His history. And it was up to him—and that gaggle of Arkies, even Molly Moore—to make sure no one would bury it again.

The rare ficus DNA buried in Florence Jenkins's shoe had become a clue in a critical page in that history. Randall knew he had to continue this investigation by providing Molly with the ficus specimen from Alexander's greenhouse.

Heading back to his aunt's house in Cairo, Randall felt something different. With each block, he sensed a looming trap. The secret behind his mother's death seemed entangled in other crimes. The abandoned blocks of Cairo haunted Randall as well. The boarded-up houses looked like giant tombstones. He had been old enough to remember the fallout of the campaign against segregation and the gutting of an American city by white flight. Many of the historic buildings of his youth had been torn down, as if the town's tragic history could be erased, buried, and paved over with asphalt.

Randall brought his car to a halt a few blocks from Liz's house. His mother had taken him to the Eighth Street corner when Randall was a child in the late 1960s, but old enough to understand the violence of the world around him. He would never forget the slow rise of her finger as she pointed at the arch over the street, welcoming its citizens. The same arch, she would recount, where a Black man had been strung up and hanged in 1909, a mob tugging at the rope until it snapped, and then his body dragged and scattered in the woods.

Nearly sixty years later, Randall could still hear his mother quietly explain that another Black man's body was hanged in a jail cell, teenage Private Robert Hunt on leave from the military, who had been stopped for a broken taillight. His beaten body belied the police report of a suicide. No autopsy had ever been done.

Randall felt his mother's hand squeeze his own. Her words had seared into his conscience with a plea, and a warning, that he had never fully understood as a child: "Don't let anyone bury this history."

46

His back against the wall, Randall sat on the guest bed in the small bedroom, a laptop computer on his knees. He had taken off his shoes at the back door, in order to not wake up his aunt. She had left on the lamp on the nightstand. With only a fan in the room, he had stripped down to his undershirt.

Like any good preservationist, Liz had left in place the framed photos on the cabinet to the side of the bed. A black-and-white photo of Randall's grandfather on a Mississippi River boat; a photo of his mother, Florence, as a young woman in her school uniform; and then Randall's wedding photo. It made him shake his head. Only an aunt 350 miles away would leave up a wedding photo from a marriage that lasted three years and ended up in divorce. And a child—Teresa.

Randall reached over and picked up the framed photo. He blew off a layer of dust. The wedding party looked harassed by the heat. Another wrongheaded summer wedding. Randall's ex-wife, Gloria, was radiant, though. He would always remember that. Her beautiful strapless dress. The elegant way she sashayed down the church aisle. They had been high school sweethearts, and marriage had seemed the logical next step in their twenties, even if both knew their love had never grown beyond their high school ways. As they lined up to take wedding photos, he was just going through the motions, as much as he wanted to believe in their marriage.

It had been hard enough to get through the late-night courses for his law enforcement studies. He had even given up his dream to become a lawyer. Once he became immersed in detective training, Randall moved on in a way he couldn't describe to Gloria. Family life didn't suit him—or at least family life with Gloria. She wanted peace between them and the time he couldn't give her. He found himself returning home late at night, even with the arrival of their baby daughter. His wife had accused him of straying off with other women, but that wasn't Randall's problem. The high school sweethearts no longer shared a bond. He had fallen out of love before they had even married.

The loss of his mother had derailed Randall in ways he could never explain. As a young detective, Randall had scrambled to use his connections and resources in Chicago to find an answer to her disappearance, but his inability to uncover a shred of evidence had always made him feel like a failure. Indeed, he felt like he had failed his mother and his family.

He placed the photo back on the cabinet. When Gloria divorced him three years later, taking custody of their child, Randall vowed to get his act together and reengage as a father. He made the vow every year, as Teresa liked to remind him.

Randall needed to sleep. It was 2:00 a.m. Something agitated him, though, which kept him from turning off the light. There had been too much to sort out, too much to enter in his notes; too much had happened that day.

Randall made five files on his laptop: Gen. Will Alexander, Alison (find last name), Sheriff Charles Benton, Sandeep, and Molly. And then he added another: Florence Jenkins.

The ping of an email startled him. It was a message from Nikki, at 2:20 a.m.

CHECK THIS OUT, FROM MAD DOG.

The Mad Dog email started on an unusual note: "Lots of 'heavy heavy' on this character."

Randall clicked on the attachment. It was a huge zip file. The highest-level internet he could install on his last trip was still working. As Randall began to cull through the documents, he scrolled down a series of military records and intelligence reports. Mad Dog had done his homework well.

Randall pulled his finger off the cursor when he saw a headline in the subject box. It was in caps: COMMANDER WXA UPDATE

RETIRED GENERAL WILLIAM X. ALEXANDER, FORMER HEAD OF MILI-
TARY MISSION OPERATIONS IN HELMAND PROVINCE, AFGHANISTAN,
IS LEADING PRIVATE SECURITY UNIT TO DEVELOP CUTTING-EDGE
DRONE AND WEAPON TECHNOLOGY IN ALEXANDER COUNTY, IL.
     ALEXANDER LINKED TO OSI CRIMINAL INVESTIGATION ON MISSING
PERSONS AND WEAPONS IN PANAMA.
     GENERAL ALEXANDER REMOVED FROM MISSIONS POST IN
GREECE DUE TO A NONCOMPETITIVE BID FROM HIS SON'S COMPANY.

Nikki or Mad Dog, or someone, had annotated the next document.

Retired army corps of engineers general criticizes security at base.
St Louis Post Dispatch. WEAPONS AND MISSILE COMPONENTS
UNACCOUNTED FOR MISSING FROM NATIONAL GUARD BASE IN MIS-
SOURI. General William Alexander testified recently at a congressional
hearing in Washington that the Whitman Air Force Base in Missouri . . .
nuclear storage bunker was not properly built and secured. It lacked
recommended fail-safe security components that have been used in
other projects he has built.

Randall rubbed his eyes. He wasn't sure if his weariness was playing tricks on him. He clicked on another file in the cache of documents. It was a copy of a newspaper clipping from a report by the Southern Poverty Law Center in Alabama. Randall recognized the photo immediately. In small type, the report noted the participants at a rally.

GENERAL WILLIAM ALEXANDER. SPEAKER AT THE STORM FRONT
WHITE NATIONALIST GATHERING IN STONE FORT, ALABAMA.

Wiping at his eyes again, Randall struggled to focus on the clipping and photo. He was too tired. But he couldn't pull himself away from the computer, and the documents. Alexander stared back at the reader from a news clipping, flashing his rugged looks and wide grin.

One final ping came from Nikki, a text: Miss u Nikki.

Randall's tired eyes pried at his mind again, sending him down to the bed. He clicked on the text to respond, writing: Miss u 2. What more could he say to Nikki?

Exhausted, he placed down his phone. He didn't send the text.

47

———

ALEXANDER FARMHOUSE
ALEXANDER COUNTY, ILLINOIS

From the road, it appeared like an imposing mansion or one of those two-story plantations that had enough columns and French doors to hide centuries of secrets and an occasional scandal. Three large sugar maple trees stood to the side like markers of time; a century-old oak tree on the opposite side presented a clearing where a small circle of metal chairs looked like they had not been used for decades. The sprawling, historic Alexander farmhouse may have had a wraparound porch and graceful columns for a turn-of-the-century Southern flavor, but Gen. Will Alexander considered the windowed and vaulted greenhouse to the side of the mansion his prized possession. At least, that is where he spent most of his free time outside of his office and field assignments.

This morning was no different. With his head buried under the leaves of an exotic golden trumpet plant, the general tended to his beloved collection of rare species, especially those he had planted around an ornate fountain and altar dedicated to his late wife. The morning light struck through the windows with the aura of another world. It reminded Alison Foreman, who stood to the side, of a tropical rain forest trapped inside a huge shipping container made of glass. She unbuttoned her blouse to the middle row.

Alison was on a mission, an intelligence mission Gen. McCarthy would have insisted, and she knew it required a certain chutzpah to get past Alexander's aura of personality, which set its own boundaries. The only way to dislodge any information from such larger-than-life figures, she knew from experience, was to let them do their own talking. Such men never knew how to stop.

Gen. Alexander didn't just have a green thumb. He was raising an army of exotic birds of paradise.

"I picked this jade vine up for my wife years ago," he called out to Alison, who seemed bothered by the encroaching vines, "when I was setting up a counterintelligence facility in the Philippines. Hell of a facility, classified. We had all of Asia wired. Yeah, I picked up a plant for that woman in every war zone I ever worked in."

"Lovely," Alison said.

She didn't have a green thumb or green desire in her body. But the tenderness Alexander lent his plants affected Alison. The general coaxed each leaf and plant with the joy that their very life depended on his saintly touch. He reminded her of an eccentric farmer more than a war veteran general. It was hard to imagine the general as a military firebrand in these moments, back in his native haunts.

"The key is keeping plants clean," Alexander went on, trimming one bush. "This tropical vegetation needs a lot of space to grow. Mold can be especially difficult, too. I learned that from a life of digging a lot of bunkers."

"Gen. Alexander," she tried to interrupt. "The cyber team at Scott Air Force Base has picked up unauthorized surveillance in the area. We believe it is . . ."

"Them damn Arkie kids," he said, trimming more dead material from a mandarin citrus tree. "I knew it. Oh, now, some bugs have penetrated the area."

"Sir?"

Alexander looked up from the bush.

"It's those Arkies, the kids at the road site," he said. "They've got drones. But we got drones, too, monitoring them. I never thought much about it but could be we need to shut them down."

"Absolutely, General," Alison said. She positioned herself opposite of Alexander, as he dug out an area around a purple-stemmed plant. "Sir, are you aware of what is transpiring in Chicago?"

Alexander halted his work, looked at Alison with disgust, and then picked up a watering can.

"Of course I am!" Alexander said.

Alison watched as he dripped water on the delicate red blossoms of bromeliads he had picked up during a covert war in west Africa.

"Any American president that allows foreigners to set the agenda on our military is engaging in an act of treason," Alexander went on. "Same goes for every general that falls in line."

"Sir," Alison said. She leaned over the basin of the plants, only a few feet away from Alexander. "I've always respected you. And I want you to know that you can trust me," Alison said. "I'm concerned about what's happening in Chicago, too, which is why I have come down to talk to you."

Motioning for Alison to come closer, bending down toward his exotic flowers, Alexander gently took one of the gorgeous red blooms into his palm.

"In such times as these," he whispered, "you should remind your superiors, like my old classmate Gen. McCarthy, that a general with more experience outranks a mutinous president who has been unwisely considered the commander in chief. Walter McCarthy has really disappointed me."

Alexander paused, dropping the flower, as both watched the petals disintegrate.

"A commander in chief surrenders his role when he relinquishes the duties of war instilled in his charge," he went on. "It is the solemn duty of the military to take over such duties when such a president surrenders." He paused again. "Do you understand what I am saying?"

Alison nodded. She desperately wanted to wipe off the sweat from her brow, but she froze in attention.

"This so-called summit is an act of surrender, the mere concept of disarmament is surrender," Alexander continued, raising his voice, "and it must be stopped at all costs."

"At all costs," Alison repeated.

"You saw it with your own eyes. We were three years ahead of the Russians. Three years! We could equip our drones and planes tomorrow. And because of an accident, which didn't take place on American soil, this stupid, harebrained president, who knows nothing about military strategy, is throwing the security of this country in the garbage . . . like it's some act of peace."

The general stood up.

"It's not peace, it's about giving up! Disarmament is just another word for surrender."

"Surrender," Alison said.

Alexander loved soldiers who repeated his commands. He winked at Alison, convinced she was precisely the mole in the military brass he had been hoping to convince.

Bounding to his feet, Alexander stepped to the side of the altar to his wife and motioned for Alison to follow him. He moved with a passion and a mission that marked his steps in the field. Alison had noticed this about Alexander; he moved briskly, on a deadline. Brushing off the dirt from her pants, Alison fell in behind Alexander, who walked a few feet. "Let me show you something," he said, and then waved her toward a hidden storm cellar door that had been built into the greenhouse floor. The general then reached down and opened it up.

48

The steel-cased stairway astonished Alison, as she descended behind the storm cellar door. It felt like it had been built for earthquakes. There wasn't a creak in any step. The stairway wound in a circular way, wide enough for two people, descending in a silo-like fashion for several yards. A caged lift appeared on a platform, the door opening on cue, as Alexander held out his arm for Alison to follow. It could have been an elevator cage for several industrial sites or even apartment complexes.

That was the funny thing to Alison. The whole complex seemed so safe and well-built and strangely inviting.

"Built them for nearly forty years," Alexander said as the door closed on the elevator, and he pushed a red button. "Name a conflict, and I've been underneath it. I know they're the safest place to be because I'm the contractor."

As they descended, a wide-awake Alison now asked, "Very impressive, sir. Tell me, where are we going?"

Alexander grinned and winked. He liked surprises. But he could hardly keep this secret.

"Nice and cool down here," he said.

Within seconds they had arrived a hundred feet below, stepping off into a large concrete corridor that opened into a passageway. Lights illuminated the passage. A bunker of huge scope came into view.

Walking in silence, Alison was impressed by a steel door that opened on Alexander's verbal command. It was a bunker door. Alison noticed an

204

old sign bolted to the wall: America Calling, Take Your Place in Civil Defense. Next to it was a black-and-yellow fallout shelter sign, which featured the radiation symbol of three triangles in a circle.

"Very impressive, General," she said as they walked down another hallway. "But why here, in southern Illinois?"

The question appeared obvious to Alexander. An armed guard on command saluted as they passed.

"This is my home base, always has been," he said. "Alexander County is named after my family. You have to understand, homeland security starts at home. So, while I built missions and bunkers and missile sites around the world for presidents, sheiks, and even dictators for decades, I felt it was a duty to protect my people down here from any kind of domestic unrest or war. This is the safest place in America."

"If you don't mind me asking, General," Alison said, "who paid for all of this?"

"The United States Civil Defense Act of 1961," Alexander said. "The taxpayers of this country paid for this by order of Uncle Sam. And you know more than anyone the Russians still have six thousand missiles targeted at us."

Walking through another steel door, with cameras and monitors at the entrance, they moved into what appeared to be a small operations center. Video screens, monitors, and computer equipment lined the walls, where two operatives controlled the situation. Another guard stood at the door.

"Right this way," Alexander said.

He took Alison into an adjoining room, which impressed her as more of a video or recording studio than a military commander's office. A couple of leather couches straddled the side walls. A rug covered the middle of the room with a colonial design. Potted plants hugged the ends of the couches like a living room. Up on an elevated stage sat a desk and a chair, framed by a large digital backdrop that changed iconic images from around the world every thirty seconds. With cameras sitting to the side, Alison could imagine the setting as perfect for a remote TV interview.

Then it hit her—this was where Alexander had been doing many of his interviews on Fox News and other networks. It seemed harmless enough to Alison. Alexander was a bunker-building crank who couldn't resist digging another bunker, even in his own backyard.

As Alexander spoke on a phone to an underling, he directed Alison to take a seat on one of the couches. Within seconds, a young operative came into the room and turned on one of the wall screens as Alexander sat near Alison.

"We also do our own communications and intelligence work down here," Alexander explained. "Intelligence of a different sort. We've got all we need to create our own messages and videos for distribution through global media. We've also got the ability to send the highest level of secret communications to our partners worldwide. We have our own satellite transponders."

Alison didn't look like she followed.

On Alexander's command, the young operative switched on a video on the wall. Footage of Russian submarines and spy ships at sea filled the screen.

"Is this real?" Alison asked.

The operator nodded at Alexander, who approved and clicked on his keyboard. A close-up of the Russian ships and sailors came into focus.

"Damn, these kids are good at this," Alexander gushed.

A deep narrator voice-over in another voice suddenly filled the room with the power of surround-sound speakers.

"Operating near the vital undersea cables that carry almost all global internet communications, Russians have carried out exercises for potential attack on those lines in times of war. According to US military intelligence, Russia is also building an undersea drone capable of carrying tactical nuclear weapons that could be used against harbors or coastal cities."

"Once you finish the edit, get that to Shawn's people at the network," Alexander told his operative, who nodded and left the room.

Alison struggled to understand.

"Sometimes I've got to rein them in, you know," Alexander said. "These kids can hack into the wrong networks sometimes." His voice trailed off, somehow distracted. "Trigger some things they shouldn't trigger. Unintended consequences, so to speak."

Alison shook her head, unsure what Alexander was saying. But the idea of military-trained hackers unleashed on their own concerned the intelligence agent. She looked back at the operative working on the Russian weapons system clip.

"General, I need to ask you something," she heard herself say.

Alison couldn't help but wonder if the general and his hackers had been involved in the Siberian nuclear disaster. The thought fled her mind, almost too bizarre to imagine.

The general, though, didn't have time to answer any more questions. Sheriff Benton entered the room from another door on the opposite side of the room, looking shocked to see Alison with Alexander.

"Don't worry, Sheriff," Alexander spoke up. "Agent Foreman is one of us."

Alison nodded at Benton with an uneasy look of camaraderie.

49

Only days from the opening of the Global Arms Reduction Summit, joint security exercises between the Chicago Police Department, the Illinois State Police, and the National Guard, the US Army, the FBI, Secret Service, and lead Homeland Security teams had turned McCormick Place into a hive of hardware. All of it—all 2.6 million square feet of exposition space, the six huge ballrooms, the 173 meeting rooms, the winding hallways and staircases, the endless glass portals that stared out to Lake Michigan with their reflection. With the attendance of the heads of state of the world's military superpowers, it demanded a level of security unseen in the annals of summitry.

The irony of deploying military tactics in defense of a conference on disarmament didn't elude anyone. Anti-ram blockades and fences had been set up around the parking lots and main entrances. Blast-proof barriers had been added to the selected ballroom and meeting halls. Windows had been retrofitted with ballistic window film that could withstand bullets. All extraneous entrances and exits had been sealed; the labyrinth of stairs and meeting rooms had been divided into security divisions.

Tromping in unison, squadrons fanned out to their blocks of security, toting automatic weapons. They replayed heightened security exercises. They surrounded the expansive convention grounds. No one moved inside McCormick Place now without a photo badge.

This was only on the ground level. An aerial view granted an entirely different picture of McCormick Place, starting with the platforms set up for antiaircraft artillery.

The view of the sky—or the monitoring of that aerial vision—was not only in the air. Coast Guard ships with radars encircled the shoreline of Lake Michigan, dispatching cutters from Calumet Harbor. Dolphin helicopters hovered off nearby pads. In a secret underground location, the Secret Service and FBI had set up the massive Multi-Agency Communications Center (MACC) base of operations in Chicago, as computer operators monitored the airways.

In this moment, however, an unmarked white windowless forty-foot trailer sat a few blocks down the harbor from McCormick Place in an empty parking lot. It was attached to a huge diesel semi engine with a generator set behind the cab. It was impossible to see the driver past the special one-way glass in the cab.

Secret Service agent Ford sat at the metal table behind a screen that separated the driver from the back of the van, inspecting his operations. He watched as an agent typed at a keyboard, tracking the air traffic coordinates that shifted on the screen. Three other operators sat at their own stations, all wearing headphones, checking the computer screens and radar equipment attached to the inside wall of the van. A map of Chicago stretched across the wall, where a red circle outlined a route from O'Hare International Airport to McCormick Place. When a low beeping sound resonated from the side station, Ford looked up from the computer operator.

"We've got a violation of the outer ring airspace between the ten NMR and thirty NMR," one of the agents said.

Ford bent back in his chair and looked at the screen of the operative. In the upper corner of the screen he could make out a small drone flying along Lake Shore Drive.

"Keep tracking location," Ford said.

"Tracking toward Promontory Point," the operative responded. "Drone, sir."

The drone sighting rankled Ford. This was precisely the kind of security breach that he had warned others to anticipate. Ford watched as the agent typed in a few words.

"Sending coordinates," he said.

Not quite five miles away, three Chicago police cars descended on a lakefront park area. It was Promontory Point, a popular picnic spot on the lake. Being a weekday, the crowds were sparse, though the day was beautifully clear and warm. The lake stretched out in a celestial blue. Pulling their cars to a skidding halt, the cops fanned out, guns pulled, and then closed in on a man of apparent Indian origin who stood by a picnic area with a remote control in his hands.

"Put your hands up," the first policeman called, holding his pistol with two hands.

The older man, with gray hair, wearing thick black glasses, a pair of khaki pants, and a buttoned-up shirt, dropped the remote control, and then raised his hands. He looked terrified.

One of the cops wheeled around when a scream erupted on the other end of the picnic area. They all aimed their guns, expecting an intruder.

"No, stop," the older man shouted.

A little kid raced out of the playground toward the old man, and then he clutched at the man's leg.

"What in God's name is going on here," the older man said, reaching down toward his grandson. "I'm Dr. Chandrasekhar, a physicist from the University of Chicago. You're scaring my grandson."

Lowering their guns, the cops watched as a small helicopter drone dipped in the sky, and then soared to a crash in the lake. Chandrasekhar put a hand to his forehead and groaned.

50

___

Even if he wanted to erase the stress of the last days and unwind from the tension and battles at the dig site, Sandeep was in no mood to party. He opted for a jog. It was good to be back in Carbondale, and to take a break from the crowded trailer at the archaeological site.

Running was a part of his daily regimen. He loved to depart from the SIU campus, head across nearby trails, and then take the back road to the Carbondale reservoir.

He passed under the canopy of the forests. Dropping onto the rural road, Sandeep jogged on the narrow shoulder, and then marked off his time on his phone counter.

Perhaps it was time to throw in the towel on this Moore Creek project, and head back to Canada. Sandeep had already put in enough time to justify a couple of articles. He had mounds of data, literally. While he admired Molly Moore's ambition, he wondered if it was worth the problems of remaining part of her crew. There were too many strange people—and cops—connected to this dig. It made the archaeological site in Syria seem like a playground.

A rumbling car in the background caught Sandeep's attention. He looked over his shoulder.

A white van drove past him at a slow pace, giving him a wide berth. Sandeep appreciated the attentiveness. Drunk college students could be the worst.

Then the van screeched to a halt, reversed, wiggling back toward Sandeep.

The back doors of the van banged open like wings. Three men in cam-ouflage leapt out, trotting toward Sandeep. He knew he was in trouble.

He careened to the side, sprinting along the road, and then hopped over the overgrown bushes, racing through the field like a hurdler. Tripping on a mound of dirt, and then a prairie dog hole, Sandeep stumbled to a stop.

A hand the size of a bear claw clasped on to his shoulder. Two more sets of hands fixed around his arms and body. He didn't bother to struggle.

Sandeep was dragged back to the roadway and pushed into the vehi-cle. A gag plugged his mouth, plastic cuffs bound his wrists, a hood was placed over his head. The back door closed with a thud. He fell back in the darkness. When the van jerked and sped off, he tumbled to the side with a feeling of horror.

As a car passed in the opposite direction, the driver waved at the van, as he did to all local cars.

51

From the edge of a promontory park, a ten-gun salute blasted from replicas of Civil War cannons. The riverfront crowd watched as smoke curled from the ends of the barrels.

Joined by a large, deputized posse, Sheriff Benton instructed one of his officers to unfurl an American flag. The deputy attached it to the flagpole, and then raised it with a slow, dramatic solemnity. Another round of cannon salutes erupted. An assortment of veterans and Civil War reenactment enthusiasts sweating in their wool uniforms saluted the flag as it waved into the midday heat. Despite being a Union stronghold, the crowd included a gaggle of Johnny Rebs in baggy Confederate uniforms. Modern deniers had a way of restitching history.

With his deputies and the posse in the background, Benton walked up to a podium that had been trucked out to the park. Setting up their cameras, the local and regional reporters, as well as the handful of national media correspondents who had driven over from St. Louis and Louisville, weren't entirely sure what was transpiring. The assembly line of posse members, all dressed in camouflage and hunter's garb, took on an air of a police lineup. There was only one difference from a true lineup: these men also carried weapons, holstered handguns, and even automatic rifles.

The Civil War relic behind them dignified the setting with a historic quality, casting the sheriff and his posse in the light of upholding an old tradition. The Civil War actors helped, too. This exact spot was the southernmost staging ground of Gen. Ulysses S. Grant for his campaign.

Alexander loved the smell of the cannons, albeit the blanks. But it was the tradition of the moment, with his troops, mustered by Benton, taking part in something bigger than themselves—something historic—that excited the general. They were a continuum of a great legacy that should not be broken. This certainty in the moment, in their actions, filled Alexander with pride and an unshakeable righteousness. He felt deep in his bones that they were doing the right thing. That he needed to step up and show the nation the level of courage that his ancestors had shown on the Civil War battlefield, and in every other war.

If only his son, Tom, could be here, as well as his beloved late wife, Marian. It was one thing to be in the boardroom of big corporations, making deals, or on the battlefields in foreign countries, or even storming our nation's Capitol in Washington, DC. But to stand your ground in your homeland and to defend your home territory and make it the front lines of an epic battle; that was the true calling of a soldier for Alexander.

Taking in the picturesque scene, the press didn't possess the only cameras. A crowd surrounded the event in horseshoe form, holding their phones aloft, registering the event in real time. One of Alexander's operatives had rigged up his own live streaming device, beaming the event to social media outlets around the world.

"We declare Alexander County will not uphold or participate in any proposed federal gun control act," Benton read from a document. He looked at the reporters for a moment, to gauge the impact of his statement. He tugged at his hat needlessly, and then continued. "We disavow and refuse to enforce any new gun laws and regulations."

Leaning against a tree on the outer edges of the crowd, Randall thought he had misunderstood the announcement. When a chorus of cheers erupted from the crowd, including yelps from a few citizens who withdrew their guns and raised them in the air, the Chicago detective realized that Benton had declared his defiance of the new gun laws recently announced by President Adams. It wasn't just buffoonery. It was a chilling act of rebellion.

A reporter raised her hand, looking around at the other journalists, with a curious grin.

"To be clear," she said. "You're declaring your refusal to obey a federal order?"

Benton shook his head, as if she didn't understand.

"My refusal to obey an unconstitutional order to disarm American citizens, yes," he said.

"Apart from updating registration and background checks," the reporter went on, looking around at the dumbfounded faces of the rest of the media, "the proposed gun control act is actually a volunteer buyback program. What exactly is it that you're refusing to enforce?"

Benton paused, glanced over at Alexander, and then continued.

"Let's be clear," he said. "Registration is simply the first act of confiscation. That is not constitutional nor acceptable. As Gen. Alexander has noted many times, military officers swear an oath to support and defend the Constitution, not necessarily the commander in chief, and as the law enforcement chief in this county, I affirm that oath, and our constitutional right to bear arms. I am an oath keeper."

52

Molly, holding a stuffed box, yelled over her shoulder. "Pack as much as you can in the truck." She was racing to get to her lab in order to test the ficus. Randall hadn't stopped texting her about it.

Danny nodded, carrying a crate to the open end of a pickup truck. The desecration of the dig site had necessitated preserving whatever the team could move to a safe location.

Surrounded by stacks of tagged and labeled bones, skulls, and ancient artifacts piled on the tables in the old barn, Molly had been working at a manic tempo. She selected the materials carefully. She placed the whole collection of pots into boxes. The sacks of shards were left behind like unmatched pieces of a puzzle. A collection of femur and tibia bones lined another box. When Danny returned, Molly reached over to the table and handed him a box of skulls.

"Careful," she said. "We've got to go."

Danny nodded, wiped at his forehead under his cap, and then picked up the heavy box with both hands. He had taken the job at the archaeological site as a part-time curiosity; unemployed, he had been laid off from his factory job on the other side of the river. Never did he think he would be carting skulls and body parts. But working with Molly had given Danny a new burst of confidence. He felt like his opinion mattered, and his sixth sense for operations contributed to the archaeological team in a way he had never considered. Molly had never put him down, like his bosses at the factory did. She never told him to cover up his tattoos. The Arkies even liked his heavy metal tunes, especially in those exhausting moments of carting the artifacts to the barn, when every jolt of energy was needed at the end of the day.

"You're in good hands, cuz," Danny said.

No one else was around. Exhausted by the turmoil, the other Arkies had gone to Carbondale for a break. The barn, as well as the entire archaeological site, felt hauntingly empty.

Danny charged back into the barn with a tired but dedicated look.

"Can you handle the rest?" Molly said, walking toward another car. "I'll call you later. I need to go."

"Got it, boss," Danny said. He looked at the mounds of pottery, and stacks of ladders, boards, and equipment. There was no way he'd be able to empty the barn by nightfall.

"I'm going to my lab," she said. "I need to get in touch with Sandeep and the others; bring everything there."

She darted out the doorway in a way that made Danny feel nervous.

53

A chorus of questions peppered Benton, after the initial shock of the refusal-to-obey announcement had been registered. The national media outlets, including a reporter for the AP, who had anticipated spending the day on the river with a fishing rod, notified their producers. Photos and statements circulated on social media. Local reporters recognized the media stunt would take on national implications.

Pleased with the attention, Benton held up both hands, attempting to quiet the crowd. He smiled. He removed his hat, ran a hand through his thin hair, and placed his hat back on with a thrust of confidence. He was beginning to like this.

"Cairo is a microcosm of what is happening to our nation," he declared. "While our citizens received threats, witnessed attacks, and invoked their right to defend themselves, we are now living under a Washington administration that is hell-bent on denying our rights and taking away our weapons of defense. How can we ask our citizenry to give up their sole source of defense—our guns?"

"What threats?" asked another reporter, standing in a long dress, holding out her microphone.

"There are terrorists in our midst," he said.

Benton paused, realizing his comment scurried around the crowd with a twitch of doubt. There was no "midst" to the reporters. The park was virtually empty, outside of the press conference. The town of Cairo appeared to be nearly abandoned to the visiting media. The rural county had fewer people than a state fair.

"To live in a gun-free zone, as this president insists," he went on, "we are effectively setting up kill zones."

"Terrorists?" More than one person shouted out a question. Benton's cryptic response provided more questions than answers.

While other reporters raised their hands, the woman in a long dress inched closer to Benton.

"Can you explain further what kind of terrorists, and what kind of threats?"

Benton quieted down the crowd again. The national correspondents equivocated between an urge to run with the sensational charge and dismissing it outright.

"I can't divulge the details right now," Benton went on, "in order to not compromise investigations, but I can say we are concerned about the illegal use of drones by terrorists in this county and nearby military sites."

Seeing Alison on the outskirts of the crowd, Randall pushed off his tree and walked in her direction. The press conference had erupted into a swirl of activity. He passed two TV reporters, who stood with their backs to Benton and the background of the park as they made live reports on the "oath keeper" announcement and the investigation into local terrorism. A few more cars and trucks—curious onlookers—had joined the perimeter of the gathering.

As Randall stepped by her side, Alison seemed startled by his presence.

"You're still in town?" she said.

Randall wasn't sure how to respond. He looked at Benton waving his arms, answering another question. Alexander had disappeared.

"You're DIA?" Randall said, stepping to the side of Alison.

"Let's say I'm a liaison with Scott Air Force Base," she said, smiling at Randall. "What about you? This part of your cold case, too?"

Turning to his right, Randall noticed a man walking around one of the recent car arrivals, and then opening the door to a parked truck. The driver of the truck had carried himself with an unmistakable presence. He had a red beard and a bearish gait.

Randall's mind was suddenly somewhere else. He looked back at Alison, who realized her question had been dropped. She grinned. She assumed she had stumped Randall. He gazed over her shoulder as the truck door closed, the engine revved, and then the truck backed out of the space.

"Hold on," Randall whispered.

Randall knew the driver—or, rather, he had met him at another crime scene.

"What's that?" Alison asked.

The truck hiccupped to a stop. The recognition was clear; Randall moved toward the truck and got a direct look at the driver's face. It was the witness from the Russian ambassador's murder in Chinatown in Chicago.

The truck made a wide turn, rattling away, barreling out of the area.

Randall didn't hesitate. He leapt past Alison, sprinted to his car, hopped in, and raced out of the park, following just enough of a trail of dust from the truck to think he had a chance. The scenic byway drive out of the park clashed with the incoming traffic across the bridge from Kentucky. A semitruck pulled in front of Randall, who desperately maneuvered and then passed it on the shoulder.

Cutting through Cairo, the truck weaved its way toward the levee road, following along the Mississippi River. It sped away until its tailgate diminished to a dot along the road, and then disappeared into the mesh of cornfields on one side and unmanaged forests on the other.

Randall lost him. He pulled over on the side of the road in a cloud of dust. He slammed the dashboard in anger. He knew he wasn't confused on the identity. He needed to tell Nikki and his crew in Chicago immediately.

Pulling out his phone from his pocket, Randall was startled by the buzzing of a text. It was from Molly.

IMPORTANT! Please meet me at the Old Gem movie theater in fifteen minutes.

Enter thru the back door.

54

___

"Answer the phone, goddamn it," Randall growled to himself as he made one last attempt to call Nikki from his car in a Cairo parking lot.

The call went straight to her message box. Then a text pinged back onto his phone. Can't talk. Just stepped into security meeting. Chief pulling me aside.

Nikki's response did not console Randall. He pounded at the keyboard on his phone.

Chinatown witness here.

Repeat: I just saw Chinatown murder witness here.

Get ahold of Mickey Berkes in military intel and find all you can about the witness.

His text seemed like putting a message in a bottle at sea.

Getting out of his car, Randall couldn't understand why Molly had asked him to meet her at an abandoned theater. This was not important to him now, but Molly's insistence had triggered him. There was still so much about Molly and her family that he didn't understand and Randall felt outraged that he was being forced to confront it. Their fates seemed inexorably entangled, and as much as that infuriated Randall, he also recognized she played a critical role in unveiling the mystery behind his mother's death.

From the outside, the theater looked decrepit, even dangerous. Peeling and cracked boarded-up windows scaled the three stories. The marquee hung off the façade like a warning sign. Moss grew up the sides of the building. The chains on the shattered French doors seemed more like an anchor than a barrier to entry.

Randall could remember going to the old Gem Movie Theatre when he was a kid. The red seats matched the red carpet down the aisles. The vaulted ceiling arched with the Art Deco design from the 1930s, when the theater had been renovated after a fire. It had been truly a gem in downtown Cairo. The title escaped him now, but the last movie he had seen had been a Richard Pryor comedy, which he had to sneak into with his older cousin.

The theater hadn't been open since the late 1970s. The seats had been removed and stored in a place few could remember. Over the last decades it had gone through scenes of abuse, infestation, and flooding. Well-meaning attempts to renovate the lobby had fallen to the wayside; the broken side doors had provided a portal to misbehavior.

Standing outside the theater now held a powerful pull for Randall. The last images of his childhood in Cairo. One of the few memories of fun. And a beautiful memory of being with his mother and father in the darkness sharing a bag of popcorn, watching a movie on the screen, as if the images were a magical door into another world.

Walking to the side of the building, Randall sidestepped the rusted fire escape stairs. He stepped over the rubble and piles of trash and bottles, looking over his shoulder, and then saw a gap in the far end that had a door.

Randall pushed on the door and entered. Once his eyes adjusted to the darkness, a few streaks of light shooting through the splintered cracks in the upstairs windows, he realized he was standing at the base of the old stage and screen, which was set back like a pockmarked target range. Birds scuttled above in the cavernous pockets of the ceiling.

When an empty bottle cascaded down the aisle, Randall reached for his gun.

It was Molly, who walked down the aisle like a true usher.

"Watch your eyes," she said. "It takes a second to adjust."

She just doesn't give up—that was the thought in Randall's mind, as he navigated the darkness.

With a remote control in her hands, she flicked on the racks of lights attached to the ceiling. In place of the seats, the terraced blocks were lined on one side with tables, topped with laboratory instruments, computers, and boxes. Crates of materials lined the walls. On the other side of the theater, a series of shelves had been set up, packed with bones, bags of shards, and other material from the archaeological dig. A few dirty couches slumped around the room.

Randall walked in a little circle.

"Saturday mornings in the summer," he whispered. "Damn, I remember this theater so well as a kid."

An awkward silence hung in the stillness of the theater as streaks of dirt were illuminated by the lights.

"This place safe?" Randall said, craning his neck at the slumping balcony.

"Safe enough," Molly said. "I've got sensors and alarms all over the place."

"Why on earth are you working out of here?"

"Because no one would ever suspect to find me here," she said. "Besides, it was dirt cheap."

Molly withdrew a small plastic pouch, and then handed it to Randall. She motioned for him to follow her to a nearby table, where a large computer screen was illuminated.

Randall knew exactly what was in the bag. He held it up to the light. The red shoe was clearly seen in the plastic.

She sat on a stool and typed on the keyboard.

"I just received the test results now. They confirmed my hunch. The seeds and pollen debris in the sole are from a rare ficus plant," Molly said, looking at the screen.

"From your dig in Vietnam?" Randall said.

"Yes, I saw this ficus for the first time in Kon Tum province on the border with Cambodia. It's called a ficus stricta. *Ficus rostigma strictum.* The specimen here came from a local planting, I'm sure."

Randall waited for the next line, knowing the answer but needing to hear it from Molly.

"It has to be Alexander's greenhouse," Molly said. "No one else would have it around here. It's too exotic to find anywhere else. Unless, of course, I'm totally wrong."

The two investigators stared at each other in a knowing way. If Molly had any real evidence that Alexander might be associated with his mother's murder, Randall would have stormed over himself and knocked down the general's door. Yet, the link to the tropical plant could almost be a ruse, even if the ficus had come from the heel of the shoe.

Molly started, "The general is a lot of things, but I can't imag—"

"You're the one who found a link!" Randall snapped. "We have to prove this."

It almost seemed like Molly was contradicting herself. Was the archaeological site so important to her that she would protect it—and her rapport with her benefactor, Alexander—over his investigation of his mother's death?

Molly placed her hand on the plastic bag with the red shoe.

She looked at Randall. "Florence Jenkins deserves this," Molly said. "She deserves justice."

In that hallowed theater of his youth, on a stage of their own making, their roles had flipped. Molly's words stung him. Florence's name had brought back decades of anguish over her disappearance, with its question over whether justice would ever be served.

"Damn right she does," Randall whispered.

Molly handed the plastic bag to Randall.

"There's only one way to know," Randall went on. "We have to get a sample from Alexander's greenhouse and see if they match."

Molly nodded, stepping back toward her table.

"I know," she said. "We have to test what's in that greenhouse."

"Sure you now want to do this?" Randall said. "I can handle this myself."

Reaching over to her computer, Molly clicked on the image of the ficus on the screen, with Randall's shadow hovering on the side.

"Yes," Molly said. "I'm part of this story, too."

55

LIZ'S HOUSE
CAIRO, ILLINOIS

Molly studied the fringe on the old lampshade casting a historic spell over the sitting room. The green velvet couch was a family heirloom. The three paintings on the wall, framed in rustic gold, had been done by a great-uncle in the 1920s who had become well-known in New York City. Leather-bound books lined the bookshelves in the corner.

Randall's aunt moved with a certain formal hospitality in harmony with her old house. When she finally sat on the Victorian-era parlor sofa with her nephew, Randall felt like he had been welcomed into the home of his ancestors.

Pauline had arrived on the heels of Randall and Molly. Protective of her elderly mother, Pauline had a way of showing up when anyone visited the house.

"Do you honestly understand what you're asking her to do?" Pauline said, her voice angry. "Put herself in the middle of an investigation? At her age? With someone who has never done anything to us, and only treated our family well? Damn, man."

Liz appeared a bit shaken by the possible implications of Alexander being connected to Flo's disappearance.

"Oh my, Pauline, settle down," Liz sighed.

"We're not accusing the general of anything," Molly said.

Pauline looked at Randall with a grin.

"We? She part of your police force now?"

Randall sighed, expecting his cousin's wrath.

"This woman has the facilities to test the soil and plant material," he said. "We're just running samples for a test. Nothing else."

"Nothing else?" Pauline scoffed. "First, you come down from Chicago thinking you know more than anyone down here. Now you want to knock on the plantation owner's door, ask to enter his private property, and test his plants to see if he had any part in killing your mother? And you don't think anyone will notice? Damn, man."

"It's for my dear sister," Liz spoke up. "It's for Flo."

Pauline hesitated a moment, looking away, and then she pointed a finger at Randall.

"You don't know what it's like to live down here," she said, her voice quieter. "The shit we put up with. You're not going to get what you're looking for. They're not going to let you play this game down here. Don't you understand that? Someone else is going to get killed before you figure that out, and that's why Liz ain't playing no part in this."

Randall didn't react. His eyes were elsewhere—perhaps on Commercial Avenue, walking with his mother, going to get some ice cream as a child. His mind had already been made up a long time ago. With that straight expression etched across his face, he could listen to Pauline all day and not get flustered by it.

"Show me that picture again," Liz said, speaking up.

Randall held up his cell phone for his aunt as she lowered her reading glasses to get a better view. The iPhone glowed in his hand.

"Molly here says it's an exotic plant from Asia or the Pacific Islands," Randall said, using his finger to enlarge the image on the phone. "Here's another photo."

"Oh, that's a fig," Liz said. "Sure is. At least, that's what the general always called it, his strangler tree, his stricta fig."

Molly looked at Randall, who still held the phone. He nodded.

"That man sure loves those plants," Liz went on. "I think I was the only person he ever trusted to take care of his greenhouse, knowing, of course, of my own gardening."

"I remembered that you tended to the general's greenhouse," Molly said.

"Off and on," Liz replied, sitting back on the couch. "You know, he used to travel more than he does now, so he needed someone to give him a hand and water his plants." She leaned toward Molly with a casual gesture. "His wife, Marian, and I were in a book reading group at one point, and when she passed on, well, the general didn't really entertain too many people at his farmhouse. He didn't trust anyone but me. He's particular about his greenhouse."

Placing his phone on the coffee table, Randall sat back, sizing up his aunt, like he would another detective in his office.

"Liz," he said. "Would you feel comfortable paying a visit to the general? I need a sample of the plant. It's for Flo. We need to know if there is a connection to where she was before she disappeared."

"I'm warning you, man," Pauline said.

"Hush," Liz said.

Randall's aunt understood the implications. But it did almost seem ridiculous to her. She had spent too much time at the general's house, among his wife's friends.

Liz took a breath and nodded.

"I saw him, not too long ago. Of course," she said.

"Good. Thank you," Randall replied.

At first, Liz didn't realize that Randall had meant an immediate visit. The urgency in his voice, though, dispelled any hesitation. Randall looked at his watch with the anticipation of an appointment. Liz got it. Raising her hands to signal her understanding, she rose to change her clothes, and by the time she had returned to the sitting room, Molly and Randall were already standing at the door.

"One second," Liz said, wearing a casual summer dress, with a purse draped on her arm. She disappeared into the kitchen. "I have something for this."

Randall and Molly had something, too. They knew it was necessary to monitor Liz's movements and safety. Liz returned from the kitchen with something in a paper shopping bag.

Randall placed an iPhone inside Liz's dress pocket.

"We want this to transmit from inside, right here," Randall said. "Take pictures if you can, too."

"I understand," Liz said. She was hardly a newcomer to smartphones; Liz had created extensive photo albums of her garden varieties.

56

Liz drove herself, of course. Her old Mercury Grand Marquis remained as pristine as when she purchased it more than two decades ago with her retirement funds from the school district, where she had been the librarian for forty years.

Driving out of Cairo, Liz realized that it had been a while since she had taken a ride into the rural areas. The area appeared to be in a state of disarray. She passed the detour for the unfinished Ft. Defiance Highway, and the unmarked turnoff to the archaeological site. Slowing the car to pull off the rural two-lane, Liz waved to a guard who sat inside a guard booth at the entrance of a wide but single-lane blacktop road and then brought the car to a halt. It was a gated community for a community of one: the historic Alexander farmhouse.

"Well, hello, madam librarian," the security guard said as Liz rolled down her window. He was a gray-headed man, with an expansive gut to match his years in an immovable desk job.

"Well, hey, Richard," she said. "How's Geraldine getting along these days?"

Listening to Liz's conversation through their transmitter, sitting in his parked car by a nearby barley field, Randall looked over at Molly with a nod.

"Mighty fine," the security guard said. "Our forty-fifth anniversary is coming up right near next month."

"Well, isn't that something," Liz gushed. "Listen, I'm taking the general a little sweet today, for an impromptu visit. Is he around?" She pointed at a large rhubarb pie wrapped in foil on the passenger seat.

"He is, but no one is supposed to enter," the guard said.

Liz smiled at him. Richard, the guard, glanced over this shoulder. He knew a camera stationed on top of the guard post monitored every conversation. But this was Liz, as everyone knew her.

"You'll be quick, right? Think he's in a meeting, but you can leave the pie with me if no one answers."

The huge wraparound porch was empty. Two dogs buried themselves under the steps for a bit of shade, without a raised eye of concern over Liz's ascent above their heads. Three other cars and trucks were parked in the dirt clearing to the side of the old farmhouse. Under the early afternoon sun, no one dared to dally outside.

Her knock on the door didn't draw any response. She tried again. Shifting the pie pan in her hands, she adjusted her purse and aimed one last knock. The door opened with a jerk as a security guard in camouflage stood to the side.

"Who the hell is that?" came a voice in the background.

Liz recognized the voice. It was the general.

"Tell the general that Liz has brought a rhubarb pie," she said, at ease with the situation. "And I need a little clipping from the greenhouse."

Before the guard could say a word, Alexander had appeared in the hallway like a shadow. His hair was disheveled. His haggard expression betrayed his swagger of confidence that normally moved his presence around a room with vigor. Liz thought Alexander looked troubled. If anything, he looked disoriented to Liz, sleep-deprived and agitated.

"Lizzy," he said, stepping up to the door.

"Good afternoon, General," she said.

"We're in the middle of an important meeting," he went on, and then stopped himself. "Well, my Lord, is that a rhubarb pie?"

Liz handed him the pie, making an exchange for the keys to the kingdom.

"I thought this might be nice on a day like today, General," she said.

"Thank you so much," he said.

Alexander received the pie, and then turned back to the door.

"I'm sorry to bother you, General," Liz went on, "I was just thinking about dear Mrs. Alexander, and I said to myself, I want to get a clipping of the schizanthus in your greenhouse to remember Marian."

"Certainly, Lizzy. Nice of you to think about Marian. You know where it is, right?" he said.

Back in Randall's car, the detective held up a thumb of victory to Molly.

Alexander had backstepped to the hallway. "Yes, well, just go and do it, Lizzy. I don't have a lot of time right now, but I'm sure you know where to find it."

"Thank you, General."

As Liz turned to step down the porch, Alexander leaned through the doorway, holding the side of the frame.

"Hey, Liz," he called out. "I met your nephew." He paused, looking around the porch. "I was informed about your sister by the sheriff. I know this is a terrible moment for you all. You let me know if he needs any help."

"Oh, I will, General, thank you," she said.

Alexander's reference to Randall eased this new concern brewing in Liz's mind. She had always enjoyed a nice rapport with the general. Everyone in the area did, too, for the most part. He had always made it a point to ask about family.

Over Alexander's shoulder peered a towering presence. His red beard was visible. The huge man wore a ball cap and a dark T-shirt. Liz didn't recognize the burly man. He wasn't local, that was for sure. She knew everyone in town who had worked for the general over the years.

"Give Liz a hand, Thomas," Alexander said, "and make sure she finds what she's looking for."

"Thomas, okay," she said.

Even with the windows cracked open, the greenhouse felt like a sauna. The vaulted glass ceiling captured the rays; the humidity dripped down the vines and branches like a waterfall. With Thomas tailing behind her, Liz entered the greenhouse with a knowing approach, and then headed toward the back of the building. Alexander kept his tropical exotics in the back, near the altar he had created for his wife.

It didn't take Liz long to spot the glossy leaves. Alexander had years ago potted the three ficus trees, strangler stricta figs, which now stood about six feet tall.

"Seems like Cambodia, right here in Cairo, Illinois," the bearded Thomas said.

"You a gardener, Thomas?" Liz said as she reached over and clipped a few ficus leaves.

Thomas couldn't tell or care about the difference between a schizanthus butterfly flower and a tropical tree from Vietnam. He knew how automatic weapons mowed down jungle foliage.

"Hell, I mowed some grass," he said.

A storm door behind the altar suddenly opened as two technicians in jumpsuits with tool belts emerged. They looked at Thomas in surprise, and then headed toward Alexander's home.

"It's okay," Thomas said to Liz. "Tornado shelter down there. Doing some repairs."

For a moment, it seemed to Liz like the altar came alive.

Making sure she also got a clipping of the flower she had mentioned to Alexander, Liz moved on with the sureness of a horticulturist.

"Oh, look," she said. "The orchids are blooming. I need to take a picture of that for my album." Pulling out her phone, Liz snapped a series of shots of the different plants, showing all corners of the greenhouse and the altar, and then landed on Thomas.

"You done?" he said.

Within minutes she was in her car. She flicked on a vintage CD of the Staple Singers, and Mavis's thunderous voice shook the old sedan. Looking over at her purse, which bulged with the leaves, Liz finally sighed.

57

Samples of the ficus leaves covered part of a small tray. A large computer screen sat to her right as Randall watched Molly at her microscope.

Picking up the iPhone, Randall flipped through the images of the plants and flowers that Liz had taken. On the screen the blurred image of a large man's back was in the foreground, but Randall could see the outline of a doorway to the side of what appeared to be a statue or altar. He scrolled to the next photo, which showed a towering Thomas beside a small fruit tree.

"Jesus Christ, he's with Alexander," Randall whispered.

Molly gestured for Randall to take a look. Randall bent over the table and fixed his eye on the microscope.

"By extracting the pollen, we can study the designs, and determine the identification of the species. Look here," Molly said, referring to her computer screen's side-by-side images of the pollen. "From your mother's shoe and Liz's new cutting," she added. "The outer skin of these pollen grains is incredibly resistant to decay, and can be preserved in humus."

Molly looked at the screen, and then back at Randall. Her expression was somewhere between disgust and terror. Randall didn't need to ask.

"There's a clear genetic connection between the Alexander greenhouse trees and Flo's shoe," she said.

Randall nodded, stepping away from the table. He lowered his head, and then he kicked at a clump of cardboard on the ground. He heard Molly typing at the keyboard of the computer.

"Do we need to get this to my lab in Chicago to confirm this?" he said.

"Times have changed," Molly said. "We have verified it here. You don't need to go to Chicago." Turning her back, she clicked on another computer. "Check this out."

The computer screen, just to the right of the microscope, unveiled various radargrams, which looked like squiggling lines and color-coded indexes to Randall.

"This is the ficus?" he asked.

"No," she said. "This is something else. The more layers you dig, the more you find how little things have changed." She touched the lines on the screen. "This darkness connects to Alexander. These images are from Sandeep's remote sensing operations. He keeps going on about it, but I never really paid attention. I'm sorry now."

"Why?"

"Because all of this action is under Alexander's greenhouse."

"What are these? Satellite images?"

"Some are satellite images available to the public," Molly answered. "But the most intriguing ones are from our ground-penetrating radar, what we call electromagnetic radiation."

She clicked on a few more images, which lit up the screen in various designs.

"Looks like an ant farm," Randall said.

Molly continued to impress Randall with her technical insights. She had a self-assurance that made him pay attention. He knew Molly was a straight shooter, and he knew she was laying her cards out on the table.

"Same concept as an ant farm," she went on. "Sandeep is so friggin' brilliant. He stumbled onto what he saw as a large tunnel system in the area. I thought it was a pipeline or mine. The area is honeycombed with old underground passages." She clicked on another image. "But this one is different, and this is what intrigues Sandeep."

"Looks like a bunker," Randall said.

"Two bunkers, actually, separated by a tunnel system."

"Where's Sandeep?" Randall said. "I have to talk to him if these are his findings."

"I think he's taking a little time off," Molly said. "That interrogation really shook him."

She touched the screen.

"How far is this from your dig site?" Randall asked.

Molly overlayed the dig quadrants and turned to Randall. The new image on the screen enhanced the underground structure.

"This is directly underneath the far end of our site, near the old Henson farm."

58

The main summit security preparations took place in the after hours of the night when a few lonely cabs and Uber drivers fought over a straggling tourist or a drunk patron stumbling out of the Velvet Lounge on Cermak Road. Dressed in black, the security forces along the lakeshore and Near South Side could have been mistaken for street cleaners as they welded shut sewer lids, set up traffic barriers, and roamed the park and Northerly Island along Burnham Harbor. Armored military vehicles had already set up along the highway exits to McCormick Place.

A parallel layer of security cloaked all of Chicago. Secret drones monitored the Loop, looking at elevated train platforms to the vast southside railroad yards. The hotels of the diplomats, journalists, and onlookers were being tracked. Cameras captured the passing traffic that had been diverted into a narrow course of control.

However, in the underground chambers of the McCormick Place conference center, where operations took place around the clock, time took on a different meaning. There was no night or day—there was only high alert. They were less than thirty-six hours away from the crush of the summit arrivals.

The nightly meeting of the summit security units always took place at midnight. No one really understood why. The meeting took place in secret, in a hidden meeting room that didn't appear on any maps of the conference center.

Introduced by Secret Service head agent Ford, Chicago Police chief Daniels stood at the front of the packed table of local law enforcement agency representatives, as well as the security chiefs for the FBI, Secret Service, military intelligence, and Homeland Security.

Nikki stood along the side wall in her usual street attire, which somehow stood out among all of the uniforms. The two Russian officers, sitting near the front, were particularly formal. Nikki noticed the Russian entourage was sitting next to an American general, Gen. Priest.

"As you know, the mayor provided authorization to deploy surveillance cameras throughout the city and in the air," Daniels was saying. "The highest state security measures are in place."

Everyone in the room had already been briefed on the unmarked white vans parked in front of the portable cell phone towers.

"FBI and Secret Service have standing authority to jam cell phone signals under Emergency Wireless Protocols, SOP 303," Daniels went on, nodding at the feds, who appeared to be indifferent to his announcement. They didn't need permission. "We will remain in contact with the MACC, Multi-Agency Communications Center."

Daniels clicked on his remote to show live video of passengers entering the Metra at key locations in Chicago.

"With the Metra Electric line passing under McCormick Place," he said, "passenger traffic during the summit will be closed to the public."

The next slide was old news, but Daniels insisted on reminding the feds of Chicago's commitment to rooting out any trouble in advance. Three men appeared on screen, their heads down, as they were being escorted out of an apartment complex by police officers, with their hands cuffed behind them.

"I want to reiterate that along with all the agencies gathered here we continue our diligent investigation of Ambassador Yuri Ushakov's murder. Tonight, three more suspects from a Ukrainian group have been arrested and detained for questioning. This is based on tips we have received from multiple agencies in the last week."

Nikki looked at the Russian officials for any reaction. There was none. They didn't even take notes. Within minutes the Russian entourage left with Gen. Priest.

Her phone suddenly vibrated with a series of messages. Nikki assumed it was Randall again. It was still hard to wrap her mind around the bizarre sighting of the Chinatown witness in southern Illinois, over 350 miles away.

But it wasn't Randall.

"Shit, it's Berkes," she said to herself.

Backing up against the wall, Nikki held the phone to her chest. She cleared her throat as she read Mad Dog Mickey Berkes's intelligence report:

Fritz Mueller is a fake ID. Confirmed alias. According to FBI facial recognition, the suspect is Sven Thomas AKA Thomas Svenson. Long rap sheet with military. 822 Army Ranger Security Forces Squadron in Afghanistan. Discharged from US Army Sniper School. Convicted for Blackwater Security operations, Iraq, Yemen. Disappeared. Three photos attached.

Nikki scanned the men in the photos, two without a beard, that blended into the same witness photo of the shooter. It was he. Nikki knew she needed to get ahold of Randall immediately.

Looking around the security meeting, where the top intelligence figures and police veterans sat together like a network of colorful uniforms, she felt a pang of fear: If someone like this witness could slip out of their hands so easily, how could they defend a summit of global leaders in the neighborhood?

Nikki could not imagine where Randall might be. Southern Illinois was another country to her, hundreds of miles away from her basement meeting. Yet, she felt as threatened as if this illusive witness was in the room with her.

Nikki copied Berkes's text and forwarded it Randall. She added her own message as a warning:

Will inform Chief. Keep me posted. Please watch yourself.

For all the security apparatus around her, Nikki felt like there were a bunch of gaping holes waiting to be discovered, starting with Randall's own safety.

59

___

MOORE CREEK ARCHAEOLOGICAL SITE
ALEXANDER COUNTY, ILLINOIS

The vehicles arrived an hour before sunrise. They bumped into the still-muddy parking lot in front of the archaeological site and skidded to a stop. Four, and then five sedans pulled in; three more trucks of deputized militia members followed on their heels. No police lights, though. The sheriff and his deputies operated in the earth's darkness, their bodies silhouettes, their actions swift as they stretched out the yellow crime scene tape like an invisible wall around the main boundaries of the site. They swarmed the area like flanks of an invasion.

"Make room for the bulldozers," Benton said. "They should be here shortly."

Benton had issued the order in an earlier email, posting his document online to all the media: Due to online and social media threats against members of the Alexander County sheriff's office and deputized posse, all operations at the Ft. Defiance Highway Archaeological Survey would be terminated immediately, and all current archaeological sites would be covered for safety.

"The threats have been traced to an ISP—an internet service provider—on this site's location," Benton read out. He made sure that line appeared in the announcement. "Personnel connected to this site will be taken into custody."

The deputies went to the two trailers that housed the Arkies. Their weapons drawn, they pounded on the doors. One of the deputies used a handheld bullhorn as the police knocked on the doors again.

"Come out with your hands up," he called.

Danny emerged shirtless, wearing a ball cap and a pair of shorts, followed by two young women in tank tops and shorts who had been serving as volunteers.

"Come out with your hands up," the office called again.

Looking bewildered, Danny didn't say anything, unsure if he should be embarrassed for being caught with the volunteers.

Moving to the next trailer, the deputies went through the same routine, pounding three times on the door. When no one answered, a police officer rammed his way through the door, bursting into the trailer. The others could hear him stumble over bottles and cans. The cop returned to the front of the trailer, his automatic rifle held to the side, and looked at the main deputy with a look of defeat.

"No one," he shouted.

There were other Arkies, though. They were hiding in the forest along the mounds, which overlooked the archaeological site. They had fled from the back door and raced into the woods.

Freddy and Anchee buried their heads in the bush. They had climbed into the mud, topping their arms and legs with branches and clumps of grass.

"We've got to get to Molly," Anchee said.

"We've got to survive this first," Freddy said.

They watched as deputies began to handcuff Danny and the two women, amid the swirl of activity around the edge of the site. Men in camouflage dismantled the fence posts, worktables, and research stations. Others appeared to be clearing a way for more vehicles.

The police halted their work, including those who were handcuffing Danny, when two bulldozers rumbled to the front of the parking lot. A black tail of smoke whipped from their exhaust pipes. The engines of the bulldozers groaned; the metallic ring of the buckets clattered to the ground.

Benton walked to the front of the lot and waved at the bulldozers.

Freddy and Anchee could pinpoint the destination. Rolling onto her back, Anchee curled into a ball and then dialed the phone in front of her chest. Freddy pulled a large branch in front of them.

Danny didn't need to think twice about resisting.

Breaking from the deputy, who had failed to lock the handcuffs well, he darted toward the bulldozer. The police raced behind him. Danny threw himself in front of one of the bulldozers, and intentionally rolled inside the main bucket, trapping himself like a bear.

Staring with horror at the protester, the bulldozer operator stopped the machine and cut the engine.

"Molly!" Anchee hissed into the phone. "Molly, please answer. They're bulldozing the site."

Four deputies surrounded Danny by the huge shovel.

"You're breaking the law, you sons of bitches," he shouted. "Someone has to stop this crazy shit."

Two deputies reached in and grabbed Danny by the arms, wrestling him out of the bucket. Two other deputies pounced, pinning Danny to the ground, and locking his arms behind his back with handcuffs.

"You wanna play hero, Danny," the deputy said, "then you're going to have to earn it."

"Molly," Anchee whispered, crying. "Please answer the phone."

Freddy looked at her with concern. He understood the wrath of Benton and his deputies. He had watched several friends get carted off to jail for bogus crimes. Freddy had always racked it up to the sheriff's racism. But Benton now strode past the local white boy Danny with a look of utter ruthlessness.

The morning sun finally spilled into the valley. The light cast onto the steel blades of the bulldozers, which pushed the dirt walls and mounds into the archaeological pits. Freddy and Anchee watched painstaking work being covered in a matter of minutes.

"I don't know what happened to Molly," Anchee whispered to Freddy, crawling back under the mud and branches.

An eerie silence hovered over the site.

From the hillside view, it looked like some badly managed dump site, where piles of boards and mounds of plastic were scattered across the area. The bulldozers had done a poor job, leaving behind gaping holes and the lines of various sections of the dig.

Freddy wasn't sure if he felt brave or defiant or without any other choices.

"Then it's up to us to find her," Freddy said.

60

___

The pounding on her door awakened Alison at her rented apartment adjacent to Scott Airforce Base. Gen. Alexander wanted to see her early. She was not told why.

The militia guards he sent seemed adamant, though, and had insisted on escorting her in their truck. Alison drew a line. It took her several minutes to convince them to follow her in her own car, agreeing to one of the guards riding with her to the historic Alexander farmhouse. Accompanied by the red-bearded Thomas, Alison was led to what appeared to be a large pantry door off the kitchen.

It opened to a small elevator like the one the general had taken her down before. The huge Thomas, inches away, looked down at her as they descended together.

At first, Alison had thought this bunker had the air of a throwback to the 1950s, almost like the floppy disk relics that housed the ICBM missiles from yesteryear, but with modern-day technology. There was something almost quaint about Alexander's bunker obsession. He had included more finishing touches than her contractor had done on her suburban DC home.

Stepping out of the elevator cage and into the huge corridor, Alison entered the meeting room of the bunker, anticipating another bizarre but friendly meeting with Alexander over his idiosyncratic ways.

Alison hesitated a moment before further entering the room. Strapped to a chair, gagged and wiggling to get out, was the archaeologist Sandeep. Alison was no stranger to interrogations, but the researcher was a cocky amateur, in her estimation, not a suspect. His explanations of his drone photos had cleared any questions.

Alison was familiar enough with Alexander to know he always covered the bases at his operations. He had his own ways of dealing with intruders at foreign sites.

"Wanted you to see and hear what this spy has been doing," Alexander said to Alison, his voice almost too animated.

Alison nodded. Watching from behind a mirrored window, Alexander and Benton had placed the interrogation in the hands of the towering Thomas. Alison entered the side of the room and sat down.

"Once again, why have you been snooping around in places you shouldn't have been, or had no business being around?" Thomas said.

Sandeep shook his head in defiance. He looked confused. He growled and motioned for his gag to be removed. He looked over at Alison, and then at the interrogator. Thomas yanked the gag off as Sandeep cried out.

"Where am I . . . you, you, help me, what . . ."

His voice garbled into a cough. Sandeep struggled in the chair. There was something so off about the researcher that Alison quickly realized he had been drugged. His eyes swirled to the back of his head.

"We know what you've been doing," Thomas went on. "You can cooperate or we can damn well make you cooperate."

"I don't know . . ." Sandeep's voice faded out again. He shook his head; Sandeep felt like he had water in his ears.

Alison looked at Thomas, and then back at Sandeep. She realized something else was taking place in the room.

"Your drones, son," Alexander blurted out, entering the room. He looked at Alison with an air of madness. "Where are your drones? And where are your computers and radars and findings?"

"I don't have . . ." Sandeep said. He stared at Alexander, attempting to focus. "Dr. Moore . . ."

"And the images?" Alexander asked. "Have you shared your findings with anyone?

"Images . . ." Sandeep said.

Alexander stepped up and kicked a stool across the room.

Alison realized she needed to get out of there immediately.

61

GEM MOVIE THEATRE
CAIRO, ILLINOIS

Fritz Mueller was now Thomas Svenson. How that name burned into Randall's mind.

Pacing back and forth in the decrepit movie house, the Chicago detective stared at Nikki's text, feeling implicated himself for their oversight; they had dropped the ball after being at the crime scene of Russian ambassador Yuri Ushakov's murder. They should have run a background check on the witness Mueller as Mickey Berkes had now done. This was no longer a Chicago Police Department issue. This was a federal issue connected to summit security.

Randall scrolled down to his contact at the Secret Service, Agent Ford. He looked at his name and number, attempting to conjure an explanation for his own involvement in Cairo—and the seemingly far-fetched connection of the ambassador's murderer 350 miles away from the crime scene. Plausibility didn't matter, Randall told himself. It was about time now. He dialed the number, instantly receiving Ford's voice mail.

"There is a dangerous suspect here in Cairo—Cairo, Illinois," Randall tried to explain, "a former special forces militia member here who is a prime suspect in the Russian ambassador's shooting."

The minute he hung up, Randall realized his message must have seemed like an addled, off-the-wall comment from a police detective out of his jurisdiction. He should have said, "Hear me! There may be an operation here involving disruption of the summit." He somehow regretted contacting the Secret Service. He should have left this in Nikki's hands.

After spending the night going through files with Molly, Randall began to question his judgement and lack of sleep.

Molly realized she had been so focused on culling the reams of data from Sandeep's files with Randall that she had forgotten to recharge her phone at Gem Theatre. She plugged it in. The images from Sandeep's various cameras had jammed her computer's hard drive, freezing it up at times. "I've only downloaded a fraction of his work and even that I haven't really examined closely."

She turned to Randall: "I have to get my hands on critical drives that are hidden at the dig site."

Her phone dinged into existence, finally recharging enough to receive. All of Anchee's desperate calls, text messages, and photos cascaded with a barrage of warnings.

"Oh God . . . We've got to get to the site," she said, standing up, and then pushing away from the desk.

"At this hour?" Randall said. "I'm burned, ready to fall over."

"The site," Molly said, stepping over to the aisle. She could barely get out the next words. "Anchee says they're bulldozing it."

Randall's first image was someone disrupting and covering up the earth around his mother's grave.

They raced to their cars as Randall asked Molly about the various routes to the site.

"Is there a back entrance?" he called across the roof of his car.

"Why?" Molly said. She opened the door to her car. "I don't need to enter from the back. I'm going after them. How dare they come onto my site. I'm going to kick their asses."

"Listen," Randall said. "Don't be stupid, kid, wake up. This is bigger than your site now."

Molly froze with the warning. Then, with a bolt of energy and incredible intensity, she responded. "Follow me. Park off the blacktop, about a half mile from the main entrance. Look for two tall sycamore trees. There's a side trail there that leads up to the hill, which overlooks the site. That's where Anchee and Freddy are waiting."

62

The morning sun glared in the mirrors of their cars.

Molly arrived first, finding Freddy and Anchee huddled in the forest above the site. They looked shell-shocked, not saying a word. They all stared below.

The bulldozers may have been gone, the sheriff and deputies long departed, but two guards watched over the leveled site. It reminded Molly of old photos from coal mining strikes in the region, when National Guardsmen had been called in to patrol the mine sites with their rifles and bayonets.

The oblivion before them was bewildering to Molly. She gazed into a different site—a site no longer under her control. Randall was right. This was no longer about archaeology, but modern-day human conflict.

"Bastards," Molly said. After creeping up the mound, Randall lowered himself down by Molly as she muttered in anger. "They think they can destroy the evidence."

"This is a general's war against the truth," Randall said.

"We've shot some of it on our phones," Anchee said.

"Where's Danny and the others?" Randall asked Freddy.

"They arrested him and some volunteers," Freddy said, "but he just texted me a few minutes ago that he's been released. He was heading back to his family's place in the country." Molly adjusted a little backpack on her shoulder that she had brought with her.

"Arrested for what?" Molly asked.

"And Sandeep?" Randall piped up.

After last night's discovery in the theater, he believed Sandeep held the clues to so many missing pieces. Molly had tried him several times with no response.

"We haven't heard from him," Freddy said. "We've called all morning, but his phone is off or dead."

"He'd gone back to Carbondale yesterday," Anchee added. "But we didn't hear from him all day or night either. Which is strange."

"Yeah, that's not like Sandeep," Molly said.

"No text, nothing?" Randall asked.

Freddy shook his head. "Something's up," he said.

Randall sized up the guards below. Automatic rifles. They weren't deputies but deputized militia, which made them more dangerous. Nikki's update from Berkes added another factor. Randall knew most of these guards, like Thomas, the Chinatown witness, were trained soldiers. He was dealing with combat veterans, not a gaggle of underpaid watchmen.

Randall didn't just need another plan. He needed some clarity in a place that seemed to operate on conspiracies and made its decisions at the end of the barrel of a gun.

There was no reason to risk a confrontation, especially when the damage had been done. Benton's jurisdiction, as flimsy as it was on legal grounds, would stand in Alexander County.

"Alexander let this happen here," Molly said. Her voice sounded clear, but devastated.

Randall shot Molly a glance. The Chicago detective knew the local sheriff couldn't have carried out such an audacious task without the complicity—or even the instructions—of the local baron. The general was also the contractor to build the federal highway.

"We need to know where this is going," Randall said.

Molly knew Randall already had a plan in motion in his mind.

"This isn't just about your mother?" Molly whispered.

Pointing below, Randall nodded in agreement.

"Those are militia goons down there, and not county deputies."

"True that," Freddy added.

Molly reached down and opened up her backpack and pulled out an iPad. She also withdrew a small camera and handed it to Anchee.

"This find, now this dig seemed so important to him. It doesn't make sense. Why would Alexander let this happen?"

"What if he doesn't know?" Anchee said, snapping photos of the bull-dozed field.

"Alexander knows everything," Molly said.

Squatting to the ground, she typed on the keyboard. Randall bent down and watched her.

"I need to talk to Sandeep," he said.

"We can try and track Sandeep's phone," Molly said to Anchee.

"What if it's dead? Can you still track it?" Freddy asked.

"We're not tracking his phone," Molly said, "but a sensor unit on the phone. Just in case someone dropped their phone in a hole or mud with important data on it, I attached sensor units to all of our phones. It's a location-positioning system. It's based on dead reckoning."

"Dead reckoning?" Freddy said.

Anchee intervened.

"You calculate someone's position by using a previously determined location, and then you advance that position based on estimated speeds over a certain time and space," she said, pointing at the iPad. Satellite images with GPS location data appeared over the position of Sandeep's phone.

"These images are like time splices," Randall said. "Where'd you get this stuff?"

"From a coal mine in Kentucky; my dad is a manager there," Molly said. "He has state-of-the-art equipment for finding miners underground. I borrowed some of it for us."

Randall marveled at the complexity of the software.

"I'm getting something here," Anchee interrupted.

"So, where's Sandeep?" Freddy asked, looking at the small screen.

Anchee stood up, carrying the iPad to Molly, who showed it to Randall. It was a blur. He looked at the researcher for help.

"It's not exact, but I think his phone is out in the Henson farm woods," Anchee said, pausing for a second. "Oh my God, it's under the woods."

"Under the woods?" Freddy echoed.

"Oh no, please, God, no," Molly said. "Sandeep isn't buried."

"Or in a bunker," Randall said.

63

___

BUNKER #1
ALEXANDER COUNTY, ILLINOIS

Alison turned away as Thomas roughly carted Sandeep out of the interrogation room. The researcher's legs wobbled. It made Alison cringe at such amateur tactics. She had no idea where they were taking him. Moving quickly into the hallway, she saluted two operatives in the main command-control room, where an embankment of screens and computers flickered in front of them showing various locations. Alison hesitated for a moment.

A remote transmission of a live event was taking place on one screen. It appeared to be in a warehouse of sorts. Elements of Alexander's militia were unloading crates of unmarked material. On another screen, though, Alison followed the footage from a camera mounted on a drone. It was definitely in downtown Chicago, as it circled around the warehouse district.

"Wow, where is this?" Alison asked the operator, pointing at the screen with the drone.

He looked over his shoulder with smile.

"The old Sears warehouse. Pretty cool, huh?"

Alexander's voice boomed into the transmission from the warehouse.

"Careful, goddamit," he shouted.

Alison could hear Alexander's live voice, but not see him, which indicated to her that he was in the next room, orchestrating the transfer of crates from a semi on a loading dock. There were no markings, or at least nothing Alison could see clearly from her distance. She shook her head, thanked the operative, and then made for the door. She heard Alexander's voice again. It made her hesitate at the doorway, one foot in the hallway.

"For Christ's sake, you're not loading bricks, Lamar," Alexander called out. "You're handling sophisticated technology and if you damage it in the process, it will be useless, and we will fail!"

The general continued his directing, as Alison realized she was free to slip away.

"Chicago," she repeated to herself. "Sophisticated technology."

Holding her emotions inside, Alison looked at the ground, and walked down the hallway to the bunker's elevator. A guard stood outside the door, nodded politely, and then muttered to himself out of boredom. Alison kept walking to the elevator door, where she resisted looking over her shoulder. She held her breath; the light on the elevator illuminated like an alarm in her mind, but it took an interminable time to open, and she didn't allow an exhale until the door closed and she was left alone in the small compartment.

"Sophisticated technology," she said to herself, looking down at her feet.

She knew a camera was in the elevator. Her moves were being monitored. Alison could feel a streak of sweat ball around her forehead, and then drip down the side of her face.

She didn't flinch when the elevator door opened, stepping out to the hidden hallway off the kitchen pantry in the Alexander home. Acknowledging the guard, Alison moved through the general's world knowing she was facing her next communication with those above her.

It wasn't until she was a mile down the rural road before Alison pulled over and then reached for her iPhone.

Her encrypted text to Gen. McCarthy was brief: Urgent. Contact ASAP.

Then, finally, she let out a quick harsh scream. Her intelligence mission had unveiled a nightmare.

64

The shades had been drawn along the wall of windows. Two lamps cast a shadowy feel about the room. The last-minute invitation had been cryptic, at best.

McCarthy had summoned his collaborators—Priest and Egerton—out of the disarmament summit negotiations, despite the embarrassing repercussions. His message was urgent: we have a situation with Alexander.

There would be no card game today. The generals, however, understood one another's strengths and weaknesses with a twitch of their eyes, the placement of their heads, and the intensity of their grips on the cards after years, even decades, of playing poker together. Kindred souls, Alexander had called them, in his twangy accent from southern Illinois, and there was almost a religious element to their rapport that had transcended any game and manifested itself on the global battlefield.

Each had their own approach. Gen. McCarthy preferred the standard "brothers-in-arms" motto, as a fourth-generation soldier and war veteran who held his cards close and rarely took chances. Egerton tended to exaggerate, reclaiming his Texas ranching roots, but he was the first to call anyone's bluff. Priest, as head of the Missile Defense Agency, may have been more conservative with his moves, raised in the strict New England home of an accountant, but he didn't hesitate to bet big, when the opportunity presented himself.

No one had really figured out Will Alexander at the poker table—or on the battlefield.

Now facing a large screen on the wall, Gen. McCarthy sat at the table in the downtown hotel room with a sense of unease; their poker game had blown up into an all-out brawl. This was no longer an exchange between kindred souls or brothers-in-arms. It had become a story of betrayal.

Sitting back in his chair, at the head of the table, waiting for their arrival, McCarthy thought back to the first time he had meet Alexander, over forty-five years ago in basic training. McCarthy had laughed at Alexander's antics; he was a practical joker who thrived on taking risks, even if it cost him a day or two suffering some kind of disciplinary action. Alexander was different from the rest of the recruits. His monied southern Illinois swagger gave him the corridor, while everyone else stood to the side. The other teens in training looked up to him as a leader, because Alexander's sheer brawn was unmatched. He was the kind of true believer you'd want on the battlefield, and when they went into combat, Alexander racked up more medals than anyone else in his company.

Alexander's military might wasn't his only tribute. His ability to size up combat situations, and engage on logistical challenges in construction and infrastructure, led to his appointment to the US Military Academy, where he earned degrees in civil engineering and military arts. Alexander didn't want to just wage war; he relished the details of laying out the battle plan, especially the building of underground operations that would support any ground assault. He became the ultimate bunker builder. Understanding the chemistry of hardening concrete to withstand nuclear attacks and silo reinforcement, one of his prime assignments had been to oversee the creation of Saudi Arabia's vast military infrastructure.

Within a short time, Alexander had moved up the ranks of the Military Mission of the US Army Corps of Engineers to become its commanding general. He had a genius about his deployments that everyone recognized, in whatever country or conflict.

McCarthy knew Alexander never really retired. He had shifted his interests to the private sector and made a fortune.

Either way, McCarthy still considered Alexander the best man in the ranks when it came to warfare. And that concerned him.

"What's the meaning of this, McCarthy?" Egerton said, entering the room. Priest followed right behind him.

McCarthy didn't say anything until the door slammed and the guard returned to his post outside the room. His secret office in the tower may have been convenient, but it didn't assuage Egerton's and Priest's concerns about his ability to command their covert operation.

"Alison Foreman should be with us shortly," McCarthy said.

"The hell," Priest said. "I need to get back. I left in the middle of a session with the Russians, Gen. Gagarin, and the Chinese."

"We have another problem on our hands," McCarthy shot back. "An inside problem."

"Alexander? I told you that nutcase couldn't be trusted," Egerton said, slamming the table.

In that moment, the screen flashed, and Alison materialized from a remote location. Her intrusion silenced the others. Egerton shook his head in disgust.

"We have been following Alexander," McCarthy began, "to make sure he doesn't go rogue and destroy our plans with his crazy interviews in the media. We're talking about a threat to our immediate security.

"Alison," McCarthy said.

"Generals," she replied.

She was speaking from a white room, with no furniture in the background. She looked unnerved, which was a shift from her usual steely presence.

"Gentlemen, I've been monitoring Gen. Alexander regularly over the past few days," she said. "At first, it seemed like he was merely disgruntled about his canceled military contracts for Gunnor's drones and was content to spout off on the news. We all know he's a character and enjoys the attention."

"For years we've known this about him," Priest said. He readied to leave the room.

"You may not be aware of the fact that he runs his operations out of an underground bunker," she went on.

"Of course, he's a goddamn bunker builder," Priest laughed.

"But his operations are much more . . ." Alison paused for a moment. "More insidious than we had calculated. Alexander dispatched two trucks to Chicago this morning."

"Trucks?" Egerton asked.

"Here's the video," Alison went on. She reached for her keyboard.

She disappeared from the screen, as footage from a surveillance drone showed two semitrucks, with dragster logos on the side of the containers, scurrying along an Illinois highway.

"You forwarded the vehicles' plates to MACC?" Priest asked.

"They have them now," Alison said, returning to the screen. "But there's more. It's pretty clear Alexander is setting up some sort of serious disruption of the summit."

"Disruption of the summit," McCarthy finally echoed.

He looked back at the other generals.

"The presidential parties and final negotiators arrive tomorrow!" Priest yelled.

"Will Alexander has lost it," Egerton shouted, "and I don't know why we didn't shut him down years ago."

"This is what I was afraid of," Priest added.

"Holy fucking shit, you need to deal with Alexander directly," Egerton said to McCarthy. "Take him out, if necessary."

"Take him out," Priest repeated.

Alison stared back from the scene, awaiting orders.

"One more thing," Alison said, her voice wavering. "There's a Chicago cop down here who's tracking Alexander as well. I'm not sure how much he knows, but I know he's also part of the summit security."

"A Chicago cop? What the hell? Get him out of there, Alison," McCarthy said. "Remove him from the scene before he connects any dots. I'll deal with Alexander."

65

Abandoning the dig site, the crew scrambled uphill. Molly collapsed at the foot of an oak tree, not far from their cars. The stress had finally caught up with her. Anchee and Freddy rushed to her side as she dissolved from exhaustion. Looking over his shoulder for anyone in sight, Randall squatted by Molly as she pulled her knees up to her chin, Consolation was not one of his strong points.

"You'll get your site back," he said, wringing his hands.

Molly looked up, wiping at her face streaked with tears.

"I don't care about the site," she said. "I care about Sandeep. What if he's dead?"

As Randall stood up, he held out a hand to Molly, who clasped his and pulled herself up. Anchee and Freddy flanked them.

"We'll find him," Randall said. "But it means I need you all to be more than a forensic lab."

"What do you mean?" Molly asked.

By dusk, Randall had given the Arkies their new game plan. Freddy and Anchee took Molly's car and headed for Gem Theatre, where they would act as the communications link, continuing to track the sensor on Sandeep's phone.

Instead of going straight to the general, as Molly had insisted, Randall wanted to drive Molly back to Harriet's cabin, to the shed where she and her team had smuggled most of Sandeep's equipment, computers, and drones. They needed to retrieve the backup on any of their drives, in order to know as much as possible about whatever was underground.

"I need to make a phone call first," Randall told Molly as she opened the door to the passenger side of his sedan. She nodded and dropped into the car, shutting her door.

Walking down the dirt path, Randall took a deep breath. The next call would be a tricky one. His message to his main contact at the Secret Service, Agent Ford from the disarmament summit, had not even been acknowledged. Randall assumed it been deleted, even too absurd to believe.

Randall knew he needed to get in touch with someone else on the federal level about spotting the sniper Thomas. Even that military intelligence agent he had met—what was her name, Ellen or Alison or Allie-something? Randall couldn't even remember. But her appearance at the sheriff's station somehow placed her in a different box. He turned to his last resort.

During the election he had met another federal agent, the head of President Adams's Secret Service team, who also shared a Chicago connection. They had exchanged numbers. Randall had mentioned his childhood link to Adams, which seemed quaint in that moment. Six months later, Randall wasn't sure if the agent would remember him from their last encounter onstage at an Adams rally, but he had no other choice.

"Randall Jenkins, from the Chicago PD, we met at the Grant Park election rally," he found himself explaining. "I know this is going to sound strange, but I'm down here in southern Illinois, and I'm tracking a suspect from the murder of the Russian ambassador, which might have implications for the summit."

The rest of the call was brief. And very confusing. But at least he got through. Randall knew his quick report from 350 miles away probably made no sense to the agent. Randall could hear commotion in the background. The agent agreed to pass on the information and Randall's number but warned him that his call was far down the list of security exigencies. "We're getting a threat a minute, as you can imagine, but I'll do my best."

"You okay?" Molly said as Randall climbed back into the car.

Turning over the key in the ignition, Randall looked concerned. He felt like he had forgotten something. Or rather, his words again had already been forgotten or misunderstood.

Looking over at Molly, Randall attempted a smile of indifference, and then pulled the car into reverse.

"He thought I was calling from Cairo, Egypt," he said, "but I . . ."

The midday news burst on in midsentence, as he turned on the radio in the car.

"As President Adams stated, the treaty would effectively attempt to eliminate and destroy the world's stockpiles of nuclear weapons, provoking outrage in some quarters, triggering serious concerns in the intelligence community over the impossibility of verification, and the possibility of treaty and conference violence and disruption, including terrorist attacks from those elements opposed to destroying their nuclear arms . . ."

As they drove back on the rural route darkened by the thick forests, a white van tailgated Randall's car for a few hundred yards, and then barreled ahead, passing on an open stretch of road in the valley.

"I'm so worried about Sandeep," Molly interjected.

Randall didn't respond. He then watched another van appear in the rearview mirror, gaining on him like the other van. Coming around a curve, Randall had to hit his brakes, when he noticed the first van was now going slowly.

"There's a bag on the floor; reach in and give me the pistol," Randall barked to Molly.

"What?"

"Hurry up," Randall pushed.

Molly reached down, and then handed the gun to Randall. The intentions of the two vans were clear. They planned to sandwich Randall. The winding road kept them from boxing him off.

As he stuffed the weapon into his belt, the van in the back clipped their bumper.

"Oh God, oh shit," Molly said.

As they took another curve Randall accelerated, attempting to pass the van in front. Randall barely hugged the edge of the pavement, going too fast when the van cut him off. Randall reached down, grabbing his gun, preparing to fire. But it was too late. Just as they turned another curve, the van from behind revved its engine, smashing into Randall's sedan, knocking them off the road. Then it disappeared ahead.

Sliding off the roadside gravel, the sedan cascaded over the edge, flipping into a thick cypress swamp beside the road. The windshield cracked as it struck a limb; the car plunged into shallow black pools. Somehow buttressed by a stump, the car then wobbled until it rolled upright.

Water rushed in from the side as Randall frantically unlatched his seat belt and reached over at Molly, who appeared trapped as waves spilled into her lap.

Molly struggled, screaming at Randall for help, ripping at her belt, which was stuck in the crushed side of the car.

Randall leaned back and kicked out his partially broken window. The swamp poured into the seats like a waterfall.

Randall climbed out of his window, pulling himself across the front of the car until he reached Molly's side, and then he reached in and yanked her belt free. As the car began to slowly sink, Randall grabbed on to a tree branch. His arm appeared in front of Molly, pulling her out.

"Get out, Molly!" he shouted.

The two of them, stunned and exhausted, hugged the knobby edges of an ancient cypress tree and witnessed the back end of the vehicle vanish into the muddy swamp, sucked below by an unknown force. The rest of the swamp hovered in a moonlit green glaze as the towering cypress, tupelo, and gum trees enclosed them like vultures. Molly eased herself off the stump, stepping onto a bridge of branches until she reached firmer ground. Lowering herself into the water, she carefully waded across to the forested side of the road. Randall followed behind her.

Molly had no idea she had a cut on her face. Wrestling a handkerchief out of his pocket, Randall handed it to Molly, who placed it onto her face like a muddy gauze.

"What else hurts? You okay?" he asked.

"I'm alive, if that's what you're asking," she said.

Her feistiness encouraged him to move on.

Emerging out of the woods on the edge of the road, their clothes and shoes drenched, Randall realized they weren't alone. The white van was now perched one hundred yards away, facing in their direction, its bright lights glaring. Randall studied the van, and then looked back at the swamp.

"Get off the road," he said to Molly, pushing her aside.

Randall yanked the drenched handgun out of his belt. Leaning against a tree on the side of the road, Molly hesitated from moving further into the swamp. She focused on the van.

The silhouetted figures of two gunmen emerged from the vehicle. The towering figure of Thomas Svenson stepped from the passenger's side. Randall recognized him. His unmistakable image now lined up like the perfect suspect, from the Ft. Defiance gun rally to the ambassador's shooting in Chicago. Randall was certain this time. He now had a name for this bearded devil who had accompanied Liz to the greenhouse.

"Get back in the swamp, damn it," Randall shouted.

"And let them shoot you?" Molly cried.

One of the gunmen raised his rifle and took aim. Randall readied to shoot back when the thump and roar of Motörhead's "Ace of Spades" came through the darkness.

A pickup truck suddenly barreled around the bend, arriving a few feet to the side of the road, and then it swerved to miss Randall. The truck screeched to a halt. The music cut to an end.

Staring down the new arrivals, the gunmen by the van paused. The lights of the two vehicles squared off.

It was Danny, hanging outside the passenger's window in a truck full of other young men, like members of some heavy metal band. Randall didn't take his eyes off the gunmen by the van, however. He felt like he was trapped between two ends of a burning bridge. Danny stuck out his head through the window, seeing skid marks and road scars as he strained to take in the scene.

"Hell, Molly, is that you over there? You okay?"

"Danny? Thank God," Molly said, pushing off the tree. She still held the bloody handkerchief to her face. She pointed at the gunmen at the end of the road, who backstepped to the van. "They drove us off the road and tried to kill us."

Danny looked at the men around the van, who held their weapons to the side, and then he nodded at his friends in the truck.

Danny got out of the pickup. The driver leapt out, cocking his Winchester shotgun. Danny reached in and withdrew an assault rifle. Two others jumped out of the back, reaching for hunting weapons. The driver shouted at the gunmen by Thomas Svenson's van as the four men aimed their guns.

"Drop your weapons, assholes."

"Hell yes," Danny added.

"Who are these guys ?" Randall asked.

"They're sure as hell not locals."

As the towering Thomas signaled a retreat, his crew jumped into their vehicle, backed up, and spun away.

"So many of these militia types around here now," Danny went on. "We best get you out of here and get Molly home."

Randall reached over and brushed the blood from Molly's face. She looked like a kid to him. A kid someone had just run off the road and attempted to murder. She frantically dug into her pocket, and then withdrew a little plastic bag and held it up.

"I still have the ficus," she said.

Looking at her as she held the evidence to his mother's murder, he wondered if Molly was so threatening to Alexander, Benton, and their henchmen—or if he was the real target now?

"Molly," Randall said, almost in a whisper. "Have you done something I should know about? Why would someone want to get rid of you?"

Molly shook her head.

"I don't know," she said. "Honestly, I do not know."

Climbing into the back of the truck, a shivering Molly took a towel from Danny, which was stenciled with the letters "ACJ." Danny winked and smiled. "Just got out. It's a gift from the Alexander County jail."

66

Holding Molly in her arms on the porch, a blanket draped over her soaking back, Harriet watched Danny and his friends park their pickup in a clearing by the entrance of the homestead, beside a grove that served as the driveway to her cabin. It was dark now. There was a thick haze in the air. On Randall's command, Danny and his friends flanked out along the country road as guards, keeping an eye on any lights in the valley.

Harriet's chest heaved in anger and desperation. She navigated Molly around Earl, who stood at the door like a sentry.

"What the hell were you doing?" she cried at Molly's back. "Why the hell have you pissed off so many people? Give 'em their damn jobs."

Molly didn't attempt to respond, still absorbing the attempt on their lives and the uncertainty of Sandeep's safety. She was too lost to answer.

Earl closed the screen door as they entered, unsure if he should come outside. Three steps from the cabin door, standing in an opening in front of the forest, he was only a tiny silhouette in this natural world.

Out of the darkness, Randall emerged. Jutting out from his undershirt, tucked into his belt, the magazine of his pistol peeked out.

"I warned you," Earl said.

"Someone just tried to kill me, and Molly, " Randall said, slamming Earl against the wood cabin. "So, no more of your bullshit." He ripped a pistol out of Earl's belt, and then backstepped. "You tell me now what's going on. Understand?"

Losing his balance, Earl fell, slumped against a few logs. He got to his feet, brushed off some dirt and bark from his undershirt, without taking his eyes off Randall.

No one exchanged a word. Randall slipped Earl's pistol into his belt, and then withdrew his own handgun. Rubbing the back of his neck, Earl nodded, held up his hands, and then lowered himself down to a stump he had always used to split logs.

"It's been going on for years," Earl said. "Not just now."

"Alexander?" Randall said.

Earl peered up with a sad, almost lost expression.

"Yeah, Alexander. All of them," Earl said.

"Years? What do you mean, years?"

"Yeah, talking years, way back. I was just twenty-one years old," Earl began. "Just out of prison and twenty-one years old. Did three years for dealing some dope and couldn't get a job with no one on the outside in my county. I'd been marked as trouble, you know, so my uncle helped me get hired on to a construction job outside of Cairo." Earl took a deep breath. "He was a plumber, taught me everything I know. He needed help on what he called a special job."

Earl didn't have gray hair or a gut in those days. He had kept his long hair pulled back and tucked under a Louisville Cards ball cap. The time in the prison camp had not diminished his muscles. His uncle had sought out his help for a reason; Earl understood how to keep quiet, he had a felony record hanging over his head and a probationary period that made him vulnerable, and he was strong enough to carry all of the equipment.

"It was a huge hydraulic pumping enterprise," Earl said.

He would never forget the entrance to the site in the middle of the woods. As a younger man he thought his uncle had gotten lost on a backcountry road, where the bramble overgrew the road so much that it scratched the side of the truck. Leaving the vehicle at the side of the road, Earl hoisted a huge rack of pipes through a trail. His uncle, a no-nonsense Vietnam veteran who still walked ramrod, reminded him to be quiet. Then the drainage ditch outside the barn and grain silo came into sight, where a storm cellar door appeared.

"It was part of the old Henson farm, the farm with the big silo next door. Alexander had bought the whole place."

Earl assumed it was a storm cellar for tornados—a common addition to most farms in the area.

"My uncle said they were always having leaks at this job," Earl went on, "because of the contours of the underground site. The fools built this huge bunker near a watershed and all sorts of underground waterways."

"Underground site?" Randall asked. "A mine?"

"No, this was a real underground bunker. They called it a bomb shelter."

Randall took a seat on an old rusty metal chair, across from Earl. "Bomb shelter?"

"That's what they told us," Earl said. "There was plenty of money around to build one in those days. Civil defense, you know."

The pipes leaked so much at the construction site in that period that Earl found himself often at the storm cellar, and then at the formal entrance to a bunker at a farm building that appeared to be a storage site for heavy equipment and tractors. Earl got used to the protocol. An armed security guard in fatigues would pat him down. He had signed an agreement to keep his work private—or secret, for that matter. Not that he had any desire to blab; truth was, Earl hardly knew anyone in the area.

"Not sure if my uncle set me up, but as an ex-con they knew I was on probation and anything could send me back to prison. I did my pipe-fitting job and kept my mouth shut."

One morning, Alexander emerged and greeted him in his garrulous fashion. In his mid-thirties, Alexander moved like an ambitious colonel in those days. He was funny, boisterous, but in charge. Earl had no idea who Alexander was—only that he strutted like a general in training, commanding everyone with a certain inimitable verve that made him seem important. Earl's uncle referred to him as "the colonel," and mentioned that Alexander was rarely in town, since he served in conflict zones around the world for the Military Missions division of the Army Corps of Engineers.

"He's a bunker builder," his uncle had said. "And this bunker has leaks."

It was all part of the joke to Earl back then. He kept the job to stay out of trouble and to provide himself with enough money to build a new house in the woods. Whether he was descending a tunnel at the storm cellar, crawling his way through the hydraulic system or the shelter's vast corridors to plug or find a leak, or entering Alexander's bunker through an elevator shaft, he never understood much about the scope of the place.

Earl also knew he had not seen the entire complex. Two large steel blast doors blocked the bottom entrance to another tunnel.

Randall crossed his arms. Earl picked up a stick of kindling. He drew a small circle in the dirt, and then a larger circle. He connected the two with a line.

"Buster Moore arrived in his truck one afternoon, near the large building they called the 'equipment shed,'" Earl went on. "Summer day, and it was hot and muggy, and it had been raining for a few days, so they called me about some leaks."

"Buster Moore?" Randall echoed.

"Molly's grandfather," Earl went on. "I could see a Black woman on the passenger side of the pickup truck. It was a '69 Ford. Daredevil red," Earl remembered.

It also had a gun rack. Those details remained etched in his memory like a threat.

"I was supposed to unload some pipes and stuff from the back of the pickup," Earl went on. "Buster Moore ordered me, 'Hey boy, unload this truck.' He was a real asshole. As I was getting things, I saw the woman had a camera and was leaning out the window, taking photos."

Randall felt his chest tighten.

Earl nodded.

"Yeah, it was your mother."

Earl remembered Alexander and Benton coming out of the equipment shed, flanked by a couple of guards. Benton was one of Alexander's private operatives then. Up to this point, Alexander had always seemed like a charitable sort. To Earl, he was almost boyish in his ways.

That all changed with Buster Moore—and Florence Jenkins in the truck.

"Alexander started cussing out the old man Moore for bringing 'that troublemaker' onto the site," Earl went on. "But Moore gave it back to 'em. Told them to go to hell. That he was only supposed to drop off the equipment and get back to town, and he could give whoever the fuck he wanted a ride.

"Then Moore started arguing with Alexander about money," Earl went on. "Something about not being paid. He was accusing Alexander of stiffing him."

Earl hesitated in a sullen moment of silence. He scratched at the dirt with the stick, and then drew a childlike outline of a truck.

"She had a camera in her lap," Earl said, looking back at Randall. "Alexander shouted at Moore, and then demanded that the woman get out of the truck."

Randall didn't know if he had the stomach to hear the rest, but the veteran detective nodded at Earl to continue. "Go on." He looked at Earl's slump; the confession had been beaten out of him.

Randall couldn't care less about some bunker site. He wanted to hear the rest of the story about his mother.

"I didn't really understand what the big deal was at the time," Earl continued.

"Because it was a bomb shelter?" Randall asked.

"You're not listening, man. Because it was Alexander's secret project, his private facility, okay?" Earl shot back.

"I want to know about my mother," Randall said.

Earl turned around and leaned against the house. He looked offended. He knew Randall now considered him a suspect.

"I emptied Moore's truck and carried a load of piping to the equipment shed, then into this big elevator shaft," he went on. "I could hear shouting in the background. When I returned to ground level, I saw them taking away your mom," Earl went on. "Three guards. They had put a hood over her head."

Randall stood up, glaring at Earl. This image of his mother burned his chest. He didn't want to believe Earl.

"A hood? And you did nothing?!" Randall shouted.

Earl wiped at his eyes.

"I didn't know what was happening. I saw Benton and a couple of gunmen take your mother and haul her away. I had no idea what happened to your mother. I thought they'd run her out of town. Alexander stomped on her camera with his boots, and then ordered a lackey to pick up the pieces and throw 'em in the scrap metal pile. Another guard restrained Buster Moore."

Earl looked down in silence.

"Old man Moore was outraged, cuttin' a rusty," he added quietly. "I don't think he really knew what was going on. He was just delivering some material. They got him back in his truck, aimed a gun at his head, and told him to drive away and forget that he had ever come here." Earl paused. "They aimed the same gun at me. Said I was a dead man if I ever told anyone. Dead man. Bodies had been dumped in the swamp or river for less. I never told anyone—not even my uncle or Harriet. I feel so ashamed. It's haunted me ever since. You gotta believe me. I had no choice."

Randall knew the follow-up story. Buster Moore had been found in his truck in the woods the next morning, after suffering a heart attack on a hunting trip. No one questioned the sheriff department's discovery. No autopsy had been conducted.

"They just buried the bastard," Earl said.

"And they buried her," Randall said.

Earl's sniffles received little sympathy from Randall.

"I didn't know, man. I didn't know what happened to your mother," Earl went on. "And I've been too scared to ever find out."

"Where did they take my mother? " Randall barked. "Alexander's farmhouse?"

Earl shook his head. The rhythmic tick of the cicadas felt like an accelerated heartbeat.

"I have no idea where they took your mother, you gotta believe me," he said, his voice faint. "The thing I saw was the truck pulling away, all that dust swirling. They vanished like it never happened."

Randall paced back and forth, and then shuffled out toward the backyard, under the vast night sky. Another ripple of rage spilled into his chest. This was one cold case he had always hoped to solve—and yet, the pain of resolution was breaking his heart.

67

—

Despite the dangerous situation, onlookers edged to the curb of the dark side streets on the southeast side's industrial area, anxious to witness some gruesome finale. It may have been nighttime but a shower of lights had illuminated the area like a circus ring.

All eyes focused on the billowing smoke, which spiraled out of the shattered front windows of the old warehouse. The scene was surreal to Nikki. Voluminous waves of water cascaded off the fire truck's snorkel. It reminded her of a rock concert, with the smoke machines that covered the stage with intrigue, even if everyone knew the act was on their way. She held her phone up to her head.

"Nikki, can you hear me?" Randall wasn't asking. He was shouting.

Another fire truck arrived, however, unleashing a further blare of sirens. Nikki watched the firemen leap off the side of the truck, axes in hands, and then disappear into the haze of smoke and water cannons.

"Thomas Svenson, the witness to the shooting of the ambassador," Randall kept trying to say, or at least this was what Nikki thought she had heard.

"Hang on," she said.

The Chicago detective moved to the opposite side of the street. She pressed the phone closer to her ear, still unable to hear the faint voice amid all the noise. It wasn't just Randall's call that had made her cross the yellow-taped line and move away from the action as two more fire trucks and their sirens bellowed into place with craned ladders. A growing

266

military presence unfolded from trucks that blocked the corner of the South Chicago street like a showroom for heavy armaments.

"Damn, Randall, military intelligence is taking over here," she said.

"Military intelligence?" Randall asked.

"Yes! They tracked trucks with militia and weaponry arriving here from downstate."

"Downstate?" Randall said. He understood its geographical connection immediately. "Listen to me. Thomas Svenson, the witness to the Yuri Ushakov murder, tried to kill me. He's a merc, a killer with Gen. Alexander. He needs to be identified as the suspect in the assassination of the ambassador. And Alexander, I'm now sure, is connected to my mother's death."

Nikki felt a jab in her heart. She didn't understand the string of associations. Randall seemed to be throwing random connections at her. None of this made sense. Pacing along the street, Nikki felt overwhelmed by this disconnection with her partner.

Was Randall coherent? Had his mother's tragedy ripped apart his mind? Or had he actually stumbled onto something? Nikki felt deeply for her partner, and yet she was faced with a horrible decision of trust.

"What, your mother's death?" she shouted. "He tried to kill you? Why didn't you tell me? You just said you wanted to confirm his ID?"

"He's down here," Randall's voice rattled. "The witness. He's down here. I know he's connected to Alexander."

Nikki stepped aside for two military officers, who attempted to move away onlookers. The confusion took a toll on her mind. She tried to sort out the names amid all the noise.

"What does a military general have to do with your mother's death?"

"You need to get me through to the chief," Randall said. "Something connected to Chicago is happening down here. There is an out-of-control militia operation here and that goon is part of it. He was no witness. I think he's the shooter."

"Okay, okay," Nikki said, relenting.

She crossed the street. It was too loud all around her.

The flurry of Randall's claims churned into the noise, into a blur that seemed almost ridiculous. While a militia in Cairo threatening Chicago might have raised eyebrows among her colleagues, Nikki trusted Randall's judgment. She always had. But Nikki had never known Randall to be so

verbally unguarded. He had always possessed a veteran detective's sense
of suspicion; Randall was a stickler for facts, not outrageous assumptions.

"Get ahold of yourself, Randall," Nikki said.

She knew the police chief was out of reach. Still, she entered the
smoking warehouse, where Daniels himself had arrived from a summit
security meeting to monitor the situation. The charred confines of the
building looked like an armory. Sheets of broken glass now covered the
remains like glittering cases. Boxes of chemicals, fertilizer, and explosive
components had been stacked to the ceiling; crates of weapons were lined
against the walls. In the middle of the main warehouse room, Daniels
had walked up to the smoldering remnants of several drones, which sat
in the middle of the room like forsaken argyles. He kicked a piece, which
landed to the side of Lt. Delich.

They both stared at the mound under the rubble. It was the charred
remains of a man in a mechanic's jumpsuit.

The SWAT team leader appeared in front of Daniels and yelled, "These
drones exploded like fireworks. Someone detonated these explosives. Probably this stupid SOB."

The bomb squad chief Lt. Delich muttered, "We're on it. We're tracking
sources now."

"Chief," Nikki called out. "I need to talk to you about Jenkins."

"Jenkins? Where the hell is Jenkins now?"

Suddenly, a large team of FBI and bomb removal agents from military
intelligence entered the warehouse, pushing Nikki aside. They declared
the building was contaminated. They moved every fireman, SWAT team
member, and Chicago policeman out of the building in seconds. In the
haste, Nikki lost track of Daniels, who was hustled out of the warehouse
and into his SUV, racing toward his next meeting.

Standing across the street again, Nikki couldn't pull herself away from
the smoking building. Surrounded by a crowd of onlookers, she had never
felt so alone and confused. She called Randall.

His voice on the end of the line was distant.

"Nikki, I can't get through to the chief. What did Daniels say?"

"Randall, listen," Nikki said, watching as a group of military agents in
jumpsuits and gloves entered the building. "Things are upside down here.
Daniels is swamped. I couldn't talk to him. He was pissed at being shoved
aside and left. I'll get to him again and try to let him know what you found."

She went on, knowing her voice was being drowned out. "The summit security is off the charts, do you read me? I'll do what I can to get through, but you've got to keep it together. Please!"

"I need to talk to him now," Randall shouted.

"Damn it, Randall," Nikki said. "Get ahold of yourself. It's fucking madness here."

68

A huge monitor on Alexander's office wall stretched with the backdrop of McCormick Place in Chicago on the TV screen as the Fox News reporter shifted to the side camera. She looked at the audience in a serious manner as the cable news chyrons rolled across the bottom with the latest headlines: Disarmament Summit Looms. Weapons Stocks Plunge. Negotiators Say Final Agreement Details Still Unsure.

"We're expecting President Adams's arrival in Chicago momentarily, so in the hour up ahead we'll check in with what the president plans on wearing for the opening here at the Chicago International Global Arms Reduction Summit," the newscaster continued, "and we'll be back with more inside coverage after this message."

With an expansive Pentagon photo as the backdrop behind him, Gen. Alexander sat at his desk on a raised platform like a news anchor. Instead of a jacket and tie, he wore his last blue uniform from when he was a general in the Military Missions of the US Army Corps of Engineers, his left side covered in eight rows of medals, ribbons, and insignia. Alexander knew the rules—as a retiree, he was only allowed to wear this uniform at funerals or military parades.

He considered this wartime service.

As the commercial break ended, an image from the nuclear disaster, with a graphic network logo and military soundtrack pounding, blinked onto the screen, and then back to Alexander and the reporter.

Staring straight into the camera set up in front of his desk, which was operated by one of Alexander's militia, the general continued his interview with Fox News. He remained calm, measured, and professional in his assessment of the tentative disarmament summit agreement.

The news anchor reintroduced the general with all of his credentials and began the questions by asking about Alexander's recently published position paper on US military strength.

"It is simple and clear: the cost now for laying down our arms is the sum of weakness, stupidity, and capitulation that will absolutely lead to the extinction of our American way of life," Alexander intoned.

This was no rant; the general sounded like he was making a sober assessment on the battlefield. "This inexperienced American president is effectively offering to surrender our nation to the whims of the world's dark forces. We must do everything within our power to stop this madness of disarmament. The bottom line is here: disarming the United States of America will ultimately cost our survival."

"Thank you, General," the newscaster said, pausing, looking at her notes. "General, your final thoughts as this vast security apparatus prepares for the imminent arrival of the president and her motorcade to McCormick Place, where she will greet this unprecedented gathering of foreign leaders and their negotiators."

Alexander looked straight into the camera.

"I'd say this is an unprecedented gathering of failed leaders and military traitors at a summit that should be stopped before it gets out of hand."

69

Standing in the corner of the cabin, watching the TV, Harriet lit a ciga-rette, the ash burning between her fingers.

"Lord have mercy, the general is on the TV right now," Harriet shouted.

Randall appeared from a back room with Earl. Having changed into one of Earl's T-shirts and jeans, he looked more like a local now. Molly sat in a rocking chair to the side with her arms crossed. Everyone focused on the TV screen as Harriet raised the volume.

"We have an oath and obligation to our country first," Alexander con-tinued. "This is not the time for surrender. This should and will not happen, if sanity prevails. God bless those who understand and support a mission away from this madness."

Randall had heard from Nikki and seen security notices and alerts emanating from Chicago.

"He's mounting an operation to stop the summit," Randall whispered.

"In Chicago?" Molly echoed.

Earl sat down on a stool.

"That's his bunker," he shouted. "See that vent, and the valve for the sprinkler? I put that in." He paused. "He's in his bunker."

"His bunker?" Randall said.

"He's got to be stopped," Molly whispered.

Randall looked over his shoulder at Molly. Her face was resolute. A fearlessness and anger emanated from her with a fierceness, which Randall shared. This strange connection between their families had twisted their lives in ways Randall and Molly could never understand; they both felt a powerful reason they had been called back to Cairo.

Returning to the cabin had worried Randall since Harriet's place had no phone service. He had called Nikki from down the road, where Earl had shown him a valley that picked up reception.

"Isn't there anyone you can call?" Molly blurted out. "The feds, or state cops, or someone?"

"I have," Randall said. "The heads of the summit security team. They're overwhelmed in Chicago and we're running out of time."

Out of his territory, and with little proof or evidence in hand, Randall knew he couldn't simply pick up the phone and call in state troopers. His frustration with the Secret Service was bad enough. The feds in nearby St. Louis would have laughed at his claims.

Those claims made perfect sense to Randall—those Cairo mercenary trucks sent to Chicago undoubtedly with weapons and drones, the killer of the Russian ambassador in Alexander's militia. The signal from Sandeep's phone. And then, of course, the murder of his mother.

He paused for a second, before nodding at Alexander's image on the TV.

"We've got to deal with him ourselves right here," Randall said.

"Now you listen to me," Harriet declared, "you're done messin' anymore with these people. You hear me? You still don't understand how things work down here."

"With Benton as county sheriff," Earl said, "they've got their asses covered. State troopers don't even come down here. This is Alexander County. Alexander's County, got it?"

A pounding at the front door jarred everyone in the room. Rising off the couch, Randall pulled out his gun. Earl already had his aimed at the door. Randall nodded, moving slowly toward the door. He motioned for Molly to hide in the corner with Harriet. Across from Randall, Earl stood on the opposite side of the room, his gun fixed on the door. Another three pounds on the door thundered.

"Who is it?" Randall called out. He aimed his gun with both hands at the door.

"Dude, it's us," came a voice.

Looking over his shoulder, Randall saw Molly bounding for the door. She recognized the voice. As Randall stepped back, Molly flung open the door.

"Thought we'd never see you again," Freddy said as he embraced Molly. Standing to the side, Anchee carried a backpack. She hugged Molly next as the two of them entered the cabin.

"We waited for an hour," Anchee said. "So we tracked your phone."

"To a swamp," Freddy added. "We were worried."

"A swamp up the road, you're right," Molly said. "Ask him . . ."

"We don't have time," Randall said.

He pointed at Anchee's computer backpack. He knew the Arkies were always connected.

"Can you get online with that?"

Anchee nodded. "Satellite should work."

Molly felt relieved to reconnect with her team. Randall had two less to worry about. Around the couch and coffee table, Randall and Earl on the sides in chairs, Anchee withdrew her computer from her bag.

"What about Sandeep?" Molly asked.

"Not a thing. I also left messages with his mom in Canada," Anchee said, opening the laptop.

Randall had instructed her to pull up the images from Sandeep's files again.

"We were hoping you had news," Freddy said.

Molly shook her head.

"You trust him completely?" Randall suddenly asked.

The mere doubt regarding Sandeep surprised the others. Molly nodded her head. She didn't want to even consider the question.

"Tell me what you got," Randall went on.

"These are the images from Sandeep's last drone survey," Anchee said. "I just downloaded them tonight."

She nodded at Randall. "I think you need to see this video footage."

Standing behind the couch, Randall and Earl stared at the fuzzy digital night images on the screen. A line of huge trucks rolled into a gated and guarded backwoods site. In the darkness, one barely could make out a farm building and grain silo. Perhaps a large shed or hangar. Anchee replayed the video, enlarging the images, and then zoomed out for a clearer angle.

"Look closely," Anchee said. "Alexander's crew has been loading his compound with deliveries from somewhere. Perhaps the river docks."

"Looks like crates of weapons or something," Molly said.

"Stop there," Randall said. "Go back three seconds."

Anchee clicked on the keyboard. The drone video relaunched. Two figures emerged out of the darkness near one of the structures as a large semitruck came to a stop. A man's face came into focus for a second—perhaps two seconds. Everyone registered the image in their own minds.

"Thomas Svenson, that's him," Randall said.

"Same guy from the swamp," Molly said.

"Where is this?" Randall asked.

"About a mile away from our dig," Anchee said.

"Anchee," Molly said, winding out of the couch. She walked toward the corner of the room, looking out the same windows that had drawn Harriet. "Do you know the correct codes in Sandeep's system?"

"Know them? I wrote most of them."

"Sandeep's laptop is buried in a box on the shelf in the theater," Molly said. "It's labeled Archaic Period 691."

"Archaic Period 691?" Anchee said. "That's the password he set up for our radar program."

"Exactly," Molly said. "I need you to go into his files and walk me through what you find from a tunnel system he located in the last few weeks."

Randall looked at his watch. It was past 1:00 a.m. It didn't seem wise to be driving with this crew into the center of Cairo, and hiding out in the abandoned local theater, at this hour. On the other hand, he reckoned, standing up, it was also the perfect time.

"We have five hours until the sun rises," he said, making for the door.

70

The moon rose over Lake Michigan with a spectacular sheen of calm as the shoreline and city skyscrapers emerged from the tip of a helicopter drone. There was no serenity inside the underground MACC, however, which hummed through the night with tension well before the sun rose. An emergency meeting of security heads had been rescheduled earlier by the Secret Service to 10:30, bringing together the Chicago Police Department with all state and federal agencies, in order to review final summit arrangements.

Secret Service agent Ford scooted to the edge of his seat as police chief Daniels, his team including Nikki, and their FBI and military intelligence counterparts sat around a long table in the meeting room. No one looked happy or truly awake, except for Ford, who acted more frustrated than confident. Behind Ford was an interactive map of the city of Chicago.

"These intercepts are ongoing," Ford said, reading from a list on his clipboard. "We just received details of potential terrorist threats to the area from our Joint Intelligence Group."

Ford looked outraged. On the side of the room, Nikki saw Ford glaring at Daniels and herself. "Listen, Chief Daniels," Ford said, "is a Detective Randall Jenkins under your command?"

The police chief felt put in a strange position, somehow without his usual iron-fist control over his intelligence sources.

"Yes, he's one of our detectives," Daniels responded. "Jenkins happens to be down in southern Illinois for family leave." Daniels looked at Nikki. "I was just updated by Detective Nikki Zanna that Detective Jenkins has identified a suspect in the Russian ambassador's Chicago murder. The suspect is alive and seen down in Cairo, Illinois. The detective thinks this subject is connected to a terrorist plan here in Chicago. Sounds like bit of a stretch, but Jenkins is on it."

"Jenkins is your detective?" Ford shot back.

"Randall Jenkins, yes, one of my best veterans," Daniels said.

"Sure about that?"

Daniels cleared his throat. "What's your point?"

Ford inhaled a deep breath through his nose, stepped back, and then put both of his hands on his hips.

"Our intel says Jenkins is being traced to a terrorist plot himself," Ford said.

Daniels looked like he had been punched.

"He's with his family right now on a personal issue," he said, though unconvincingly.

"Is he?" Ford shot back.

"That's impossible," Nikki blurted out. "Where the hell did you hear that?"

Daniels put out his arm to restrain an infuriated Nikki.

"You are?" Ford said.

"Detective Nikki Zanna, Jenkins's partner."

Ford looked harassed. He didn't have time for this. He spoke into his lapel.

"Get Murphy up here," he said, adding to Nikki, "One of my agents will be here to talk to you shortly."

71

—

Molly yanked off the quilts she had casually used to cover the large computer screens. Anchee and Freddy rifled through Sandeep's files. Connected by a cable, Anchee ran a search on Sandeep's computer, typing the passwords and codes onto her own keyboard. Sitting back on stools, the glow from the computer screen cast a light on Randall and Molly as they filed through the stacks of printouts.

Randall held up one paper, which was no more than a series of lines on a graph, without any labels or names or even a single word.

"Radar, remote sensing charts," Molly said, looking over his shoulder.

Randall and Earl tried to make sense of the research. Something in this inscrutable map, Randall felt, explained the layout of the underground facility—and locating Sandeep. Standing by one of the shelves of artifacts, Earl turned, and then held up something he didn't recognize. It was an effigy figure.

"This was carved in coal," Earl said.

"Check it out," Anchee suddenly said.

Both computer screens showcased the same image; Sandeep had acquired a unique digital X-ray of a large underground facility. Anchee pointed to the right.

"The LIDAR images are like a three-dimensional pop-up display," she said. "And this is a series of ground-penetrating radar images."

"Look like the habitations of underground insects," Earl chimed in.

"Can you separate the images?" Randall asked.

Anchee typed on the keyboard.

"Let me try this," she said.

The screen filled with lines of deep red images, yellow marks, and purple streaks, which cascaded down into dark pockets of black. Randall compared it to the printed-out digital images, including a map.

"There," he said, pointing at the black pockets on the screen. "Molly, isn't that where Sandeep circled this entire bunker layout and made maps?"

Molly nodded. She put her finger on one of the maps.

"Then there are two bunkers," Randall said, moving his finger over to another darkened area.

"That's right," Earl said.

Molly didn't look convinced.

"Tell me what these red lines represent," she said.

"The piping system," Earl said, looking over Molly's shoulder. "And that feeds the sprinklers. It all leads to a drainage system in the bunker that connects to an underground waterway."

"That pipeline leads straight to the bunkers," Randall said, looking at Earl. "Both of them."

Randall stood up from the stool.

"Sandeep's hopefully still alive down there," Randall said, "and whatever Alexander's planning in Chicago will be executed from those bunkers."

"Sun is about to rise," Molly said. "Let's take my mom's car, to be safe."

Randall turned to Earl.

"Would you still know how to turn on the sprinkler system below?" Randall asked. "Can you flush them out?"

Earl nodded. "With the right wrench and some magic powder," he said.

Randall looked around at the crew, and then asked, "Are you all willing to go on with this?"

"My truth is now," Earl spoke up. "I've never been more willing."

"Hell yeah," Freddy added.

"Totally agree," Anchee said, looking up from the screen.

"We're all together then," Molly said.

Randall stepped back; he realized the streak of light cutting through the darkness of the theatre rimlit this team in front of him. This was not a row of spectators. They surrounded him with a solid back of support. They were committed to finding their colleague, the truth, and the madman with his militia.

72

———

Gen. McCarthy had given Alison the opportunity to relinquish her duty and walk away from the assignment. He recognized the danger in sending her back—belowground. They both recognized an even greater risk in not following up. Nor had Alison ever backed away from an assignment in any part of the world. She didn't plan on starting now, in godforsaken southern Illinois. This intelligence agent would carry out her mission until it was accomplished.

Alison didn't come unprepared. She and McCarthy had briefed the commander of Scott Air Force Base on her concerns. Backup had been called. Less than four miles away, stationed at the local National Guard armory, Col. Sam Scalise and an Air Force special operations ground force pararescue team waited, securing their subsurface communications with Alison.

Alison arrived early that morning at the historic Alexander farmhouse, where she was escorted to the underground bunker. She had contacted the general and laid out an excuse for returning with inside information about Sandeep and the negotiations happening in Chicago. Smiling at the armed escort as he accompanied her down the elevator and through the steel doors to the main control room of the bunker, Alison maintained an aura of calm and an aloof innocence, as if she had no idea what was transpiring underground. Men with guns always assumed women didn't understand; so, Alison played that role carefully.

Alison knew she had crossed a line on her last visit to the bunker. Witnessing the interrogation of Sandeep had placed her in the presence of

Alexander's increasing madness. And she knew a Chicago plot by Alexander and his henchmen was afoot—and yet, the details remained hidden under the layers of this underground bunker.

As she stepped past the steel door, the unmistakable figure of Thomas appeared in the hallway, across from the entry to the main control room. Wearing fatigues, carrying a pistol in his holster, Thomas operated like a veteran of multiple wars. He nodded at the guard to leave.

"Listen, I need to see the general now," Alison said. "I've uncovered information on that foreign researcher he needs to know."

Thomas smiled. He was at least a foot taller than Alison. His beard topped her head.

"Until further instructions, the general says you are to remain in our 'talent' room."

Thomas's hand clasped on to Alison's shoulder with the strength of a bear trap. She flinched.

"You have no authority to hold me," she shouted. "Do you know who I am?"

Pulling her steadily down the hallway, Thomas nodded.

"We do, indeed," he said.

73

ALEXANDER FARMHOUSE WOODS
ALEXANDER COUNTY, ILLINOIS

The grove of eastern red cedar trees didn't provide much cover, but Randall and Molly left her mother's car in the clearing. It was a chance they had to take. It was close to the objective: Alexander's greenhouse. Randall looked at the coordinates on his phone. It amazed him that his iPhone survived intact and was working after being submerged in the swamp. He had used a hair dryer to dry out the connectors and recharged it when he got to Harriet's cabin.

He sent a text to Nikki and his bosses at the CPD, with the expectation of shooting an arrow at the sun:

Apprehending murder suspects at these coordinates. Backup and support needed ASAP. Follow up with all federal and state agencies. Critical: Do not alert local Sheriff.

But the delivered icon never appeared; the text didn't appear to have been sent or received. And then a red alert hung on the text—no reception. The text stared back on his phone like a map of his isolation. Message did not deliver. With Anchee's satellite connection, this confounded Randall. What if a strike or some crisis had already hit Chicago? He tried to shake off that thought, dismissing it as some glitch. How many crimes had never been solved because people did not get the information? How had history been shaped due to a missed communication?

The morning sun had already unleashed its wrath. The southern blanket of humidity added a layer of weight. Randall wiped the sweat from his forehead. Earl's hand-me-down long pants clung. A camo backpack from the Arkies rested on his shoulder.

Placing a tiny earbud in her right ear, Molly followed by Randall's side. It took her a moment to program her backup phone. It was an underground mining cell phone from her father's operations. She adjusted the wire on the green backpack. A microphone dangled along her cheek. Molly's tank top exposed a long scar on her shoulder. It had happened in Vietnam—a strange accident at an archaeological site, which she had never explained well. For some reason, it was reassuring to Randall, as it spoke more of Molly's fearlessness than frailty.

"Do you hear me?" Randall asked, checking his microphone.

"Ten-four," Freddy's voice chimed in from the theater.

"We hear you," Anchee added, "and we see you."

Freddy had been busy. He was on one hand a protégé of Sandeep, but he was also a self-taught wizard with this level of surveillance tech. Freddy hung a portable screen on the Gem Theatre stage, in order to project the live video stream connecting the Arkies' small phantom drones to the receiver and satellite dish that Molly had hidden on the roof of the theater. Behind the shambles of the building, the bright blue sky of the Alexander County valley spread across the stage.

Sitting at a lab table, Anchee verified the coordinates on the screen, and then focused the drone camera on Randall's location. Anchee could see sweat going down Randall's back as he walked out of the cedar grove.

Entering into the thicker woods, Molly motioned for Randall to follow along the faint path. This wasn't a human trail, which made her feel more confident. Molly had grown up hunting with her father. She knew how to track anything—on two or four legs. She pointed out a cluster of leaves. "Keep your hands to yourself," she said. "Poison ivy everywhere."

Randall shouldered his way through a bush. At a little clearing, Randall checked the coordinates again. He fingered his earbuds, which bothered him like annoying insects.

"Anything from Earl at the other end?" he asked.

"Negative," Anchee's voice responded. She monitored the drone's screen, where a blinking red light indicated movement. That was Earl—somewhere. "You're a half mile from the greenhouse," she went on, talking to

Randall. "No cars, trucks. Farmhouse appears to be unoccupied. Don't even see a dog on the grounds."

Freddy had never seen the Alexander house, even though it had once been profiled in the local Cairo newspaper when he was a kid. Now on the Gem Theatre stage, the live stream from the drone projected the picturesque layout of the home, the sweeping wraparound porch, and the greenhouse at the far end.

Randall and Molly saw the roof of the farmhouse in the distance at the same time. Randall squatted in front of a block of bushes as Molly huddled by a pile of three fallen trees that provided decent cover under an old oak tree. Inching closer for a better view, Randall could make out the greenhouse. The sprawling farmhouse had an eerie silence about it. Perhaps it was the morning interval. Only the buzz of insects was audible; the natural order of things had been brought to a standstill.

Randall moved quickly and crouched next to Molly.

"Any signal activity from the house?" Randall asked Anchee from his transmitter.

"No cell phones, no Wi-Fi," Anchee said. "Nothing, though we've picked up a security sensory system within thirty yards of the buildings."

Randall gave Molly a telling glance.

"I thought you were archaeologists, not NSA hackers," he whispered.

"Past is prologue," Molly said. "We have to be both."

Molly's quiet voice was cut off by the crack of a broken limb, and then the smashing of bushes. It sounded like a grunting elephant approaching. Randall gripped his trigger. The branches to the right of Molly started to rustle. Randall aimed his gun.

"Goddamn it," Molly hissed.

She waved off Randall, recognizing Danny's grunt before his hand pulled back a leafy branch. Wearing camouflage bib overalls and a floppy safari hat, Danny toted an automatic rifle like it was a machete in the tropical forest. Three other armed men in camouflage flanked behind him.

"Reporting to duty, cuz," Danny said, crouching down by Molly as his sidemen followed. "Sorry, we're late. Freddy's coordinates were a bit off. You've met Chester, and these are my partners Roy and Corky."

"Why aren't you with Earl?" Randall whispered.

Danny brushed off his comment with a wave of his hand.

"I left him with the best two shooters in the county," Danny said, "including Wayne Evans, who could have qualified for the trap skeet team in the Olympics."

Randall pushed forward quietly.

"Skeet team," he said. "Let's keep moving."

"I was more worried about you city folk," Danny whispered.

74

No one stood when Gen. McCarthy entered the room. Everyone knew his role with President Adams was critical. They understood this meeting would be quick. Everyone was expected in the summit hall within minutes.

Sitting at a conference table, the two other generals, Priest and Egerton, looked stiff in their uniforms.

"The hell's going on, McCarthy?" Egerton said, rubbing at his neck.

"Alexander has gone rogue," he said. "We've lost contact with Agent Alison Foreman."

"Will Alexander has gone rogue all of his career," Priest interrupted. "That's what the military trained him for."

"But he's not our rogue anymore," McCarthy said. "He's lost it. He's intent on stopping this negotiation."

"So much for Alison Foreman, your most capable operative and spy," Priest added. "I never thought she was too capable or smart."

"And our plans?" Egerton shouted.

"Our plans are still on, damn it," McCarthy shouted. "I've ordered a special ops force from Scott Air Force Base to neutralize him. In Cairo."

"Cairo?" Priest said, from the couch. "That's a world away. Isn't the threat in Chicago?"

"Nothing's a world away anymore," McCarthy said, glancing at his buzzing phone, and then at his watch. "It's the president. I've got to go."

He spun around and faced the two other generals.

"The next minutes will make or break us. Keep it together, gentlemen."

McCarthy then stepped out the door.

75

The city center had been on lockdown by 4:00 that morning, including the lakeshore neighborhoods. Helicopters swirled around the skyscrapers with the confidence of migratory birds. Squadrons of police, SWAT, and Army units lined the streets from the Loop to Hyde Park, standing shoulder to shoulder in battle gear.

Apart from the crowd, Lt. Delich found Nikki, who surveyed the area with a few other plainclothes officers from an embankment of large cement blocks. Delich walked over and then shouted into her ear.

"Drivin' me crazy how MACC has been testing cell phone jammers," he said. "We're gonna be back in the sixties without any reception."

"No wonder I haven't received any outside messages, except from the summit security," she said.

"Nonstop cyberattacks, that's what MACC's been fending off," Delich added.

Nikki had no idea this sweeping jam had momentarily included Randall's desperate call for help in his text—or her own calls. After the meeting with the Secret Service and accusations about Randall, Nikki had tried to contact her partner but she had only received his voice mail.

His silence worried her. This kind of disappearing act had never happened in their years on the force together. Nikki considered the worst-case scenarios—that Randall was hurt, dead, or had gone rogue.

"Where are you, Randall Jenkins?" Nikki said to herself.

As much as she dismissed Ford's comments about her partner as nonsense, Nikki desperately wanted to hear from Randall to dispel any concerns.

With McCormick Place glistening and a crisp blue Lake Michigan as their background, the media set up their crews in cascading rows of cameras. Satellite vans encircled the area, creating their own wall.

Nikki and the rest of the security team recognized that some kind of delay was unfolding. The summit timeline had been broken more times than a promissory note. The Chinese and Russian heads of state were finally now arriving. The turmoil behind the scenes with teams of military and State Department personnel, exhausted with last-minute language tweaks and positions, could only be lost to conjecture.

"Something's up," Delich said. "A friend of mine is in the White House security pool, and says the president's team is panicking. He thinks the summit might be faltering."

76

A computer monitor sat perched on Alexander's desk with a map of McCormick Place center. But Alexander wasn't paying close attention to the screen content. Instead, he sat back, puffed on a cigar, and affected a regal poise. He then threw his uniformed jacket onto his desk. Standing up, he reached into a closet and pulled out his ready-for-battle flight suit. He had expected this moment to come; he dropped his drawers, undressed, and then pulled on his fatigues. With a final zip, he was ready to go to war.

Muting the TV, Alexander clicked on the camera attached to his computer monitor. He set the cigar into an ashtray, and then wiped a bit of grit from his front teeth. Running a hand through his hair, Alexander looked into his image on the computer monitor.

He looked good.

Alexander hesitated, and then went back to watching the coverage of the disarmament summit, obsessively checking to make sure that it was still there—and ready to be ended. A guard looked at the general for a command.

"Sir?"

"Bring them in," Alexander said.

The door to his office banged as a guard shuffled in with Sandeep, who continued to look bewildered, his turban gone, his long hair flowing down over his shoulders. His hands were cuffed behind his back. Pushed from behind, Alison stumbled in next, followed by the towering Thomas.

Alison had never felt so powerless. She had thought Alexander's band of mercenaries were clueless boobs. But they were armed now, and in charge.

"General, I demand an explanation for this treatment," Alison said. "Gen. McCarthy would never . . ."

A guard motioned for her to quiet. Alison pushed him away.

She stepped toward Alexander, who hadn't bothered to notice her, too preoccupied with his current mission.

Two guards descended on Alison, clasped their hands on her shoulders, and pulled her back. They placed her on a chair in the far corner.

"Sit him up," Alexander said to the guard who held on to Sandeep. "Get the camera on him. And put that goddamn rag back on his head."

After setting up a blank screen in the background, a guard turned the camera toward a chair in the corner. The other guard shoved Sandeep into the chair. Unlocking his hands from the cuffs, the guard handed Sandeep his turban and then signaled for him to rewrap his hair. Overcome by the force of power, Sandeep obliged, wrapping the turban in a methodical manner.

Alexander remained focused on Sandeep. Alison's presence meant little to him.

"Son, tell me again what kind of drones you were flying?" Alexander said, staring down at Sandeep.

Sandeep looked over to Alison beseechingly. He struggled in his stupor to understand what Alexander was referring to, as if he had done something wrong at the archaeological site, but he wasn't quite sure of what.

Alison recognized that he was still drugged. A guard kicked Sandeep in the shins.

"Answer the general's questions, as we reviewed," the guard said.

"We flew a Walkera Voyager 3," Sandeep said, licking his lips in thirst. His words were issued in a monotone voice. "And a DJI S1000 octocopter."

"The next question is the most important," Alexander said, bending down in front of Sandeep. "Answer it as you have been told and you and your friends will survive. Understand me?"

Stepping back from Sandeep and the camera, Alexander placed his hands on his hips.

"And what did you tip the drones with?"

Sandeep's eyes widened. He stared at the camera with a blurred vision.

"Make it easy on yourself," Alexander continued. "Repeat what we instructed you to say."

"We loaded them with chemical weapons and mustard gas canisters stolen from the Blue Grass weapons depot in Kentucky," Sandeep said, his voice breathless.

Alison closed her eyes, testing the grips of the guards. Did the archaeologist understand what he was saying—or doing?

"Good boy!" Alexander smiled.

He spun around to the operative in the control booth, who waved a thumbs-up.

"Edit me out, upload it with additions and encryptions, and release it immediately," Alexander commanded.

The general turned toward Thomas.

"Tie him up and put him back in the hold," Alexander said, and then he walked back to his desk. "And get me McCarthy in Chicago."

"What about her?" Thomas asked, pointing to Alison.

"In there," Alexander said, pointing to the control room. "She might be of use."

The dome-shaped ceiling of the control room had once beguiled her; now it terrified her. It was no longer the rather ornate executive office of a bunker and construction operation, as she had assumed. It was a military command and control room—and a military operation was in play.

Thomas stationed an armed guard by her side as he sat at the control panel. Alexander joined him soon after, standing behind his immense shoulders and issuing a series of commands.

"Does this look familiar?" Alexander asked Alison.

A look of horror swept across her face. She recognized the Chicago grid.

Alexander and Thomas had worked together on covert operations for two decades. The burly guard had the bearing of someone who would execute the general's orders without flinching.

Linking up with their operations chief in Chicago, they worked the board in the bunker like they were in the Windy City themselves.

On the aged wooden floor of an open warehouse, dressed in black, wearing masks and gloves, the technicians who had orchestrated the laser demonstration for the generals in the strip mine were now unfolding another large fleet of small drones on a huge sheet of canvas. It looked like they were simply setting up an art installation on a drop cloth. The brushless motors, the landing gears, the boom and props, and especially the GPS modules—all of the parts came together in a runway of drones.

Then, gloved hands carefully handled a metal-framed cylinder device, which had been kept inside a velvet case. This was the heart of the Gunnor laser. A glimmer of its glass core turned to purple in the prism of the light. It looked beautiful. Mounted on the drone, it took on the shiny aura of an orb.

77

___

Randall had agreed that Earl would wait in the hillside forest buffer that separated the Henson farm and its compound from the nearby woods. He didn't realize how long it would take to get there. There were too many armed guards, all of them in sight of the targeted storm cellar that knelt on the end of the property like a forgotten lean-to. A quarter mile away, one of the entrances to the largest building functioned like a revolving door as men in uniform arrived and departed in vehicles.

Adjacent to the huge building was a grain silo, which spired over the area like a concrete medieval relic of authority.

Earl didn't recognize anyone, until Sheriff Benton arrived in his county sedan. The sheriff sat in his car for several minutes, perhaps on the phone, and then emerged, looked around the confines, and finally entered the building.

"Let's go, we're late," Earl whispered, "and when I whistle, you follow. Keep your belly next to the ground."

Two camouflaged caps appeared in the underbrush—the rest of Danny's partners. As veteran bow hunters, the two young counterparts were accustomed to hiding in the forest crevices for an eternity, without a sound, waiting for a buck or fleeting chukar to come into range. Today they had rifles.

Lugging a heavy bag onto his shoulder, Earl took a deep breath and then bolted across the edge of the field. It was the fastest thirty-yard dash he had ever done in his life. He dropped to the corner of the storm cellar, which looked more like an overgrown mound. A maple tree had grown to the side of the concrete slabs, and unmanaged stalks of grass had covered the door.

Cutting through the brush, Earl reached for an old rusty lock on the door. The rust meant that no one had used this storm cellar in years. He pulled out a pair of heavy-duty bolt cutters, and snapped them onto the lock, which then cracked as he wrestled it apart.

Looking over his shoulder, Earl puckered his lips and uttered a duck call familiar to his local hunters. No guard had come out of the building since Benton's arrival. Darting from the forest buffer, the two figures in camouflage ran twice as fast as Earl, and then slid by his side.

A guard stepped out of the main building as the cousins dropped behind the storm cellar.

"Whew, that was close," came a voice.

Taking off her cap and wiping her brow, a young woman shook her head at Earl. This partner was Danny's cousin Mattie, who had recently returned from her covert tour of duty in Iraq and Syria.

"Well, look who's here," Earl said.

"This war shit never ends," she said.

Ramming his shoulder against the front of the storm cellar, which had been jammed with dirt and weeds, Earl pushed open the door. A spider-filled black shaft leading to an old metal storm drain appeared.

"Watch the entrance and the farm building for me," he said. "Just use your whistle if you see any movement in our direction."

Relieved to stay aboveground, the hunters stationed themselves by the cellar door, their rifles by their sides.

78

Freddy watched the projection on the Gem Theatre screen like it was an actual Saturday matinee showing. Anchee had split the screen into two parts—Molly and Randall and Danny's crew at the Alexander farmhouse, and a blank screen for the still-missing Earl.

"Heads up, you're not alone out there," Anchee said, her voice urgent. "I'm picking up some major presence from the phantom drone."

"It's just Danny's other crew," Randall's voice echoed. "Another crew is guarding Earl."

A close-up on Freddy's computer screen tracked the two new guards with Earl on a map, with the live streaming images from another drone.

"Uh, we're picking up some kind of a mobilization, lots of traffic, near the Henson farm about a mile away."

"That's right near Earl," Molly responded. "Can you follow up?"

"Something is down with our system in his quadrant," Anchee said as she furiously worked at her computer.

"Send the nano," Molly said.

Freddy was already on it. He stood at the edge of the theater door, with a small drone in the cup of his palm. It looked like a tiny sparrow. Freddy clicked on the drone's camera.

"Do your thing, baby," he said, and then waved at Anchee.

The drone disappeared into the sky. It wasn't alone.

The theater stage screen showed Randall, Molly, Danny, and his team cautiously approaching a shed near the greenhouse. Their movements had been quiet. They hid behind the shed for a few moments to gauge their presence.

Randall peeked to the side of the shed. He held his gun by his chest. No one was in sight. Steam covered the greenhouse walls like a sauna. He nodded for Molly to proceed.

"Disable the security," Molly said.

Anchee clicked at her keyboard.

"Give me a minute," she said. A vehicle was heard in the distance.

"We don't have any more time," Randall said. "We've got to go now."

Nodding at Danny and his crew, who had moved to some bushes several yards away, Randall made a dash for the greenhouse. Three automatic rifles covered his approach. He crouched at the side of the building, around the corner of the side door. The top part of the door was glass, affording a view into the greenhouse.

Molly soon followed, dropping at Randall's side with a jump. Danny held up his head, and then gave a thumbs-up.

At the Gem Theatre, a moment of panic set in.

"I need more time to reboot and code this security system," Anchee pleaded.

Randall didn't hear her. He stretched over to the glass door, cupped his hand to block the sun, looked inside, and then stepped back. Using the handle of his handgun, he smashed in one of the window plates with a clean swoop.

Randall reached inside and unlocked the door.

"Going in," Randall said, disappearing into the mesh of plants and trees.

Tracking behind Randall, Molly gave a final order to Anchee and Freddy.

"If you lose contact with us, you know what to do."

79

Sector 6 had been violated.

The huge stacks of monitors inside the nerve center of the bunker now displayed a pulsating visual alarm as the bunker sound transmitters triggered sharp sonic alerts.

Thomas rose from his seat in the control room, scanning the array.

"Call in the breach!"

With her hair in disarray, Alison looked bewildered by the upheaval around her.

Grabbing an automatic rifle, Thomas motioned for Alison to sit in the corner of the room on a bench, and then reminded the control booth operator to keep an eye on her.

"Don't let her out of your sight."

Alison was impressed that Alexander had installed the latest security equipment and technology. But it was too much for one person to handle. Twenty screens flashed images of guards moving in the tunnels and bunker rooms and aboveground at the main entrances. Monitors flashed images of the greenhouse. Obsessed with tracking the origin of the movement that triggered the alarm, the control booth operator focused on the keys and knobs on what looked like a mixing console in a recording studio. His nervousness made him clumsy. He glanced at Alison, worried she was grading his efforts.

In two of the camera monitors to her left, Alison saw Thomas and three militiamen scurrying down the tunnel hallway. The monitor above it, though, scanned the images from a different room, which appeared to be covered in plants. Alison recognized it immediately—the greenhouse.

But Alison didn't just see a room full of flora. A door with broken glass was behind Randall's figure, which darted to the side of the greenhouse, soon followed by a woman that Alison recognized. The archaeologist Molly Moore. Alison remained motionless. She knew she had to make a split-second decision on tactics, and whether she agreed with it or not, she recognized that the Chicago cop might be her only way out of this mess.

"I'm trained in security operations," Alison told the armed control booth operator, who was overwhelmed by the system. "You want a hand with a few of these monitors?"

The operator nodded, waving his hand for Alison to take Thomas's seat at the console on the left end.

Alison knew precisely what to do—or rather, what she could do to clog up the system to buy Randall and his people some time. As Randall's and Molly's figures disappeared, and Danny and three men with rifles ran across the camera's view, she shot a casual look at the guard on the right, and then reached for a switch next to the monitor: REBOOT PROTOCOLS.

The monitors suddenly turned black, the system alarm went quiet, then the greenhouse monitor came up again with nothing flashing. The guard looked at Alison, convinced she had figured out the security alert.

Alison flinched when the door swung open. Thomas stood to the side, controlling Sandeep with one hand. Thomas didn't look any more pleased with Alison at the control board as the operator snapped to attention.

"Looks like a glitch, sir, a false alarm," the operator said. Thomas pushed Sandeep to the side of the room.

"Watch him."

Then he motioned at Alison. "Get out of there."

Rising from her seat, Alison acted indifferent.

"Software in the security system needed updating, happens you know," she said. "Trips the alarm as a test. We deal with this all the time."

The guard sat back, throwing his hands behind his head, nodding to Thomas.

"We're good."

80

ALEXANDER GREENHOUSE
ALEXANDER COUNTY, ILLINOIS

The greenhouse was as lush and humid as a jungle, with enough cover to hide an elephant. Randall reached over with a large tropical leaf and covered the lens on a camera above the windowsill. He and Molly crept through the rows of plants and trees, the vaulted ceiling and windows above them like a nave, and then they pushed past the draping flowers and deciduous branches that blocked their way.

"Find that altar," Randall said, brandishing his handgun. Danny and his armed posse slid into the greenhouse. Randall looked all around and shuddered at the reality that his mother was in this glass container, standing or lying near some ficus before she died.

"There's a lot of human movement underground," came Anchee's voice from Gem Theatre. Anchee stared at the flickering monitor. "Again, there is movement afoot under you."

In one corner of the arboretum, Randall approached an angel standing several feet high. At the bottom of the altar sat a framed photo of Alexander's wife, Marian Douglas Alexander, smiling in her wedding dress, holding a bouquet of roses. He waved Molly over to his side, and then whispered, "This is what Liz saw."

Randall led Molly around to the back of the altar, which was framed by a four-foot-high bas-relief. It was very ornate. It looked like a medieval tornado safety door to Molly. A religious staff appeared to be a handle. She grabbed it; the latch began to slowly open.

"Wait," Randall said, putting his hand on hers.

He waved over Danny and his boys. They were ready. Weapons in place, Randall ripped aside a rug covering a section of the floor behind the general's altar's wall to look for sensors or booby traps. He studied the deck, and then rose from his bent knees.

Randall nodded at Molly.

Pulling back on the handle, Randall opened the hatch door, revealing a winding metal staircase.

"We found the rabbit hole," Randall said into his microphone. "Keep tracking us."

Molly stepped around Randall, looked back over her shoulder, and began to descend the industrial staircase into the darkness. Randall reached for Molly and held her back, motioning for Danny and his partners to follow his lead, keeping one watching the rear.

81

MCCORMICK PLACE
CHICAGO, ILLINOIS

As he flew above the lakefront, the sprawling McCormick Place roof complex reminded a Coast Guard helicopter pilot of his training days in northern Virginia, where he had once entered the airspace over the Pentagon. Given the role of the military brass at the summit, McCormick Place effectively loomed as the focal point of the Department of Defense now—and its future.

The military police, flanked by Chicago officers in riot gear, stationed the media hub far enough from McCormick Place to control for security, and yet, the conference center remained a perfect backdrop for the thousands of cameras set up in a seemingly unending row. Jostling for space, reporters burned their time by juggling their microphones and giving obligatory updates on the upcoming summit. Social media outlets scrolled with more questions than answers.

"Ensuring the safety of the summit leaders, of course, remains an ongoing process," one newscaster reported. "As one military analyst reminded me, over five million drones are in the American skies on any given day. Nearly a million drones were sold over the Christmas holidays. However, security leaders have assured us that nonmilitary or nonpolice drones will be unable to operate near the conference."

The split screens of the television newscast included a pulsating countdown clock to the summit opening. In lieu of any hard news or insights from the negotiators, pundits took their turns in the little boxes of interviews, where the horrifying images of the Bardiche disaster in Siberia and in Mongolia, as well as the military buildup that followed with great public outrage, continued to return nonstop as a reminder of what was at stake at the summit—a global nuclear war. Missiles from all the nuclear powers were shown as graphic comparisons in megatonnage, range, and numbers. Worldwide supporters of the summit spoke of the huge benefits that cuts in military spending could deliver to the world, including the reinvestment of the United States's nine-hundred-billion-dollar weapons budget into greatly needed social programs for health coverage, education, housing, jobs building high-speed trains, the long-awaited development of new minigrids for renewable energy, regenerative agriculture initiatives, and other desperately needed infrastructure. The Great Shift, as Adams called it.

A clip from President Adams ran several times, becoming viral on social media and all networks. She sat across from the Joint Chiefs of Staff in the Oval Office, looking straight at the camera, framed by the three large south-facing windows. Adams looked calm, but resolved, in her pose.

"In this very moment," she began, "nuclear weapons are moving on air, sea, and land in a triad of potential destruction. There are more than thirteen thousand nuclear weapons in play, and yet ninety percent of those are in the hands of two nations—Russia and the United States. In a time of nuclear weapons and advanced weapons systems capable of death, chaos, and the unthinkable collapse of our ecosystems, the Bardiche tragedy has reminded us that human error is a formidable deadly enemy. With this historic summit accord, we will commit our nations to no longer being the 'destroyers of worlds,' as J. Robert Oppenheimer reminded the nation of our nuclear burden in 1965 after having supervised the Trinity nuclear test and witnessed the tragic results of the bombing of Japan. Oppenheimer called on us to be makers of a viable future through disarmament."

A newscast looked back at the history of weapons programs, including a black-and-white photo of Gen. McCarthy, flanked by Gen. Alexander, at the unveiling of a new Minuteman III missile silo.

As an international convoy of diplomatic vehicles snaked through the city, passing the waves of protests, the cheers of supporters, and the gazes of onlookers, discussions abounded about the possibility of complete nuclear disarmament and a world at ease. Was a world without stockpiles of weapons of mass destruction possible?

A defiant crowd of supporters for former president Waller answered that question, hunkered down on one corner, raising America First flags and a massive banner that proclaimed, "Build the Weapons. Disarmament is Surrender."

Sirens blared and police lights flashed as convoys with Russian and Chinese flags on their vehicles, along with those of other world and UN leaders, were ushered along the lakefront.

When they arrived at McCormick Place, the bank of media cameras captured their arrival with the frenzy of a red-carpet runway.

And then, finally, a news flash cascaded down the feeds of social media as it crossed the TV screens in virtually every household, office, bar, and gathering spot in the United States—and around the electrified world—with a breathless headline:

COUNTRIES AGREE TO HISTORIC DISARMAMENT ACCORD.
DETAILS OF SUMMIT TO COME.

"As this historic summit finally takes place," began a TV newscaster, "negotiators have reportedly come to a preliminary agreement on massive weapons reductions, including the scrapping of our nuclear stockpile and the elimination of several new high-tech first-strike weapons systems, including the US laser weapons programs."

82

The steep stairs below the trapdoor in the greenhouse made Molly feel claustrophobic. At the landing, however, was an elevator.

"No," Randall said, shaking his head.

One foot down from the landing on the staircase, he looked over his shoulder.

He had gone through too many pursuits to trust a mechanical box in the hands of a control room. Randall would never forget a misstep in a service elevator in the underground pedway linking buildings in Chicago's Loop district.

"That elevator is a trap," Randall whispered.

Molly let go of a deep exhale.

"This whole place is a trap," she murmured.

Randall and the team turned and descended eighty-eight more feet down the dark winding staircase, hands pushing off the walls. It seemed more fit for a submarine. Before them appeared the entrance to a large concrete and rock-cut tunnel. The hum of transformers and fans permeated the air, evidence of a huge operation. Randall motioned for everyone to stop as they considered their next move.

"We wait now for Earl to start his operation," he whispered.

83

Standing alone in the back of an open-air boat on the Chicago River Canal, a faded blue awning above his head, a young man in a black ball cap and dark clothes aimed his remote controller at the warehouse on the opposite side of the canal. The captain of the boat had idled the engine. Another tourist boat floated fifty yards down the river.

"Commence operation," came a voice.

It was Alexander's southern Illinois drawl, loud and clear.

"Wilco," the young man responded.

It was a beautiful afternoon, the sky clear—perfect for flying.

The young man in the ball cap turned left on the controller's yaw, and then moved the pitch forward, engaging the throttle. Alexander and Thomas had set the coordinates.

Twenty remote-controlled drone helicopters rose from the floor of the warehouse as huge doors opened. Emerging one by one, the drones scuttled along the river canal like a flock of geese, rising incrementally along the canal toward the edges of the buildings.

Operating the controls from the boat, the man in the ball cap signaled the departure back to the control center. The first wave had been launched. The boat coasted in the opposite direction. Watching from behind, the man in the ball cap moved the stick to the right, ramping up the throttle.

At first, it would have been hard to see the second launch. It emerged like a closed flower, and then unfolded into dark shoots. Six tiny bumblebee drones rose, hovered, and then sped across the canal in haste.

Hundreds of miles away, standing behind the array of monitors and controls inside the bunker studio, Thomas and another operative to his side, Alexander commanded the operations.

Alison now was cuffed to the seat by Thomas. He didn't trust her movements inside the control room and didn't want anyone else to waste time on disposing of her. The last guard dragged Sandeep out of the room and locked him down. Alison knew her most important task in the moment, apart from staying alive, was monitoring Alexander's aims. She looked for an escape route; she scoured every inch for an opening to send a message back to Chicago.

Alexander didn't even bother to look over his shoulder. He could control events in Chicago right from here.

"Mount the package," he ordered, then nodding to Alison. "Now for a little demonstration of our weapons they want to eliminate."

He instructed the operative to tap a key on the console, and then pointed at the screen.

"Today, we deploy our high-output mobile. The Thunderbolt."

"Fuck your laser weapons!" Alison suddenly said aloud.

Leaning on the right side of Thomas, Alexander finally glanced over his shoulder. He motioned for the guard by the door.

"Get that wet blanket out of here," he said. "I'll deal with her later."

At first, Alison resisted the guard's attempt to remove her as he struggled to unlock the cuffs. She was a veteran of too many wars herself. But she was unarmed. She pushed back on the guard's clutch, until he overpowered her.

"Come on," he demanded.

"Mount them on two," Alexander called out to the control booth operative. "The rest are decoys."

"General?" Alison shouted. "You can't be doing this. You *really* don't understand what's going on at the summit."

The laser terminology brought Alison back to the image of Alexander on the old strip mine bombing range. He had been so celebratory that day; his chest brimmed with victory. Alison saw that same gusto in the general's poise now. The battlefield had been moved to a new location.

Standing up, Alexander looked amused by Alison's outburst.

"I understand perfectly what's going on. These generals are traitors," Alexander bellowed.

"They want what you want, believe me," Alison pleaded. "This agreement won't pass, let me explain."

"No time for more bullshit capitulation scenarios," Alexander said.

Gaining a glimpse of the monitor, and the live stream of the drones, Alison seethed with regret for failing to call Alexander's bluff earlier on. Why hadn't she realized what had been happening? And now, where was McCarthy's airbase backup?

"You know why we need to protect bees?" Alexander suddenly said, strutting across the room toward Alison. She closed her eyes, shaking her head, trying to block out the insanity. "See, if you worked with plants, you'd understand this, Alison. Bees are the great pollinator. And it's thanks to them, making sure the strong plants survive, that our civilization continues. We can't leave pollination in the hands of our enemies. We're going to make sure that our superiorly armed country prevails so that we will thrive."

Shifting back to the screen with the drones, Alexander raised his hands like a conductor, his voice chillingly calm.

"Get them, my little darlings."

84

Clad in their respective uniforms, without hats and without smiles, Gen. Walter McCarthy, the lead negotiator for the US Joint Chiefs of Staff, shook hands with Russian general Nikola Gagarin, chief of the Russian Armed Forces, in an undisclosed meeting room at McCormick Place.

A powerful solemnity awaited the world leaders in the great treaty conference hall, where flags from 193 countries dangled on a stage in the front of the expansive room like a legion of royal horns trumpeting with historic fanfare.

If the Atomic Age had truly begun in the afternoon of December 2, 1942, at the University of Chicago with Enrico Fermi's team, creating the first controlled chain reaction in a secret location under the old Stagg Field stadium stands, then a new age of a world without nuclear weapons was to unleash its own chain reaction of peace here at McCormick Place in Chicago. The nuclear bomb had come full circle. Or so it was hoped.

That had been the symbolic agenda of President Adams in selecting the neutral Chicago location, away from the turmoil of the United Nations or the politics of the White House. She had wanted to the bring the world back home to where the initial key step in the Manhattan Project had led to the first nuclear weapon, and where a final handshake would eliminate all nuclear weapons from the earth.

Therefore, the quiet entrance of President Adams and her negotiating team, including Gen. McCarthy, from a guarded side door to the treaty conference hall almost took the other participants by surprise. The media had been set up at the front entrance. Instead, her arrival had been choreographed in secret, alongside the stealth maneuvers of the Russian and Chinese leaders. The security team had insisted on decoy convoys through the city, while separate helicopters had escorted the presidents from O'Hare and landed in the middle of Soldier Field.

Recognizing the historic moment, the world leaders assembled in the great hall rose to their feet in applause, almost in a ripple effect, as the American president was ushered to the front of the room. Looking sober and resolute, President Adams stood with her hands to her sides, overwhelmed by the spontaneous reception. She nodded vigorously, and then raised her arms in solidarity.

The president had worked hard to restrain her mounting concerns about whether the agreement would hold. How could she "quietly trust the Russians," in the words of her Gen. McCarthy, "without having her hand on the biggest stick?" Her national security advisor had questioned whether the agreement had been clear in the translation, sending a chill down her spine. She had a promise from her Russian and Chinese counterparts, that much she knew. But she also knew promises could be broken, especially unclear ones.

The Russian and Chinese leaders were scheduled to arrive within minutes.

The split screens on the network feeds erupted into the split opinions over the peace agreement. The news anchors readied for their television parleys, rehearsing, then lowered their voices with each live report. They gazed into the cameras with expressions of fearful anticipation. The viewers awaited the news, expecting a conclusive verdict.

"Given the disparity in warheads and this recent Bardiche nuclear disaster," one news commentator said, "anything less than total disarmament will not satisfy the nonnuclear world or the global community. Getting the major nuclear powers—the United States, Russia, and China—to totally disarm is a huge leap for its military and political leaders."

85

Earl had slithered through sewers and climbed into underground pipe-lines in the past. But this time was different. He felt like there was a time bomb strapped to his gut. It was more of a burden; the need to atone, to redeem himself from the secret he had held inside for decades; and now, to make good on his promise to Randall to raise the dead and cleanse the earth below.

Lugging his backpack of equipment with him, he climbed down a lad-der into the chamber of the hydraulic pumping system below the ground. Cobwebs and weeds dragged along his face. It had been years—decades, more like—but when Earl reached a flat concrete landing, he remembered the first time he had set foot on this property. He knew exactly where he was. In fact, he had built the mechanical workings of this chamber and it felt like home.

Earl placed the heavy bag on the slab gently. He wasn't just carrying his usual wrenches, pipes, and tube cutters. Anxious to make sure they remained dry, he unfolded several sticks of dynamite he had stored for many years from a stump-removal job.

Loosening up the old rusted valves, Earl recalled what Randall and he had discussed. He had to set off the sprinkler system, which would trigger the evacuation alarm. Then make the rats flee the ship. The rest would be in Randall's hands.

The valves to the pipeline hadn't been touched in years. Earl and his uncle had set up the hydraulic system, after the initial construction of the underground site, as a way of redirecting any flooding from the bunker.

Their pipes shifted the runoff to a drainage site, about a hundred yards from the storm cellar. The dynamite guaranteed that any frozen and rusted valves would play no part in stopping the desired flushing and flooding.

With his headlamp ablaze, sweat and debris on his face, Earl could smell the musk of an underground water system. The last valve at the bottom of the landing was stuck. Earl gave it one last push and opened it.

When water slowly started flowing, the pipes began tapping. Earl had no idea how long it would take for the stream to reach the sprinkler system. He felt a chill go down his spine with the expectation of this controlled flooding and its results.

86

Randall spun around in the underground tunnel, wiping the water from his nose. The wait was over. The sprinklers started to unload small drops onto their heads. The dangers around the corner remained elusive. Randall and Molly knew they had no choice but to expect the next step in their plan, which Earl was tasked to achieve.

"They should be coming at any moment," Randall whispered to Danny and his crew.

At the bottom of the staircase, the Arkie team hid in the corner of a landing next to the elevator. Fluorescent lights flooded the area like a stage as water droplets continued to fall on cue. The veteran detective looked around the low ceiling and corners. He knew someone had to be watching them on a security monitor somewhere.

Standing on the bottom step of the staircase, Molly pointed at the ceiling of a side entryway, which led to another hallway. Earl had informed them of an emergency exit. In a wedge between the wall and ceiling perched a camera, like a greeting crew at the bottom of the stairs.

Aiming his pistol, a silencer already attached, Randall took out the camera. Then he hit the ballast on the first set of lights. The tunnel went dark.

But it wasn't quiet.

"Get ready," Randall said. "The big water's coming."

Danny looked spooked by the comment.

"We're too far underground. I've lost contact with Anchee," Molly said.

"Get back and make contact above," Randall whispered. "If you don't hear from us in fifteen minutes, then go. You know what to do."

Molly hesitated. The urgent shrill of voices grew. The stomp of oncoming boots followed like a drumbeat. This was more than a handful of guards.

He placed a hand on her shoulder.

"Go, we've got this part. You need to get out and see if you can reconnect us and Anchee. You need to know what's happening on the outside, and keep Earl in the loop."

Molly didn't budge, so he shook her.

"Anchee and Freddy are our Wizards of Oz," Randall said, his voice more adamant. "Go! We all have a different part to play."

Nodding her head, Molly held out her hand to Randall. He clasped it, and then pulled her in for a quick embrace. Molly was terrified, and Randall knew it. No matter what happened below, Molly needed to make it out alive and tell the story.

"Twenty minutes?" she said.

"Okay, twenty minutes." Randall nodded.

"I'll see you then," she said.

"You will," Randall said. "Now go."

Stepping back, Molly placed her hand on his shoulder, and then pushed away, scrambling up the circular staircase as fast as she could.

87

An agent with the summit security team at the MACC at first wondered if his sleep-deprived eyes were playing tricks on him. He blinked. Then he shook his head and set down his coffee.

Nearly 370 miles away, the large-screen monitors on the walls behind Alexander's desk showcased this spectacle. The skyline of Chicago came into view. Alison couldn't believe what she was watching.

The drones glided up the river and turned south, revealing the grand corridor of Chicago's Magnificent Mile stretching down Michigan Avenue in shades of limestone and glass. Art Deco skyscrapers gave way to Gothic designs as the white terra-cotta exterior of the cathedral-like Wrigley Building awaited its nighttime illumination. However, the greatest sight may have been in the reflection of the glass windows of a high-rise on Michigan Avenue. Passing like birds in formation, the migration of a drone army flanked out in silhouettes along the seventieth floor of a building. A man in his pajamas, holding this morning's paper, looked out the window at them. On their tails, the bumblebee drones darted across the mirror reflection of the windows in a tiny flash.

Back at the MACC the swarm of red lights in the downtown Chicago area now blew up the operative's screen. The agent turned to an operative at his side as he monitored three video screens.

"Confirm violation of the outer ring airspace between 400 and 800 coordinates?"

"Negative," the operative answered.

"The fuck?" the agent said, scooting back in his chair. "Agent Ford," he said, in a more urgent voice. "Agent Ford, heads up here now!"

The swarm of red lights transformed into the brigade of drones on the monitors. An alarm on the screen shrieked. Two agents in the room shouted in front of their computer screens as the security apparatus mapping airspace turned into a spider's nest of signals.

Ford leaned over the shoulder of the first agent.

"Jam the field," Ford called out.

"Coordinates locked in," the tense operator said. "There are twenty of these suckers."

"Jam the field!" Ford barked.

Tracking the quadrants of the drones, the computer operator emitted an electromagnetic field blast from the top of both the John Hancock Center and the Waller International Hotel, attempting to disrupt the GPS and ISM radio frequencies in the area.

Everyone at the MACC watched the screen. Their work was in the hands of those controlling radio waves now. Their own surveillance drone followed the threat with real-time images. The drones continued on course, carrying a barrage of firepower along the avenues. Then something invisible happened, as if time had been frozen. The drones suddenly swerved, faltering with a bop of their front pitch, until they cascaded with a dramatic dive toward the ground. Icons on the screen followed the falling drones.

Back on the streets, the sirens of the Chicago police and federal security blared as a team of bomb and chemical weapons disposal experts fanned out in the area of the drone coordinates. An old man with a cane, walking his dog along the canal near the DuSable Bridge, watched as one drone after another crashed into the river like victims from a duck hunt blast.

"Got 'em," said the first agent.

Ford blew out a stream of air. "Too close."

Not all the drones came down, though. The bumble bee drones powered above Michigan Avenue, barely visible to the eye.

"We didn't get them all," said the first agent, his voice desperate.

The agent at the security station stared at a new red signal on the screen. It was faint but consistent. Her mouth dropped open again. Along the same trajectory of the other drones, this new line of resistance had reemerged on the screen on the outer edge of the Loop.

The operator spun around in her chair, too shocked to speak. Standing a foot away at another monitor, Ford looked at her with the turned brows of a translator, reading her silence.

"All hands on deck," Ford shouted, leaping toward the blinking screen.

"Drones have penetrated the outer ring airspace," the agent said.

She clicked on the array of knobs and switches, and then typed into the keyboard.

"Bring 'em down," Ford shouted. "Bring 'em down."

"Trying, sir. Trying. It's within the McCormick Place perimeter now."

"Come on, damn it." Ford pounded on the table. "Throw everything you got."

"We're trying, sir," called out the operator on the opposite side. "Locking on the microwave."

Three microwave dishes atop McCormick Place swiveled like giant radars, searching for a target. The transmitters sat on top of twenty-foot shipping containers.

Back in the security room, the operator carefully maneuvered the controller and joystick in front of the split screen, which showed the coordinates of the drones in the right corner, and a live image of the bumblebee drones in flight filling the left. The swarm headed south over Grant Park, the grand museums, and the colorful array of sailboats docked on the lakefront. Their target: the cathedral glass walls of the Grand Concourse of McCormick Place.

They soared under the massive roof like tiny swallows.

On the top level by the escalators in the Grand Concourse, a young man with China's negotiating team stopped and stared at what he thought were birds flying under the rafters. The mounting toll of wildlife crashing into the skyscrapers had been a concern in his Chinese city as well. But these birds were different.

The laser weapon installed on each of the drones revved into action. The electrons ignited as the light emitting from the lasers emerged in waves, rolling into a powerful narrow beam.

The young diplomat watched in awe as the birds somehow transformed themselves into dragons. The beam of light fired repeatedly until that fire turned into a stream of red.

"Detected and identified," the operator at the security office called out.

"Now," shouted Ford.

The operator's fist pushed the joystick down as the four-foot tall transmitters on top of McCormick Place unleashed a swath of microwave radiation that lit up the screen in red beams.

In a sudden pop, a large blast of laser light swept the side of the huge wall of the convention center. The young diplomat and a dozen others around him dove to the floor. The nano drones dropped, their laser beams blinking into darkness. The machines plunged to the ground below in a powerful blast, shattering into a thousand pieces on the exposition center's balcony and street.

Inside the command center, the security screen lights announced an end of the tracking.

"What the hell was that?" the agent said, her head dropping.

The computer operator glanced at Ford, who held a hand to his forehead. He looked like he was ready to collapse.

"This is just beginning," he said. "Get me Gen. McCarthy."

88

Alexander stared at the computer screen in disbelief. His chest swelled with outrage at what had just happened in Chicago. The rest of the guards in the room craned their necks around, staring at the dripping sprinklers.

"You told me your Chicago team could override any electromagnetic wave," Alexander bellowed to the technician at the controls.

"The problem was not on our end," the technician answered. "The jamming frequencies were changed at the last minute."

The general couldn't believe what had happened to the drones. His drones. His lasers. Years of development and planning had been vanquished in a matter of seconds. For the ultimate planner on the battlefield, this was more than a nightmare scenario to Alexander. It was a humiliating loss.

But Alexander was not defeated.

When a drop unfolded with a splash on the screen, Alexander looked over his shoulder, almost offended by the structural defect. He had engineered for this; he knew that someday he could be pushed to the edge. So, with required security he had prepared for what could happen from human or nature-made threats or problems right in his cavern.

"General, it's the fire system. Water on the control panel," Thomas said.

The general glanced upward.

"Cover them, damn it, and find out what the hell triggered it," he said.

Thomas watched as Alexander flipped a switch and transparent shields emerged from the walls and covered the control panels, creating a windowed bunker on one side of the room.

"What triggered this?" Alexander barked to Thomas.

Thomas shook his head, wiping the drops from the screen.

"We're checking."

"Now, send a team above," Alexander screamed.

The lights in the control room flickered; the power was cutting off. Two guards stormed into the control room. They looked panicked.

"Sprinklers are on across the tunnels," one bellowed.

"We're losing contact with the radar," Thomas added.

"Contact the duty engineer above," Alexander shouted. "Deactivate the sprinklers. It's got to be an electrical control problem."

Alison had been moved to another location down a nearby hall, where Sandeep had been cuffed to metal bars on the wall and saddled to a chair. The "talent room," she surmised, was the interrogation or holding area. As the guard slipped out of the room, Sandeep and Alison could still hear the shouting in the adjacent main control room. There was a crash from a chair being thrown. Alexander's voice boomed under the door.

With drops of water falling around him, Sandeep watched in a daze as Alison cut the thick plastic ties around her wrists by wiggling against the sharp corner of a metal cabinet.

A streak of blood dripped down her arm.

The booming noise of an exodus had begun. Sandeep turned to his side when he heard the rustle of guards outside. They shouted in a clear fit of panic.

"Got to get out of here," she said, holding the palms of both freed hands in front of her. But Alison hesitated. She knew the corridor was the last place to be right now.

A cadre of men, including Alexander and Thomas, stood outside as Sheriff Benton appeared in the hallway. Their shouts sounded too close, as if the door had speakers on it.

"We've got incoming military on our ass now from the Scott base," Benton announced.

In the storage room, Sandeep wiggled in the chair, and tried to repeat with his restraints what Alison had accomplished. But it didn't work. She listened to the outside conversation, not lifting a finger to help Sandeep.

"Scott?" Alexander sounded more offended than concerned at the military threat.

"General," Benton went on. "We've got to deal with a special operations unit in movement from Scott Air Force Base."

The hallway fell dramatically quiet. You could hear the troubled breathing of Alexander.

Sandeep looked frantically at Alison, who grasped at her bleeding wrist. She held a finger to her lips. Then she wiped some of the water from her face.

"We have our options," Alexander said. "A punk platoon of Air Force privates and a lieutenant will not stop anything."

Then Alexander, forever the general, led the team out of the control room as he commanded.

"Right now, we're taking this to the next operational level."

Alexander strode farther into the tunnel hallway. The others followed. Their footsteps echoed.

"Svenson, Benton, we have the means to crank this up," he called out.

His voice drifted down the hallway.

Sandeep and Alison could hear two technicians from the control room pass their door, following Alexander's crew in another direction of the bunker.

Water had collected on the floor like a sheet of glass.

"Kick in the generator and start the pumps," Alexander's voice bellowed down the hallway. "I've installed the best hydraulic system in the world."

It was the last thing Alison heard.

She hesitated for a final moment at the doorway. She looked back at Sandeep, his arms strapped behind him. Alison nodded goodbye and then disappeared.

89

Three military trucks, including a medium-sized tactical vehicle fitted with a 12.7-millimeter machine gun, barreled down the narrow state highway 3. Locals assumed the vehicles were engaging in some sort of off-base exercises, which they were, though the orders from Scott Air Force Base commander carried a seriousness none of the soldiers had ever experienced.

Another special ops team followed the convoy from the air, trailing behind in a Pave Hawk helicopter, equipped with a gunner team.

"The operational plan is to secure and safely shut down an Alexander County civil defense bunker that has been taken over by former military operatives who are armed and extremely dangerous," the aerial team leader announced.

The military team and their trucks had hardly passed two county lines when a huge semitruck appeared around a bend from the opposite direction, and then slammed on its brakes, sliding and flipping onto its side.

Coming around a blind curve, the first two military trucks collided with the semi, which had just jackknifed on the narrow two-lane highway. The last military truck, including the tactical vehicle, smashed into the back of the first trucks, launching all of them off the road and into the swampy ditch.

The scene in the ditch was a sorry one, especially for the gunner riding in the Pave Hawk helicopter, who watched the unfolding scene in horror from the sky. He saw the tires of one truck disappeared into the muck.

Two men were injured. Climbing out of the trucks, soldiers gripped their weapons in a daze, unsure what had happened. Several soldiers rushed with fire extinguishers to help rescue the semitruck driver, whose upturned cabin and engine puffed out waves of smoke.

No one in the military vehicles—or intelligence command—would ever know that the truck driver had been dispatched by Sheriff Benton. Rocky Ryan, a militia member and former expert Hollywood stunt driver, was capable of this trick; he lay on the road edge faking his injury.

Ordered to continue the mission, the Hawk helicopter flew on.

90

Panicked voices echoed through the winding tunnel system as Randall slid into a wedge between the tunnel entryway and the stairway landing. Their rifles brandished in the air, Danny and his two friends stood along the wall.

"Hold here," Randall said to Danny and the others, who huddled behind the steel railing at the end of the staircase. "I'll give the order."

Randall could hear the murmuring of arriving guards. The sounds of a military operative's words were unintelligible. The red laser flicker on the barrel of his assault rifle poked out of the darkness a hundred yards beyond, and then moved toward the same staircase. A sliver of daylight emanated from the top of the staircase like a waning moon.

Randall's team, hidden in the darkness under the stairwell, watched a guard pass, then another, the stomps of their boots on the metal staircase drowning out their frantic voices. Randall counted six guards, who clambered up like a herd of spooked horses. He prayed Molly had darted far enough ahead of them and escaped.

The echo of the guards aboveground was fleeting. It suddenly turned silent. Randall peeked around the corner, only to be face-to-face with the terrified eyes of the last guard, and the clutch of his two hands raising a rifle.

Hammering the guard from the side, Randall knocked the rifle from his hands as the guard collapsed into the darkness like a bale of straw. Randall aimed his pistol at him. The reticle of the red light from the guard's weapon shined on his own face as a target. Lying on his back, the guard raised his hands.

"Who's behind you?" Randall whispered, throwing a quick look over his shoulder at the staircase.

"No one," the guard moaned. "There's been an evacuation alert."

Randall kicked him.

"Bullshit," he shouted.

"I mean, no one is left on this end," he said. "The others went the other way. We got out of there when the sprinklers filled the main chamber."

"And the general? The others?" Randall aimed his pistol at the guard's forehead.

"There's another escape on the other end," the guard whimpered.

91

—

In the shadows of his headlamp, Earl imagined Randall breathing behind his neck, like a ghostly presence pushing him closer to the abyss. Earl knew it was now or never.

Crawling to his feet, he pushed his duffel bag to the side, exposing the Colt 4, a turbo version of a handheld smoke generator. He knew it would be able to reach the ventilation system needed for flood control. He remembered that the air ducts and hydraulic systems in the bunkers below were full of shafts that diverged in different directions. Slowly twisting the smoke canister into a groove on the top, he clicked on the power. That would get things started below.

Earl began unfolding his sticks of dynamite laced together with straps. It was old-school—the newer mines preferred ammonium nitrate and fuel oil mixes—but it worked all the same. Earl knew what to do.

Gathering the explosives into a bundle, Earl crept along the cellar tunnel, and then stopped at one passage. Having prepared a simple cord fuse for each load, he would have little time to climb out and escape. Crouching in front of a small door, he flipped the latch, and then turned back to his bundle. Two stacks of wrapped corded dynamite bumped off the shaft walls with an echo. A few feet down, Earl dropped another stack with a longer fuse into a second shaft. This would be backup. There were never two without three, as the saying went.

Earl took a deep breath and turned off his headlamp, leaving him in an eerie moment of darkness. He was ready. Earl was no longer dealing with the sprinkler system. He wanted to unleash the fury of the underground river. The Shawnees called it the panther of the deep.

The agreement with Randall was to flush out the bunker. Send them scrambling like rats. Earl had one more tool at his disposal.

He ignited a minitorch and focused the flame, as if making an offering.

"May the bundle of twigs be strong," he whispered. "Bring it all down, in the name of justice."

Bending over, Earl lowered the flame to the two fuses until they sparkled with success. Looking at his watch, he calculated the delayed fuses.

And then he bolted from the cellar.

Outside the storm door, the new recruit Mattie whistled from a distant tree. Emerging from the entrance, Earl dashed across the hillside, finally throwing himself to the grass.

"Wait, is that Molly Moore?" Mattie called out.

Through her riflescope, Mattie watched Molly, a hundred yards away, racing across the pasture area from the opposite side of the farm.

Whistling toward her, Mattie held up her rifle and waved at Molly, who immediately made out the hunter in camouflage.

As the last truck of escaping militia and guards tore out of the building and the hangar's dirt parking area, spiraling up a dust devil in its wake, the facility now looked deserted.

The hunters mounted their rifles, turning toward the main building, covering for Molly as the archaeologist raced to their perch at the forest clearing and then dropped at their feet. Earl pulled Molly to his side. He knew she had sprinted from the greenhouse.

"Randall is still below," she said, still catching her breath.

Earl looked stunned. He looked at his watch and timer.

"What's he waiting on? He's gotta get out."

92

As Alexander and Benton and their dwindling team advanced through the underground passageway, a deep rumble was suddenly felt resonating into the tunnels. The walls shook.

Everyone knew they were sitting underground in one of the most devastating earthquake zones in the country. Everyone knew the Big Shake had reversed the Mississippi River in 1811.

"That wasn't a quake, right?" Benton said.

Alexander didn't have an answer. It didn't matter to him.

Looking up, a light coat of dust cast from the ceiling. Alexander flicked off the dirt like lint; his county sheriff stopped in place. A creek of running water at their feet already scared everyone.

"Move it along, Benton," Alexander shouted, looking over his shoulder. "These walls were built to withstand a nuclear bomb."

The declaration didn't comfort the sheriff. It terrified him with a new reality. Looking frantically around, he hustled to catch up with the general, Thomas, and the others.

They passed a huge open blast door and then entered a steel-enforced control room. They stepped into the second bunker. It was smaller, and yet it contained more equipment and hardware than the communications array in the first bunker. Benton stood to the side, his hat in his hands, looking around at the banks of command and control technology along the walls. It seemed like he was in some spaceship.

Alexander and Thomas took seats next to two technicians at the control panels like they were piloting an F-35 fighter jet into war.

327

In that moment, after a lifetime of loyalty oaths, Benton felt the sharp pain of real warfare for the first time. This was a war of their own making, and the sheriff wasn't quite sure he was up to the task of actual combat.

Then he stopped, confronted with a preview of the next order of business. The image on a large monitor in the middle of the room left Benton breathless.

In the middle of the huge adjacent grain silo sat a massive ballistic missile with the radiance of all its might.

"This is one bullet that can change the world," Alexander added.

At the board, Alexander replaced a working operative and made some settings with the alacrity and the touch of a pipe organ master with wartime experience. He then quickly moved through a steel door with Thomas into the entry of the huge silo vault. The missile crew was finishing fueling, tightening hoses and connections.

The silo had been updated since Benton's last visit to the second bunker, when the silo was an empty concrete hangar, totally devoid of this aging rocket and warhead.

That had all changed now. The structure and equipment had been modified. New hardware had been installed. No more floppy disks. This was a deadly live missile in an ingeniously camouflaged silo.

Benton stared in awe. He had seen the silo many times over the years, but without the placement of the actual missile.

"Your boy Jimmy Joe and his guard buddies came through," Alexander said to Thomas. "They are true patriots, and they will be taken care of for the rest of their lives," he added.

"They've got so many goddamn missiles across the river at that Missouri arsenal, and we only needed one," Thomas said. "They were cheap, too."

Alexander entered the chamber for a moment, checking the pressure on the massive engine. He ran his hand lovingly on the missile's surface. Here was the ultimate weapon. The missile's skin still seemed fragile to him, but he had put his faith in those metal casings, marketed to the military for their resistance to corrosion and extreme temperatures.

The general then turned and gave a thumbs-up to Thomas, reentering the control room.

Alexander's voice came slightly muffled over the speakers.

"Lord, I've been preparing for this day to come for forty years."

93

Randall stopped in his tracks, realizing it was Earl's second huge boom of dynamite finally sounding across the tunnel. The walls seemed to wobble, though he wasn't sure if his eyes were playing games on him. The cascading drops of water were starting to take a toll on his nerves.

"We need to get out of here," pleaded the guard who had been dragged along with them.

"Tell us where we find Alexander," Randall demanded.

"I told you, I have no idea," came the plea.

"Tie him up and gag him," Randall said as Danny and his squad in fatigues dragged the man into the shadows.

Everyone looked scared. Growing puddles of water began to bog down this tunnel. An acrid smell tickled their noses; there was a mist in the air. Earl's smoke generator was on.

"Jesus, Earl," Randall said. "Pray his magic powder doesn't wash us away."

Randall listened intently as one of Danny's cousins coughed.

"I'm smelling dynamite," one said.

The roped-up guard was placed on the floor of the tunnel.

Then Danny held up his rifle, aiming the scope and red dot sight into the tunnel. Randall spun around.

"Don't move," Danny said.

Randall saw his target, and raised his gun as well.

Out of the mist, a shrouded figure emerged from the darkness. It was

Alison, whose hair was soaked like she had been walking in the rain. She scrambled up another metal stairway, fleeing for her life.

"Goodbye, you piece of shit," Danny whispered, who withdrew his rifle to the side.

94

There was new commotion outside of the silo and farmhouse that erupted with a flurry of panic. More militia, guards, and technicians were being flushed from the buildings by the power of water. Watching with scopes from a distance, behind an earthen mound and a maple tree for cover, Earl and the young hunters possessed a sense of victory—and a foreboding sense of disaster.

Molly, instead, felt a pain across her chest. The rumble of the two blasts didn't simply unnerve her; it set off a time clock of survival for those underground. There was no Randall in sight. No Danny and his crew. No Sandeep.

"Look, she's there, too?" Earl said, watching the individual guards flee.

It was the woman from the county jail—Alison—who appeared out of a side door of the farm warehouse. She followed the other guards and then hopped into the back of a truck.

Molly turned to the only source of hope.

"Anchee," Molly gasped as she clicked at her phone. "Anchee, do you read me?"

The reception had dropped. Earl and the two hunters crouched around Molly, unsure what to do or say. Staring at the main building and silo, Molly felt a strange sensation. She pointed at the huge grain silo, her chest still heaving from the run.

"There's hasn't been grain on this farm for a terminal silo to be rebuilt like that in a hundred years," she whispered.

The hunters stared at the silo in a moment of confusion.

"Is that you, Molly?" a faint voice came.

Adjusting her earbuds, Molly stood up in a natural move, hoping to improve her reception. Anchee's voice got stronger. Molly had never felt so relieved to be in touch through technology.

"Anchee," she gasped.

As she spoke into her microphone, Molly faced the huge grain silo and building site.

"Molly, thank God, we've got you again," Anchee said.

95

As the spray of water rained on their heads, Randall and Danny and his crew lit up the dark tunnel with the lights on the end of their rifle scopes. Creeping toward a large steel door, which had been the portal of exit and entry for the other technicians and militia, Randall was reminded of times he had trudged through the night shift on some abandoned freight train tunnel.

"Keep moving," he whispered.

Danny and his crew didn't look particularly nervous at the circumstances. They looked wired and ready for a fight, maneuvering through the tunnel like it was only an obstacle course.

At the end of a hallway, Randall found the heavy steel door.

The studio door was half open, flickering light and shadows. Past the door, the mist-filled tunnel was flooded with an array of fluorescent lights. Randall almost felt blinded at first.

Randall stepped back into the hallway and into the abandoned control room.

All of the screens still blinked with their operations.

"Look at this," Danny said.

He stood at the doorway into another room. The great Pentagon photo stretched in the background, behind the door on a platform. It was Alexander's office. Several chairs had been strewn around the room. A blue uniform sat on the couch in the corner. Puddles of water had collected in the room, and on the tables.

No one was around.

333

The evacuation of this bunker worried Randall.

A noise came from a door at the opposite end of the control panel. A light beamed underneath the door. A muffled voice sounded.

"We're not alone," Danny whispered.

Aiming his gun at the door, with the sharpshooters to his side, Randall turned the knob. Sandeep, his arms tied behind his back on the chair, dropped his head and felt a sliver of relief for the first time in days. His face was streaked with the water from the sprinklers. He looked up and seemed more sober now.

"Thank God you're here," he said.

"Where are they?" Randall said with an urgency in his voice as he cut the cuffs and released Sandeep. "Where's Alexander?"

"There is a second bunker," Sandeep said, his voice faint. He rubbed at his freed hands. The water on his face had somehow helped to break his drugged state. "Look at the monitors."

Pulling Randall along, Sandeep limped over to the control room monitors and board, which he recalled from his interrogation. Still weary, his technical understanding and training had never left his fingers. Sandeep activated one of the overhead screens. Bunker #2.

Randall watched over Sandeep's shoulder as the live images on the screen followed Alexander pacing back and forth on the metal floor in the missile control room of the second bunker. Sitting nearby, Thomas operated one of several control panels with another armed technician. Benton stood along the wall. Two technicians darted from the silo room.

"I knew it," Sandeep groaned, finally able to catch his breath. He pointed at the black-and-white images on the screen. "I think they're loading rocket fuel." The last words from Sandeep rattled Randall. He couldn't believe the screen image was real.

"Is that a fucking missile?" Randall barked.

As Sandeep switched images on the screens, the missile silo came into view. It felt like an unveiling to Randall.

Rising with the sleek edges of an enormous cylinder, the encased missile mounted into the shaft with the airframe. First the rocket's flange section, the fuel capsule, and finally the warhead. Two technicians hovered around the base of the rocket booster, continuing to load the fuel mixture into a steel-cased housing. A readout on the filling tank was studied by Sandeep.

"The propellent is rocket fuel, a powder and perchlorate mix," he read aloud.

"Can you get us there?" Randall barked.

Sandeep clicked at the rest of the monitors. The security cameras all looked the same—the same battleship concrete sprayed gray walls along the tunnels.

To Randall, the underground system was like a maze. He knew they could waste valuable time going in the wrong direction.

The vast chamber underground remained empty, except for a military truck, which had been parked at the ramp of an escape tunnel. Danny pointed at the truck on the screen.

"Why don't we take that truck and get the hell out of here?"

Randall had already made his decision. It was the same decision he had made back at the FBI lab in Chicago: his mission was to get to the source of his mother's murder and apprehend this devil. Now the mission was compounded even more with worldwide consequences.

"If you want to leave, go ahead," he said.

Sandeep traded looks with Randall and Danny and his three partners.

With a slight nod, Danny added, "I meant, we can take that truck after we finish our business."

Moved by the courage and loyalty of his team, Randall pointed toward the hallway and made for a side tunnel. "This is what your images showed us, Sandeep. Alexander's got to be this way," he said.

Sandeep looked at Danny, and with an air of accepted fear followed Randall's splashing footsteps down the hall.

96

―――

Freddy pulled up Molly's image on the live stream from the drone. He could see her position by the forest. Projecting it to the screen on the Gem Theatre stage, he could even make out a piece of wood in Molly's hand. He saw the hunters to her side.

"Listen, Anchee, can you . . ." Molly began to speak, but Anchee interrupted her.

"You have to get out of there immediately, Molly," Anchee shouted. "All of you."

"Randall's below," Molly answered. "He needs our help. Alexander has launched some sort of military operation underground."

"Ya think," Freddy said sarcastically.

Shifting away from Molly, the drone projected a new image on the screen. The live feed was wobbly, and then it cleared to a stunning aerial view of the grain silo. There was a gray platform covering the top of the grain silo. The outer structure was cylindrical, with hemispheric ends. The cover was slowly opening in the middle, unsheathing the barrel of the silo.

"Look at the silo," Freddy said, pointing at the theater screen.

"My God," Anchee said.

Freddy continued, "That looks like a missile and a warhead to me."

"Tell me about this silo!" Molly shouted, putting a finger on her earbud.

"The silo," Anchee said, her voice breaking. "That's not a grain silo, Molly. It looks like a missile in there."

Flanked by the hunters, Molly watched debris fall from the top of the silo as it slowly opened, grinding with a high-pitched metallic squeal. A few birds circled around the rim of the silo as nests and feathers dropped, flying across the building tops and then toward the buffer of trees, like they had been rustled from a long perch.

"Anchee," Molly said. "Can you knock down the transmitters in this area, or jam whatever signals are coming from underground?"

"No, no way," Anchee gasped.

"But you're operating a drone right above me, correct?" Molly went on, staring at a birdlike shape hovering near the silo.

It wasn't a bird; it was their drone.

"Yes," Anchee said.

"Then you've got to send that drone straight into the silo, and link and record your live stream to the world," Molly said. "Every news site you can find."

"Molly, you've got to get away from there," Freddy shouted.

"Do as I say," Molly said, her words sounding like an order. "We need to show the rest of the world what Alexander is hiding."

The drone rose, guided by Freddy, and then aimed to look straight down the opening of the silo. It revealed the tip of a huge missile.

"My God," Anchee said again as Freddy continued. "It's really a missile's warhead." Anchee's voice broke. "It's too risky. If we crash in that silo we could risk detonating whatever they have in there."

"I think that's just what she intends," Freddy said, standing next to Anchee.

97

No one knew that Earl had still been counting down. Finally, the third and last of his delayed fuses had burnt down and ignited.

The walls shook, and then shook again. The lights flickered in the control room.

Alexander turned toward Benton, even as the operator at the control booth looked over his shoulder at the general in bewilderment. Thomas stood up from the desk.

"That shaker sure was no quake," Benton said, his voice weak.

"Didn't you hear me?" Alexander shouted. "This facility is steel reinforced and suspended with shock isolation. Walls of Jericho might fall, but we'll be just fine."

There was a detached madness about Alexander that now terrified even Benton. He had never witnessed someone so calm about facing what was before him: launching a firestorm of unthinkable power.

The darkened tunnel came to an end. Randall slowed his pace to a halt as the light of the second blast door and the control room beyond came into view. A stream of water continued by everyone's feet.

"General, there's flooding in the silo housing," Thomas's desperate voice, changing registers, yelled back from the control room. "It's not the sprinklers. This is a waterfall."

Another technician then screamed.

The last guard shook his head, and then bolted from the room. He didn't go far. He ran directly into Randall in the corridor, who collared him and smashed him down to the wet pavement. Danny disarmed the guard, who then crawled up against the wall, and without a word or resistance, ran down the hallway in terror.

The water had now risen to four inches. Randall turned to Sandeep, Danny, and his team.

"Ready, go," Randall said.

Alexander didn't expect the fleeing guards would return. He had no respect for men who turned tail at the first glimmer of the bayonet. But when a flank of rifles pointed into the missile control room, followed by Randall and his handgun, Alexander sat back in his chair in complete surprise. With his feet soaked in water, Thomas turned and raised his hands.

The sheriff thought he knew better. As Benton reached for his gun, Randall shot him in the shoulder, tossing the groaning sheriff against the wall.

Alexander disregarded the water on the floor. Perched on an elevated platform, the control center appeared like an island in a sea of turmoil. The screen hung over Alexander's head like a frame. The control panels were protected by a transparent glass.

"Lord have mercy," Randall said.

He was not referring to Benton, who knelt in the corner, bleeding and whimpering. Randall saw the silo chamber in full view. It hadn't looked real on the monitor—now it swirled with life and vapors around it. The missile stood out like a spire on the landmark Chicago Temple building, except it was immense and even more powerful in its repose. And it was real.

"Well, the prodigal son has finally come home," Alexander smirked, standing up from his chair.

"You're insane," Randall said as he put his pistol to Alexander's head. Everyone saw Alexander's gun sitting on the console of the control board—though not out of reach.

"It's over, General," Randall said.

Pointing his gun, he motioned for Danny's boys to tie up Thomas, the technician, and then the slumped Benton.

Alexander didn't reach for his gun. As more water now rushed around his shoes in eddies, the general flicked a switch on the left side of the console.

Everyone suddenly saw an amber flash ignite the liquid propellants in the base of the missile, releasing a gust of smoke in the silo chamber. The boosters were ready.

A timer appeared on the control board: four minutes, twenty-four seconds. The chamber rumbled slightly.

"Might as well put down that gun, son," Alexander said. "Sorry, but you're out of your league. We've already put in the coordinates for the boost phase. Whether you like it or not, I have a little present for your friends in Chicago."

Alexander nodded to Sandeep.

"And the world will have enough of your video and your fingerprints all over it, my friends," he added.

"Shut it down!" Randall roared.

He hadn't moved the gun an inch from Alexander's head.

"Who do you think you're fooling with that little gun?" Alexander laughed. "I've got a bigger one. And it has a nuclear warhead."

He paused and widened his smile, overjoyed by the moment. The timer was already at three minutes, forty-eight seconds. Alexander reached down to the control board, toward his pistol.

Randall cocked his gun.

Alexander scoffed, pausing, and then he motioned at Thomas, who still had his hands tied behind his back.

"You put that thing down," Alexander said, looking at Randall with a deranged look, "and perhaps we'll give you a chance to run, like your mother. She found herself in the wrong place at the wrong time, just like you. And here you are, underground, just like her."

Randall locked on to Alexander's gaze.

"Give it up, son," Alexander continued to goad.

All of the years of waiting, all of the sleepless nights of wondering, and all of the days of searching for any sign of his mother's life and death now came to a dead end of time. There was no consolation here, only darkness. No resolution or peace, only the forever unresolved question of why she had been lost in a world replete with monsters like Alexander.

Randall whipped Alexander with his pistol. The general fell to his knees, splashing in the water.

"The dead bury the dead, you fool," Randall said as Alexander struggled to his feet, slipping in the water. "My mother is not through with you yet."

Another explosion rocked the room. Electrical sparks flashed. The lights flickered again.

And then everyone heard it. Its roar sounded like a huge furnace had been fired and ignited. The rocket fuel at the base of the missile set off a series of flames. Red lights cranked into operation on the control panels.

"Our reckoning has come," Alexander called out, blood pouring from his lip. "The war has just begun."

The timer read: three minutes, sixteen seconds. Thomas tried to make the first diversion. Launching his body, he slammed into Danny's chest, and then he head-butted one of Danny's sharpshooters, who collapsed to the water on the floor.

As Randall shot Thomas, dropping him into the corner, Alexander pushed off the floor and grabbed his handgun from the console. The veteran detective didn't hesitate.

Two more shots rang out in the control room.

The general fell on top of his control panel.

Moaning, one hand clutching at his side, Alexander turned to Randall with a look of agony—and victory. And then his eyes closed.

The madness of the moment was almost too much; the absurdity of a bunker in the bunker builder's backyard; the front lines of a war that had come home to roost. Randall glared at Alexander in rage. His mother's murderer would not witness his main trial now.

As water splashed around his feet, the lights turned off for a long moment. Only the silo's glow from the missile launching pad remained illuminated—and the timer, now at two minutes, sixteen seconds.

Randall saw the aura of the missile clearly. The missile was alive.

Pushing Alexander's bloody body from the control panel, he frantically searched the computer board for any link to the missile. The liquid fuels readied for a rapid launch. The boosters collapsed. Randall clicked randomly on a few knobs and buttons, and then smashed his hand down on the console in frustration. It was no use.

"There's got to be a way," he shouted.

The power to the room suddenly dropped.

Water tugged at his legs now.

"The red switch on the left," Sandeep shouted.

Randall lunged for the switch on the control panel, pulling it down. The smoke from the silo had completely filled the silo chamber. Fire lashed from the jet vane. The combustion system roared. His last-ditch effort had no effect.

"Get out of here," Randall shouted. "Get to the escape tunnel."

As shorted wires crackled with fire, Danny helped up his cousin from the floor, and then they made for the door, splashing through the water, disappearing with the crew down the exit tunnel. Sandeep and Randall followed as parts of the flooded ceiling and walls fell around them.

No one looked back. No one saw Alexander's body floating in the water among his men, like a captain who had gone down with his ship.

98

___

The huge grain silo started to shake as pieces of its concrete siding dropped to the ground. Smoke streamed from the main building. The ground itself seemed to be trembling. Molly, Earl, and the hunters all feared they could be blown up any second.

With a combination of horror and awe, Anchee and Freddy watched the last video images of their whizzing drone as it entered the silo like a bat, fluttered along the walls, forever aiming at the eye of the nuclear warhead.

The tough little machine crashed off the top of the warhead, then slammed to the silo chamber, falling violently, smashing into and puncturing an opening on the side of the missile.

No one had any idea that rocket fuel had started spraying out. That the little drone had made its preemptive attack with the precision of a killer bee. That was the last image from the drone. Their screen in the theater turned black.

The vapors of fuel in the silo room hovered along the blast doors with the pressure of the ages. The rapture of the blast did not come from the encased warhead, but the detonation of the fuel and launcher. The killer bee drone sputtered with enough current to ignite the massive fuel supply of the missile.

The bunker builder, it seemed, had failed to anticipate this reality in the design of his final project.

The initial explosion across the region shook like an aftershock of an earthquake.

Not knowing what more was inside this huge weapon silo, Molly and the hunters raced back into the forest buffer, where Earl had left his truck.

"Run for it now, damn it," Earl shouted.

"Where's Randall?" Molly cried out. "And Danny and the others? We can't leave!"

"Take the back road, now," Earl shouted from his truck window.

The trucks bounded away.

At the hillside view overlooking the Henson farm in the valley, the support team vehicles stopped as they watched the grain silo split in half. Idled in their trucks at a saddle in the road, they watched in silence, shocked by the huge concrete walls crumbling before their eyes, revealing the still-standing missile.

A militia truck suddenly emerged on the side of the collapsing building, driving out of a smoking ramp exit, and then Molly got a view of the driver.

"Oh God . . . it's Randall," Molly said.

It was Randall and he wasn't alone. Danny bore down with both hands on the steering wheel. Sandeep hung on, exhausted. The others in Danny's crew ducked their heads.

The truck sped away as the silo and rocket completely collapsed to the ground. A wave of dust pushed across the farmyard. The rest of the buildings ignited.

A groundswell enveloped the earth.

Molly and Earl and the others watched as the entire compound rumbled and then collapsed. Cascading against the steel-enforced walls, the warhead of the missile wobbled, readying for detonation, and then lodged against a collapsed mound of limestone.

The nuclear warhead remained immobile as a land mine, encased in safety features that kept the fissile reaction from taking place. As the earth slid over the warhead, it would maybe become an artifact in an archaeological site of the future. A remnant of a culture capable of ending human existence. An archaic weapon as futile as a stone or bronze or steel sword in the burial grounds of war.

Earl saw Randall's truck barely making it past the edge of the explosion.

"It's over," Earl called out. "Get the hell out of here!"

99

The tense faces from the vast security apparatus scanned every corner in the conference center as helicopters encircled the compound from the lakefront to the side streets. There was an awkward air of uncertainty everywhere. No updates had been released. Military and security spokespeople could not be found. The debris from both of the drone attacks, swept away by military units, had remained an unexplained phenomenon.

Standing in front of the ornate doorway to the great conference ball-room, a row of TV reporters sought to fill an increasing time gap in their live reports. "We are told that President Adams remains in session with her negotiators," a CNN reporter said, speaking into the camera. "The delay, according to our sources, is a disagreement over two technical points, dealing with classified future nonnuclear weapons systems, which is keeping the Russian premier from accepting the prenegotiated treaty. We'll keep you up-to-date on the latest news once we confirm with Russian officials."

Her Secret Service detail and several soldiers escorted President Adams out of the great conference ballroom in such a rush that most of the participants didn't even witness the moment—or the humiliation.

Only a handful of people near the back doorway picked up on the sudden departure. Gen. McCarthy, flanked by military police, had joined the perplexed president in the hallway. The scene confounded the security agents on both ends of the area. No one knew what was going on, except for the general. McCarthy held his hands before him, as if they had been emptied. The president appeared livid. On the side wall of the hallway, two other generals, Priest and Egerton, watched the improvised meeting between the president and her military negotiator erupt into a shouting match.

"You set this up, didn't you?" Adams said, facing off with McCarthy, with a fierce urge to pin him against the wall. "You changed the agreement, you bastard. You pushed the Russians into a corner with demands you knew they wouldn't accept. And demands I never asked for."

McCarthy stepped away from Adams, glanced at the others, and then held his own.

"You have no idea what's involved with these negotiations."

"I know what's at stake," the president shouted. "And you blew it, intentionally."

Two of the president's advisors stood at her side as her finger-pointing at McCarthy became so unyielding that one of the advisors sought to restrain her.

The president understood the general's ploy, in cahoots with the Russian brass, as lip service gave way to a political maneuver outside of her control.

"You're done," the president hissed at McCarthy. "I promise you that."

Within seconds, she marched away from McCarthy and the rest of the military brass as her entourage of White House advisers and Secret Service agents hastily made for the exit.

The meeting between the president and McCarthy remained private for less than a minute as the doors of the great ballroom flung open. The shocked representatives of the conference understood it was all over.

Within minutes, hackers and news media had tapped into the intercepts sent throughout the rest of the summit's vast security apparatus.

"In a stunning turn of events," a news reporter said, looking over her shoulder at the streaming crowd, as if to confirm words she feared to use, "the Chicago summit for global disarmament collapsed today, as American and Russian negotiators failed to bridge lingering disputes over weapons reductions. We still don't have details, but . . ."

To her left, a French reporter added as the camera's light cast a glow around her, "The world has returned to the arms race."

Shouts in Russian, Chinese, Arabic, and Spanish, among untold languages, sounded around the conference center in a similar tone of chaos. An agitated Secret Service and their agency counterparts heightened their security measures as crowds hemorrhaged on the verge of all out panic. The security apparatus for the Russian and Chinese counterparts propelled into action, removing their leaders within minutes from the center. Cadres of diplomats retreated to their McCormick Place rooms. The media chattered in the background in scores of languages. Without any real information, disinformation took a new form as pundits threw in whatever toxic sound bite they could conjure, as if the breaking of a disarmament accord had been a disaster foretold. The *New York Post* threw up a new headline: CIGARS Blows Up on President.

Inside the remote MACC, Nikki felt frozen in place. Everyone around her had stopped what they were doing to check their social media or watch the cable news alert blaring in the corner of the room. She looked at her phone: no messages from Randall. Nothing.

Stunned by the news, Nikki moved out into the wave of summit participants, who scuttled through the bewildered crowds for the exit doors. It felt like rush hour on the underground train.

Walking outside in a scrum of military police, Nikki watched from the curb as the generals—McCarthy, Priest, and Egerton—loaded into a bulletproof military limo waiting for them at a private entrance on the side street adjacent to McCormick Place. She wasn't alone. A crowd of reporters had managed to elude security agents. A journalist with National Public Radio raced to the car, sticking her microphone in front of the door, jamming it from closing.

It caught McCarthy's attention like a hook.

"Any comment, Gen. McCarthy, on the possibility of restarting the talks?"

As Priest and Egerton bent into the back seat, McCarthy offered a pained smile.

"We are deeply disappointed in the failure of this summit, and truly hope we can with all good intentions reconnect, but I believe our new president has discovered the reality of the world here in Chicago. We live in a world in conflict, and we recognize the necessity to modernize our weapons systems for a new era of defense and security."

McCarthy climbed into the car without another word.

100

―

Harriet was waiting for them on her porch. The two trucks barreled through the narrow hedge and overgrown trees. Molly leaped out of the truck and ran to Harriet. Earl, Anchee, and Freddy straggled out of the seats with the relief of having made a great journey.

"Get inside now," Harriet shouted.

She wasn't talking to Molly, who clutched at her embrace. Harriet was calling to Randall, who stepped out of the militia's military truck with a look of exhaustion.

Danny and his crew unloaded from the opposite side with the haunted expressions of veterans from another world.

Inside the cabin, everyone huddled around the TV, which held their attention with the power of a flaming fireplace they had lit to dry out. Harriet pointed at the screen in horror. First Sandeep, then Molly, Anchee, and Danny, and then Randall and Freddy. The freeze-frame photos were almost too clean, edited and enhanced. Their individual photos were framed—like wanted criminals, still at large. The doctored video of Sandeep proclaiming the attempted attack with drones was eerily terrifying.

"Is this AI work?" Freddy asked, his voice almost a whisper.

"Meanwhile, along with an attempted terrorist drone attack on Chicago, the military and FBI have launched an investigation of an underground cell of terrorists in southern Illinois, where a massive explosion in a restricted weapons facility has taken the life of Gen. William Alexander, who had been at work on a top-secret military project."

"What's going on?" Molly said as her hands went to her mouth.

"We're the cover," Randall said, under his breath. "It was a setup."

Barging in the front door, Earl stomped into the cabin, his chest heaving.

"Military vehicles are coming up Ozark Road, headed this way," he shouted.

Randall didn't pause. He knew this wouldn't be sorted out in a rendezvous with the military. He knew there was no phone call he could make to explain what he had just experienced.

Randall knew this decision had been made a long time ago—not his decision, but the ripple effect of an ignored history, and its players who had never been held accountable. The unearthing of his mother's bones didn't merely reveal a secret; it had opened a window into a history of denial.

"Is there another way out of these woods?" he asked.

"Let's go," Earl shouted.

As the others raced out the door, Randall took one last look at the TV screen and their photos as Molly hugged Harriet. The back door slammed. The room became empty, with Harriet staggering in the middle, unsure of her place; unsure if she was an accomplice or suspect among the background chatter on the television screen.

Epilogue

The media cameras jammed the press conference held in the small briefing room. The news release had been vague, but intriguing.

Gen. Bill Egerton, head of Intelligence, Surveillance, Reconnaissance, and Cyber Effects Operations for the Air Force, stood at the podium, with a screen behind him. On the side of the room, dressed in black, Tom Alexander from Gunnor, Inc., looked despondent; the loyal son could barely manage to stand. Alison Foreman held his arm, caressing his back in a sisterly way.

Walking up to the podium, the base communication director handed Egerton a remote control for the screen. Picking up a stack of folders on a nearby table, she started to hand out the materials for the press.

The first of several photos projected on the screen: Gen. Will Alexander, retired commander of the Military Missions in the Army Corps of Engineers.

"In the service of his country," Egerton began to speak, "we must recognize Gen. Will Alexander, a decorated war hero, who neutralized a terrorist plot to attack Scott Air Force Base and the National Geospatial Intelligence Agency with drones. Although several classified investigations are underway, it is clear this attack was in coordination with an attempted terrorist attack on the Chicago International Global Arms Reduction Summit. We offer our deepest condolences to the Alexander family for the general's sacrifice in the defense of his country and our gratitude for his forty-two years of unparalleled service."

Egerton nodded at Alison, who gave one last stroke of concern to Tom Alexander, and then joined the Air Force general at the podium.

"Good afternoon, my name is Alison Foreman, with the Department of Defense's Defense Intelligence Agency." She used a laser pointer, aiming the beam at the screen, which projected a photo of Molly and the Arkies at the archaeological dig.

"Working with Gen. Alexander," Alison continued, "we infiltrated and thwarted the plans of the terrorist group that had posed as an archaeological team in Alexander County."

As Alison continued to speak, she aimed the pointer at a series of freeze-frame photos of the Arkies. Released directly onto social media outlets, the photos included Anchee, setting up a LIDAR scanner that looked like a grenade launcher, then a freeze-frame photo of Freddy inserting soil moisture measurement system devices that resembled explosives into an embankment; a photo of Sandeep, perched above the site at a covered table of computers, showed him adjusting a drone.

"The Cairo archaeological site was used as a cover for international terrorists, who included Pakistani and Chinese extremists, working with American militants and Black radicals, and as the secretary noted, had planned to attack the National Geospatial Intelligence Center with sophisticated drones equipped with chemical weapons, as well as Scott Air Force Base and the private operations at the Ft. Defiance Airborne Laser Complex. This group of terrorists worked with and coordinated the thwarted drone attack on the McCormick Place convention center during the Chicago disarmament summit."

A photo of Randall appeared on the screen, showing him smashing the greenhouse window, then a photo of Molly speaking into her microphone inside the greenhouse room. Alison had made sure all of the security cameras at the greenhouse had been saved to her cloud.

"While some of the identified terrorists died in a massive underground explosion at the Ft. Defiance company compound, there are suspects still at large and considered dangerous," Alison went on. "Working with the FBI and all law enforcement agencies, a national search has been launched."

As the press cameras flashed, the reporters barraged Egerton and Alison with questions.

LAKE SHORE DRIVE
CHICAGO, ILLINOIS

Sitting on a bench along the lakeshore, looking at the zigzag slips of sails cutting through the expanse of blue water and sky, Nikki had never felt so adrift in her life. No one in the department would talk to her. The fallout of the security summit had left the police force in disarray; her chief had left town on an extended vacation. The image of Randall in the news as a reported terrorist had issued an eruption of rumors over his shadowy legacy on the force.

Nikki had spent the last night walking the streets, hoping to somehow arrive at a resolution or even the right moment in her life.

Then a ping burst from her phone. She didn't bother to look at it. Just more harassment, she assumed. More pushback from the police department or even her friends.

It wasn't until later that night, after she had turned off the lamp by her bed, her phone still illuminated, that Nikki checked her email. An encrypted message appeared. The message had no ID, but the words were clear:

> Tell Teresa I love her. Much to sort out. Miss you. You will hear from me one day.

WHITE HOUSE ROSE GARDEN
WASHINGTON, DC

President Elaine Adams, after reviewing a highly classified FBI memo about the events in Cairo, issued a memorandum to her national security staff. "This is clearly a scam, a lie, and a conspiracy that goes beyond the summit fiasco," she wrote. Adams knew Randall too well. The memo raised more questions about Alexander's links to the Pentagon and extremist groups. Demanding a thorough investigation into the Chicago and Cairo terrorist events, the president appointed her national security advisor to lead a special commission on military contracts and protocols as she implemented the replacement of the prior administration's top military brass.

Now flanked on her right side by her vice president, secretary of defense, and national security advisor, Adams straddled the podium in the Rose Garden with both hands, underscoring the resolve of her decision. It was a bright blue morning, rays of sun casting onto the steps of the White House in the background. The two decorated generals to her left, both of them draped in extensive medal ribbons, stood with their hats in their hands, the differing colors of their uniforms distinguishing their branches of service.

"I am happy to announce my choice for the next chair of the Joint Chiefs, Gen. Anne Marie Robinson, one of the most admired officers in our military," Adams said, recognizing the Air Force general's former leadership of the North American Aerospace Defense Command and the United States Northern Command. "With the retirement of Gen. McCarthy," she continued, "Gen. Robinson and her new vice chair, Admiral Sherry Morgan, commander of the US Naval Forces, will begin a new era of military challenges in the world."

The symbolism in Adams's choices was not lost on anyone in the audience, including the press. In a rapid series of events, McCarthy had disappeared without a word or formal ceremony. His assistant secretaries had been dismissed as well. The headquarters of the Joint Chiefs of Staff at the Pentagon had gone through the biggest turnover of personnel since World War II.

"As commander in chief," Adams went on, "I was elected by pledging to make our country a leader in eliminating nuclear weapons worldwide. As commander in chief I look forward to working with Chairwoman Robinson and Vice Chair Morgan to shape a more responsible defense policy and budget including the reduction of all weapons. We continue to make a commitment for the elimination of nuclear weapons, and a renewed global summit for disarmament."

The president thanked the new appointees, and then withdrew from the podium, refusing to take any questions from the press.

CEDAR SWAMP
ALEXANDER COUNTY

The leaf-covered canoes cut quietly through the swamp, navigating the towering cypress and tupelo trees buried in rows like elephant feet. Earl, the seasoned river guide, knew the sandstone bluffs and limestone glades by memory. He led the others like ancient travelers coming upriver, nearly invisible under the thick canopy.

Anyone could get lost for an eternity in the back pockets of the Shawnee forests. Never identified, the local hunters who had participated that day at the silo disappeared back into daily life. However, after hiding out for two weeks in a series of caves in the Shawnee National Forest, the buzz of the helicopters fading each night, the Arkies, led by Molly and Randall, had decided it was safe to return to the waterways, in search of a new plan.

They knew it was time to move on.

Randall, in the stern, paddled and guided through the isolated hidden water as Anchee and Sandeep stroked ahead of him. Gently cutting through the water to the side, Molly and Freddy paddled the third canoe, next to Earl and Danny.

It was not quite twilight. The calm hour of the evening, before the wilderness reclaimed its own ways.

Randall looked back at Molly as she pulled on her paddle.

"We're gonna find allies and figure this out," he said.

She nodded.

"So, for now, we'll survive like the people who preceded us," she said, pulling her canoe in a current beside his own boat.

"Hopefully, not hidden and underground," Randall answered as he turned to the opposite side of the canoe and dug into his stroke.

In the distance, the spiral of a drone hovered above them, like a bat searching for its evening repast.

Acknowledgements

———

Deep gratitude to the dedication of our editor Carl Bromley, who has graciously shaped and shepherded this novel, and to the entire Melville House Publishing crew for your extraordinary efforts: Dennis Johnson, Valerie Merians, Janet Joy Wilson, Hanna Lafferty, Michelle Capone, Sofia Demopolos, Michael Barson, Sammi Sontag, and our fabulous copyeditor Peter Kranitz.

Special thanks to the indefatigable Larry Becsey and Emma Alban at Intellectual Property Group, and Murray Weiss at Catalyst Literary Management, for all of your work.

FROM ANDREW DAVIS:
My parents Metta and Nate Davis, who met in the theater and raised their kids to fight for a world without war, finding dignity and justice for all. My sister Jo Friedman and brother Richie Davis who have lovingly participated in so many aspects of my career.

My dear wife Adrianne Alexis Partida Davis, who has supported and put up with me for over forty-five years, nurturing and creatively raising our delicious children Julian Reed Davis and Gena Pilar Bezdek. Our kids' loving partners Alex Bezdek and Jenna Savage Davis gifted co-parents to our own more delicious grandchildren.

Jeff Biggers, whose *Reckoning at Eagle* Creek made me realize I had found a truly gifted writing partner and soulmate who clearly understood the depth of history in southern Illinois.

John Wier, my early mentor at the University of Illinois who introduced me to the historic Koster archeological dig that became the basis of this story. Studs Terkel and Haskell Wexler, who beginning in 1968 had faith in me that allowed incredible opportunities to pursue relevant stories that might entertain and change the world.

Peter Dekom, my brilliant attorney and consiglieri and Larry Becsey, my agent and manager at Intellectual Property Group who have been by my side for over 45 years. Writer filmmaker Michael Gray and producer Jim Dennett who hired me as an assistant camera person and collaborated with me for five decades. Ian Masters broadcast journalist, political commentator, author, screenwriter and documentary filmmaker. Peter Macgregor Scott my great producing partner who made magic happen.

Other partners: Mary McGlone, Tomlinson Holman, Tamar and Josh Hoffs, Teresa Tucker Davis, Lowell Blank, Tommy Lee Jones, Dov Hoenig, Dennis Virkler, Mike Medavoy, Max Youngstein, Terry Semel, Bob Daly, Dick Cook, Steve Spira, Bruce Berman, Lorenzo di Bonaventura, Arnold & Anne Kopelson, Joel Wayne, Alan Horn, Louis Sachar, Cary Granat, Michael Flaherty, Phil Anschutz.

Advance readers Scott Spencer, Jen Sovada, Roger Sutton, Zoe Hoenig, Rick Kogan, Suzanne Austin, Paul Brickman, Arne Schmidt, Joe Medjuck.

My brothers from the South Chicago neighborhood Mike, Jerry, Howie, Albert, Buzzy, Sonny.

FROM JEFF BIGGERS:

Unending gratitude to Andy, who not only made this book possible, but a nonstop adventure of fun, intrigue and constant astonishment. I would like to thank my southern Illinois family, as always, and the long walks and talks with Sam Stearns, Gary DeNeal, the lunch crew at Morello's restaurant, the brilliant work of photographer and historian Preston Ewing in Cairo, and readers Jennifer and Justin DeMello.

And per sempre, grazie Carla, my jo, for keeping the faith, keeping the ship afloat, and keeping me inspired for the next adventure: *Así cuando los dientes de la literatura trataron de morder mis honrados talones, yo pasé, sin saber, cantando con el viento, hacia los almacenes lluviosos de mi infancia, hacia los bosques fríos del Sur, indefinible, hacia donde mi vida se llenó con tu aroma.*

Live at the Sweet Home Chicago Heartland Café—across a lunch table in the backroom of this once vital hub, our authors' collaboration was hatched, thanks to our dear friend Michael Gaylord James.